By SHELTER SOMERSET

NOVELS
Between Two Worlds
Between Two Promises

On the Trail to Moonlight Gulch

Published by DREAMSPINNER PRESS
http://www.dreamspinnerpress.com

ALASKA HUNT

Shelter Somerset

Dreamspinner Press

Published by
Dreamspinner Press
5032 Capital Circle SW
Ste 2, PMB# 279
Tallahassee, FL 32305-7886
USA
http://www.dreamspinnerpress.com/

Alaska Hunt
Copyright © 2012 by Shelter Somerset

Cover Art by TL Bland
tbbland@cox.net
http://thruterryseyes.com

ISBN: 978-1-61372-671-6

Printed in the United States of America
First Edition
August 2012

eBook edition available
eBook ISBN: 978-1-61372-672-3

To Walter

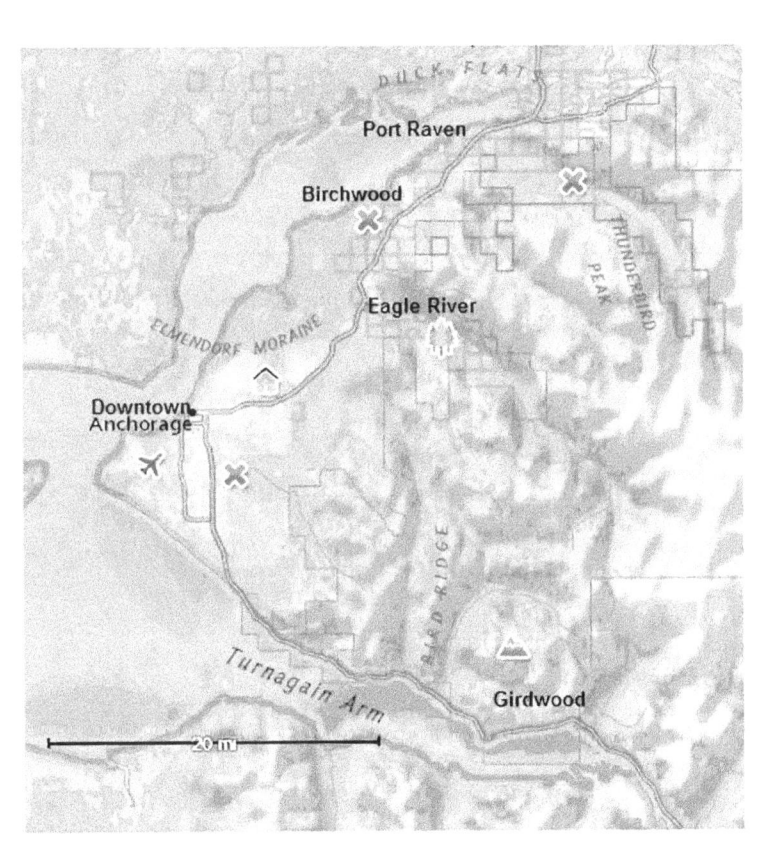

CHAPTER 1

RAGE filled her. Pounding, penetrating rage. Tearing into each muscle fiber. Pebbles and twigs crunched under her weight on the unfamiliar, primitive road and seemed extra sharp and irksome. Smells on the wind carried the first certainty of spring. The incessant overcast sky would release no more snow in the boreal forest footing the mountain ranges, but horrible, stabbing rain might come at any time. Flashes of red blazed across her vision. Winterovered berries grew along the road. But no time to stop and gorge the way she'd like. She had to keep moving. Voices inside her head pushed her, encouraging her to find the scent. Furious determination ruled her every movement.

Throbbing in her head made each step like a blast of thunder. Did her agony have to do with waking from a deep sleep? She was annoyed, waking cold and dizzy. Wrathful resentment toward everything in her path burned her eyes. Even hidden things bothered her.

A ground squirrel burrowed beneath her. Irritated, she stopped and dug into the permafrost until she found a cache of pine nuts and squirrel droppings. Where had that squirrel escaped to? A rustle jerked her head. The squirrel was hopping away over the duff, scraping along the decayed leaves, a sound similar to a giant beast snapping in half the lofty aspens and spruce.

She lurched for an adolescent birch tree. Bit into the trunk to ensure the tree paid for the squirrel's cunning. Tried to shake it from its roots. The leaves rattled like a thousand gurgling streams. Her teeth reverberated with pain and agony against the hard wood. How had she let that ground squirrel escape? She stopped. The familiar rancid smell forced her to refocus. She loomed closer. And angrier.

Panting, she loped onward, unconcerned for sharp branches poking into the sensitive flesh around her ears and nose. She must reach that reeking animal. Over the years she'd grown accustomed to the sickening odor. But the past several weeks she'd wanted to destroy whatever emitted that stench. She detested the putrid stink more than the beating in her head.

Mosquitoes swarmed her eyes and nose. The warming weather always brought them out in force. They used to chase her and her mother and brother clear across the brush and into the wide streams. Funny how she should consider that now, after many years. She remembered those days better than some might guess. When they bored into her skin and laid their eggs, the hatched larvae would eat into her stomach and cause unbearable diarrhea. They'd once almost killed her. But she'd survived worse. She bit at the buzzing pests, chomped at the rancid air.

The ancient slug in her right shoulder came alive with a burning fury. Long covered in scar tissue, the bullet brought back suppressed, painful memories. A hunter had wounded her. The recollection made her angry. Angrier than when it had happened her second summer. Her mother and twin brother had been killed by the same madman.

Trauma from that incident coalesced into fresh rage. The red flashes burned into her retinas. Hatred coursed through her muscles and bore into her bones. She began huffing, needing more and more oxygen to match the increase in her heart rate and her loathing for the world and everything in it.

She lifted her head, beating with heavy, excruciating pain, and sniffed the soggy air. Hoary steam shot from her nostrils and mouth. The encroaching forest burst with every sort of creature, tormenting her with their chatter and fussiness. The lengthening days allowed more time for foraging, hunting, pestering. Overhead, she snapped at the warblers chirping nonstop from the tree branches overhanging the road.

She pushed headlong, her snout low and sweeping from side to side. Her ears heated with blood, and her eyes smoldered. She opened her mouth a tad, sucking in the odors. When the wind shifted from the west near where she knew a large arm of water rested (but had never seen), the smell intensified. One singular stench she'd learned to loathe. She must reach it.

Losing concern for stealth, she turned into the forest and increased her pace, stomping the vegetation and chasing away ptarmigan foraging on salmonberry buds. She wanted to kill those birds. Their chirping buzzed like dozens of heavy chainsaws. A grinding, mind-piercing screech. Worse than all the blustery wind in the world combined.

Scent from the creature rose clearer, along with the sight of a large and square object. One of those abodes the rank creatures lived in. The creature fussed inside. Instinct demanded she circumvent the cabin downwind. She kept her head low, her eyes piercing at the structure through a marsh filled with tall grass and saxifrage. Again, no time for grazing the protein rich grasses. She must inspect inside that cabin. She'd never done it before. Her nature always instructed her to avoid such places, even during her first spring when she'd been a curious suckling. But now, she had to discover what lurked behind those wooden walls.

Without warning, the door opened. She crouched behind a cluster of tall grass and watched. The man peered around, carrying with him his heavy stench. His eyes widened, searching. Did he smell her presence?

The man hesitated, scurried inside. Sniffing the air, she rose above the blades and tasted the wind for answers. Yet what questions did she have? Mere curiosity for what lurked inside the abode? The voices in her head goaded her, pulling her through the marsh. Patches of grass and saxifrage flattened under each heavy step. Red rage flashed before her eyes.

The stench grew stronger. She dug at the dirt by the cabin, huffed, shuddered, and jumped onto the door, wetting herself. Little did she care if the man reemerged, armed with his weapon, ready to kill. She bit the door, swiped at the handle. Rustling inside irritated her. The smell of fear exploded around her. The man creature, filled with terror, was scrambling about, pushing aside objects that made horrific scraping and clanking sounds. She must stop those horrible sounds.

She jumped at the door and pushed it open with a sharp shatter. The rusty metal hinges ripped off the doorframe, and the door hung limp like a broken tree branch. The man cowered in a corner, his eyes wide and his teeth gnashing. A rifle, poised in the man's arms, trembled and reeked with a long history of bloodshed. She jumped for the barrel and bit hard as the first shot blew off part of her snout. Blood gushed over her jaw and down her neck and chest. Enraged with pain and hate, she lurched for the man creature with what remained of her mouth, snapped his arm, shook him until the rifle fell with a loud thud to the floor.

Agonizing screams from the man echoed through her head. She jumped on top of him, bit into his head, neck, back using her powerful molars. The man's arms flailed out. He struggled, tried to push against her. He reached under his stomach. A long, shiny object, clenched in his white fist, came at her. Why hadn't she noticed the creature carried a hunting knife? They almost always did.

The knife plunged deep into her lung before she had leapt sideways. The man jumped to his haunches, his eyes white with fear and fury. Hatred saturated the cabin. She wanted to snap the man's neck, but her jaw grew limp and painful. She could hardly see through the blood and rage obscuring her vision. Stench of the man surrounded her, as if a dozen or more of them circled her. She lurched backward, snapped at her sides, below and above. At whatever appeared to move.

The man grabbed for his rifle. He fired off several more shots. Splintering hot bullets ripped open flesh. She leaped for the man again, pinned him to the floor. The man's excruciating cries resonated against the walls and ceiling and inside her head. He flailed, kicked, punched. But his resistance incited more anger. She bit and bit, scratched and dug. Bones snapped and crunched in her claws. The man creature weakened. She sensed life had oozed out of him. She sniffed the man, licked the blood. Anger receded. Seconds later, it rose again. She thrust her disabled jaw into the corpse, ripped off flesh with what remained of her molars. Overcome with hatred, she dragged the body across the floor and out of the cabin.

TROOPER Zanebono Fusca gazed at the remains of what resembled a man. The partially eaten corpse, stripped of its clothes, no longer had a face. Even the genitals had been chewed off, yet what remained of the well-developed pectoral muscles left little doubt the deceased was male. A wildlife investigator with the Alaska State Troopers for five years, Zane had never laid eyes on anything more gruesome. What struck him and the other investigators on the scene as uncanny was the large grizzly, approximately three hundred pounds, lying dead fifteen yards away, spread out like a bear rug, as if man and bear had arranged an interspecies murder-suicide pact.

He figured at least twelve hours had passed since the grizzly had attacked. Rigor mortis in both the man and bear had already set in. The bear, unknown to any of the present officials, lacked a collar or tag. Might be a rogue sow entering new territory with its cubs and becoming hyperaggressive. But no sign of cubs zigzagged across the muddy soil. The single tracks proved the bear must have stayed near its kill, feeding whenever it fancied. Typical bear behavior. Some bears, so guarded over food, would even sleep on top their kills.

But this bear hadn't attempted to conceal its kill, like most. Plentiful grass and brush grew nearby for a cache. The entire scene loomed more and more bizarre.

Dr. Greg Gomez, the wildlife biologist on the scene, had spotted the bloody sight from the helicopter. Zane, Greg, Jasper Bohler, a warden with the Alaska Department of Fish and Game, and fellow wildlife trooper Dana Chernikoff had been conducting a routine spring moose count in south central Alaska, when the doctor had hollered above the roaring turbo and pointed out the window.

They'd landed in the small meadow filled with saxifrage by the cabin, eager for a closer look. By the expressions on everyone's faces, no one had an inkling what might have spurred such a horrific attack. They were waiting for the state medical examiner to helicopter in for an on-scene preliminary assessment of the man's body. He would probably learn as much as anyone else.

Strange to find himself surrounded by such bloody remains and still experience a certain peace and comfort from the verdant green of the Alaskan boreal forest. Zane had always been drawn to Alaska's vast ruggedness, and first realized he'd wanted to live there in the fifth grade at Cranston, Rhode Island's Brownridge Elementary School when he'd learned its location on the United States map.

The Chugach Range loomed through a clearing in the trees to the east. An aura of yellow sun spread across the washed sky above the peaks. Half-dollar-sized mosquitoes buzzed around the carnage, a clear sign that May in Alaska had arrived. Although temperatures hovered near the midfifties, Zanebono could see his breath.

He shuffled to the cabin and reexamined the gaping door. Deep striations would have proved the bear's stature and power, even if they had no carcass. Zane wondered if the victim had been habitually feeding the local bears, and one had decided to help itself. Made sense. Bears were high-brained mammals. One or two exposures to a positive stimulus provided enough conditioning. Food—the most powerful stimulus of all.

Inside, Dana searched for the victim's identification and collected evidence from the ransacked cabin, no larger than a one-car garage. The bear had left nothing untouched. The mattress ripped to bits, furniture turned into piles of lumber, curtains from the one window torn to ribbons. Puddles of blood covered the wood floor. Must have undergone some struggle. By all appearances, the victim sustained himself by trapping and hunting small animals. Probably one of those hermits living in the Alaskan bush to seek a life away from people. Zanebono related to the trapper's wanting to stay far from the madding crowd.

Dana, wearing her nitrile gloves, lifted a bacon sandwich with two or three human-sized bite marks from the floor. "The bear most likely interrupted the victim's breakfast."

"Odd that it would do all that butchering, but leave a bacon sandwich untouched," Zane said.

"You find any identification on or around the body?"

"Nothing. Maybe the bear ate it."

Zane followed the blood trail to the trapper's corpse, watchful for any missed clues. Evidence suggested smaller mammals had fed off the corpse. Zane swatted mosquitoes from his view. "Can't even imagine what might've sparked all this," he muttered to Greg and Jasper.

Greg, squatting next to the body, collected bear hairs from the countless wounds with tweezers and inserted them into a biohazard baggy. Young for a professor. Less snooty than his colleagues. Zane liked working with him more than anyone else from the University of Anchorage.

"The bear was angry, that's for sure," Greg said with a strained voice.

Zane scratched under his trooper's cap, rubbed his temples. "Had it been starving?"

Greg gazed at the dead bear and shook his head. "It sure doesn't appear it was starving. A big, healthy bear. As big as any female grizzly I've seen."

"Maybe it had an extra-large appetite."

"There's no shortage of berries around here, and the spring salmon runs are more abundant than ever," Jasper said. "No need to tear down that hermit's door and devour part of him."

"And the bear left all those cans and smashed boxes of food untouched," Zane said, growing more puzzled. "Along with a bacon sandwich."

"What about defending her cubs? You think that's what happened?" Jasper said. "Maybe the sow chased him to his cabin after she spotted him out hunting or something."

"Nope," Greg said with a definitive shake of his head. "Take a look at it. It's not lactating. Teats are near shriveled. If it birthed during the winter, the cubs hadn't survived without milk. Definitely some kind of an offensive attack."

The ensuing silence highlighted their bewilderment.

Black flies fed off the numerous scat droppings Greg examined around the body, at least ten pounds worth from what Zanebono ascertained. Digested bear hairs, long and lustrous, encased the small piles. Looked normal for scat. Zane was unsurprised to find pieces of the trapper's clothing imbedded in the feces, since bears have ultrafast digestive systems. Greg squat-shuffled from pile to pile to take a few more samples for DNA analysis.

"Not diarrheic like I'd expect from a grizzly," he said. "Especially after what it had eaten."

They gathered around the dead bear. Dana was already bent over the grizzly's melon-sized head, pulling open what remained of its jaw and examining the teeth. Pristine molars glistened in the overcast sky above the birch and white pine. The trapper had blown off the canines and incisors along with half of the snout. Zane peered inside the gaping mouth. Other than the bloodstains and hair stuck in the gums, the molars appeared spotless.

"I'm surprised her teeth aren't in worse shape," Dana said. "Based on the size of her, I'd guess she's at least ten years old and would have some wear."

"No apparent gum disease or abscessed teeth at all, from what's left of them," Greg said.

"That rules out chronic pain from tooth decay." Zanebono had theorized the bear might have attacked out of redirected rage from chronic tooth pain, which sometimes occurred. He went down the mental checklist of other possibilities. "What about broken bones, any other old injuries that might've caused so much pain it couldn't stand it and went berserk?"

"Only the fresh wounds from the attack," Greg said. "That might have spurred it to attack more ferociously, but the question remains what started the whole thing."

Another scan over the carnage, and Zanebono had no doubts the bear had ambushed the trapper inside his cabin. Yet what might have prompted such an unprecedented assault? The bear appeared as healthy as any bear in a zoo.

Jasper snapped photographs. "Perhaps she's got meningitis or osteoporosis," he suggested.

"We'll find that out once we get it back to the lab," Greg said.

"Amazing she was able to tear flesh with nothing but molars," Dana said.

"Certainly was in a rage," Greg reiterated. "It used its carnassials for all they were worth."

Dana let the bear's jaw snap shut and stood. "This is a strange one, fellows."

"Won't be easy keeping the press from turning ballistic," Zane said.

Dana giggled. "They'll love it, no doubt."

"I won't blame them this time." Jasper lowered his Nikon and shook his head. "This isn't normal."

"Normal is a tricky word," Dana said, her hands on her curvy hips, pushing against her tight navy blue trooper's slacks. The Glock sidearm and Stratos phone on her belt accentuated her curves. Zane had always found her attractive. Too bad she'd been pushing him away more and more lately.

"Ugly, that's for sure," Greg said. "Hadn't witnessed this much gore since I used to watch those splatter films as a teenager."

Dana waved mosquitoes from her face and winced. Her brown eyes, light like tiger's-eye, sparkled with disgust. "Smells like hell too." She hoisted a biobag full of evidence she'd retrieved from the cabin and handed it to Zane. "This is all that might help identify the victim. A couple of notebooks with curled edges and five spent rifle shells. No other identification. No photo, passport, driver's license, checkbook, wallet. Nothing. Fingerprints or DNA might show who he is, if he's got a criminal history."

Zane grabbed the biobag and peered over the grounds for the umpteenth time. Typical trapper's shanty. Few modern contraptions. A place he'd like to call home, minus the gore. A rusty snowmachine, about ten years old, semicovered with a canvas tarp, sat on the side of the cabin by the woodshed. Blood splatter left an irregular heart shape on the canvas. Ironic, he thought.

He sighed into the soggy air, leaving a waft of silver breath. "One hell of a way to start the summer."

CHAPTER 2

ZANE sat at his desk at regional headquarters near downtown Anchorage the day after the attack and shuffled through paperwork, the least appealing part of his job. Officially, no state agency investigated bear attacks. Curiosity—and a dead body—had led them to land the A-Star at the trapper's cabin. Loose agglomerations of interested parties came together for the concern of public safety and to quell media curiosity. And in the case of the AWT, for protection of wildlife. But this time Fish and Game had unloaded the paperwork on his department since the mounting evidence suggested the grizzly had attacked unprovoked.

"This one's your girl," Jasper Bohler had told him after they'd left the attack scene by the trapper's cabin. "You figure out what went wrong with her, if you want."

Zane had sarcastically reminded him that some guardians of Alaska's wildlife believed bears never attacked unprovoked. Regardless, Lt. Jasper had left the bloody mess in his lap. Zane understood Fish and Game's call of duty tripled with the winter breakup, and they sought ways to shed excess workload.

Amanda O'Connell, the flirtatious and pudgy office assistant, smiled at him as he groaned over the mound of files. She often embarrassed him by commenting on his dark Ivy League hair and "pecan brown" eyes. She had more of the Irish in her than Yupik, Zane supposed. A glance through the glass partition into Col. Wallace Lund's office showed his boss engaged in a heavy conversation with the public relations liaison, Lt. Karen Flecks. They'd have much to discuss before releasing information to the press about the fatal bear mauling. He considered himself lucky to sit on the other side of the partition, despite the crushing paperwork on his desk.

Zane still waited to hear from Greg regarding the bear's necropsy. In the meantime, he hashed out theory after theory of his own on what might have provoked the attack on the victim, nicknamed "Trapper John." Zane's speculation that Trapper John had been feeding the bears wavered after interviews with nearby neighbors—the closest a quarter mile away—revealed they'd never known him to mistreat bears. Even more puzzling, none of the neighbors had experienced bear troubles.

Zane was pondering the trapper's idyllic life, ending tragically, when his telephone rang. "This is Trooper Fusca.... Okay.... Really? Hmm.... Sure.... I'll look for it.... Thanks.... Bye." He peered at Dana, sitting at her desk across from his. "That was the Bureau of Investigations. They got the medical examiner's report on our Trapper John. They're going to fax it for our records."

"Did they find anything unusual?"

"Only that the trapper had advanced pancreatic cancer and would most likely have died by the end of summer anyway. What do you think about that?"

Dana frowned. "I'd rather die from cancer than have a bear partially eat me."

"I don't know," Zane said, studying the popcorn ceiling. "If I had a choice, I might take death by bear."

"You men love to be sacrificial lambs."

The medical examiner's report curled from the facsimile machine fifteen minutes later. The autopsy confirmed that Trapper John (officially known as John Doe 11-5, the twenty-third fatality from a bear attack in the white man's recorded history of Alaska and the fifth unidentified man of 2011 found dead), had died between eighteen and twenty-four hours before his discovery. Numerous laceration and abrasion marks crisscrossed the outline of the body. Despite dozens of broken bones and a crushed vertebra, the victim had expired from exsanguination. Massive blood loss. The medical examination verified what the bloody scene had revealed—a vicious struggle had ensued between bear and man. Neither had come out victorious.

"Poor guy," Dana said. "I hope we find out who he is."

"You mean was."

Initial prints taken from the three remaining fingers uncovered zilch. Trapper John had not lived the life of an ex-con on the edge. The missing person's clearinghouse had already posted an "unidentified body" announcement on their website, including aerial photographs of Trapper John's cabin and a few items of his clothing for easier identification. Since he'd worn no wedding ring (at least, no sign of a ring had turned up in the bear's scat), he would most likely remain an unknown for quite a while. Trapper John's neighbors had no idea of his identity other than a possible first name—Ted. The AST still awaited a full name from the municipal clerk, who might have a plat description of the cabin property on file, including the owner.

The faceless trapper was a good guy by all accounts, without a criminal background, seeking to mind his own business in the Alaska bush apart from mainstream society. Zane had come to Alaska for the same reasons.

Yet, as his own life had proved, Alaska sometimes forced a grim dose of reality on its human and animal inhabitants. Death and heartache, as much a part of life as the wind and the changing seasons, clamped its fangs on Alaskans more often than not. Zane had experienced that firsthand too.

An hour later, Greg called Zane with word the bear's necropsy was about to begin at the University of Anchorage's Department of Pathology. Without delay, he raced across town in the AWT's Escalade, seized two years ago in a drug raid, before any more interruptions kept him from observing the procedure.

He made it to the lab the moment the pathologist, Dr. Eugene Orowitz, was slicing along the bear's thorax. Zane glanced around. Stainless steel stretched from wall to wall and floor to ceiling. Storage racks, trays, everything pristine and icy cold.

Zane had observed necropsies in the past and had prepared for the unspeakable stench. He held a handkerchief splashed with Polo cologne that he always kept in the Escalade's glove compartment over his nose. He sidled up next to Greg, one of the chief biologists with the university's Department of Biological Sciences, and a colleague. A biologist with Fish and Game also attended.

Dr. Orowitz proceeded to pull pieces of clothing from the bear's intestines and stomach. They matched those worn by Trapper John and what they'd found mixed with the bear scat at the scene. Greg mentioned this fact to the doctor. A few fingers and other unidentifiable human remains followed. Dr. Orowitz shook his head. "Quite a mauling," he murmured. "How long did the ME say the victim had been deceased?"

"Between eighteen and twenty-four hours," the biologist with Fish and Game said.

"Our lady's been deceased about sixteen hours," the doctor said. "Rigor mortis has already passed. She must've been feeding a while after she'd killed the victim. She's got partially digested human remains throughout her digestive tract."

"Any sign of a wedding ring?" Zane asked, wanting to learn the hermit's identity more than anything.

Dr. Orowitz lifted a clump of fluid-soaked fabric with forceps. His eyes screwed up. "None that I can detect. Victim must've been single. Lucky no wife would have to identify his body. The bear had quite a feast. Anything left of the man?"

"The bear fed off the entire body, bites here and there," Zane said into his handkerchief. "Much of his arms and legs and face were completely gone."

The pathologist flashed his dark eyes above his thick moustache and dropped the soiled remnants of clothing onto a tray. "Quite extraordinary considering the condition of the grizzly's muzzle. Bear must've been right on top when the victim fought back. She's got a stab wound in her side, penetrating the middle right lobe of her lung. Has a few more bullets in the abdomen. The victim fired off quite a few shots. Amazing the bear had lived long enough to feed off the man, considering her injuries."

A meditative silence followed the clink of three slugs into a stainless steel vessel. The subsequent hum of the florescent lights underscored the exceptional eeriness of the attack.

"Odd...."

"What's that, Eugene?" Greg asked.

"The sow looks at least ten years old, but doesn't appear to have ever given birth. Uterus is completely intact, no stretched cervix."

"Maybe she's sterile," Zane said.

"Or a dyke," the Fish and Game biologist said. No one followed his snicker.

Dr. Orowitz tinkered inside the bear while the others watched in silence. He sliced off bits of organ and muscle tissue and placed them on petri dishes for later analysis.

"Big bear even for a boar, for the area," he said. "She weighs in at one-hundred-sixty-four kilograms. Well-fed and healthy. Lots of fat reserves. She's taken on quite a bit of calories since emerging from her den. No visible sign of osteoporosis, as the X-rays have already shown us. Organs are healthy. She's got some scar tissue in her right posterior shoulder. An old bullet wound, maybe six years old or more. Otherwise, in perfect shape, even for a bear half her age. How far out did you discover the victim's remains?"

"Fifteen miles northwest of Eagle River," Zane said. "South of Birchwood."

"She might have migrated from the coast," the pathologist pondered aloud, but directed the statement mostly to Greg. "Or maybe from the Alaska Range before breakup and followed the Knik Arm down?"

"It's possible," Greg answered. "But we checked feeding grounds in both areas and they're plentiful. Can't imagine why she'd want to waste all that energy and come here."

Next, Dr. Orowitz withdrew cerebrospinal fluid using an instrument resembling a thin turkey baster. The doctor would use the fluid to check for meningitis, brain tumors, and other disorders, Zane knew. He still held onto hope that some kind of brain mess might explain an unprovoked and violent attack. He hoped whatever they found wasn't contagious to other bears. As a wildlife investigator, that would be his primary concern.

What followed the lumbar procedure forced Zane to step back. He pressed his hand more firmly against the handkerchief covering his mouth and inhaled more of the Polo. The Fish and Game biologist turned his head to the side and watched from the corners of his eyes. Using a chainsaw-like instrument with a buzzing sound worse than a dentist's drill, Dr. Orowitz decapitated the bear. Scant blood leaked from the severed tissue, since most the blood had already drained from the bear and washed into the floor drain, indicated by the rubber tube inserted into its subclavian artery. The bodiless head looked like a grotesque Halloween mask.

The doctor placed the head on a stainless steel scale. Blue digital numbers displayed eight point six kilograms, about twenty pounds. "We'll do a separate brain autopsy in addition to the spinal to make sure she didn't have advanced brain disease," Dr. Orowitz said. "But my clinical opinion is she's in perfect health."

Zane lowered his handkerchief and shook his head. The necropsy thus far, if anything, reaffirmed how little they understood about the gory attack. Zane turned to Greg in the hallway a half hour later. Away from the others, he said, "What do you think?"

"Not sure." Greg gazed toward the tiled floor. "Still have to go with the theory the bear had become habituated and wanted inside that cabin for whatever reason."

"No chance it was a hyperaggressive alpha asserting dominance over a territory?"

"Usually in cases of predation of humans, the less dominant bears are the greatest threat," Greg said. "Redirected aggression, you might call it. Short man's disease, in a sense. Our bear certainly hadn't suffered from that."

Studying Greg's brown eyes, which sparkled like garnets under the florescent lights, Zane said, "Then the grizzly was basically a psycho, is that it?"

Greg shook his head and snorted. "Few of my colleagues share my views, Zane, but as you know, I believe bears are as unpredictable as humans. It's quite possible it was merely a crazy bear, like you say. We'll probably never learn. At least we know for sure it's the offending bear. We won't have to worry about another attack by a bear with an appetite for human flesh."

CHAPTER 3

Grizzly kills trapper

By LIZ SCRIBNER

A GRIZZLY broke into a trapper's cabin near Birchwood over the weekend and claimed the man's life, a mere week before the official start of the summer tourist season. The victim, identified by municipal plat survey as Theodore Krum, is believed to have lived alone. The sow thought responsible for the mauling was found dead nearby. According to pathology reports, Krum had fired off several rifle shots into the bear and stabbed it in the chest with a Bowie knife, killing it. No cubs were found in the area.

Two Alaska Wildlife Troopers, a Fish and Game warden, and a biologist with the University of Anchorage discovered the body Monday while conducting a routine moose count from a helicopter. The research team landed near the site and found Krum dead several yards from his cabin. The dead sow was a few yards from Krum. The municipal medical examiner pronounced Krum dead on the scene.

Officials wouldn't detail the nature of the fatal attack except to suggest Krum's injuries were wide-ranging. University of Anchorage's bear experts believe Krum might have been feeding nearby bears, prompting the grizzly to seek more food inside the cabin.

"It's a case we see often," Dr. Sylvia Linden, a biologist with the university, said. "Bears realize where the food comes from, and they go straight for the source."

Investigators on the scene discovered high growing brush which might have concealed the bear from Krum's view. No one else was injured in the attack, and no one has yet claimed Krum's remains.

The medical examiner's report reveals Krum had been dead at least 18 hours before the research team discovered his body. Much of his body had been fed on by foraging animals.

Nearby residents described Krum as a quiet and elusive man who caused them and the local bear population little trouble, as far as they knew.

The fatal bear mauling is the first reported inside the municipality of Anchorage since 1995, and the first bear attack in the area since three years ago, when a slew of attacks terrorized Anchorage in August 2008. At that time, three people were mauled in a span of two weeks, although none fatally.

Zanebono dropped the *Anchorage Daily News* on his desk. The issue was over. Psycho grizzly was dead. They had informed the media and public of the attack, and, despite the media's attempt to stir alarm, Anchorage residents went about their day as if nothing had happened. Or so he hoped.

The troopers still had to tread carefully when releasing accounts of bear attacks. AST's public relations department, headed by Karen Flecks, demonstrated mastery at keeping people from getting anti-bear. Angry sentiments often erupted, especially after an unusual string of attacks, like the summer of 2008 when the three separate grizzly attacks inside Anchorage's municipal limits had pushed the city to the edge.

Zane's job, after all, was to safeguard Alaska's wildlife from unnecessary harm, even if those animals sometimes displayed brutal hostility toward humans. Then there lurked the others—the polar opposites of the bloodthirsty hunters. Those who practiced an odd form of zoolatry. Many in his own department flirted with such animal worship. An Alaska without its largest mammals—even those that showed fierce brutality— was unimaginable. Yet he understood the difference between a wild animal that required respect and a stuffed teddy bear.

Zane, like many others, had moved to Alaska for its uncultivated wilderness. Surrounded by rugged, raw nature, a man had purpose. In Alaska, Zane could accomplish undertakings improbable in the rest of contemporary America. He sought his own destiny, to live without modern constraints, restrictions, regulations. Odd that he'd become a state trooper a few years after moving. A person needed to make a living, after all.

His father, an emigrant from the Calabria region of Italy, asked him the day before he left for his big Alaska adventure what he hoped to find in a vast, rustic land. "The same thing you were looking for when you came to America, Pop," Zane told him with a wry smile. His father chuckled and shook his head. The need to explore far off places might've been lodged deep in the family's genes.

Maybe his own son, on the verge of turning nine someday, might become the first human on Mars, Zane often mused.

Alaska meant more to Zane than a place to explore. To that day, he hadn't pinpointed what exactly, or how a state represented a concept. But it did. Independence from an ever restrictive society? A mere image, yet a powerful one.

He hadn't ventured to Alaska alone. He'd dragged along a new bride and a one-year-old son. His intention was to move into the bush, live a subsistent lifestyle with his woman and boy by his side. Old-fashioned, many called him. Others referred to him as "unconventional." His in-laws had called him, "Idiotic!" Perhaps all three labels fit.

Their marriage commitment after moving lasted less than two years. The sometimes harsh reality of life in Alaska—the state with the highest divorce rate—claimed yet another union. Thoughts of his ex-wife, Julie, his sweetheart from Cranston High School East, often choked his mind. He wished their life together had turned out differently. At thirty-one, he learned a man's control over relationships came as easily as spring in Alaska. In other words, shaky, at best.

He eventually settled in the Anchorage bowl (sardonically called by locals, Los Anchorage) once his marriage broke up along with winter's ice. He lived a suburban-like life, the same he might have had in Rhode Island.

Despite life's uncertainties, he was glad he chose Alaska for his nesting ground. Waking each morning to the towering, eternally snow-streaked mountains of the Chugach Range, the scent of pine, the vast wilderness stretching farther than anywhere else in the western hemisphere, filled him with arousing expectation. Maybe that's why he elected to become a wildlife investigator after one year with the AST. To protect the actual wilderness he cherished—in spite of its callous reality.

He still had no idea what had prompted the grizzly attack on Theodore Krum. At least they had identified him from the municipal clerk's plat description. Thus far, no family or friends had stepped forward to claim his remains.

The AWT may never learn what had happened, like Greg had said. Did Krum feed bears, like pigeons? If so, why hadn't the bear gone after the cache of canned and boxed food inside the cabin rather than partially consume him? Had he done something to anger the grizzly?

Until Dr. Orowitz informed him whether the bear carried a contagion that might threaten other bears, the ordeal wafted behind him like noxious car exhaust. Other pressing matters prowled around the corner. New challenges, new mysteries reared themselves.

A slap of more files on his desk. Fellow wildlife trooper Langston Banks, smiling like a demon, stared down at him with his piercing leather-brown eyes. "Reports from the gallbladder harvesting, Bono." Langston sauntered away without any other words. His uniform, worn a bit too tight, showcased a gym-honed rump that would make a moose proud. Must be keeping up with squats. Zane wondered if he still used the juice. Nice guy, but flashier than a supermodel.

Zane rummaged through the latest set of files. Recent black bear killings had resurfaced. Three blacks—a sow and two cubs—found slaughtered with bows near Eagle River two weeks ago. The killers had harvested the bears' gallbladders, leaving the rest behind. Human hunters had a place in the food chain as much as any animal, Zane believed—all part of the balance of nature—but killing wildlife to harvest organs for aphrodisiacs and sleep aids sold on the Asian market disturbed Zane. Wasteful, wanton slaughter.

Not the first time he'd faced the ugly slaughter of black bears. Every few years, the AWT nabbed greedy hunters harvesting bear organs for profit, sometimes fetching more than twenty thousand dollars apiece. Each time, the case had been solved. He had no intention of letting the latest mission end any differently.

Right when he set to organize his list of suspects, Dana, hanging up her phone, said to him with an amused grin, "That was the municipal police. We got an Alces alces stuck in a tree."

"In a tree? A little late for an April Fools' prank."

Dana ogled him over her mug of Bad Ass coffee. "The officer swore he was telling the truth."

"I guess we got to see this one to believe it."

When they arrived at 1400 E. Ptarmigan Drive—a middle class subdivision of modest ranchers and split-levels—a large group of people had already gathered around the home. An Anchorage news station filmed the scene while two municipal police officers tried to hold back the curious onlookers.

Zane gazed at the young moose (a subadult Alces alces), squirming and moaning from the sturdy branches of a white pine. He scratched under his trooper's cap. Why should he even care about those oversized rodents?

"How do you suppose it got up there? Practical joke from some neighborhood kids?"

"How would they have lifted him?" Dana said. "Even adolescent cows weigh close to a thousand pounds."

Difficult to judge the bull's age from the small set of velvety antlers it sported. Each winter, every bull moose loses its heavy antlers. From its body size, Zane guessed its age no older than three.

Zane asked the Anchorage police officer guarding the tree if he'd learned any details. The officer shook his head and said none of the neighbors saw how the moose got into the tree.

"You think it flew up there?" the officer said.

Zane chortled. "Only reindeer can fly."

The officer pointed out a woman wearing a bathrobe and head towel as the homeowner. Zane strode over to her right when a sharply dressed reporter shoved a chunky microphone into the middle-aged woman's face. The reporter stepped back and gestured for the cameraman to focus on Zane. Zane escorted the woman closer to her front door where he might question her without feeling as if he were in a reality TV show.

"You have no idea how the moose got up in the tree?"

The woman held onto her head towel to keep it in place when she shook her head. "I was getting out of the shower when Wayne, my neighbor, called to tell me a moose was in my tree. I thought he was yanking my chain. I glanced out the window, and, sure enough, there he was. I couldn't believe my eyes."

"You have trouble with pranksters around here?"

"Not that I'm aware of," the woman said.

"Do you live alone?"

"Ever since I divorced my husband five years ago, praise be to God."

Zanebono strolled to the backyard. Surveying the property, he noticed the typical Anchorage home. Five-gallon water jugs, old tires, wooden crates, bicycle chains, and a mishmash of other items cluttered the yard. No one wasted anything above the fifty-fourth parallel. Harsh winters required people hoard.

The house bordered a hillock covered in a grove of firs and pines. Large Alaskan ravens cackled from the branches. Many of the trees had toppled from past storms and created natural ramps leading to the tops of larger trees. Some of the fallen trees leaned onto the home's roof. Zane followed with his eyes the uneven canopy line of the evergreen grove to the rooftop. Screaming fire engines approached from the distance. He returned to the commotion in front, where the crowd had expanded. A second news crew had arrived, followed by a third.

"What's it look like, Bono?" Dana asked him.

"I'm pretty sure I figured it out." He waved over the homeowner. She secured her robe and scurried to his side. "Your moose might have wandered along some of those fallen trees pressing against your house, found itself on your roof, then, frightened, jumped off and landed in your pine tree out front here."

The homeowner shook her head. "That would explain it. The critter's probably too young to know what he was doing."

"Might do you and the local animals some good if you hire someone to remove those fallen trees off your property."

A municipal fire truck pushed into the scene, parting the crowd to either side of the street like a grizzly loping through a herd of caribou. The firefighters jumped from the truck. After assessing with Zane and Dana what tactics were needed to save the Alces alces, they organized their gear.

Zane retrieved the tranquilizer gun from the strongbox in back of the Escalade. He inserted the syringe dart containing the Immobilon—a combination of etorphine and ketamine. Chemically immobilizing any animal came with many risks—fatal apnea, violent tremors, even strokes—but few alternatives existed when trying to rescue a half-ton beast.

By the time he returned to the scene, firefighters were already stretching a net under the pine tree in case the rigged harness failed to hold the moose.

"You guys stand back." Zane aimed at the moose's rump once everyone had cleared. Although he had a steady hand, he wanted to take no chance anyone might get hit. The dose of Immobilon Zane used would kill a human adult within seconds. Ironically, Zane hadn't held a gun in his life until coming to Alaska. Living for a year in the bush, he'd become rather good at shooting mammals, large and small. He was a natural killer, his ex-wife had commented back at their rustic cabin in the bush.

"Here we go." He squeezed the trigger, and the usual puff of gas nudged his arm upward. The dart landed on target. The moose jerked, flinched its wobbly ears, whined, but seemed unaware of the syringe stuck in its hindquarter.

Zane lowered the rifle and raised his hand to keep everyone back. "Takes a minute before it'll go into effect."

Soon the moose's struggles waned. Its limbs drooped, and its head rested motionless against a branch. It looked like a massive furry garland.

"Careful," Zane said to the firefighters. "It's a good ten-foot drop. It'll break its neck for sure. You got about sixty minutes before it'll wake." Zane had deliberately used the word "minutes" rather than saying they had "one hour" to reinforce the urgency of the rescue. He worried they would not get the moose down in time before the Immobilon wore off.

The municipal firefighters, experienced dealing with wayward or trapped animals, rushed in with the ladder and harness to secure the animal. Two climbed the ladder, one behind the other. Three other rescuers jacked the crane on the fire truck that would lift the harness, typically used for rescuing people from Alaska's quicksand-like mudflats. Carefully they strapped the snoozing moose into the harness, ensuring its head slipped in without jeopardizing the hold the tree had on it. Cameras zoomed in on the action. The story would make a sweet end to a gruesome news week, Zane concurred, his mind sweeping over the ugliness of the grizzly bear attack from Monday.

The moose's marble-sized eyes fluttered. Its muscled snout flexed in the air. Zane's heart leaped. Maybe Zane had misjudged the bull's weight. Younger males seemed to have a higher tolerance for the Immobilon. Zane theorized high levels of testosterone interacted with the drug's pharmacodynamics. The moose relaxed. Zane breathed easier.

Neighbors, passersby, and people from across town who'd learned of the ordeal through home police scanners gathered to watch the rescue. The entire block held a collective breath. Other than the crackle from the emergency vehicle radios, the intermittent bark of an excited dog from a nearby yard, the chatty ravens, a person could have slept through the entire rescue.

The rescuers positioned the last section of the harness. Silently, the lead firefighter gestured to the crane operator. The crane ground into incremental position. The lead firefighter attached the hook to the crane hovering above the branches. Another gesture and the moose's massive shape began to lift, elegantly, like cottonwood snow.

With a steady hand, the crane operator, taking a generous fifteen minutes of finite maneuvering, lowered the moose to the ground. The crowd cheered once the bull touched the flatness of the grass. Camera crews captured the enthusiasm. The moose stirred. It lifted its head, gazed around with dopy brown eyes. In an instant, the subadult jumped onto its hooves, which always reminded Zane of a lady's pumps. The massive, delicate force of such muscular animals never failed to impress him. And upset his stomach.

The moose shook its head and trotted into the woods behind the houses, where it had probably survived for the winter scavenging on homeowner's garbage. The show was over; the crowd dispersed.

"Well," Zane said, raising his eyebrows at Dana. "Guess that's the end of that."

But not quite. One of the reporters for a local network affiliate rushed to Zane and Dana, followed by her cameraman. "Can I get your comments on the grizzly bear mauling death from Monday?" She had her microphone nearly up Zane's nose.

"The AST already issued a statement regarding the matter," he said, flinching backward.

"We're interested in what might have triggered the attack," the reporter said. "Was the trapper ambushed inside his cabin, as some say?"

"I cannot clarify more on the details other than what we already have stated," Zane said. "We have confirmed the offending bear dead, and there's no cause for alarm."

"Do you believe the bear acted unprovoked? With Memorial Day weekend around the corner, should citizens be alarmed?"

"The official report from the University of Anchorage is that the trapper most likely surprised the bear foraging in nearby brush, or had been feeding it, resulting in the attack. No need for alarm."

Even Zane did not fully believe the report. Most of the experts from the University of Anchorage, who provided the details of the attack to the AST's public relations department, disliked using the term "unprovoked" to describe bear attacks. When unsure, they usually concluded the victim had "surprised" the bear. Zane had witnessed enough blood and body parts at the scene and during the necropsy to fear something worse than a startled bear. Karen Flecks had determined to limit the graphic details of the mauling. A flesh-eating bear, even one that had been killed, would rouse hysteria in the public. Zane figured the reporter, fishing for details, sought to spread such panic.

He and Dana walked to the truck, but the reporter tried her luck with Dana. Dana, a bit more abrupt than Zane, nudged her shoulders forward. "We don't conduct official investigations into bear attacks," she said. "You should realize that by now." And they ignored the remainder of the reporter's questions, more bothersome than mosquitoes.

"You're handling the media roughly these days," Zane said to her in the truck heading back to headquarters.

"Bono, you're too soft with them," Dana said, steering the sturdy truck down the highway onramp. "You should learn to ignore them. Don't bother to give them the time of day."

"You're good at that," Zane said.

Dana gave him a sideways glance. "What's that supposed to mean?"

Zanebono chuckled. "Nothing, don't worry about it."

He hadn't meant to deliver his comment in the form of an insult. He liked Dana Chernikoff's brusque style. From the first moment the twenty-six-year-old entered the department as a rookie wildlife trooper three years ago, he respected her tenacity. One of the few Alaskan natives working as a trooper, she understood as much about Alaska wildlife as anyone. She represented the closest to the Alaska world Zane had encountered outside of his job. Her natural strength instantly attracted him and had grown into genuine desire.

"Bono, you have to get those ideas out of your head."

"What ideas?"

"I can see in your eyes. You're brooding over it again. It was one night two years ago. That's all."

"Was it that long ago?"

Seemed like last week. After Dana had learned of her father's death, Zane's comforting her had unleashed passion they'd both harbored since their first meeting. One intimate touch had led to another. He hadn't been sure a relationship would bloom from their one night of lovemaking. He'd observed her the weeks following. She'd appeared disinterested. He'd finally asked her if she wanted to date, and she had laughed.

The department didn't frown upon coworkers dating. Many were married and continued to work together. More and more women resisted Zane's noble intentions, although he'd considered himself above average in looks and personality. Even Dana had complimented him on his appearance and charm.

Why did she refuse him? Another part of the post-modern world Zane had learned to let go. He grasped as many answers for his poor social life as he did the grizzly attack.

"You sorry you and me ever hooked up?" he asked her while the warehouses north of downtown whizzed by.

"Bono, we've been over this. I liked being with you. You were a big comfort. But it was one night. One night with a good friend when I needed one."

Zane bit his lower lip. "Hard to figure out you women, that's for sure."

Dana laughed, her cheeks rosy against her bronze skin. "Harder to figure out you men."

Eighteen-wheelers heading north on the Glenn Highway ground past the Escalade. The Chugach Range towered above the northeastern horizon beyond the urban sprawl. Zane shook his head. "Maybe you had us pegged right when you said men are like sacrificial lambs."

CHAPTER 4

THE ten o'clock news buzzed in the background while Zane threw together lasagna, using an old box of Hamburger Helper, leftover ricotta cheese on the verge of spoiling, and jarred spaghetti sauce. His father would roll in his grave. But he was hungry and didn't have the time—or the patience—to make traditional lasagna the way his father had taught him. With the semblance of lasagna simmering on the stovetop, he took his bottle of beer outside, keeping the sliding screen door ajar, and sat at a cast iron table on his small porch that overlooked his patch of boreal forest.

Quarter past ten at night, and the sun, an orange orb hanging above the canopy of black spruce and firs that blocked any view of his neighbors, had yet to set. Tonight, sunset would not come until near eleven thirty. The green leaves and needles stood out against the milky sky, as stark as a punch in the nose.

He lived as far from the city center as doable inside the Anchorage municipal limits. His commute from the Girdwood Mobile Home Park along the Turnagain Arm took about an hour without heavy snow or road construction. It was worth living closer to nature, the principal reason he'd moved to Alaska.

Many of his neighbors lived in luxury A-frames silhouetted against the emerald wall of the impinging Chugach Range. Zane's was a simple doublewide built in a fifteen-unit subdivision before the ski resort up the road had opened. He bought the house on impulse for cheap ($205,000) soon after his assignment to the Anchorage office. The area had grown even in his short six years living in Girdwood. He couldn't curse the development spreading in the upper basin area. He'd moved there for the same reason as everyone else.

Theodore Krum's face appeared in his mind while he gazed at his rustic backyard. The trapper had moved to Alaska to get away from the world and its puzzling baggage, like Zane had. He'd escaped to the enveloping branches of conifers and kisses of mountain peaks. Yet Zane, and everyone else in Alaska, accepted that appearances can deceive.

The attractions that lured people into the wilderness sometimes killed them. Brutal tragedy lurked in every mountain shadow, behind every tree. Even Alaska's natives sometimes failed to prepare against their environment. He remembered reading about a Yupik man in downtown Fairbanks who'd died digging for his truck keys in the snow after a bout of heavy drinking. Police found him the next morning, frozen like a statue, his hand still reaching into the deep snow. Modern man of any race, in many ways, stood little chance against nature's fury.

Zane experienced nature's wrath a mere nine months after moving to Alaska. He'd hauled his then wife and their son, not even old enough to walk, into the vast wilderness north of Denali National Park. Zane found an advertisement for an old cabin, sixty miles from the highway, no longer used by its owner, an old trapper whose rheumatism forced him to remain near the security of town. Using money they'd saved while working during and after high school, Zane paid the trapper five thousand dollars for the use of the cramped, moldy shack for one year, a dream come true for Zane. Julie tolerated it, for Zane's sake.

Zane learned much of his skills by getting his hands grimy. Boyhood camping trips into New Hampshire's White Mountains helped. In some ways, Julie proved the better woodsman. She had a knack for finding the perfect discarded tool or a lone caribou to shoot. One day she stumbled upon a swath of berries wider than a Walmart parking lot that they fed off for months. Julie's blackberry pies, baked in their wood-burning oven, and the blackberry syrup she canned for sourdough pancakes were some of the tastiest treats he'd ever eaten.

With baby Michael on her hip, Julie would tend to the garden of potatoes and onions the old-timer had started years before. Moss still protected the roots from the cold. Zanebono would sometimes laugh, spying them. Julie reminded him of Sacajawea with little Jean-Baptiste strapped to her back. Julie, a belated hippy of the twenty-first century, relished the natural world for her child. Fear never crossed her path. Although she would rather have stayed in Rhode Island, she made the best of her new environs and flourished.

Together, the three exemplified the finest qualities of a small, fledgling family. Man, woman, and child, living in the shadow of the Alaska Range. Zane spent hours outside toiling, and Julie, when not outside herself, would be inside the cabin nursing Mikey or cooking, like a pioneer wife in days gone by.

Zane lucked out marrying a woman sturdy enough to accept his rugged dreams, despite her wishes they remain closer to family. In the end, her steadfast toughness ushered the breakup of their idyllic life in the Alaskan bush. He could still hear her voice calling for him, shrill and horrifying.

Much how Ted Krum's life had ended, Zane speculated. Now the hermit lay stored in a medical examiner's freezer, without any friends or family. But the trapper would have died alone from pancreatic cancer by summer's end, anyway.

Once again, nature proved the stronger adversary, one way or the other.

His nose told him dinner was ready. The phony lasagna was sizzling in the pan when he stepped inside the house. He plated himself a hefty portion and sat in front of the television. Hot pepper flakes and a generous amount of shredded parmesan made the meal palatable.

He chuckled when news of the moose caught in the tree popped on screen. He'd viewed himself on television a handful of times since taking his job with the AST, but he never liked the local population seeing more of him than he saw of them. Luckily, the network edited out the part where the pesky reporter asked about Monday's bear attack.

Left with an empty plate, Zane dumped it into the sink and dug into his pants pocket for his cell phone. Sighing, he speed dialed a number he rarely used. Tonight, lonely and stuffed, he goaded himself into calling. She'd been lingering on his mind lately. That time of year often awakened stirrings inside him. She answered on the fifth ring. Typical for her. Not too fast, not too slow. Even with her encumbered movement, little had changed with her behavior. Still the independent, headstrong woman.

Her calm voice indicated she understood, as always, Zanebono's calling her late at night, since his job forced him to work erratic hours. Zanebono grinned when she accepted his invitation for dinner tomorrow. He wanted to see her. Not to check on her, but to visit, for old time's sake.

He clicked off the phone and shook his head. Did he ever imagine his life would turn out the way it had?

ZANEBONO waited by his Sierra outside Julie's five-story apartment building on Fifth Avenue after a typical Thursday at work. Snow atop the Chugach Range rising to the east sparkled like strands of honey. The Anchorage skyline reflected in the glass of the lobby doors. He had left his trooper cap in the cab, and the blurry sun, still high in the sky at six o'clock in the evening, warmed his cheeks. The uneventful workday had proved satisfying. He hoped the evening would too.

He looked around and grimaced. He hated the place. Never understood why she'd chosen to live in a public assistance apartment complex. The few times he'd resisted contacting her was because of where she lived. Too many dependents. Gave him the creeps. Why did she prefer relying on the government rather than on him?

He'd have to curb his opinions in Julie's company. She liked her home. Always expressed pride in it. Inside wasn't bad. She'd invited him in a few times since she'd moved. A small, one-bedroom apartment. Dark green rug. Ochre walls. She'd made nice quarters for herself.

Zane always wondered why she remained in Alaska following her accident rather than return to Rhode Island, where she'd never wanted to leave in the first place. He figured she was rebelling against her controlling parents, who had custody of Michael.

His former in-laws had flown to Alaska to watch after Mikey, two years old at the time, while Julie recovered in the hospital. Zane expected them to stay with him while he kept watch over Julie. Instead, his in-laws absconded with the boy back to Rhode Island after two weeks. He understood. Temporarily, it would be for the best, until Mikey's mother recuperated.

But temporarily turned into a year. And when he tried to get Julie's parents to bring Michael back, they said he'd already settled in, attending nursery school, surrounded by a doting family. They labeled him an unfit father for having dragged their daughter and baby grandson into the Alaska wilds. Julie, with her reduced capacity, agreed they should keep him. He was better off in Rhode Island, where he'd have a real childhood. She never did get around to leaving Anchorage for Mikey's side. Julie flew to Rhode Island to visit him a few times (she'd always complained about the complications of traveling with a handicap) and each time relayed he was a happy little boy.

When Julie telephoned him two Octobers ago to inform him Michael would be coming to Alaska for Christmas, Zane was delighted. He didn't even mind that Mr. Gagliardi tagged along. "Too long a flight for such a young boy alone," he said. Instead, Zane relished his short time with his son, despite the awkward presence of his former father-in-law staying in one of his doublewide's spare bedrooms. He seemed overwhelmed with the ferocity of Alaska's winters and barely left Mikey's side. Julie surprised him when she stayed the night Christmas Eve, showing up unexpectedly on the special bus. Seemed like a family again, no matter how short-lived.

Zane wanted Mikey back badly, but he had abandoned trying. Everyone, including Michael's mother, worked overtime to keep the boy in Rhode Island. He supposed he should be grateful, and less peeved, that so many people cared for him.

He visited Mikey while back home for his father's funeral last summer. The boy acted aloof and shy, flinching from his hugs and kisses, as if the previous Christmas had never happened. He supposed it was for the best to leave him behind. Over the years, his ache for his son had softened into a dull pain, like a stiff neck.

The automatic doors swung open. Anchorage's reflection disappeared and reappeared in a flash. Sight of Julie in her wheelchair still caught Zane's breath. He forced a grin. She smiled back, her hair bleached and tied in a smart bun, most likely by the chatty women at her favorite salon. Funny how she still worried over her appearance. Not because she was wheelchair-bound, but because she lived in Alaska. Even at the cabin, she often dressed more like a New England college girl than an Alaskan sourdough's wife.

"Hi, Zane." She rolled closer to him, her right hand clasped onto the wheelchair control. Her arms showed better coordination than when he'd seen her last autumn. "How you been?"

"I'm good. Nice to see you, Julie." She had smeared her makeup a bit on her lips, but at least she'd tried. The scars on her face and neck, faded after several years, were barely noticeable anymore. "You're looking good." Pleasantries came easy for them. Serious talk led them to falter. "Winter treat you okay?"

"Not in particular." She giggled. "I must've kept the lights and television on nonstop. I'll never get used to the darkness."

The image depressed Zane. Gnawing emptiness ate into his gut. He grinned wider, displaying his full set of teeth. "That's Alaska for you. Ready to eat?"

She rolled alongside Zane's unhurried stride to his pickup. "I heard about the grizzly attack."

Zane frowned. "Just one of those one in a thousand things."

"How bad was it?"

"What was left of him had over four hundred separate wounds. But it's over. Bear's dead and incinerated by now, except for its head."

"Yuck. Spare me the details."

They stopped at his truck. Awkwardness inched up inside him. He knew from the past she preferred little assistance. Watching her struggle out of her wheelchair made him cringe. Only when she had no choice did she grin with her eyes rolled back and allow Zane to lift her inside his lofty truck. He folded her wheelchair and stowed it in the backseat of the cab.

The drive to the restaurant where he'd reserved a table took only five minutes, since Julie lived near the heart of the city, but it might as well have taken an hour. Awkward silences had already begun to disturb any hope for a laid-back evening. He was glad to be inside the posh restaurant located on the tenth floor of a four-star downtown hotel. He never appreciated fancy places. A country fish fry was more his style. Julie was rather lowbrow herself. Yet, for some reason, the evening compelled him to take her someplace nicer than a brightly lit roadhouse. Silk blinds covering the windows kept out the nighttime sun. He recognized the sepia photographs of the Alaska bush hanging from the wood paneled walls as the life he'd left behind.

"I saw you on television, saving that moose," Julie said once she situated her wheelchair as far under the table as possible.

Zanebono resisted an urge to help. "It's my job," he said, feeling his cheeks heat.

"Don't be ashamed. I have nothing against moose. You looked good with your dark eyes and short-cropped hair."

Was she flirting with him? Most likely not. That part of their relationship had ended long ago. They hadn't made love since before her accident, seven years ago. He never rejected the idea of making love with a semi-quadriplegic. She, on the other hand, had issues with him. The last time he'd had sex with anyone was last summer. He couldn't think about that now. Still couldn't believe it happened. First he messed around with Dana, and then…. He chuckled, unable to truly comprehend.

"Seeing myself on TV is the worst part of the job," he said, flushing.

"You looked handsome in your uniform, always did."

"You said you hated my uniform when you first saw me wearing it."

"You shocked me, that's all. I'd grown accustomed to you loathing authority." She eyeballed him from across the table. "To see you as a state trooper…. Well…."

"I still surprise myself." Zane opened his menu to conceal his badge, but only glanced at the fancy script. "I remember the first time I put it on. I worried I might pass out from hyperventilating."

"We're allowed to change, Zane," she said with a relinquishing sigh.

The waiter brought water and asked if they wanted cocktails. Both declined and requested a few minutes to study their menus. Julie stopped the waiter before he walked away.

"Can you bring me a straw, please?"

The waiter, reddening for failing to realize Julie might have difficulty using her hands, scurried off and returned with a straw and a shaky grin.

A bulky discomfort hovered between Zane and Julie with their noses buried in the menus. Same scenario whenever they got together. Zane struggled for the right words. Difficult to communicate with each other even while married. Kind and intelligent, but eerily independent, to the point he wondered at times if Julie cared if he lived or died. He held his hand to his thigh to steady his bouncing leg.

He cleared his throat, needing to fill the gap with conversation. "You were talking about taking up needlepoint during the ride over. You thinking of trying to make money off it? Sell your work on the Internet, or something like that?"

"My work?" She blew out a chortle. "For one, I'm a beginner. I only started because the lady who lives across the hall, the one who lost her legs in a snowmachine accident, got me into it. For another, my hands shake too much to make anything decent. I do it mostly for physical therapy. Besides, I don't care about money."

"They have organizations that sell work on behalf of...."

"On behalf of handicapped people?" She shook her head at Zane's burning cheeks. "You don't have to be ashamed to say it, Zane. I'm handicapped. Or handicappable, whatever the politically correct term is nowadays."

Zane lowered his head. The words on his menu merged into a meaningless black blob. "I'm not ashamed."

"I wish you would get over the past," she said. "I've never blamed you for what happened. I made my choice when I came to Alaska with you. I blamed you for how you treated me afterward. Like I was a child. You were worse than my parents."

"Hadn't I been caring after the accident?" he said.

"You were condescending." She rested her eyes on her menu, but clearly was not reading any of the entries. "It never mattered. Our marriage wouldn't have worked out one way or the other. In the long run, it was over. I think we both knew."

Alaska, always the "other woman." It could destroy weak relationships, fortify strong ones. "I guess we were doomed back in Rhode Island," Zane said, toying with his napkin roll.

"We butted heads too often. I'm selfish in that way."

Zane unfolded the napkin and studied the glint in the silverware from the subdued recessed lighting. He sipped his ice water, held it in his mouth, swallowed. "We both were."

"I like to have my way," Julie said. "Maybe that's why I never got past your bisexuality."

Zanebono widened his eyes. Moisture sapped from his mouth. "What? Why did you say that? What do you mean?"

She tittered. "No big deal, Zane. I've always known, even before we left Rhode Island. I found some porn on your computer. You forgot you had it minimized. A couple of sites with naked women and one for gay men. I don't know why I'm mentioning it now. I guess I'm tired of pretending about everything, from my handicap to our relationship."

Hot blood ran in Zane's ears. "I... I was curious. I never acted on it." He shuddered from his lie. He'd never flat-out fibbed to Julie about anything, and disliked doing it. He'd fooled around with a few of his high school buddies before he and Julie started dating. No big deal. Typical drunken episodes. He never thought much of it. Something guys did. He pushed the images aside as quickly as they'd emerged.

Julie shrugged. "Like I said, no big deal. Porn is part of male culture. I don't worry about that. I'm not an anti-sex feminist freak. Finding your porn, gay or straight, only underscored my own worries about myself. I wasn't much cut out as wife, for anyone. In a way, I can understand you."

"What do you mean?" Zane lifted his water to his mouth for what seemed the twentieth time in as many seconds. He hated his ex-wife's frankness sometimes.

"Infatuated with Alaska the way you are," she went on, "it's almost natural for a bisexual man. Everything's so rugged and masculine. Like a moose in rut that'll mount about anything. Even saw one trying to mate with a Ford Focus last autumn." She giggled. "Raw power and beauty, no need for makeup or manicuring. All very masculine. I like Alaska for that reason too, Zane. Probably the only thing I do like about it."

"I was always faithful," Zane muttered into his menu.

"I never worried about that, Zane. I know you aren't the disloyal type, to anyone. Who could you have messed around with out in the bush, anyway? The wolves? But none of that mattered. I'm better off alone. No one can give me as much attention as I can."

Allowing the reality of their conversation to sink in, Zane flashed her an anxious expression. "That's not why you wanted to keep Mikey from me, is it? Because… because of… what you said? You never told anyone, did you? Your parents?"

"No, never." Julie shook her head with what dexterity she could muster. "It's none of my family's business. I have no issue with your abilities as a father. Keeping Michael in Rhode Island is no vendetta against you. I always figured he'd fare better in the Lower Forty-eight, with capable guardians. Neither one of us has the time or means to care for him, not at his age, not here in Alaska."

The waiter returned to take their orders. Once he left, Julie lifted her glass with a shaky hand and upset it. An overzealous waitress nearby rushed over with a rag and mopped the spill from the tablecloth. Zane flushed more than Julie. With a new glass of water, Julie sipped from the straw, pretending nothing awkward had happened. She'd become accustomed to mishaps, large and small.

Zane leaned back in his chair and wanted to redirect the conversation back to the original issue. "I still don't understand why you never wanted me to care for you."

"You never did like my independence. That's why I refused to move back home. Mom and Dad wanted to treat me like an invalid. I certainly don't need that from you."

"That's not what made me want to provide for you. I loved your hardiness. Living in the bush with Mikey, you performed like a champ. Until…."

"Until I got overconfident? Until I forgot to heed your commands?"

"Is it wrong for a man to want to be strong for his wife?"

"Let's stop this. I hate when we get on this same topic. I'll be right back."

She wheeled herself to the bathroom. Zane gazed around, heated with discomfort. The lavish atmosphere changed from snug to oppressive. He longed for his coworkers, sitting in a coffee shop, gossiping and laughing under the bright fluorescent lights. A group that, although they knew more about each other than they perhaps realized, would never throw private issues in his face to taunt him.

Ten minutes later, with their orders waiting on the table, Julie returned. They made small talk while they ate. He tried not to notice Julie struggling with her fork. As always, she'd ordered a meal which required hardly any cutting—salmon quiche.

"We're close to finding the gallbladder harvesters," Zane said. Work always proved a safe subject. He chewed his venison carbonara and nodded with a swallow when Julie asked him if he was referring to the black bear slaughter. "We've narrowed the suspects down to the same culprits from a few years back. They're from a native village north of Anchorage."

"Are you sure they're the ones?"

"We're pretty sure. They're already in violation of their parole. It'll take some more investigation, but at least we have a lead. The man who runs the hunting lodge downriver says he sees them with bows in their skiff, but they never come back with any kills."

"The bears were killed with bows?"

"They use them to make it harder to track them down."

Julie gazed toward her lustrous water glass.

"What's wrong?" Zane asked.

"I was thinking how ironic. You have two incidents, one with bears attacking people and the other with people attacking bears."

Zane swallowed. That little bit of irony hadn't escaped him either.

CHAPTER 5

"I'M TELLING you, my uncle never would have done that," a twentyish-looking man was saying to Langston when Zane walked into the office the next morning. "He used to lecture me about respecting wildlife. He would never have fed the bears. Not even if they were starving. He always believed in letting nature take its course."

Langston's dark brown eyes widened at Zane. He appeared desperate for what to do. The forlorn-looking bran muffin next to Langston's steaming mug of coffee begged for attention. Amanda gestured with a grin for Zane to keep quiet.

"I'm sure he was an able sportsman," Langston said, and he shot Zane another pleading expression. Zane shrugged and went to put his leftovers from last night's dinner with Julie in the kitchenette refrigerator. He'd lost his appetite after Julie had announced she'd figured out his bisexuality. How idiotic for him to have forgotten to delete that stupid porn site. For all those years, she'd known his guarded secret.

Sitting at his desk, he kept a stealthy eye on Langston and the visitor rambling on about some topic.

"The official report is unfair," the man said. "I knew my uncle too well. No way would he have baited the bears with food. No way, I'm telling you."

Langston stretched back in his chair. A dull screech echoed through the spacious office. "Well, I'm sure your uncle abided by the laws," he said, "but it's in the past now. The report doesn't actually mean anything."

"But I would like to clear his name."

"Perhaps you'd better speak with Lt. Flecks. She's our public relations officer. Let me let her know you're here." Langston dialed

Karen's extension, spoke with her briefly, and pointed a stubby pencil down the hallway. "You can find her down there. Second office to your right."

"Who's he?" Zane asked once the visitor disappeared down the hallway.

"Trapper John's nephew."

"You're kidding."

"That's him in the flesh," Amanda said. "He showed first thing this morning, pulled in as soon as I did."

"Said a friend of his was watching satellite TV when an Anchorage station popped on with news of the attack," Langston said. "He booked the last nonstop out of Portland, got in at two this morning."

"Poor kid must be exhausted." Amanda crunched her chubby face. "Certainly doesn't show it, though."

"Determined guy," Zane said. "What made him come here?"

"From what I can piece together, he was pretty close with his uncle." Langston shrugged, bit into his muffin, washed it down with a sip of coffee. "Doesn't like that the official report states the attack might've resulted from him feeding the bears."

Zane rested his arms atop his cluttered desk and snickered. "Can't blame him. The university always issues the same excuse."

"Nothing else can explain what happened." Langston, who often agreed with the university's findings, used a tone Zane understood meant he wanted to hear no more about the bear attack. Amanda glanced at Zane with her cheery, raisinlike eyes nestled in her doughy face.

Zane shrugged and turned his attention to more files on the black bear slaughter until the nephew, escorted by a weary Karen Flecks, emerged ten minutes later.

"He taught me an awful lot about wildlife, especially bears," the nephew was saying. "They were his passion. But from a distance. He respected them too much to treat them as anything other than wild animals."

"Mr. Gaffner, I appreciate your concerns, I do, but there isn't much we can do." Karen walked him to the vestibule. "The investigation isn't anything official. No need to worry."

"But aren't you concerned about what might have happened out there?"

"Of course we are, but we've done all we can. What happened to your uncle was one of those things."

"Why does everyone keep saying that? A bear eating someone isn't one of those things."

Karen faced the resolute Mr. Gaffner with taut lips. She was a beautiful woman, one of the most beautiful Zane had known. Yet he never imagined her in a sexual or romantic way. Her skin color, of course, had nothing to do with his disinterest, as others in the office had proved. But her lesbianism did. Zane liked a challenge, but not when it came to relationships. In that regard, he sought the path of least resistance.

"Who told you about the bear consuming your uncle?" Karen beamed a glare around the office, eyes wider than walnuts.

"I didn't blab," Langston said, gulping down a bite of muffin.

"I viewed my uncle's body for myself," the nephew said. "The only recognizable feature was his hair. You can't tell me he's the victim of a run-of-the-mill unprovoked mauling."

Karen's moist honey-brown eyes pleaded with Zane. Why did his coworkers always expect him to bail them out? Col. Lund shouted for Karen. From the tone of Lund's voice, he meant for her to come to his office immediately. Another public relations emergency. They came faster than police calls. Zane finally bit Karen's baiting expression and took her place by the nephew's side.

"I'm Trooper Fusca, Mr. Gaffner," he said, taking him lightly by his arm. "Let me walk you to your car."

Puddles in the parking lot from an earlier rain reflected the surrounding spruce and pine trees. Under the pale late morning sky, Mr. Gaffner's sturdy frame remained motionless against the backdrop of lush green. He watched Zane with unblinking blue eyes. Amanda had been right, but despite the obvious fatigue in his pale oval face, he appeared no older than twenty-five. The breeze swept his light brown hair across his crinkled forehead.

"Mr. Gaffner, I'm truly sorry about your loss," Zane said, using his steady official tone. "But the state of Alaska doesn't actually conduct official investigations into bear attacks. You're wasting your time with us. Our investigation has gone as far as we can take it."

"You care more about the bears than my uncle?"

"Of course not. Like I said, we don't do official investigations, not really."

"Uncle Teddy never would have fed the bears, not even for research," Mr. Gaffner said under his breath, indifferent to Zane's insistence. "He was my mother's eldest brother. The family's black sheep. But I near worshipped him. I envied how he gave up his worldly possessions and moved to Alaska's backcountry."

"I understand," Zane said with a sigh. "I truly do."

The nephew peered at Zane. Taut skin pulled across his square jaw line, dusted with a light, shadowy beard. "I've been to the cabin. I saw what the bear did. I saw the blood splatter. There's no way a normal bear would've created all that destruction in any situation. I may not have a college degree, but I'm no idiot."

"No one is saying you are," Zane said. "But we didn't make the report, we merely issued it."

"Lt. Flecks said something about the report coming from the university."

"They do the research on these matters and provide us most of the reports, unless it involves police matters. Bears aren't typically viewed as criminals, Mr. Gaffner."

"Then I'll have to talk with them."

Zane held him back. "Those reports are templates. And if you expect to change anyone's opinion over there about bear behavior, you'll have a long day ahead of you. I'm sure you're not in the mood for that after your long night. Other than Greg Gomez, most of them believe bears will never attack without provocation. One way or the other, you won't change their opinions."

"And you, Trooper Fusca? Is that what you believe?"

Dana pulled her Ford Escape into headquarters' parking lot. She eyed Zanebono speaking with the strange man, passed them by wordlessly, her Bad Ass coffee in hand, and entered the office. Zane shook his head, rolled his eyes.

"Between you and me, no, I don't know what provoked the attack. But it doesn't matter what I believe. None of us fully understand the anatomy of bear attacks. Like everything else, they happen, as rare as they are. Your uncle was one of only twenty-three people killed by a bear in Alaska in its entire history." He inhaled, formed his hands into tight fists by his sides. "Moose stample more people in Alaska each year than bears have attacked people in the past century."

"And to me that makes everything all the more pressing." Mr. Gaffner turned for his rental car, a red compact Dodge Avenger, coated with mud.

"You didn't drive that vehicle to your uncle's cabin, did you?" Zane asked.

Although a narrow, primitive road led from the main thoroughfare near the Glenn Highway to the trapper's cabin, it lay as close to Anchorage as one could get and still say they lived in the bush. Even the sturdy Escalade would have had a tough go handling the rocky trail.

Mr. Gaffner stopped at the car door. "I had no choice. I needed to see for myself."

Tenacious, Zane thought. "You drove there in the dark?"

"The sun was rising by the time I arrived."

"How did you know where to find it?"

"I spent an entire month with my uncle at his cabin two summers ago. I can remember things. The turnoff for his cabin wasn't too difficult to find."

A flood of sympathy and respect filled Zane. "Why don't you go back to your motel?"

"What motel? I haven't even checked into one yet. I drove straight to the cabin from the airport, and from there to the coroner's, and then from there to here. Now, what is the name of this university? University of Alaska?"

"University of Anchorage."

"I'll use my map to find it." Mr. Gaffner contorted into the car and lowered the window when Zane followed him. "I wonder how those researchers would feel if a bear had fatally mauled one of their loved ones."

"They'd probably be proud." Zane wished he hadn't uttered the comment. Sometimes he had difficulty curbing his contempt for the highbrow university researchers. He placed his hand on his hip, near his Glock. Wanting to erase his last comment, he said, "Look, there's nothing more you can do. We're happy you came to claim your uncle. Now it's time you return to Oregon with his body—"

"Recovering my uncle is only part of why I'm here. I'm going to clear his name."

Zane leaned his head toward the open window. "At least take this in case you need it. You'll find my personal cell phone number. Now, promise not to get into any trouble."

Mr. Gaffner gazed at Zane's business card, tucked it in his jacket pocket, probed Zane with cunning blue eyes. "How can I get into trouble? They're only university researchers."

WITH the trapper's nephew, Mr. Gaffner, out of the way, Zane returned to his desk and the list of suspects for the gallbladder harvesting. Two of them had already served time for the same crime and had violated parole. The ex-cons, brothers who lived in a small Athabascan village on the Knik Arm, carried a lengthy record with the AST, ranging from failure to record fish catches with the state to leaving behind organs in moose hunts. In Zane's part of Alaska, subsistence and sports fishing and hunting all fell under the same mélange of regulations. Not even natives were exempted.

"Ready for some leg work?" Zane said to Dana.

They drove the Glenn Highway as the late morning sun broke high through the heavy clouds. Sunrays heated the inside of the truck. Zane lowered his window halfway. Technically, the village lay within the municipality of Anchorage, but the thirty-mile drive north from downtown and the boat ride up the Knik took more than an hour. Zane never got used to Anchorage's city limits being twice as large as his entire home state of Rhode Island. Since moving, he'd become accustomed to considering fifty miles "up the road."

Because no roads reached Port Raven along the upper Arm, they required the use of one of the AST's vessels docked at the state-owned pier. In the winter, they could snowmachine or fly into the tiny villages that peppered southcentral Alaska, but in late May, with the snow melt and muddy trails, using the waterways came easier.

"You do most of the talking," Zane said to Dana while she navigated the winding gravel lane toward the pier. They passed the Alaska Railroad tracks and a mile later came to a turquoise Russian Orthodox Church. St. Fyodor's single onion dome towered no taller than the surrounding spruce and pine trees. Zane watched it grow smaller in the side mirror.

"Why do I have to do all the talking?" Dana said above the grind of gravel and wind rushing inside the truck. "You're the lead investigator."

"These are your people."

"They're not my people," Dana said. "They're Tanaina. I'm Alutiiq. Besides, I have as much Russian in me as anything else."

"Nyet, tak u tebya ne vyydet."

"Huh?"

"I still don't understand how you can't speak any Russian or Alutiiq. I can even speak some Russian, and certainly Italian."

"Hey, I grew up in the Kenai. Besides, I have a little Irish in me too."

"Poor excuse," Zane said. "Everyone in America has some Irish in them."

Dana pulled into the parking lot by the dock, and after tightening their bulletproof vests, they hiked to the pier. The snow-streaked Alaska Range loomed west of Knik Arm. Zane piloted the airboat since he had experience boating while ripening into adulthood on Rhode Island's waterways.

Already Zane's heart rate increased and his breathing came in short gasps. He disliked traipsing into native villages. The residents often treated the brown-shirted troopers as carriers of contagious diseases. Zane hardly blamed them for wanting no part in government. Many Alaskans, non-native and native alike, worried the state bureaucracy was getting too big, with more and more regulations. But venturing onto native turf, the worst part of Zane's job, made him realize how much he earned his keep. Hostile glares, puckered lips, and frozen dark eyes sent chills through his blood.

With the icy wind rushing through Dana's black hair, she blurted, "That Gaffner kid is kinda cute."

"What are you talking about?"

"Trapper John's nephew. He's kinda cute."

"You considering dating him?" Zane snickered, steering the vessel away from the mudflats.

"He's not my type. Too blond for me. But he seemed to have a nice body."

"Is that what's important to you?"

"If it was, I'd be on him or you. But since I'm not, I merely mentioned he's good-looking."

Zane agreed. He was a sexy man. First thing he'd noticed when he'd stepped inside the office that morning. He and Dana often shared banter, but they stayed clear of open sex talk. What had prompted her to make such a comment now? Was it a figurative elbow to get him back for his recent pressing her to date? Maybe she suspected he was bisexual, like Julie. Is that why Dana had no desire to date him? He shrugged it off. What difference did any of it make?

Clouds had concealed the sun again by the time they reached the village of about seventy people, visible from the water through a grove of thin spruce. Zane inched the airboat to the village dock where several small skiffs and dories lurched in the tide. Many other boats were dry docked on the shoreline. He made sure to cut the motor before reaching the dock to maintain a low profile. Small children playing on the muddy shore greeted them with large black eyes. Two rushed off toward the village center. Curious about the strangers, the remaining children followed the two "brown shirts" into the village. Zane widened his eyes, using concentration to maintain optimal peripheral vision, the way they'd trained him at the academy on Baranof Island.

A massive snow pile sat in the center of the village from winter plowing. Dozens of Quonset huts were scattered about as if someone had tossed them into the air and let them land where they may. Mud and dirt— the village's primary décor.

Mothers and grandmothers held the children from getting too close to Zane and Dana. They ogled them with reproachful eyes. Even when Dana stooped to tickle the chin of an extroverted little girl in a pink parka, her grandmother yanked her back. Dana questioned the women about the gallbladder harvesting, but, taking their children by their hands, they pulled them inside their huts without answering.

They reached the home of the Baxters. Two fancy ATVs with fresh mud caked on the wheels and oil drippings underneath suggested the brothers still lived with their parents and five younger sisters. He glanced around, scanning for any other clues. An archery target leaned against a dilapidated shed pockmarked with arrow holes. Did the brothers use that for target practice on black bears?

Zane expected little help from the family. He rapped on the metallic door and whispered to Dana to prepare to ask questions should the family ignore him. Sweat dripped from his armpits. Two or three minutes passed before the father answered, creaking the door ajar. He and several others inside, where a television spread blue glow about the small hut, met their questions with harsh silence, far-off stares, indifferent shrugs.

"They haven't been back here in many months," the father said, after much prompting from Zane and Dana. "They no longer visit. You have chased away my only sons." And he shut the door, muting the applause and hoots from a game show.

One non-native lived in the village, the sole teacher for the past four years, a burly man from Minnesota. Known as Mr. Cheechacko to the locals, he carried his nickname, referring to him as a non-native, no matter how pejoratively the villagers had meant it, with pride. He proved less cooperative than the Baxter family.

Men like "Mr. Cheechacko" had moved to Alaska for the same reasons Zane had, and, like him, they'd found survival easier in close-knit communities. But many still maintained an antisocial stance. The teacher, the most vocal of the villagers, told them point-blank how he viewed their investigation. At least he expressed himself without reserve. Even with their hostility toward the AST, native Alaskans living in rural outposts retained the Asian trait of reserve.

Mr. Cheechacko conveyed no such cultural restraints. Spiced with a few epithets, he said, "Take your Glocks and go."

"Gallbladders have been removed from the bears, leaving the meat to rot," Zane told him. "Does that not bother you?"

Their badges glinted in the sun from a quick part of the clouds. Mr. Cheechacko glared at them.

"Your presence in Port Raven is what bothers me," he said.

They left the teacher glowering from his doorway. A middle-aged couple stepped out of a garage. Exasperated, Zane approached them next.

"Excuse me, sir," Zane said, addressing the man, since in small Athabascan villages the men do most of the speaking. "Are you aware of the bear harvesting that's taken place nearby?"

The couple kept their eyes fixed forward, their mouths taut.

"Someone slaughtered a black bear and her two cubs," Dana added. "Maybe the men arrested for the same crime a few years before. The Baxter brothers, Karl and Matthew."

"We don't mingle with the Baxters," the man said, nudging his wife to keep walking.

"Do you know where they might be?" Dana said to their backs.

"No. Now leave us be."

Farther down the muddy road, they found a group of men in their twenties hanging outside the local mercantile.

"Have you guys run into the Baxter brothers recently?" Zane asked without fanfare.

Silence.

Zane and Dana exchanged stares.

"Have you seen any Asian men around lately?" Dana attempted to reach them. "Men from China interested in purchasing gallbladders from black bears?"

One of the men, with intelligent downcast eyes and wearing a skull cap, shook his head. "Ain't nothing going on here. Go home. We don't have to listen to you. Baxter boys don't live here no more, anyway."

"We noticed two ATVs parked at their parents' house," Zane said, trying to maintain a non-confrontational tone. "You wouldn't happen to know if they belong to Karl and Matt Baxter, would you? They're awfully big for the parents and their daughters to ride."

More silence.

If Zane failed to learn answers to one puzzle, perhaps he might encourage the youths to spit out answers for another. He had little to lose. He pictured Joshua Gaffner standing by his tiny rental car in the parking lot at headquarters, determination etched on his face. "Would you happen to know anything about the grizzly attack a few miles downriver?" he asked. "The one that took place Monday?"

The apparent leader of the group flinched, yet he held his shoulders steady. Like everyone else in the village—save for the children—not one met the eyes of the troopers.

"Why don't you get while you still got your government boat to get going in," the leader said.

Zane had forgotten. Isolated villagers, white and native, often vandalized trooper vehicles—without any witnesses, of course—leaving them stranded. He stood taller and gestured for Dana to leave. "We'll be poking around for who might've killed the bears," he said. "We'd appreciate whatever help you can give us. If you run into the Baxter men, tell them we'd like to talk. Just talk. You have our number."

On the airboat back to the pier, Zane and Dana remained quiet. Trips to the native villages often sobered them. Dana, one of the few natives on the force, was as gregarious as anyone he'd met. No chip on her shoulder. Still, uneasiness lurked. Did she feel he was an intrusive white man too? Is that why she'd refused to date him? Zane found the bitter taste of contempt difficult to shake off.

He wanted to stop at the Russian Orthodox Church since the church elders often ferried and bussed some of the villagers, mostly women and small children, to the services. The priest, an austere, tall man with the typical orthodox beard and piercing blue eyes, showed hospitality only a few notches above what they'd experienced in Port Raven.

The evasive priest suggested the Baxter brothers might have moved to the Lower Forty-eight after their prison release. Zane knew that was untrue. The priest accused Zane and Dana of harassing the natives. Despite Zane's insistence the animals' welfare was their only interest, which, in turn, meant the good of the natives, the priest dismissed them.

Outside, Zane said, "I could never trust a man in a funny hat."

"You mean like a periwinkle blue baseball cap with 'State Trooper' stitched across the top?"

Zane rolled his eyes toward the underside of his bill. He got Dana's point.

CHAPTER 6

AN OLD dance tune from the nineties Zane failed to recall flowed from the jukebox when he stepped inside the Caribou Stampede Brewing Company. He gazed around the sourdough-themed brewpub, popular with tourists and locals alike. Joshua Gaffner was sitting alone in a back booth, nursing a mug of beer. Already fifteen minutes late, Zane bypassed the hostess and hurried to join him.

"Hi there," Zane said, sliding into the booth. "Sorry I'm late. I wanted to get a quick workout and shower in after work. My typical Friday routine."

"I expected to see you in your trooper's uniform."

"We're allowed to wear other clothes." Zane chuckled.

"Thanks for coming. I realize you didn't want to."

Zane gazed at the wood tabletop. "It's no big deal."

Trapper John's nephew had surprised Zane when he'd telephoned around lunchtime. Joshua had said he wanted to talk. Zane had insisted he had nothing more to say about his uncle's mauling death. Joshua's voice had sounded desperate, and Zane had no choice but to agree to meet him for a few drinks at the restaurant near his motel. Exhausted from his trying visit in Port Raven, Zane had begun to look forward to a few drinks out with a harmless stranger.

He studied Joshua's freshly shaven face. "What's up?" he asked once the waitress left with his drink order. "Tough go at the university?"

"You were right about them." Joshua eyed the suds in his beer. "Worse than I expected. They not only refused to consider other possible motives for the attack, but one of the professors called me a reactionary." He peered at Zane. "What in the world did she mean by that?"

Zane snickered and shook his head. "Told you they don't like anyone questioning them."

The waitress brought Zane's Kolsch-style pint and hurried off.

"I assumed academia was all about questioning stuff," Joshua said. "I guess I should've known better."

"Many don't like anyone to question them."

"You can say that again," Joshua said, his mouth downturned. "I spoke with a Dr. Linden. Once I pushed her against the wall—figuratively, of course, although I felt like actually doing it—she laid aside the nice chat. She basically said that my uncle had no business living in bear territory, and that he had it coming to him."

"Sounds like her," Zane said with a shrug. "She views the world either black or white." He savored the tangy flavor of his ale for a few sips. Lowering his glass and wiping the frothy moustache with the side of his hand, he said, "Did you speak with Dr. Gomez? He's the best researcher at the university, if you ask me. We've always worked well together."

Joshua shook his head. "They said he was out jogging or something."

Studying him from across the table, Zane said, "So what do you want with me? I won't be able to sway them. I've worked with them for six plus years and they still ignore most of my input on these issues."

Joshua widened his baby blues at Zane. "The troopers can do something, can't they?"

Zane drew in his lips. His restless right leg began bouncing. "There really isn't anything we can do," he said. "We lack the resources and the time to worry."

They sipped their beers in silence. Zane gazed about the brewpub, eager to dismiss his unease. As much as he wanted to help the man, he'd spoken the truth about the state tying his hands behind his back. Joshua hadn't been the first family member of a loved one killed by a wild animal in Alaska wanting more action from officials. The state wielded little control over its vast wilderness. Enter at your own risk. Zane had experienced that from both sides.

He rested his eyes back on Joshua. "Can I ask why this is important to you? It's not like the university said your uncle was a lunatic. They labeled his death the same way they do all of them. Is that so bad?"

"But even you said you didn't believe their report. Don't you want to find the truth? You're a policeman."

"Technically, I'm an investigator, and I investigate humans who harm wildlife, not the other way around. In this case, it's out of my hands."

"Can't another department help?"

"Not really."

Joshua clasped the handle of his mug, seemed ready to dive into his beer. "I don't understand. You mock the university's coddling of the bears, then you turn around and do the same."

"I'm not coddling the bears," Zane said, his chin raised. "The state of Alaska has established laws protecting wildlife, and I enforce them. Damn good laws, for the most part. I basically don't view wildlife the same way many others do."

"You mean, like pets?"

"Pretty much."

"My uncle hated people like that." Joshua's knuckles whitened over his mug handle. "He was a professor of ecology at a university for ten years, Ochoco State in Oregon. He riled a lot of his colleagues while working there. I was too young to understand, but I heard a lot through the family grapevine. When I was older he explained to me what working there was like for him, but he never liked to discuss it in detail. He left for Alaska to put it all behind him, disappeared off the planet."

The sorrow in Joshua's sleepy eyes touched Zane. "You and your uncle were pretty tight, huh?"

"I was the only one in the family he'd talk to. Never understood what caused the friction. We stayed in regular contact after he moved here, as best we could, considering he lived in an isolated cabin. He was a staunch individualist. Didn't even believe in government-issued IDs. I'd send him letters to the closest PO Box in Birchwood, but he rarely wrote back. I was lucky to have spent that summer with him before he died."

The waitress sidled next to the booth and asked if they wanted dinner. Zane and Joshua shared a look across the table, and Zane, detecting an eager glimmer in Joshua's sad eyes, said they would. The smell of grilling meat had made Zane's stomach rumble the moment he'd stepped inside the brewpub, anyway. After his gym workout, he craved some solid protein.

The waitress handed them menus, and her quick exit left a somber quiet between them. Zane listened to the latest tune flowing from the jukebox. An oldie from the fifties. This one he recognized. Johnny Horton's "Springtime in Alaska." He waited for his favorite verse to end and said, "Was your uncle some kind of bear expert?"

"He studied them since before I was born," Joshua said. "Learned in the field. That's why his colleagues resented him. He went to school later and received a PhD in ecology, but he basically only went through the motions for the degree. He'd already written papers and had earned a reputation among bear experts. When he was a teenager he worked part time for the National Park Service during summers at Yosemite, as a backcountry ranger to study bear activity. He'd go weeks without laying eyes on another human being. He liked that. He was a loner."

"I suppose the medical examiner gave you a full report."

Joshua lowered his eyes, gripped the menu tighter. "They told me about his cancer. It's all very shocking. I wish I had more time with him."

"Who gets his cabin? You?"

"He told me the summer I was up here it was mine whenever he died. He bought it from some old-timer, something like that. Can't be worth much."

"You're going to sell?"

Joshua shrugged. "I guess. Who would buy it? It'll need some fixing. After what that bear did."

Images from the grizzly attack sizzled in Zane's mind like the steaks the waitress set before the patrons at the table next to them. Joshua was right. No bear could have done what he'd seen from a simple unsuspecting encounter. According to Greg Gomez's blood tests, the biopsies, and the necropsy, including the brain autopsy, no unknown pathogen or disease had tormented the bear, unlike its victim. No contagions like rabies or meningitis. Much to Zane's relief. But if bears were as unpredictable as Zane always believed—as unpredictable as humans—who knew what might have motivated a lone bear, wandering in the forest, to maul and consume part of a person.

For a moment, Zane pushed aside the ghastly slideshow in his mind while the waitress took their orders. Ten minutes later, she set their burgers and country fries under their noses. She asked if they wanted anything else. They shook their heads, eyes gaping at their steaming plates. Zane, his mouth watering, tore into his savory meal.

"What are your plans now?" he said, chewing.

"Uncle Ted always said he preferred cremation. I guess once I get that done I'll toss his ashes around his cabin site." He grimaced and deepened his tone. "The place he should never have lived in, according to Dr. Linden."

"Be careful driving," Zane said, swallowing. "Lucky you made it in the first time with your tiny rental."

"I have no choice," Joshua said, his eyes flashing above his burger. "I have to straighten the place, get it ready."

"Then what?"

"My flight back to Portland leaves next Thursday. Unless there's something you might do for my uncle."

"I wish I could, but there isn't, not in an official capacity. I wouldn't know what else to do, anyway." Noticing a new wave of sorrow wash over Joshua's eyes, Zane wiped his mouth and added, "I suppose I could drive you to the cabin in my truck if you like, help you clean up and make some repairs for you to sell."

Joshua grinned. "You would do that?"

"Sure, why not?"

"That would be extremely kind of you."

"There's also a man who lives along the way you might be interested in meeting."

Joshua arched his eyebrows. "What man?"

"A bear expert, like your uncle. He might provide you with some more answers if you want them. The AWT sometimes calls on him to help with our bear issues. He runs a bear sanctuary along the Eagle River, not too far from your uncle's cabin, at least not in Alaskan terms. He's not affiliated with any university. Doubtful he'd pressure them to reconsider their report. His opinions aren't much different from the rest of academia, but he's a straitlaced guy, nonetheless."

"If you think he can help."

"He might shed some light on the mauling. He has a keen understanding of bear behavior, almost like he is one."

Joshua's mood lightened. They ate the rest of their meal with less talk of death and bear assaults. Zane grew to enjoy Joshua's easy manner and the way he'd purse his lips when he'd try not to chuckle at Zane's quips. After dinner, Zane escorted Joshua to his motel and drove the Seward Highway to his doublewide at the Girdwood Mobile Home Park. The nighttime May sun, dangling over Turnagain Arm, stroked his face and lulled him into a fresh sleepiness. He peered from the corners of his eyes at the Delta 757 turning into a descent for Ted Stevens Airport. A graceful bird ushering in the first slew of seasonal tourists from the Lower Forty-eight.

CHAPTER 7

Zane faced Joshua Gaffner outside his truck in the rustic parking lot of Dr. Barry Sands's Eagle River Bear Sanctuary. The hazy sun shimmered in Joshua's cheerless eyes. What else did he have to say to him? Let Dr. Sands mollify any lingering concerns about his uncle's death.

They'd already cleaned the grisly remnants from the attack at his uncle's cabin and hauled out the debris. Saturday was always a good day for odd jobs. Zane had fixed the door, using the sturdiest hinges and deadbolts, and wearing biohazard suits he'd brought along, had helped scrub blood from the floor and walls. The AST never considered the cabin a crime scene. He had no problem helping the poor man.

Why he'd offered to help, he had no idea. Perhaps he, Trooper Zanebono Fusca, enshrouded in the call of duty, had simply assisted a man who'd traveled from afar with gritty determination to rescue his uncle's reputation. Or maybe another reason lurked behind his good deed.

No doubt he was attracted to Joshua. From the first moment he'd spotted him seated next to Langston at headquarters, the typical stir nudged his pants. A ruggedly handsome man, expressing a desperate need for assistance, always captured Zane's notice. Perhaps that's why Zane had offered to help him clean the cabin. What else did he have to provide him?

They toiled mainly in silence. Little had changed since the morning Zane and his colleagues had descended on the scene. Joshua had ventured to the cabin his first night in Alaska to see the destruction with his own eyes, but Zane tried to discover any remaining body fragments lying about that foraging animals might have left behind before Joshua noticed.

Toward the afternoon, Zane became fascinated with Uncle Ted's journals. He'd already read through the ones Dana had confiscated as evidence back at headquarters, and was eager to read more. Dana had stacked the rest in a neat pile on the stove when she'd searched the cabin for the man's identification. The uncle had kept them primarily on his life in the bush and on local bear behavior he'd witnessed during his ten years at the cabin. Zane read through the legible ones (the bear had torn half the notebooks into ribbons, and others were covered with teeth marks and dried blood), while Joshua swept and organized. Nothing he found indicated the uncle had been concerned with unusual bear activity in the area or that he'd ever fed or baited them.

Based on his journals, written with a quick, determined hand, Uncle Ted had fostered a clinical appreciation for bears, studying them from a respectful distance, never interacting with them personally, like many researchers did. Zane liked the man. The two probably shared much in common, despite a fifteen-plus years' age difference. They'd sought the seclusion of the boreal forest, away from society, enjoying nature for its raw beauty, never regarding wildlife as a circus sideshow or something they saw through a television screen.

Zane and Joshua scarcely spoke after the cleanup while driving to Dr. Sands's bear sanctuary. The somberness of the occasion warranted silent self-reflection. They remained quiet until reaching the gravel parking lot.

"Let's go rattle Dr. Sands's brain," Zane said. Of course, Zane hoped the doctor might answer a few questions of his own.

Zane led Joshua past a yellow school bus from the Mat-Su Borough School District, two trucks, and a large white trailer along a path to the main building. No larger than a plank cottage, the building housed Dr. Sands's research. In the back a vast tract of private land contained large bear habitats built with charitable contributions and sizeable government grants. Zane and the AWT had delivered many of the twenty-seven rescued bears Dr. Sands had kept since he'd first opened the nonprofit sanctuary in 1995. Dr. Sands devoted most of his resources to the bears, while he and his assistant lived in less elaborate quarters in the cottage's upstairs.

Inside smelled moldy and dusty, like a research facility should. Wads of nonperishable food, paper, printer ink, boxes of contributions—

whatever a small-scale bear sanctuary might need—filled corners, desk tops, and high reaching shelves. Graphs and posters with facts on blacks, grizzlies, and coastal browns lined the dingy white walls. Glass display cases contained bear skulls and jars filled with petrified bear scat. The institute remained unchanged from the last time he'd traveled there two summers ago, when he'd needed the doctor's help isolating trichinosis in the local black bear population.

Out back, schoolchildren jumped from enclosure to enclosure to view the large bears basking in the fluctuating sun. Zane gestured for Joshua to follow him. They stepped along the stone footpath to where Dr. Sands, standing in front of one of the larger bear habitats, lectured the children on bear behavior with his signature showmanship style.

Dr. Sands exuded a tremendous enjoyment when sharing his knowledge with the public. Although a bit mawkish for Zane's taste, Dr. Sands had proved invaluable to the AWT. He'd written several books on bears, usually praising the species for its power and beauty. His latest book, *For the Love of Bears*, made Amazon's bestseller list. Since taking his post with the AWT, Zane had sought the doctor's expertise and sharp wisdom a dozen times. He and Zane were neighbors, in a sense, since they'd both hailed from New England—Dr. Sands, born and raised in Sudbury, Massachusetts, and Zane, a native Rhode Islander.

"Bears can hibernate five months," Dr. Sands was explaining to the children. "Imagine if you could sleep the winter away like the bears. An amazing evolutionary capacity. You know why bears hibernate? So they don't have to worry about finding food in tough winter conditions. During the summer and fall, they'll eat more than two kilograms of food a day to build up fat reserves for their long sleep. That's almost ten thousand calories a day."

The children "oohed" and "aahed."

"They won't urinate or defecate while hibernating, and they rarely will venture outside their dens until spring," the doctor continued with a toothy grin. "In captivity, like here, the bears don't always hibernate like their wild counterparts because they're aware there's food available for them." He chuckled. "We've spoiled them, I'm afraid, but in winter they'll often go entire days without coming out of their dens. See those shelters built between the spruce trees there? Upon the first scent of snow, they crawl inside and snore away for days at a time."

Grinning over the children's giggling heads, Dr. Sands nodded at Zane. "Leslie will show you Pingaq. She's our star bear, and by far the largest. She's a Kodiak brown and weighs more than four hundred kilograms. That's nearly nine hundred pounds." Once the children moved away down the path, Dr. Sands approached Zane and Joshua with an extended hand.

"Trooper Fusca, how are you? It's been too long."

"Hello, Dr. Sands. Good to see you again. This is Joshua Gaffner."

"Good to meet you, Mr. Gaffner."

"Joshua's uncle was the one killed by the grizzly a week ago. I'm sure you've heard about the mauling. Happened about fifteen miles northwest of here."

"I heard on the radio." He turned to Joshua. "It must be difficult for you, surrounded by all these bears. Would you prefer to go inside?"

"No." Joshua flushed. "I'm fine, truly."

"As long as they're caged, right?"

Dr. Sands's stringy hair had grown grayer and lengthier since Zane had last visited the sanctuary, falling nearly to his shoulders. Long days under the Alaska sun had still failed to add any extra wrinkles to his tanned face beyond what Zane might expect to find for a man in his sixties.

"What's prompted your visit?" the doctor asked, grinning with wide icy gray eyes.

"We're a little curious about what might have motivated the bear to attack Joshua's uncle, off record."

Dr. Sands pulled in his chapped lips. "What I heard on the news didn't indicate an unusual encounter, as far as bear mauling deaths go. The investigation suggested the victim might have been feeding the bears—"

"No," Joshua said sharply. "He hadn't been doing anything like that."

"Well, since your uncle—"

"He was a doctor," Joshua said. "Dr. Theodore Krum. A bear expert, like you. Worked for many years at a reputable university in Oregon."

"What about Dr. Krum's death?" Zane said. "Can a bear revert to such aggression? Consume a man when there's an abundant natural food source available?"

"Bears aren't like humans, Trooper Fusca," Dr. Sands said. "They don't kill for pleasure. Murder is a trait which resides inherent only within us, I'm afraid. And they certainly have no appetite for human flesh. A grizzly's diet consists of overwhelmingly vegetarian sources. Whatever caused your bear to act unprecedentedly territorial I believe only the victim and the bear would know. I haven't seen where your poor uncle met his demise, but based on the autopsy and necropsy reports you showed me, what powered the bear was her raw force, not ill intentions. In other words, it's a case of the bear not recognizing her own strength."

Zane and Joshua exchanged glances. Joshua hadn't said much. He appeared intrigued, maybe a bit awed, by the scope of Dr. Sands's bear knowledge. Perhaps he was rehashing in his mind the bloody scenario that had played out at his uncle's cabin, resulting in the mess they'd cleaned for half the day. He appeared guarded while the bears frolicked inside their spacious enclosures. Zane's attraction to his unsteady resolve grew.

"Such astonishing strength sustains bears in their rugged environments," the doctor continued. "Their power might appear aggressive to us, when in fact it's simply what Mother Nature had instilled in bears for their survival."

They stopped before the last bear habitat, one which Zane remembered housed Pingaq, the nine-hundred-pound female Kodiak, rescued as a cub when its mother fell from a cliff overlooking the Gulf of Alaska. Left alone, the first-year cub wouldn't have survived winter. Even cubs with the protection of their mothers have a fifty-fifty chance of reaching adulthood. Zane figured that's how Mother Nature had wanted things too.

Despite what Dr. Sands had stated, Zane believed the fringe research that bears, on rare occasions, attacked and ate cubs and killed competition when food became scarce. The thinning of the herd. But he held back mentioning this to Dr. Sands. Joshua should have full access to Dr. Sands's mental databank. Butting heads with the doctor might alienate him.

Pingaq wandered out of its den, lifted its head only long enough to recognize its benefactor standing outside the cage. A two-inch tan scar on its snout stood out against the coffee brown of its coat. Zane recalled reading one of Dr. Sands's earlier books, titled *Bears: Monarchs of the Forest*, to help him with his new job as wildlife trooper. No doubt, the six-year-old Pingaq lived like a queen surrounded by its ample court.

The light breeze carried the muted laughter of the children from the river. Middle-aged Sands, never married as far as Zane had gathered, suddenly had ears and eyes only for Pingaq, his four-legged prodigy.

He gazed at the bear, his steely eyes far away. "I believe I love Pingaq the most," he said, "and she me. Not the same type of love two humans can share, of course, but it is love, nonetheless. Despite her size, she lets me hug and kiss her. But even then I'm cautious of her power. The kind of power men can only dream of possessing. I understand how quickly death might come if I allowed myself even one misstep with Pingaq or the other bears." He faced Joshua with a gentle expression, the soft parenthetical lines around his goatee emphasizing his sincerity. "Do you understand what I'm saying, Mr. Gaffner?"

Joshua locked onto the doctor's level gaze. Slowly, he nodded, his lips puckered.

"What happened to your uncle was one in a million," the doctor said, "but the bear meant no harm. She only did what bears do—search for food, using the power more than one million years of evolution had bestowed her with." He turned back to Pingaq. It was lying on its back, swatting mosquitoes with its hubcap-sized paws.

"Bears do not destroy for destruction's sake," he said. "The horrible ordeal your uncle faced was the product not of an aggressive man-eating bear, but of raw power. It would be the equivalent of standing in front of a runaway Mack truck. You could hardly blame the truck for the resulting destruction."

Zanebono pressed the doctor. "If a bear's intelligence is as high as you say, as high as everyone knows, then would it be farfetched to assume they could behave unpredictably, as free-thinking individuals capable of violence, like humans? Perhaps something from their past, like a negative encounter with a hunter, might spur them to attack humans."

"Bears are incapable of revenge, Trooper Fusca. They exist, purely and without adulteration, with one simple goal—survival. What you consider a sign of intelligence in humans, others might ascribe to whims created by a society overwhelmed by hysteria. You should appreciate what I allude to first hand. Recall the summer of 2008, when the people of Anchorage wanted bears annihilated after a few nonfatal encounters?"

Zane considered the doctor's words. Dr. Sands did wield an interesting point. People were far more reactionary than any animal he'd ever encountered. He nodded in contemplation, his eyes on the ground. To keep the atmosphere light, he smiled at the bear through the mesh cage and said, "Pingaq is looking healthy."

Dr. Sands grinned. "She couldn't be better, in wonderful health."

"You've lost a few?" Zane remembered records showed the sanctuary housed thirteen bears as of November 2010. He had counted eleven from their short walk along the footpath, although some might have been resting inside their dens.

"Two died during the winter, I'm sad to report," Dr. Sands said. "It's like losing a child. But they were old. Lived a long life. Not that it makes it any easier. I only hope I was able to make their lives worthwhile."

"No doubt you have. If I was a bear, this is where I'd want to call home."

"Not the wild, Trooper Fusca?"

"Captive bears live longer and are healthier, no?"

"Yes, but at what cost? Their liberty?"

"Perhaps you're right."

The clattering children came rushing over the embankment. Dr. Sands grinned at Zane and Joshua.

"Would you like to watch us feed the bears?" he asked, guiding them back toward the cottage. "The children have been hankering for us to get started since their arrival."

"No, actually, I wouldn't," Joshua said.

"We probably should go," Zane said, sensing Joshua's increasing discomfort. "I appreciate your time, once again, Dr. Sands."

"I hope I was able to ease some of your concerns," the doctor said. "I sympathize how difficult it is to lose the ones you love, but try to keep the tragedy in perspective. She was a powerful animal, had no inkling of what she'd been doing, other than the desire to survive on her home turf. Spirited perhaps, but unaware of her own raw strength."

Joshua squinted at the doctor, his arms locked across his chest.

"But the encouraging prospect is the bear who killed your uncle is dead," Dr. Sands added. "And no more harm can come to anyone, right?"

"That's the only good news," Zane said.

They'd reached the cottage, swarmed by eager schoolchildren. Zane and Joshua shook hands with the doctor. Somberly, they made their way to the parking lot.

"Seems like a lot of people want to make excuses for the bears," Joshua said, contorting himself inside the cab of Zane's Sierra.

"When you look at them like children," Zane said, fishing for his keys from his pocket, "as does Dr. Sands, then making excuses for them comes natural. At least you got a deeper understanding into their behavior. Despite the doctor's corny emotions, he does make a lot of sense. Bears don't harm out of spite. I do believe they can be unpredictable, but from my experience, the overwhelming majority of bears will choose one of three actions when they come face to face with a human. In order of probability: run away, bluff charge, or attack. Maybe the bear that attacked your uncle had no understanding of what it was doing, like Dr. Sands said."

"I suppose," Joshua said.

Zane wanted to sweep away Joshua's brooding mood. To his surprise, Joshua flashed him an earnest smile first.

"Thank you for bringing me to see Dr. Sands and helping me clean Uncle Ted's cabin," he said. "I'm grateful for what you've done for me. I wish I could show my appreciation in some way."

Zane measured a response, wanted to laugh. "Maybe you can," he said, turning the ignition. The engine roared to life. Joshua's questioning stare tickled him. "You can allow me to take you to the symphony."

"What?"

"The AST gets complimentary tickets. I have no one to go with. No one at headquarters likes to go."

"Where?"

"Where? Anchorage, where else? The Anchorage Symphony Orchestra."

"Anchorage has a symphony?"

Zane chuckled. "Anchorage is like any American city that way. Has those fancy things. Even plumbing and electricity, you might've noticed."

Joshua snickered and shook his head. "Sorry, I didn't mean it the way it sounded."

Zane jerked the truck into gear and drove off, spitting gravel. "It's settled. Tomorrow afternoon. The symphony."

CHAPTER 8

ZANEBONO had looked forward to Sunday's concert all day. He had considered inviting Julie, but she'd never enjoyed such outings. Neither had Zane. He'd exaggerated when he'd told Joshua he fancied symphonies. He appreciated the talent behind the music, not the sappy pomp. He'd patronized the symphony twice before, once with Dana, who scoffed the entire time, and with Mikey when he'd visited during Christmas while Mr. Gagliardi spent special time with Julie, but the boy was too young to appreciate the music. Joshua might enjoy a side of Alaska few people experienced. The "haut couture" face, sandwiched between the craggy Chugach Range and the choppy Cook Inlet.

The Atwood Theater seated more than two thousand and towered five stories. White pine trim, forest green seats, and ochre satin walls sparkled in the ambient lighting. Joshua's mouth dropped the moment he and Zane took their seats on the mezzanine level. Zanebono relished his reaction.

Zane had picked him up at four o'clock sharp from his motel near the airport. He was grateful to dress down along with Joshua, who'd bought a nice pair of slacks to wear with his green Oxford at the T.J.Maxx next to his motel. Most of the other attendees, especially the high school students on a cultural excursion who filled one-fifth of the seats, wore casual sweaters and slacks. Few people, other than the tuxedo-clad ushers, stood out.

"It's so modern, yet old-fashioned," Joshua uttered, gazing around from his seat.

Zane nodded. "The city built it with donations from gold rush money."

"I like how they brought a feeling for the Alaskan outdoors inside, without forgoing the fancy stuff you'd expect for a symphony hall."

"Pretty cool, huh?"

The hall was three quarters full by the time the curtain opened. Five minutes into the overture, Joshua leaned into Zane, his breath sweet from the peppermint he'd been sucking. "I hadn't expected a tribute to the rock group Rush," he whispered.

Notes burst around them, sliding down the satin walls like snow runoff. A robust celebration of the unrefined nature surrounding Anchorage and the vastness of the human mind. Six major mountain ranges crisscrossed near Anchorage, and the music soared through the waffled ceiling to reach every one of the tallest peaks.

Each note brought a dazzling laser creation that sunk Zane's stomach. He glimpsed Joshua in the flashing lights. His wide grin and eyes proved the experience grabbed him by the throat. To Zane's relief, he'd left the tragedy of his uncle's death behind, if only momentarily.

Two hours later, the dazzling memory of the concert followed them down F Street. Drunk with wonder, he and Joshua peered through the shop windows, glanced at the towers. The sun, bright in the sky at seven o'clock in the evening, played off the street like the music they'd enjoyed.

"Hey," Zane said, turning to Joshua. "Why not grab some dinner? My stomach tells me it's that time." He never intended to make a huge night out with Joshua. But the good feelings between them, like a smooth leather strap yoking them together, bolstered his courage.

Joshua, smiling, nodded in agreement.

Zane escorted him to Sullivan's Steakhouse across the street. Thus far the evening had tumbled into one of unexpected delights. They'd left the heartache of Dr. Krum back at the cabin, behind the thick wall of the boreal forest. Tonight, Zane would try and enjoy all the enchantment a city of three hundred thousand offered.

Under the rich, dark lighting of Sullivan's, they ate thick steaks and Alaskan snow crabs, their dinner chatter light. The only sour note came when Joshua mentioned returning to Portland on Thursday, after he scattered his uncle's remains by the cabin. Joshua's mentioning his dead uncle or the impending cremation hadn't dispirited Zane. A nagging regret sawed into him, picturing Joshua leaving for home.

His burgeoning attraction for Joshua barely surprised Zane. He regarded men like Joshua "his type." A definitive masculine hardness alloyed with a noticeable vulnerability. A boulder poised on the edge of a cliff.

Julie's public apartment complex stood down the street from Sullivan's. How would she take her ex-husband dining with a man, on a date? She'd already confessed her awareness of his bisexuality. Would she express a jealous rage, insist Zane come back to her, take care of her the way he'd wanted? He'd never dated anyone seriously since their breakup, not even a woman. Funny how such impressions tickled his mind.

But how did Joshua view Zane?

Zanebono held little doubt he was gay. He could always figure out a man's homosexuality. Joshua, although far from effeminate, exuded that unique quality Zane had come to recognize in masculine homosexual men. How would he phrase it? Like a moose bull peering from behind an alder bush. His blue eyes, sharp as the lasers during the concert, revealed his soul and sexuality.

Halfway through his T-bone, Zane realized he must invite Joshua back to his home and, at some point, make his move. The notion hadn't sunk into his consciousness until that precise moment. How long had it lurked beneath his perceptions? When he'd first encountered him at headquarters Friday morning?

Admit it, Zanebono, that's why you'd offered to drive him to his uncle's cabin. Zane inwardly chuckled at his self-teasing.

Like Dana had said on the ride up the Knik Arm to Port Raven, Joshua Gaffner seemed to have a nice body. Here he sat, directly across from him at dinner for the second time in less than forty-eight hours. Fate perhaps demanded he view him as more than a bereaved nephew.

Joshua flushed, gazed toward his plate of crab legs. Might he be reading Zane's mind? Did his brown eyes give him away like Joshua's had?

"Hey, sexy boys." Two drunken twentysomething girls gyrated at Zane and Joshua when they stepped outside the restaurant an hour later. Downtown crawled with drunks most nights, even during daylight months. The Chugach Range crushed into the city like a massive emerald wall while Zane and Joshua walked to Zane's truck, parked on Seventh

Avenue, trying to forget the girls' catcalling. Zane and Joshua flushed, kept their cool.

"That one has a nice butt," one hollered, following a few feet behind.

Which of the two had they meant? Zane turned to stare them down. The girls giggled and clung to each other to keep from falling. If only they realized Zane carried the badge of an Alaska State Trooper, he chuckled to himself.

The drunken yuppies accentuated the surreal sense of the evening. The chrome-colored sky seeped into Zane's head. Zane and Joshua sparkled on the streets of downtown Anchorage in lieu of the muted street lights. Each passerby acknowledged a special aura. An impression that forced them to ogle, to wonder. Step aside like footmen.

"Hey, let's have some fun," the other girl hollered after them. "Come on. You don't want to leave two girls alone in the city, do you?"

Zane's ears burned until the blast of a delivery truck encouraging a Camry to move through a green light erased the girls' inebriated giggles. Finally, the girls stumbled down Sixth Street. The tall buildings blocked their lingering antics.

"I guess they felt safe with us," Joshua said, "or they wouldn't have been carrying on like that."

Zane stood by his truck. "I guess so. You want to go back to my place for a few drinks?"

Joshua faced him from the passenger side. His reflection in the polished burgundy steel of the hood appeared to egg him on. "I'd love to see your home," he said.

"Great. Hop in."

ZANE handed Joshua a foaming bottle of beer outside on his porch. "It's from a local microbrewery," he said. "Good beer, if you got a sweet tooth. Made with local berries."

"Thanks," Joshua said, chuckling.

"What's so funny?"

"The way you say beer. Like the 'r' becomes an 'a.' You're not from Alaska originally, are you?"

"I'm from Rhode Island." Zane sat next to Joshua, concentrating on forcing his jittery leg to remain still. "What're you giggling about now?"

"You moved from the smallest state in the union to the biggest."

"I've heard that one before." Zane chuckled. "Did you know that if you filled Alaska with Rhode Islands, Alaska's population would swell from seven hundred thousand to over one hundred million?"

"That's amazing."

Sparrows fluttered in the duff, chatted like a breezy group of teenagers. Soft shadows from the black spruce surrounding Zane's backyard blanketed the deck. Zane kicked back, held the beer more firmly. Condensation trickled between his fingers.

He wanted to wait for the exact moment to make his move. He'd had little practice lately, with either sex. The last three times with women, they'd been the first to come onto him. Dana Chernikoff had pulled him down onto her while he'd comforted her on her sofa after learning of her father's death. His last two dates had straddled him while the television hummed in the background. One jumped him after she'd confessed to beating a cocaine addiction, the other while Zane was in the midst of talking about his latest case involving illegal airborne Dall sheep hunts.

Did women turn to him for sex for no other reason than to blot out misery?

He hadn't had sex with a man since, well…. He'd rather not recollect those three times with the same man in a span of one month last summer. The experiences had been strange. Never saw it coming. Could he even consider what had transpired sex?

The hookup before that he'd met on a gay chat site, a tourist from Chicago in Anchorage to experience the Iditarod. His wife had taken ill with the flu, and he'd been tooling on the internet at the motel, bored out of his skull. He'd ached to get out and meet some "local color" while waiting for the races to start in a few days. Zane had met him at a nearby coffee shop, afterward invited him back to his doublewide. Of course he never mentioned he was an Alaska State Trooper, not even for the likely aphrodisiac affect.

Sex with other men materialized for one purpose—quick fun to pass a dull afternoon.

Zanebono figured Joshua wouldn't be any different.

"What made you move to Alaska?" Joshua asked, setting his beer in his lap after a sip.

"Probably the same reason as anyone else," Zane answered after a moment of contemplation. "I wanted to live someplace more rustic, off the beaten path."

"Is it what you expected?"

"Pretty much. A bit more worn out in the cities and towns, but life up here can be ugly in winter. People need to stockpile. No point trying to impress *Better Homes and Gardens*."

"Some of the cabins around here are pretty luxurious."

"That they are."

"How did you end up a policeman living in Anchorage?"

Zane controlled a sigh. He rarely spoke about his personal life with anyone. Julie and Mikey, locked away in his chest of memories, materialized in conversation only with Dana. He'd told her more than anyone, yet even with her the mentioning of his past happened as commonly as white ptarmigan in July.

"I tried to live in the bush, like your uncle, but it didn't work out for me," he stated flatly. "I moved to Anchorage to find a job, like most everyone else who comes to Alaska. The AST was hiring back then. I figured, why not?"

"Why didn't life in the bush work out?"

Like molten metal from a cauldron, Zane's words rose in his throat, too heavy to reach his lips. He hoped to circumvent Joshua's questions without flat-out lying. No need to detail his awful misadventures in the bush, an experience that had mocked him since he'd packed the last of their belongings from the old timer's cabin and made his final exit. Had only seven years passed? Closing in on a year to the day?

"Stuff happens," he said, pushing down the gloomy memories with a gulp of his beer. "Life's tough out there. I didn't have the proper survival skills, I guess." Flashes of his short year in the bush raced past Zane's mind, like an icy wind blowing across the tundra. He'd failed not only himself, but Mikey and Julie. Especially Julie. Look at her life. Living in a government housing project with a wheelchair her only means of getting around.

Eager to shift the conversation into a more pleasant topic, Zane fired, "What do you do?"

"My father runs a kitchen remodeling business back in Portland. Guess I've been working for him since I was a kid. I used to answer phones, take orders. Now I mostly go out on job sites as the foreman."

"Good to have a family business during lean times."

"We're hanging in there. If people are going to spend when the economy is rotten, they'll remodel rather than throw money at a brand new home."

The booze reached Zane's head, filling him with warm courage. "Do you mind if I check out your eyes?"

Joshua flushed. "What for?"

"I want to check something." Zane leaned closer, widened his own eyes to take in more of Joshua's baby blues. He smelled the hops from the beer on Joshua's breath. "What I suspected," he said, leaning back in his chair.

"What did you suspect?"

"You have beautiful blue eyes."

The pounding of his heart, the burning of his ears. Zane wondered why he didn't date more often to experience the arousing sensation of foreplay.

Joshua's silence, utterly still, calm, settled over the deck. Sparrows called out to them, carrying the moment on their winged songs.

"In all honesty," Joshua said, "when I called you the other day, I had more on my mind than wanting to figure out how you could help my uncle."

"You did?" Zane grinned.

"I wanted a chance to see you again. I got a vibe from you."

"Well," Zane said, peering at the forest abutting his backyard, the bottle of beer poised between his legs. "Why don't we do something about that, then?"

WITH the nocturnal sun streaking through the tears in the tinfoil Zanebono affixed to his bedroom windows each spring to keep out the incessant sunlight, they kissed and groped. Joshua's questioning looks pierced Zane while they tumbled and rolled on his king bed. Stares of wanting, confusion. Was it really happening? How had they figured each other out? How had they gone from the parking lot of AST headquarters to Zane's bed in such a short time?

Zane dismissed Joshua's mystified glances, pulled him closer, covered him with his probing tongue, fingered the elastic of his tight whites and the muscular mound of flesh beneath. Joshua relented. Squirming and groaning, he allowed Zane's weight to press on him. Zane roved his nose over his neck, cheeks, finding his lips with his own. He was about to enjoy more swipes of his tongue when his cell phone on the night table went off.

Greg Gomez's personal ringtone. Oingo Boingo's "Weird Science." If Greg telephoned after hours, he had something urgent to share.

As difficult as it was to break his lip-lock with Joshua, he reached for his phone and flipped open the top.

"What is it, Greg?"

Greg's voice came through low, somber, grave. "Another fatal bear attack, Zane. This time a black got two people."

Sickness gurgled inside Zane's stomach. He sat upright in a flash. "Where at?"

"Twin Peaks. A group of hikers discovered their bodies with the bear guarding them. One of the hikers shot the bear on the scene. I was doing a late run in Bicentennial Park when I received word from Fish and Game. I'm here now."

Zane absorbed Greg's words. "How far in?"

"About a mile."

"Want me to head up there?"

"It'll be dark by the time you get here from Girdwood. We have the situation under control. Meet me at the university tomorrow morning?"

"Sure thing, Greg. Thanks for the heads up." Zane clicked off the phone, dazed. Tomorrow was Memorial Day and they already had three fatalities from bear attacks in less than one week. Joshua's pleading stare failed to pull Zane from his stupor.

The summer of '08, all over again?

CHAPTER 9

Two hikers dead after second bear attack

Third fatality in less than one week baffles officials

By LIZ SCRIBNER

A FATAL black bear attack in Chugach State Park claimed the lives of two hikers Sunday night. Husband and wife, Harold Bloomington, 52, and Vishva "Vee" Rakesh, 39, of Wasilla, were pronounced dead on the scene. They were the second and third fatalities from bear attacks this week, marking a frightening start to Alaska's illustrious summer season.

Hikers from a high school hiking club enjoying the Memorial Day weekend discovered the bodies on the popular Twin Peaks Trail around 9:30 p.m. According to official reports, the bear was guarding his kill when the teenagers encountered the bloody scene. The Department of Natural Resources has posted warnings on the trail until further notice.

Jason Carlucci, 18, one of the hikers from Mountain View High School in Anchorage, said the group frightened the black bear down an embankment by shouting and throwing stones. Officials called to the scene found the bear lying dead from gunshot wounds in nearby bushes.

No details of who shot the bear have been released.

Some witnesses said the adult black bear appeared to have been eating the victims, although officials would not verify the claims.

"We'll examine the condition of the bear to rule out pathogenic causes for the attack," Officer Jasper Bohler, a warden with the Department of Fish and Game, said. "But it appears the couple was at the wrong place at the wrong time."

Dr. Sylvia Linden, a biologist at the University of Anchorage, said the bear attack most likely resulted from a surprise encounter.

"The hikers were on steep terrain, and they probably surprised the bear while he foraged for berries," she said. "Bears have been known to use whatever force they deem necessary when defending against human encroachment onto their food sources."

Twin Peaks Trail is popular for berry pickers, and bear sightings are not uncommon, although this is the trail's first fatal bear attack on record.

Dr. Barry Sands, author of several books on bear behavior and operator of the Eagle River Bear Sanctuary, said that it's unlikely the bear attacked without some provocation.

"Human reaction to a bear encounter is usually what dictates how the bear will behave," Dr. Sands said via phone from his sanctuary. "If you run, the bear will run after you. If you hold your ground, the bear, in all likelihood, will turn and walk away. If you leave the bear to do his business, he will reciprocate."

Black bear attacks on humans are especially rare, Dr. Sands said.

Sunday's attack comes six days after Alaska Wildlife Troopers conducting a moose count discovered the bear-ravaged body of Theodore Krum, 46, near his Birchwood cabin, less than 30 miles from Twin Peaks. Officials ruled Krum's death the result of a surprise encounter with a grizzly. Krum had shot and killed the grizzly.

Officer Bohler insisted the two bear attacks are unrelated and that anyone found retaliating against bears will be prosecuted using the full force of Alaska state law.

"They make my uncle and that couple look like bear stalkers," Joshua whispered, gazing at the headline in the *Anchorage Daily News* that lay askew on Greg Gomez's desk.

"They comprehend as much as anyone else," Zane said, matching Joshua's low voice. "That doesn't stop them from writing." The AST would have to work overtime quelling public hysteria, Zane feared, his head cocked at the newspaper along with Joshua's. Unlike in 2008, the latest slew of bear attacks had resulted in fatalities—three of them. A sidebar story written by another reporter raised fears of a tourist backlash. Zane shook his head. It was going to be a long summer.

Greg was speaking on the telephone with someone official. He'd been on the phone when he'd gestured for them to step inside his office. Zane figured he was talking about the latest bear attack. The university's spring semester had ended last week, but from the clutter in Greg's office, he appeared swarmed with work. Greg's dank basement office, with one small clerestory window, magnified Zane's unease. Trapped with no means of escape.

Zane glanced around, making sure to keep still to avoid toppling the columns of books and papers on the floor. Textbooks on bear behavior, including a few of Dr. Sands's, were dog-eared or lying butterflied page down. A paper he remembered Greg having written a few years ago, about aggressive predatory behavior of the North American black bear, lay on top of a stack of books. An obscure wildlife journal had published the article. The mainstream media had given his theories minor publicity. But his colleagues had derided him for his views. He recalled Greg joking about their reaction. Zane peered again at the *Daily News* and shook his head.

Zane's cell phone went off. He stepped into the hallway to avoid disturbing Greg. Dana was calling about the bear attack. She was confused. No one at headquarters had any information. And where the hell was Bono? He regretted not telephoning and explained that he'd wanted to square things at the university before heading into the office. He instructed Dana to help Karen rein the publicity machine from galloping out of control.

Normalcy was the choice weapon against panic. The equilibrium push. For every action was an equal and opposite reaction. Calm begets calm. Zane clicked off his phone and stepped back inside the office the moment Greg replaced the receiver.

"Well," Greg said, nudging the newspaper on his desk for a better look, "the media didn't waste any time plastering the story on the front page. Complete with sidebars."

"It's all the radio was talking about on the drive over here," Zane said.

Greg ogled Joshua.

Zane's neck and ears warmed. "This is Joshua Gaffner," he said. "Joshua, this is Dr. Greg Gomez." He allowed them to shake hands before saying more. "Joshua's uncle was Dr. Ted Krum, the trapper who owned the cabin near Birchwood."

Greg's mouth gaped. "I'm sorry," he said. "I had no idea. I'm familiar with some of your uncle's work with bears. I recall reading his writings while working on my doctorate at Texas A&M. He was a rogue scholar."

"Thank you for your efforts trying to piece together what might have caused his death, Dr. Gomez," Joshua said. "Trooper Fusca tells me you're the only voice of reason here when it comes to bear research."

Zane and Greg exchanged amused glances.

"Coworkers butt heads with each other in every field, I suppose," Greg said. "My colleagues' views are valid in many respects, and they certainly understand the science, it's that…. Well, there's an old saying: Beliefs shouldn't be idolized."

"Good words to live by," Joshua said.

"What's the real deal, Greg?" Zane said, wanting to steer clear of mawkish sentiments and face the issue at hand. "Give me the bear's profile."

"*Ursus americanus*," Greg said flatly. "Adult male, about fifteen years old, two hundred twenty pounds. Good health from empirical observation. No tags or collars. We're checking its blood right now for meningitis, rabies, the litany of pathogens."

"What's the MO?"

"I arrived on the scene right after I heard from Jasper," Greg said, "but I didn't learn much. A lot of people had already stomped evidence. *Daily News* got most of the story right, except for who emptied five shots into the bear. One of the teens did that. Claimed it charged the group. From the looks of the attack scene, I'd say the boy had justification."

"Was it another surprise encounter?"

"The couple was found lying fairly close together, indicating the bear went for them fast and furious," Greg said. "They most likely never saw it coming before it was too late. Barely any defensive wounds from what the autopsies reveal, unlike Dr. Krum."

"No trouble with bears in that area before."

"Even stranger," Greg said, scanning the untidiness in his office, "the couple did have plastic jugs full of berries, like Dr. Linden said. But the berries were found strewn next to the couple, untouched. Clearly the bear wasn't after any of them."

"Is what the paper says true, Greg, about the bear consuming the victims? Like with Dr. Krum?"

Greg inhaled, kept his eyes averted. He glanced at Joshua from under his brow, as if wondering if he should go into a graphic account since a bear had mauled Joshua's uncle in the same manner.

"Don't worry about me," Joshua said. "I've seen my uncle's body and cleaned the blood from his cabin. Whatever you say can't bother me any worse."

Greg sat at his desk and sighed. "Some of the kids say they witnessed the bear consuming the victims, while the rest insist it's untrue," he said. "Scat from the area didn't reveal much. But there were definite signs of feeding, from my observation. The attack was too fresh for any decomposition. Rigor mortis hadn't even set in. Fish and Game took a score of photographs. The medical examiner has the bodies now. The autopsies should tell us more." He shook his head. "Strange, black bears are almost entirely herbivorous. Why not eat the berries? If it hungered for meat, ample opportunities for rodents were available."

"Déjà vu," Zane said.

"If I hadn't seen the first attack scene with my own eyes, I wouldn't believe the similarities," Greg said.

"You and I both agree that bears are capable of attacking without provocation, Greg. But this is getting bizarre."

"I suppose it's a coincidence. What else?" Greg glanced at his wristwatch. "We're doing a necropsy in about fifteen minutes. Care to observe?"

"You know I do." Zane turned to Joshua. "I better call a taxi to take you back to your motel."

Joshua shook his head. "I'm not leaving until I understand what's going on."

"You can't witness the necropsy."

"Then I'll wait."

Zane sighed. "All right. I'll give you a lift when we're through, okay? I'll fill you in with any developments along the way."

Joshua flashed him a terse smile. "I'll wait for you outside on the steps."

"Is he a male model?" Greg said on the way to the pathology lab.

"Excuse me?"

"Joshua Gaffner. Good-looking man."

Were Zane's ears tricking him? Why would Greg utter such a comment? Did he suspect he and Joshua had been on an all-nighter and that's why he'd brought him to Greg's office on a Memorial Day morning? Greg had never married. Was he confessing his sexuality to Zane?

Dumfounded, Zane said, "People seem to think so."

Greg opened the lab door for Zane to walk though, winking as Zane brushed past him. Langston followed not too far behind and sidled next to Zane.

"What are you doing here, Banks?" Zane said, relieved to shake off Greg's odd insinuations.

"As soon as I got into work, Lund told me to drive out to the university. I guess he didn't realize you were already here."

"I drove straight here before going to headquarters. Didn't have time to keep anyone abreast."

"What's that nephew doing here?" Langston nodded toward the blind-covered windows. "I saw him outside when I came in."

Zane lowered his voice. Blood pulsated in his cheeks. "He's with me."

"This early?"

"He wanted to talk about his uncle," he said, speaking mostly the truth.

"He's snooping into the case?"

"There is no case." Zane peered around the lab. "Or at least there wasn't until now."

"It's a mere coincidence," Langston said. "Two separate bears. That's all."

"Karen will have her hands full, regardless," Zane said.

"Wouldn't want to be her. Here comes Dr. Orowitz."

For the next hour, Zane observed Dr. Orowitz conduct the necropsy with his signature precision and detached air. A replay from the last necropsy Zane had viewed. Although he uncovered less clothing bits in the bear's digestive tract, Dr. Orowitz agreed with some of the students' observations—the bear had consumed parts of the victims. He lifted chunks of human flesh from the bear's stomach and laid them in stainless steel dishes. The doctor emphasized the health of the black bear. Teeth near perfect for its age, claws scarcely worn. To Zane's relief, the doctor decided against decapitating the bear. The lumbar would reveal enough of the bear's brain condition.

Zane had no new information to share with Joshua during the drive to the motel. The silence between them emphasized Zane's preoccupation about the latest attack—and with Joshua.

After Greg's call last night, Joshua had stayed at Zane's house, but they hadn't finished what they'd started. Neither considered making love appropriate after the latest news. Instead, Joshua had dozed in Zane's arms, his tight whites glowing in the dim light that seemed to bleed through the walls, while Zane had spent most of the night falling in and out of sleep, until the sun rose around three thirty in the morning and he'd fully awakened.

Zane, in no mood to reflect on their abbreviated sexual encounter, hoped Joshua understood nothing could come from their interaction. From the way Joshua had clung to Zane last night, he wondered if Joshua had already become too serious.

Zane had never imagined having a relationship with a man beyond sex, although a few times he toyed with the notion that living with a man in the bush might come easier—and in some ways more sensible—if he ever considered moving into an isolated cabin again. In modern society, a male-male relationship wielded too many complications. Dana, Julie—if they would only relinquish clinging to their independence, Zane would find peace and happiness with either of them. Joshua was easygoing enough. Yet he couldn't imagine their relationship moving beyond a few one-night stands. Pulling into the motel's drive-thru, Zane worried Joshua wished for more.

"I'll talk to you later," was all Zane said before leaving him in the wake of his exhaust by the entrance.

Had he been too callous? No, he concluded as he pulled onto the westbound lanes of the Seward Highway. He'd demonstrated pure professionalism and sincerity with Joshua Gaffner, minus their minor sexual interlude. He'd supported him in his time of need, helped him when no one else could, entertained him during lonely hours. What more might Joshua have expected?

Steady disorder greeted Zane when he stepped inside headquarters. The phones had been jumping off the hooks all morning, Amanda lamented.

"We're getting calls from as far away as China," she added, wiping her brow with the back of her pudgy hand. "Amazing how fast news travels these days."

"And China's getting our news today tomorrow," Zane quipped. "Talk about speedy."

"Huh?"

Zane chuckled and sat at his desk, already loaded with paperwork. "Never mind."

Media inquiries were keeping everyone busy. According to Amanda, she and Dana had repeated the same, mind-numbing phrase to callers all morning: "We don't know anything. We'll issue a preliminary report when we get one."

"One newspaper in Japan has already labeled our summer season as 'The Summer of Blood'," Dana told him with disgust.

Zane rolled his eyes. "Let's hope no one takes the news seriously."

Lund had escorted one pesky radio reporter to his car, Amanda said, snickering.

"Was he cute?" Zane said with a sneer, quipping how suddenly everyone noted handsome men.

"Not as cute as you, lover boy," Amanda said, winking as she answered yet another external phone call.

By noon, the University of Anchorage's standard report squeezed from the fax machine: Black bear attack likely the result of surprise encounter spurred by berry picking in prime bear territory. Karen Flecks had the official statement posted on the AST website. She and Col. Lund insisted everyone again keep the man-eating rumor hushed. Zane grew skeptical. Was the decision in the public's best interest? Then again, considering the attacks were unrelated, what did anyone have to fear? No conspiracy among bears to attack and eat their victims existed. Incidents like that didn't happen. A horrible coincidence, like Langston had said in Dr. Orowitz's lab. The public's—and the bears'—best interest remained in Zane's obeying his commanding officers. Keep his mouth sealed.

Zane nudged the entire ordeal aside. Psycho bear number two, as he unofficially referred to the black, was dead. Shot and killed, like the first, this time by one of the high school hikers packing a .357 Magnum. Zane's biggest worry—a possible backlash. That's when the AWT would have to step in with might. His job was to protect bears from a whole list of possible retaliatory actions.

The more he considered Karen and Lund's directive, the more he accepted their rationalizing.

Dr. Sands had been correct in what he'd told Zane and Joshua during their visit to his bear sanctuary on Saturday. Bears did not seek revenge. Humans did.

CHAPTER 10

UNTIL area residents brandished pitchforks and torches against the local bear population, the most pressing issue in Zane's lap was the gallbladder harvesting. The investigation had sputtered to a dead end. More than once Col. Lund had voiced his dismay with the sluggish resolution. No one had learned the whereabouts of the Baxter brothers, the primary suspects. Zane dreaded another trip to Port Raven. Six years with the AST and he still hadn't grown used to venturing into the native Athabascan villages.

Too many expressed contempt for Zane and his badge. A bone-chilling mistrust for uniformed government agents. Oddly, the closer to Anchorage the isolated villages lay, the more negative his receptions had been.

When he'd lived in his dream cabin north of Denali, his one-time visit into far-flung Kalida (three hundred miles from Anchorage and seventy miles from the nearest road), the solicitous villagers had treated him like a superstar, especially the teenage girls. Considering the dire circumstances for his trip, he supposed anyone would've shown him kindness.

And at that time he hadn't worn the "brown shirt" of the AWT.

"Ready for another fun-filled excursion into Port Raven?" he said to Dana as she strolled from the women's restroom.

"I'm for anything that will get me out of this office," she said. "I don't want to hear another phone ringing for the rest of my life."

He and Dana left for Port Raven late Tuesday morning with the threat of a thunderstorm hovering over the Mat-Su Valley. A drizzle followed them along the Glenn Highway and up the Knik Arm in the airboat. The wetness made Zane wish he hadn't replaced his polyester uniform with heavy painter's pants and flannel shirt. Dana grumbled in the cold wind in her tight blue jeans and crimson sweater.

"They've seen us before, Bono," she said, her nicely groomed eyebrows knitted. "What difference does it make if we're out of uniform?"

Zane grinned without comment. He'd decided before leaving they should change into plainclothes to blend in with the villagers. Of course they had to identify themselves with visible badges affixed to their Turtle Tracks bulletproof vests, but by removing the wall of formality—government-issued uniforms and baseball caps with "State Trooper" blazoned across the crown—their trip might go easier.

The excursion into Port Raven, though awkward, proved more productive than last time. They again failed to locate the Baxter brothers, but two villagers agreed to answer Zane and Dana's questions. They admitted to seeing the brothers. The father had lied when he'd told them during their last interview he hadn't laid eyes on his sons for months. The two villagers said the brothers stayed with their parents. Whenever they left the village, they headed south on their ATVs or hopped in their skiff and wouldn't return for days. One villager said that the brothers kept a Toyota pickup truck on an old battered road three miles from the village, and he suspected that's the direction they headed on their ATVs. Neither had witnessed any suspicious people associating with them.

At least the information provided Zane and Dana with an idea of the brothers' activity. No doubt they were up to no good. But what?

Zane navigated the vessel against the increasingly choppy Knik waters back to the AST's pier. As much as Zane disliked visiting Port Raven, the half day spent there had taken his mind off the recent bear attacks—and the baby blues of Joshua Gaffner. He realized he should reconnect with Joshua. Too much had passed between them to pretend they'd never met. The turbulence in his own life (a turmoil that matched the shifting waters of Knik Arm) drew him to Joshua. He liked him enough to want to pay him a considerate good-bye before he returned to Oregon. Maybe even finish what they'd started Sunday night.

Once back at headquarters, he resisted calling him. Perhaps he shouldn't get any more involved in his life. A few hours after Zane had dropped him off at his motel, Joshua had telephoned without leaving a message. Zane hadn't bothered to return his call. By now Joshua would assume Zane had moved beyond him. Another chance encounter, a streaking comet.

Zane rested his head in his hands at his desk. Phones rang, people chatted. He noticed only the throbbing confusion in his head. And the grisly images of partially consumed bodies that intercepted his thoughts.

What had he been thinking when he'd hit on Joshua Sunday night? Bad idea to take advantage of someone susceptible like Joshua. But wasn't his combination of vulnerability and determined grit what had attracted Zane to him? The same features he'd liked in Julie? And Dana?

And Alaska itself?

Joshua had said he planned to leave Thursday—in two days. Could it hurt to see him one last time?

Zane's mind swirled in a vortex of indecision. He hardly noticed the phones beeping and commotion leaking down the hall from Karen Fleck's office where she still juggled callers from around the world demanding information on the fatal bear attacks.

When Zane's cell phone went off near six o'clock with the generic ringtone, he recognized Joshua's cell number. This time he answered. Zane apologized for not having returned his call, but Joshua expressed understanding, considering the tragedy at Twin Peaks.

"I'm sure you've been burdened with lots of extra work," he said. "Even if you don't *officially* investigate bear attacks."

Joshua had been busy himself, he said. Busy taking care of his uncle's remains. He had his body transported to a mortuary where he'd requested a cremation for tomorrow morning. Without a wake or funeral, the way Uncle Ted had wanted it. The hermit-college professor eschewed organized religion. No surprise there, Zane thought.

Zane had almost laughed at himself, listening to Joshua recount his hectic day. He'd imagined Joshua Gaffner sitting alone in his motel room aching for Zane. All the while he'd driven his tiny rental car around town, taking care of business. Zane asked him if he wanted dinner. But it was Joshua who shot him down.

"I still have a lot to take care of here. Maybe I'll see you tomorrow before I leave."

The bottom of Zane's heart fell open. "I'll drive you to the cabin," he said without forethought. "I'll help you scatter your uncle's ashes. With all this rain we're supposed to get, your Avenger won't make it to your uncle's cabin, anyway."

Silence. "That would be great," Joshua said, his voice rising. "Thanks."

"Tomorrow around noon? I'd like to stop and talk again with Dr. Sands along the way, if that's okay?"

"Sounds good, Zanebono. See you then."

Zane clicked off the phone. Appropriate action, he theorized. Help him out. They'd already become semi-intimate. He grinned. He liked how Joshua had spoken his name. Few people referred to him by his full name, obscure even in Italy. His father had insisted on the name, meaning "the good one," against his mother's wishes. She'd wanted to call him Marcello, after her favorite Italian film idol.

"Zane," Dana said, lifting her head from the mouthpiece of her desk phone. "There's a downed moose on Glenn Highway, milepost seven. The driver is okay but wanted to report it. He said he's already left the scene and he's certain the moose is lame. The mother is apparently lurking in the woods making a racket. You want me to take care of it?"

"No." Zane shook his head, his thoughts commingling into a clear focus of his duties. "I'll go."

He rose from his chair, slipped on his jacket, instinctively reached for his Glock. Another part of the job he hated. Euthanizing wildlife struck by high-speed vehicles. He shuffled out of the office, realizing how moose roamed the streets of Anchorage—and everywhere else in Alaska—like pesky hazards.

He pulled the Escalade out of the parking lot when the first flash of lightning and thunder rolled over the Chugach Range.

CHAPTER 11

STORMS from the previous night had passed out to sea. Typical uneven clouds remained, crowning the surrounding snow-streaked mountains. Zane, driving along the Glenn Highway to Dr. Sands's bear sanctuary, grasped the steering wheel more firmly whenever Joshua raised the issue of the bear attacks. He must abide by his superiors' directive and keep his mouth shut. Joshua was too much of an insider already.

"If a lone rogue bear stalked the woods it would make more sense," Joshua said. "Like it was a nut out to kill anyone in its path. But two separate attacks by two different bears and three people killed in the same way? Doesn't make sense."

Zane peered out the windshield. Wet blacktop reflected spruce and gray sky. His knuckles whitened over the steering wheel. "Nothing in life makes sense," he said for what seemed the hundredth time the past twenty-four hours. "You hear about things like this all the time. Happens in Florida with shark attacks. In a span of a week three or four people are bitten or killed, and everyone suddenly starts conjuring shark conspiracy theories. The CIA has programmed them to be assassins, or global warming is triggering them to seek revenge on mankind."

Joshua shook his head. "You might have a point. But I still say something is odd—"

Zane was grateful when dispatcher Clarice's voice crackled through the radio and disrupted their conversation. Another moose hit. This time on Jewel Lake Road across from Anchorage International Airport. An RV struck it while the driver was pulling out of a rental lot. Tourists were streaming into Alaska for the season, regardless of the notorious bear attacks. Rental agencies near the airport leased thousands of RVs each summer. He'd already passed five of them before reaching milepost ten. Langston's voice announced he was headed for the scene. Zane felt more remorse for the unwary tourist than he did for the moose.

The last dispatch silenced Joshua. He gazed out the window at the blur of slick forest racing past. From his reflection in the glass, Zane guessed he'd fallen into deep contemplation. His uncle's death must be pressing on his mind. Or was he pondering other issues?

Neither had mentioned what had happened between them Sunday night at Zane's house. What was either to say? In a creepy way, Greg's disturbing call had come at an opportune moment. Zane probably shouldn't have allowed their intimacy to escalate.

The exit for Eagle River Loop Road loomed ahead. Zane steered off the highway and followed the road until he turned right at the small blacktop lane abutting the river. With the sprawl of Eagle River behind, the lane rollicked with frost heaves. To their left the raging river gurgled with the recent rains and snowmelt. Joshua pointed out a subadult black bear fishing for salmon along the bank.

"Bears seem different now," he said, his voice solemn.

Zane had to admit, he shared the same unpleasant, wary emotion.

Fifteen minutes later, Zane pulled into the shabby parking lot of the bear sanctuary. Uncle Ted's ashes rested in an urn on the floor in the backseat of the Escalade, nudged between two small sacks of calcium and magnesium acetate. When they exited the truck, a sunray burst through a band of clouds and highlighted the gold trim on the urn. Perfect placement. Zane wanted to share the moment with Joshua, but decided to remain silent. The principal issue at hand—speaking with Dr. Sands about the latest bear mauling deaths.

"I want you to keep yourself busy enjoying the sanctuary," Zane said to Joshua while they hiked to the cottage past the familiar two trucks and white trailer. "What Dr. Sands and I have to say is official business."

"You didn't mind last time."

"Circumstances are a bit different now."

"I'm not leaving your side. Besides, I know as much as you do."

Joshua was right, Zane admitted. He sighed. "All right. But you have to promise to keep everything between us."

Zane found the doctor tinkering outside the bear exhibits when he and Joshua approached him from the cottage footpath. This time, he did not greet them with an extended hand and smile. His gray eyes proved he'd anticipated their visit.

"I heard about it, of course," he said, gazing at the ground. "The media's been hounding me since the morning after it happened. I can tell you what I've been telling everyone else, that it's a pure coincidence. Unless you wish to blame poor bear management by humans. But like I've said a thousand times, bears simply do not attack out of revenge. Humans are the only animals who can carry a grudge."

"The MO is identical to the last attack," Zane went on. "Including partially eaten victims."

"Now that bit of information I hadn't been privy to," the doctor said, eyeing Zane under his bushy silver eyebrows.

"We're trying to keep it out of the media, like last time."

"Come with me while I feed Pingaq, we can talk."

They walked along the footpath beside the doctor, waiting for him to speak. Zane understood by the way Dr. Sands gazed at the ground that the gears of his mind cranked like an open watch case.

"If only we had scarce food sources to blame," he said finally. His eyes shimmered in the fluctuating sun when he glanced at Zane. A sad, pleading expression. "Poor salmon runs, a dearth of pine nuts, anything like that. But there have never been more abundant food sources since I'd come to Alaska fifteen years ago, carrying with me my dream of opening a bear sanctuary."

"That's Fish and Game's take," Zane said. "Jasper says there's more salmon in the Anchorage basin this spring than some previous autumns."

"Perhaps that's the problem," Dr. Sands said. "The ample food sources are bringing in more bears, increasing the chances for human-bear encounters."

"But no one has reported any nonfatal encounters," Zane said. "Only these three deaths. But that still wouldn't explain the nature of the attacks."

Dr. Sands stroked his goatee, shook his head. "Very troubling. Very troubling."

"What if the two bears came from the same mother, and shared similar DNA?" Joshua asked, surprising Zane.

Dr. Sands chuckled. "The unfortunate bear who killed your uncle was a brown bear, a grizzly, and the one who mauled Drs. Bloomington and Rakesh was a black. There's no possibility of a relation."

"The two recent victims were doctors also?" Zane asked, unaware of the tidbit until Dr. Sands had mentioned it.

"Research biologists, like me. They retired at a young age. Weren't especially regarded for their expertise in wildlife biology." He turned to Joshua. "Unlike Dr. Theodore Krum."

Zane eyed the bears in their elaborate cages. Two subadult blacks snoozed side by side in the shade of a spruce tree. He remembered when Fish and Game rescued the cubs two years ago after a boar had killed their mother while she was defending them. "How are your two youngest males?" He pointed to the dozing blacks.

"Since their rescue they've been doing fine." Dr. Sands ogled the bears. "They've prospered well. Look at them sleeping like babies."

Joshua stepped to the cage, his fingers woven through the mesh fencing. One of the bears stood on all fours, wandered a few yards downslope, and urinated.

"Aren't you afraid one of your bears might attack you or one of your volunteers?" Joshua asked.

"Like I mentioned last time, we take due precautions," Dr. Sands said. "I don't fear them attacking, I fear their strength. Anyone with sense should. Please, no offense, Mr. Gaffner, but I often wonder if those who are victims of bear attacks possess much sense. They must understand the power behind these animals. The slightest encounter might result in instant death."

"You're absolutely certain we're not dealing with a case of rogue bears attacking for no reason," Zane said, following Dr. Sands to Pingaq's habitat.

"There's always a reason," Dr. Sands replied with a scant curl of his lips. "Life is the reason, the drive to survive. Death is often the result. Unfortunately, for both man and bear."

Zane reflected on the last few days. The bear attacks, the two moose struck by vehicles. His having to euthanize a calf only yesterday evening. Once again, he conceded the doctor had a valid point. Life begets death. The way Mother Nature—or God—had had it planned from day one. Humans, like every other living creature on earth, exerted little if any power over the inevitable outcome.

"Have you heard about the latest gallbladder harvesting?" In coming to the bear sanctuary, Zane had also wanted Dr. Sands's take on the black bear slaughter. He might nudge Zane on the correct path to find the culprits. Zane noticed red emerging over the doctor's ears.

He clenched his hands by his sides. "I am aware of the recent slaughter," he said. "I can't tell you how it sickens me that people kill animals for no reason other than sport or for a few organs to sell on the market."

"This time the culprits used bows," Zane said. "Shot from a tree, judging by the angle of the entry wounds. I almost wish they'd used rifles. That way we'd at least have some ballistics to go on. Clear case of baiting too. Things like pizza, donuts scattered around."

"Shame people do this." Dr. Sands shook his head, his lengthy hair brushing his shoulders. "You almost wonder why bears don't seek revenge against humans. They are such innocent creatures in the big scheme of things. They are not predators. It's humans who prey on the innocent."

Zane lifted his chin at Joshua, sending him a subliminal message to remain patient. "If you learn of anything, you'll let me know?"

"Certainly, I'll be the first to inform you."

They reached Pingaq's habitat. The Kodiak loped back and forth, clearly distressed. It huffed and bit at the ground, tearing grass and dirt. The sun burnished the two-inch scar on its snout. Surprised by its antics, Zane instinctively held Joshua back, despite the sturdy mesh cage keeping them and the nine-hundred-pound brown bear separated.

Dr. Sands used a sharp tone in a foreign tongue to calm Pingaq. "Tace! Audi! Sedo!" The bear hesitated, grunted, and eventually obeyed its keeper's command. Grumbling, it lay next to a boulder, its marble-sized eyes alert.

"She's having one of her days," the doctor said, chuckling. "You understand how women can be."

"Maybe it heard us talking about the gallbladder harvesting," Joshua uttered in a mocking tone.

"Everyone has a bad day," Dr. Sands said, laughing off Joshua's comment, "but when a bear has one, there's enough raw power to topple small trees."

"I sometimes feel like that." Zane grinned. "Especially Monday mornings."

"I suppose we should wait on her feeding," Dr. Sands said. "Don't you agree?"

They returned to the cottage. Inside, Zane glanced at the boxes cluttering the floor and shelves. More deliveries. Dr. Sands, a popular man of research, had garnered support from around the world. Paper towels from Maine. Sugar from Brazil. Syringes from Florida.

Joshua shot him a weary expression Zane had learned to recognize meant, "Let's get out of here."

"Dr. Sands, we have to get going," he said, inching toward the exit. "We're heading to Dr. Krum's cabin, in fact."

"More investigating into the attack?"

"I'm spreading my uncle's ashes," Joshua said beside Zane.

"He couldn't ask for a better resting place."

"We'll be seeing you, Dr. Sands," Zane said, shaking the doctor's calloused hand. "Thank you again for your assistance."

"My pleasure, Trooper Fusca. I only hope your next visit will come under more pleasant circumstances. Now be careful on those hazardous roads," he hollered after them. "They can get awfully muddy and slick."

CHAPTER 12

JOSHUA twisted open the urn, uttered a few words—"Good-bye, Uncle Teddy"—and scattered the ashes. Zane figured Joshua would have gone through the same motions by summer's end anyway. The medical examiner had discovered Dr. Krum suffered from acute pancreatic cancer. Returned to the earth, Zane contemplated as the wind carried the remains over the small meadow and into the forest.

"I don't usually pray," Joshua said. "But I think I just did."

Zane replaced his trooper's cap on his head and patted Joshua's shoulder. "He's probably in a better place," he whispered, unsure what else to say.

"I wish my family had been here. I still don't understand why Uncle Ted and everyone had become alienated from each other. My mom and her family held the same sentiments as a lot of people—that Uncle Ted had it coming to him for living out here. At least my dad wired me money to cover cremation costs."

Ravens overhead squawked and whined. A lonely cry echoing through the boreal forest. Zane needed to leave. He probably shouldn't have driven Joshua. Officially he was on duty, although a lawman and his responsibilities never took time off. He glanced down the narrow foot trail about one hundred yards where he'd left the Escalade.

"We better get going," he said.

"You go ahead. I won't keep you from your duties." Joshua shuffled toward the cabin. "I'd like to stay here awhile, spend time around my uncle's belongings."

"I can't leave you out here with no means of getting back."

"You can pick me up tonight. I'll be okay. Besides, I should probably get used to living here alone."

"What do you mean by that?" Zane tucked his hands into the pockets of his jacket and edged closer to Joshua.

"I decided I'm going to stay, at least for a while. I've canceled my return flight for Thursday. That's the reason why I called you yesterday. I was kinda thinking out loud."

Zane gawked at Joshua. "How will you be able to get in and out? You'll have an easier go in winter with the snow. And you can't rent a car forever."

"I've already bought a used truck. It's parked at the motel."

"You what?"

"A 1998 Ford Ranger. It's got eighty-seven thousand miles, but I doubt I'll need to drive much. My uncle didn't have a car the entire time he lived here. If he needed supplies or wanted to get his mail he hiked to Birchwood, or sometimes took the snowmobile in winter."

"What about your family's business?"

"I talked to my dad, and he said he can go on without me for a while. I'm due for a vacation. Not that I'll get much of one with everything going on." He held Uncle Ted's urn closer to his chest. "Something isn't right, Zanebono. I can feel it. And I want to hang around to stay on top of things."

Ice cubes lodged in Zane's throat. "What do you guess is going on, Joshua?"

"I'm unsure. But I'm considering going to the press."

The icy lump evaporated into a burning steam. Blood seared his neck. "You can't do that. You promised me you wouldn't. I brought you to Greg's office and to Dr. Sands's assuming you were on my side."

"I am on your side, but I'm also on my uncle's side. Shouldn't people learn about the gruesome details of the attacks?"

"For what purpose? They weren't premeditated. Bears can't commit crimes like humans. You'll only achieve spreading hysteria. That could pose more harm to both the public and the bears." Zane stepped closer. "Your uncle's dead. It was a freak accident. Don't go blowing it out of proportion." He stopped, his words scattered by his feet like spent shotgun shells. "I'm sorry," he said, flushing. "I didn't mean it that way."

Joshua scrutinized him, his blue eyes moist. "I'm staying," he said, turning back for the door. "I'm going to move in here for a while. Legally, it's mine."

"What if you get injured out here? How will you get any help? You're not experienced with wilderness first aid."

"What did you do when you lived in the bush?"

Zane cringed. What *had* he done? Failed miserably? Destroyed his wife's life? A measly first aid kit hadn't saved Julie. Zane, a neonate of the woods. A fool. "It's not the same thing," he uttered under his breath. "You'll be alone here."

"I can't afford to stay at the motel any longer, and I'm not going back to Portland." Joshua laid his hand on the door handle. "The cabin isn't so remote for Alaska standards. Glenn Highway is only ten miles from here. The Alaska Railroad is even closer. I can sometimes hear it when the air pressure is high. And I can hike to Birchwood in less than an hour."

No way could Zane offer him to stay at his doublewide, despite his mobile home having three bedrooms. That would be generosity overkill. "Rent a place short term in Anchorage, a sublease," he said. "The city is loaded with them."

Joshua peered at Zane over his shoulder. "I already looked, and most are either way out of my price range or in worse condition than my uncle's cabin. I'd rather be here, anyway. The cabin needs a lot of fixing up if I'm to put it on the market at some point…. *If*, that is. Who knows? Maybe I'll grow to like living out here, like my uncle. We did have a lot in common. Don't worry," Joshua added, reading the meaning behind Zane's wrinkled forehead. "You don't have to feel obligated to do anything more for me. You've gone beyond the call of duty. I can hike out to the highway later tomorrow and hitch a ride to the motel for my truck."

Zanebono followed Joshua inside the cabin and watched him set the urn on the table and scuffle around the stove, getting ready to prepare something to eat. "You're crazy. I knew the first time I walked into headquarters and heard you speaking with Trooper Banks. You're crazy."

"You want some lunch?"

Zane dropped into one of the chairs Joshua had rebuilt after the grizzly's rampage. Shaking his head, he snorted. Joshua stuffed shreds of newspaper under the logs in the wood burning cast-iron stove, struck a match. Flames leaped inside the firebox.

"I'm taking you back to your motel," Zane said evenly. "You can drive that crappy truck you bought here if you want to come back. I can't stop you. But I'm not leaving you here if I brought you."

Strands of dark blond hair brushed Joshua's forehead when he turned to peer at Zane. "Fine. But I'm coming back tomorrow. In the meantime, does canned ravioli sound good? My uncle didn't have many culinary skills, but he kept tons of canned food."

Joshua secured the firebox, set a dimpled pot on the stovetop, and used a hand crank to open a can he'd retrieved from a high shelf. A whiff of cold tomato sauce tickled Zane's nose. Smelled like his boyhood home back in Cranston. Difficult not to grin at Joshua's determination.

"Still don't understand why the bear didn't rip open more of these cans, if it was food it was after," Joshua went on. "My uncle never baited or fed a bear in his life."

Zane nodded. Silently, he studied Joshua. Tall, strong, swift around a cabin.

"We'll need some more wood," Joshua said. "Good thing Uncle Teddy kept a large pile by the cabin. Should last me most of the summer, if I choose to stay that long."

Zane wanted to grab him from behind, hold him close, run his tongue along his nape. Finish what they'd started Sunday night. Joshua stood a few inches taller than Zane. But his height didn't bother him. He liked manhandling men a tad larger than him. He was on duty. Inappropriate to do that. Instead, he headed for the door.

Zane dug through the large woodpile in the shed beside the cabin, selecting choice logs. Memories from his time with Julie rose inside him, like the smoke curling from the chimney. He pictured their small cabin shadowed by the Alaska Range. Julie cooking at the wood burning stove, baby Michael playing with his toy truck on the floor, and Zane outside collecting firewood. He missed those days of subsistent living.

Allowing the fantasy of his living in the bush to wash over him, he inhaled the aroma of the wood fire and gazed through the clearing toward the Chugach Range. He needed the reprieve. For a minute. Even in the form of a daydream.

So what if he did have the confidence to try again? He had a job now, requiring his full concentration—often even while he slept. How many times had a solution to a crime come to him through his dreams? Like that time when he'd jolted upright in the middle of the night, realizing the Kenai Dall sheep poachers had been renting Forest Service cabins in small parties under different surnames to throw off authorities.

Law enforcement absorbed most of his life now. Besides, he'd proved a better lawman than woodsman.

If he'd failed to survive in the woods, how might Joshua expect to succeed?

"Your uncle lived in a beautiful area," Zane said, stepping inside the cabin and spilling the logs into the corner near the stove where Joshua stirred the ravioli. His movements were purposeful, sturdy. He placed his hand on Joshua's shoulder. "About Sunday night," he said.

"What about it?" Joshua kept to his task.

"About what happened."

"You mean the bear attack?"

"With us."

Silence. "It was nice with you the other night," Joshua said into the pot, "even if we never got to finish what we started." He dropped the spoon in the steaming pot and faced Zane. "I like you a lot, Zanebono Fusca."

"You're hard to dislike, yourself."

"You're not dating anyone, are you?"

"I'm... I'm not dating anyone seriously at the moment. Why do you ask?"

"Curious."

"Do you have a boyfriend back in Portland?"

"We broke up last Christmas. That's how things go. He two-timed me, not my style." Joshua scraped the bottom of the pot with the wooden spoon. "When I was here a few summers ago, I told Uncle Ted I was gay," he said after a brief pause. "My family knows, but they don't ever mention it. Uncle Ted once asked me what type of guy I hoped to meet." He eyed Zane. "I've only known you a short while, but I'd like to learn more, if you give me a chance. Since I'm staying in Alaska, we could see each other."

Zane dropped his hand to his side and stared toward his Danner boots. Joshua was foolish to stay, but Zane, happy somehow that he'd cancelled his flight home, imagined them spending more time together. Women showed him little interest these days. Why not try with Joshua?

"I've never dated a man long-term," he said.

"I've never lived in a cabin alone," Joshua said. "We're even. I guess you can say we're both pioneers."

Joshua flashed Zane a full set of whites. Zanebono grinned back.

CHAPTER 13

ZANE reexamined the crime scene photos taken of the slaughtered black bears. A sow and two cubs. Illegally harvested for their gallbladders. Mother with three arrow holes in her upper back, the two cubs, each with two in their abdomens. All three facing the branches of the towering spruce trees, their paws extended in rigor mortis, reaching for final salvation from the heavens. But wildlife cannot expect deliverance, can it?

Perhaps they might on earth. That was Zane's job, he supposed. He studied the photographs in earnest. The adept marksmen had removed and confiscated the arrows and extracted the bears' gallbladders with precision, leaving behind scant blood. The perpetrators were experienced. They'd committed this crime before.

The Baxter brothers still stood out as the primary suspects. The only ones in Anchorage with a recurring conviction for gallbladder harvesting. The first time, they'd been found guilty of a misdemeanor—leaving behind an unharvested carcass. A high-priced attorney Zane suspected worked for the Chinese buyers had managed to convince the judge no hard evidence connected the brothers to any gallbladder dealers. Zane had been a rookie then. The second arrest, the AWT used an informant who'd helped land each brother a five-year sentence.

The state had released them from the Wildwood detention center in March. Soon after, the gallbladder harvesting had begun again. Had they regrouped and committed their crime for a third time?

Investigating the brothers was as much to eliminate them as suspects as it was to nab them, he'd told the villagers and family members many times. Each lead must meet a logical conclusion. None had bought it. This time, law enforcement scoured for answers on its own.

Zane wanted to use an undercover agent and set up a sting, but Col. Lund argued the brothers might be too savvy to swallow the bait a second time. Zane offered an alternative plan: stake out the primitive road where the two villagers had said the brothers parked their truck and tail their movements, and add a trooper to patrol from the water to follow if they took off in their skiff. After a briefing at headquarters, Lund agreed to the stakeout.

Friday morning, a fellow wildlife trooper, impersonating a bird watcher, loitered near the primitive road while Zane kept to the water in an unmarked motorboat, pretending to fish for hooligan. Appropriate name for a fish. He *was* fishing for hooligans, but of the human variety. Fish and Game warden Jasper Bohler waited at Merrill Field downriver, ready for any word to hop in his helicopter. Easy to lose someone in Alaska's expansive and roadless terrain without air support.

Zane's lonely unmarked motorboat rocked on the whitecaps of the Knik waters. A brisk wind blew off the snowcapped Alaska Range one hundred miles west. He pulled his trooper cap snug near his ears and tightened his life jacket around his torso. The radio crackled with updates from the undercover bird watcher, Trooper Marlton. Quiet thus far. Zane reported the same.

Brackish sweeps of salt air, pungent and thick, stung Zane's cheeks. Cirrostratus clouds churned with a gray, wet presence, concealing a fuzzy sun. Nothing new for south central Alaska the first few days of June.

The village dock appeared still. The brothers' skiff, tethered to the dock, ebbed in the current untouched. On the water, authentic fishermen hooked hooligan and chum from shoddy dories. Everything ordinary. Zane steadied into a squat and spied the village through binoculars. Port Raven remained motionless as a glacier.

Minutes turned into hours. The blurry yellow sun arced toward the southeast where it wouldn't fall until near midnight. Marlton reported no unusual activity. Wind had settled and left a transparent mist over the Knik. The village dock lurked in the fog like a forlorn spirit. Two children built sandcastles by the shore. Small, dim figures sandwiched between sand and sky.

Zane's damp trooper's pants chafed his thighs. He needed a new pair, a size or two bigger. Too many lower body workouts at the gym had bulked his legs. He'd been hitting the gym harder and more frequently after a lull during the dark months, since losing his workout partner, Langston, last summer. After what had happened between them, who could blame them for ending their gym partnership?

And now Joshua played a prominent and unexpected role in his life. He'd promised him they'd "date." How did that happen? Somehow, when he'd walked into headquarters that Friday and taken notice of the strange man speaking with Langston, he foresaw. They were destined to connect. But how long would their junction last?

Wednesday night, Joshua had driven his impulsively purchased truck to the cabin after Zane had dropped him at the motel. He feared for him living alone in the bush. The rawness of the Alaskan wilderness mocked mawkish sentiments. Was Joshua, six foot and sturdy, tough enough— tougher than Zane and Uncle Ted—to face the challenges?

He had to concentrate. Focus on the mission at hand. Personal issues must remain at home.

He peered through the binoculars for the umpteenth time. Sensitive tissue around his eyes throbbed from the eyecups. Movement from the village dock. Finally. Zane stood, ready to act.

The Baxter brothers were untying the skiff. Zane radioed Marlton. He agreed to remain at his post. Next he alerted Jasper for a possible air chase. The suspects boarded the skiff (it appeared they carried no hunting bows) and motored ahead across the Knik at top speed. White froth churned in the skiff's wake. Zane loosened the throttle and followed.

The brothers turned a sharp starboard for the narrowest part of the Arm. Zane increased speed and raced after them, keeping a reasonable distance to throw them off his chase. Why were they heading north? Zane had assumed they'd used the boat to go downriver closer to downtown and meet their buyer at a posh hotel.

Zane hardly believed their next move. The skiff lunged to port and surged for the remote western shore. Zane closed in and idled the motorboat a hundred yards from the shoreline. He reported his coordinates and informed Marlton and Jasper of the suspects' moves.

Were they headed for some kind of obscure meeting place between the vast and barren Alaska Range and the Knik with only a splattering of villages? A beige Toyota pickup truck, parked near the gravel parking lot abutting the mudflat fishermen used for a boat slip during high tide, piqued Zane's suspicions. The truck's windows, dark and obscure, reflected the billowy clouds. Through his binoculars, Zane saw no driver. He concentrated on the license plate, but he could read only the first two letters and the last digit. He jotted them down anyway: "XR" and "7."

The brothers motored to shore and crossed the mudflat like experts, centering their line of gravity to prevent the glacier silt from pulling them under, all while dragging the skiff behind them. Zane kept his binoculars focused on their movements. By the time they reached the drier sand, a young woman in a hoodie (he could not see her face, but her figure gave away her sex) had jumped out of the pickup and rushed to help moor the skiff. She'd left the cab door open, and inside Zane noted a loaded gun rack mounted on the rear window. Not too incriminating in Alaska. The three pulled the skiff behind brush. (Why did they do that? To keep anyone from stealing it or to hide their whereabouts?) A minute later, they scrambled inside the truck and headed down the desolate road.

"We need helicopter pursuit," Zane called into his radio. "Fast, Jasper."

Zane, unleashing a torrent of coordinates of his location, motored to shore and moored the boat on the beach. Within five minutes, Jasper set down the A-Star on the clean beachfront near Zane.

"Tan pickup truck, heading north on Goose Bay Road, license plate number XR and 7 something," Zane told Jasper as he climbed aboard and strapped on the headphone. "Try to make it casual, like we're doing a moose count."

"What are they doing this side of the Arm?"

"They might have gotten a heads up of the stakeout and are trying to throw us off," Zane hollered into the mouthpiece above the roar of the rotor blades. "Who knows?"

The terrain receded and rolled. The road appeared and disappeared behind thick groves of aspen and spruce through sporadic subdivisions of the Mat-Su Valley closer to the Knik. To their left towered the Alaska Range, a crystal-like kaleidoscope of prisms and spires that draped the entire western horizon. Triumvirate and Capps Glaciers jutted eighty miles southeast, a monumental shelf of ice and snow drifting millimeter by millimeter into Beluga River. A clearing in the trees provided view of the vehicle and driver casually moving along the primitive road. The suspects appeared unaware of the airborne pursuit. The truck traveled the speed limit, steady.

"They're probably going to cut back down into the Anchorage area through Wasilla," Zane said with the binoculars pressed against his eyes. "Wait. They made a left. There."

"I got them in my sights. I'll hang south of them."

They followed for several minutes while the suspects headed west, into even more remote and barren country. The truck gained speed, a desperate spray of gravel spitting from the back.

"They're getting away," Zane said.

"They must've gotten suspicious of us," Jasper said. "I'll hang left seven o'clock." He veered a sharp left, the front of the helicopter near parallel with the earth.

The Baxter brothers and their female driver led them farther west, closer to the foothills of the Alaska Range. The trees concealed the narrowing road, save for small patches. Zane shifted and turned in his seat to get a clearer view with the binoculars. He still could not get an unhindered view of the license plate.

"They turned another right toward Fairview," Zane shouted. "They must be familiar with the area, because it's the last right before the road dead ends. Quick, head twelve o'clock."

Peering through the binoculars, Zane couldn't believe what came next. He lowered the binoculars, shook his head, gave another look. His eyes hadn't deceived him.

"There's a naked woman running down there," he shouted into the mouthpiece.

"A what?"

"I'm not kidding, Jasper. Two o'clock. She appears in distress. There's a burly guy, ran out of a nearby cabin, like he's in pursuit of her. We'll have to land and check it out." Zane shifted the binoculars and took one last look at the beige pickup speeding back toward the Mat-Su Valley out of their sight. "Dammit," he said. "We'll lose them now." Col. Lund would give him hell for the wasted resources.

"I'm setting down south of the scene," Jasper said, guiding the helicopter onto rocky soil.

"Looks like a domestic dispute," Zane said.

He hated abandoning the Baxter brother pursuit, but they had to aid the woman. No other law enforcement deployment would touch ground in time to reach her. The man chasing the woman was now on top of her. He glanced at the helicopter as he was about to yank her head back by her long strawberry blonde hair.

Heart racing, Zane jumped from the helicopter and crouched toward the couple, inching closer and closer, eyes wide like craters. Jasper covered his back.

"Hands up," Zane shouted, pulling out his prepped Glock and fighting the tunnel vision. Were there others inside the cabin? A meth lab perhaps? "Hands over your head now. Step away from the lady."

The man, dressed only in dingy white boxers, hesitated long enough that Zane moved his finger closer to the trigger. He'd never shot anyone in the line of duty and hoped to avoid having to. For now, the woman, wincing underneath the hefty man, was his number one concern.

"Step back. Step back."

The man raised his arms and obeyed Zane's command. The woman, thin and frail, scurried away like a spider. Curled in a ball to conceal her nakedness, she threw her head into the crook of her arm and sobbed. Jasper raced to her side and draped a jacket over her while Zane aimed his gun at the man.

"I didn't do anything," the man said, shaking his head. "I was going after my woman."

"Are you presently armed?"

"Where, in my shorts?"

"Anyone else in the cabin?"

"Only me and that godforsaken bitch live here."

"Turn around and put your hands behind your back." Zane holstered his sidearm and cuffed the man. "What's going on here?" he demanded, yanking him face forward.

"That bitch is driving me crazy," the man said. "She been disrespecting me for too long. Won't even cook."

"I live like a slave," the woman spat. "I'm sick of breaking my back for that pig."

Zane guessed the couple's profile. A rough sourdough, one of those who sought to escape society, but not for the same reasons as Zane and Uncle Ted and the vast majority of others. Once Zane ran a check on the man, he was certain he'd uncover a lengthy conviction record. All his pathological rage narrowed on the one woman who he'd somehow convinced to live with him. A lonely lady most likely suffering from a lack of self-respect and few choices of where to live.

Jasper helped the woman to her feet. She spat at her offender. "I hate you," she said, her voice quivering. "I hate you. I hate you."

The man squirmed in Zane's grasp, wanting to get at her.

"I hate you more, bitch," the sourdough fumed. "You worthless bloodsucker."

The woman returned his glare. Blood trickled down her nose. "Why don't you roll over and die?"

"Shut your face, bitch."

"Settle down, or I'll arrest the both of you," Zane said. "Now let's head to the cabin. Keep straight ahead. Stay clear of each other."

Inside, Zane and Jasper calmed the couple long enough to learn their story. The couple, Deborah Smyth and Grason Boyd, had shared the cabin since last summer. Grason had been living in the bush for twelve years. Longing for companionship, he moved to Palmer for a month until he found a willing partner. The long winter had proved nightmarish for the new lovers. Holding a rag to her bloody nose, Deborah, dressed in a robe, recounted endless days of verbal and mental abuse. Grason snickered, unleashed expletives.

"She's a mooching princess, like all of them."

"I'm not staying here one more minute," Deborah screamed. "I'll hike out if you don't take me with you. I'll swim across the Knik." She loathed her new boyfriend, but insisted she did not wish to press charges against him.

"We don't have a choice," Zane said.

Boyd tried to stand with his cuffed hands but Jasper pushed him back into his chair. "You have no right to haul me in."

"By law we're required to take you in if we suspect domestic abuse," Jasper said. "We caught you in the act, Boyd."

"But she had it coming to her. The state can't rule over my personal affairs."

Zane ignored Boyd's rants and turned a softer voice to Deborah. "You have any place to stay or somewhere we can take you?"

"I got family in Palmer. Set me down wherever you're going. They can pick me up."

In a rush, Deborah dressed and packed her one small duffel bag. Zane removed Boyd's cuffs long enough to allow him to throw on some clothes. While Jasper escorted the woman to the helicopter, Zane replaced the cuffs on Grason, read him his rights, and pushed him ahead.

Before stepping onto the helicopter, Boyd turned to face Zane with a sinister grin creeping above his scraggly dark beard and said, "You know why I moved out here? Back in California, I was wee close to becoming a killer. Even got to the point I believed I might be doing God's work. Studied the best way to do it. Gun, knife, strangulation? Then I decided against it. You see, Trooper Fusca, I'm a good citizen. I've committed the kindest act a human being has ever done for mankind. I voluntarily removed myself from society before I followed through with my plans. And here society's laws require you bring me back. Ironic, ain't it?"

Grason Boyd laughed sardonically, and Zane shut the door on him. An icy chill rolled down Zane's spine.

Alaska could be a bitch.

CHAPTER 14

THEY summited Magpie Peak as puffy gray clouds whizzed past them.

"This is amazing, Zanebono," Joshua, resting beside Zane, hollered above the blustery wind. "How high are we?"

"About six thousand feet."

"Awesome view of Turnagain Arm and the other peaks through the cloud breaks."

Zane enjoyed Joshua's excitement about his first overnight hiking trip in Alaska, although he'd informed Zane he'd backpacked numerous times in Oregon and Washington. When Zane had mentioned to Josh—as he now found himself calling him—that he and two of his AWT colleagues, Dana Chernikoff and Langston Banks, had planned their yearly overnighter in the Chugach Range to burn stress from their law enforcement jobs for that weekend, Josh had wanted to tag along.

Neither Dana nor Langston had asked about Joshua's presence. They understood Zane had taken a concern for him. Helping distressed family members of an animal mauling victim sometimes came with their duties. Still, Zane had detected a glimmer in Langston and Dana's brown eyes whenever they looked Joshua's way. They were scrutinizing him, wondering what else linked him and Zane.

Joshua had proven himself a natural outdoorsman. He'd handled the sixteen-mile hike along the Crow Pass Trail from the trailhead like a champ. And he'd ascended the strenuous two-hour side trip to Magpie Peak—which required occasional non-technical rock climbing—effortlessly. A hardy man, Zane acknowledged.

He'd probably make a more worthy sourdough than Zane had.

"Wish we could take in the view all day," Zane said, embracing Josh against the chilly wind and the latest burst of flurries. "But we better head back. Dana and Langston will worry if we're gone much longer."

The canopy of clouds broke once they reached the old abandoned mining camp at tree line. Temperatures lifted back to the midsixties, and the wind calmed. An hour later, their camp appeared in a small meadow where new growth of white spruce, birch, and cottonwoods poked above the blackened permafrost. A lightning-ignited forest fire five years earlier had carved out a wide swath of forest along the south facing slopes. New stands of trees and fireweed painted the landscape emerald green, yellow ochre, and ruby red.

A smaller crowd than normal for that time of year camped at Crystal Lake. Zane wondered if the bear attacks kept the hikers away. A five-member family with a Labrador retriever who'd hiked behind them from the trailhead had claimed the Public Use cabin. Another three families camped among the trees with easy access to the privy. A hundred yards from their camp, Zane had earlier spied a man and his grammar school-age son assembling their camp. Now they were fishing together for rainbow trout. Envy buzzed around Zane worse than the black flies and mosquitoes.

Stress from the past few weeks had forced Mikey to the forefront of his mind. He hadn't spoken with his son since March. Could he convince his in-laws to send him to Alaska for a few weeks? It was nearing summer break, and Zane had a few weeks of vacation due. They might go camping or fishing, like the father and son down lake.

Mikey's birthday peered around the corner. Nine years old in July. Zane usually sent him a card with a slightly larger check than usual. He sent a check each month for Michael. And once a year he sent him his Alaska Permanent Fund check, which ranged from one thousand to three thousand dollars. No one asked for his help anymore. Julie never wanted alimony. The few times he'd sent her a check, she'd never cashed it. Eventually, he'd stopped bothering.

He wanted to call his in-laws and request that Michael fly up for at least a week before school started in September. He was in no mood to listen to their excuses.

"Why don't you fly down for a few days, Zane?" his father-in-law would say.

"Of course, Zane can see him," his mother-in-law would say from the background, as she always did, never talking on the phone with Zane herself. "We've always encouraged him to visit."

Now she'd probably add, "We're not sending a boy to Alaska with all those bears killing people. It's all over the news. The Summer of Blood. We'd be insane if we sent him up there, especially alone."

They'd find some excuse or another. Zane supposed he understood. Anchorage, five thousand miles from Rhode Island, was quite a distance for a boy to travel alone.

And there *were* the bear assaults to consider, although everything had remained quiet since Sunday.

"What took you guys so long?" Dana stretched by the campfire, her figure slim and taut in her nylon hiking pants. "We worried you fell off the mountain."

Zane blinked at her. "You and Langston should've come along."

"I don't mind the climbing," Langston said from his supine position on a fallen spruce by the fire. "It's the cold wind up there I hate."

Zane warmed his hands by the campfire. "Been busy getting dinner ready while we were gone?"

"We were waiting for you guys to cook it for us," Dana said. "You have all the energy."

Joshua and Zane caved to the pressure to fix dinner, since they'd packed the food. They made Italian-style Tuna Helper in tinfoil over the open flames of the campfire, with a side of day-old rolls and gorp.

"Not bad," Dana said. "I like the hot spicy flakes."

Shortly after dinner, Josh handed Zane a twig.

"What's this for?"

"Toasting marshmallows," he said.

Zane chuckled, and watched him hand sticks to Dana and Langston. Josh fit in quickly with his colleagues. They seemed to like him. To Zane, he'd transformed from a "loved one of a victim" to a…. Were they really boyfriends? Thus far, they'd had little time for any dates since the symphony, much less to make love.

The sun shifted a notch westward and shined down on their camp. They toasted marshmallows, ate s'mores. Always the wildlife trooper, Zane focused one eye on the lake's campers. He noticed Dana and Langston behaving the same. They ensured no one disobeyed state fishing and environmental regulations. They wore their state trooper caps to ensure the campers recognized they worked with the AST. Some smiled respectfully, a few grimaced. Zane kept his Glock concealed under his jacket.

Joshua bit into his gooey treat, waved at the mosquitoes. "I'm afraid if I open my mouth, I'll eat a mess of mosquitoes."

"We call those Alaska's state birds," Zane said.

"Takes some getting used to," Joshua said. "But I must say they're less here than at the cabin."

"Most people in Alaska hole up in the summer and stay away from the bugs," Langston said. "Winter's when real Alaskans have fun."

"Really?"

Dana wiped melted chocolate from her chin and nodded. The only Alaskan-born among them, Dana comprehended the state's stalwart culture more than any of them. "Winter is when we snowmachine, ATV, ski, snowshoe," she said. "It's a time for carnivals, games, lots of different kinds of activities. Even those who live in the bush visit neighbors by snowmachine or dog sled."

"What's fifty miles between good neighbors?" Zane snickered. "When I lived in Rhode Island, we almost never chatted with our neighbors. In Alaska, people will travel hundreds of miles for a friendly visit."

"You plan on staying at your uncle's old cabin long-term?" Langston asked Joshua. "Even through winter?"

"I'm trying to come to terms with everything," Joshua said. "You still believe my uncle caused the attack, Langston?"

Zane cringed. They'd managed to sideswipe the issue of Joshua's uncle and the bear mauling deaths during the hike to Crystal Lake from the trailhead and Zane wanted to keep it that way.

Langston shifted on his haunches. His brown eyes mirrored the flames from the campfire. "I've worked at this job for four years, and I truly believe that bears never act without provocation. I'm not alone. Most academics agree. There's a lot of evidence to support our views. I'm not saying your uncle had it coming to him, but I'm sure he could have been a bit more careful. Maybe he left out some food. You can't live in the boonies without leaving some mess around, attracting bears over a period of time."

"Not everyone's a slob like you, Banks," Dana said.

"I'm speaking intellectually."

"Langston has a college degree." Dana snickered. "He's full of hot air, like all those highbrows at the university."

"What do you have against people with college degrees?" Langston scoffed. "You're an anti-intellectual."

"The anti-intellectuals are the so-called intellectuals themselves." Zane reflected on the journals left by Uncle Ted. Most of what he'd written concerned bear behavior and life in the bush, but he'd also flirted with the topic of academic dishonesty and cronyism he'd experienced while working at Ochoco State University in Oregon. Zane had noted the darker handwriting, more indented in the paper, when he'd scribbled about how his own colleagues had bamboozled him out of tenure merely because of his unpopular views. Zane hadn't put much consideration behind his scribbling. Now he spoke on Dr. Krum's behalf.

"When the universities eschewed rational scientific research in exchange for pandering to the government for grants," he said, "that's when intellectualism took a nose dive."

"That's bull," Langston said, his brow full of more grooves than the sprawling Chugach Range. "You have no idea what you're talking about."

"The human race has come full circle," Joshua said with a light air. "We started off worshiping animals as gods, and here we are doing it again. Can't we ever be original? But I have a better idea. Let's tell riddles."

"I hate riddles." Langston kicked at the duff.

"But you're an intellectual, Banks," Dana said with a giggle, licking sticky chocolate and marshmallow from her fingers.

"And an officer of the law," Zane added. "Your job requires that you solve riddles. I'll go first." He stretched his legs, eager to leave the jittery topic of wildlife management behind. With his boots edging the campfire, he allowed the flames to stir his mind. "Okay, I got one. It has a hole in the middle, is weighed by the pound, and comes in a variety of sizes."

"A donut," Langston blurted, his bottom lip still hanging low.

"Take time to ruminate."

The crack of the fire filled the contemplative silence.

"A crater?" Dana wrinkled her nose.

Zane shook his head.

"I got it," Joshua said. "Dog."

Zane threw back his head and clapped his hands. "That's right. Good for you, smart guy."

"I don't get it," Dana said.

"You're such an intellectual. Figure it out," Langston said.

"Dog," Joshua explained. "The hole in the middle is the letter o. Dog pounds weigh dogs when they arrive. And they come in many sizes."

"We're going to play those kinds of riddles, huh?" Dana leaned back against a log. "My turn, and I have a good one. This'll get you back. Listen up. You can shoot it, but you can't skin it or eat it."

"The breeze," Langston mumbled.

Dana kicked dirt at him. "How did you figure it out so fast?"

"You stiffened when the breeze picked up off the peaks. I figured you were thinking about it. Makes sense."

Dana reached over and slapped his thigh. "Maybe college did you some good after all, Banks."

Langston's mood lightened. "Okay, my turn. This is a good one. If you turned the letters one-hundred-eighty degrees to the left, it would be brand new."

Everyone fell silent. Dana mumbled the riddle to herself over and over.

"I cede," she said.

Zane and Joshua insisted Langston hold off revealing the answer, wanting more time to ponder. A few minutes later, they both shrugged and shook their heads.

"What's the answer?" Zane asked.

"Zoo," Langston stated, grinning.

"Zoo?"

"Get it? If you turn each of the letters in the word 'zoo' one-hundred-eighty degrees to the left, you spell 'NOO'. Brand noo. Understand?"

"Stupid as hell, Banks," Dana said.

"You were grasping for straws on that one," Zane agreed.

"Went over your heads," Langston said. "Stop bellyaching."

"Now it's my turn." Joshua straightened his back, widened his eyes. "It starts off big, can be sharp, and is never first."

Each one repeated the riddle. After several minutes, pensive expressions turned into wide grins.

"I'm clueless," Zane said.

"I'm not telling." Joshua chuckled.

"You have to," Dana moaned.

"You've got the rest of the weekend to chew on it."

"On that anticlimactic note," Langston said, standing with a crack of his bones to match the lapping flames from the campfire. "I'm off to bed. Silly riddle games are more tiresome than you guys."

"Sleep tight, Banks," Zane said, his words ushering him toward his tent. "Don't let the mosquitoes get you." Normally he'd tease him about bears, but this time, considering the recent bear attacks and Josh's presence, better judgment censored his words.

Dana yawned, stretched, and said she wanted to turn in too. She slumped behind Langston, climbed inside her two-man tent, and zipped the flap shut tight after a hearty, "Good night, guys."

Alone, Zane smiled at Josh. They remained silent, staring into the waning flames. Many of the other nearby campers had faded off to bed like Dana and Langston. The lake, quivering with the breeze, glimmered in the orange glow of the sun hovering above the northwestern peaks. Close to ten o'clock, Zane figured. Daylight for another two hours.

Times like these, Zane relished Alaska the most. Quiet solitude in the outdoors around a campfire. He could buffer the worries growing inside his mind. Out in the wild, his soul nestled between peace and wisdom. A rush of need surged in him, like the wind that raced off Magpie Peak. He wanted to take Joshua in his arms and hold him, in front of whoever's eyes remained alert. No concerns here. Under the fullness of the late night sun, he slid along the log and edged closer to him.

Joshua pushed his shoulder against Zane's arm. "Why do you study all those foreign languages?" he asked.

"What?" Zane glanced at him.

"At your house," Joshua said, "I noticed the study guides and CDs on foreign languages. Italian, German, Russian, Mandarin Chinese."

Zane chuckled. "I guess I like to understand what my enemies are saying, wherever they might come from."

"Who needs college?"

"Right, who needs college?" Zane chuckled.

He patted Josh's shoulder, wanting to protect him from his own confidence. He'd failed to save his ex-wife from hers.

Julie, like his son, had filled his mind lately. It was near that time of year. Especially after the incident with the hermit and his terrorized girlfriend, he wondered if he and Julie would've turned into a Grason Boyd and Deborah Smyth. People moved to Alaska for a whole slew of reasons. Zane had wanted to live side by side with Mother Nature rather than as a passive observer living the life of a modern consumer. He hadn't sought to escape from the law. Funny how he'd *become* the law.

The past few days he'd squelched the urge to call Julie again. Many years had passed since their divorce. She'd rather they saw each other less and less. His wanting to dine with her a few weeks ago had been selfish.

Few needed or wanted Zane. Dana did not wish to date him. Julie, both before and after the accident, had refused his help. His son was better off without him, living with his grandparents in Rhode Island. Did the animals the state paid him to protect even require his aid? Did they deserve it?

"You're far away," Joshua said.

"The outdoors makes me ponder life, I guess."

"What else does the outdoors make you do?"

Zane soaked in the blue of Joshua's irises. They flickered in the scant glow from the fire like aquamarine gemstones. "Makes me an animal," he said, tickling Josh's ribs.

Joshua squirmed and chuckled. "In that case, let's hit the tent."

After dousing the fire and ensuring their backpacks were secured in the spruce branches away from bears (and peering around to check the other campers had done the same), Zane used the privy and headed for the tent where Joshua waited.

Sleeping arrangements had pressed on Zane's mind ever since Joshua had decided to join the backpacking excursion. Would their sharing a tent stir curiosity? Disapproval?

Joshua, snug inside one of Zane's extra sleeping bags and naked from the waist up (and probably from the waist down), greeted Zane with a wide grin when he crawled inside the tent. Orange sunglow from nylon fabric washed Josh in a golden hue.

Zane slipped off his Glock, stripped naked, and slid inside his own bag.

"You lack experience with men, don't you?" Joshua said, resting on an elbow and eyeing Zane.

"I've hooked up with a few." Zane tucked the bag around him. "And hardly any since moving to Alaska. Why do you care?"

"Curious what your type is."

Zane chuckled. "Same as yours. Rugged and handsome."

"So you have a thing for police officers too, like me?"

Zane turned away, cheeks burning. "I didn't join the force out of some fetish, if that's what you mean."

Joshua prodded him. "You've messed around with a fellow cop, haven't you?" When Zane refused to answer, Josh sat stiffer, exposing his sinewy waist. "I want details," he said.

Actually, Zane had "messed around" with two fellow cops. Dana, the first, would hold no interest for Josh. The other he'd kept as a guarded secret since it happened, almost a year ago. Each of his encounters with his colleagues puzzled him. They'd materialized unexpectedly, like a rainbow in the Alaskan winter. "It's a long story," he said.

"Tell me."

Zane sighed. "Don't go blabbing about it to anyone."

"Who would I tell? Go on."

"I'm ashamed to admit it now, but I used to give Langston steroid injections. I didn't want to. He'd insist. He's that kind of guy. Persistent. He has belonephobia, a fear of needles. He'd bring me the hypodermic loaded with his dose, and once or twice a week I'd give him a shot in the ass. Usually after working out together."

Joshua snickered. "Hot. Did you ever do any?"

"I dabbled at first, but only a couple of times. Seemed silly to go to such extremes for only a few extra pounds of muscle."

"What happened? Couldn't resist his beefy rump?"

"Last summer, after we finished our workout," Zane said, flushing, "we went back to my place to shoot him up, routine. That particular time, Langston said, 'while you're down there....' Well, he basically begged me to do him. Right there. At first, I assumed he was joking. You know how guys act. But he kept insisting. He said a side effect of steroids is a craving for anal sex, on the catcher's end."

"You're kidding?"

"That's what he claimed. Never heard of it before. I can't recall experiencing the urge when I was on the juice, but I hadn't done near the amount as him. Anyway, one thing led to another, and I did what he asked. We did it two more times over the next month."

"That's wild. Did you ever do anything more?"

"Nope, just anal, me doing him, the same way, quick and purposeful."

Zane acknowledged to himself the first time he'd beheld Langston's rock hard brown rump poking out at him that he'd had a difficult time passing up his invitation. Before he fully comprehended what Langston had asked of him, he'd lowered his own shorts, his arousal brushing against Langston's cheeks.

"Show me what a stud you are," Langston had moaned while he'd grabbed onto the kitchen counter. "Go ahead. Give it to me hard, stud."

The experience drenched him in a surreal sweat, as if they did nothing more intimate than play touch football. Five minutes later, spent and panting, he hardly believed what passed between them. Langston, however, hiking up his shorts, grinned and shrugged. During the next month, he asked Zane to satisfy him twice more, using the same voice he'd use whenever requesting Diet Coke.

It was always mechanical, with Langston bent over his kitchen table. Except for that one time when Zane tossed him onto his back on his favorite armchair and they did it in the missionary position. Instinctively he leaned in and kissed Langston on his mouth. Langston did not turn away.

Zane merely stared at him after each time, trying to catch his breath, since he'd always oblige Langston's demands to drill him harder and faster.

"You can ask any scientist," Langston would declare afterward. "Anyone of them will tell you a side effect of steroids is the need to get plowed in the ass. I swear I'm no homo. It's biological. It's the hormones. Keep your mouth shut about it, all right?"

Zane never got around to asking "any scientist," and certainly harbored enough self-respect to avoid approaching Greg Gomez about the subject. Langston had never married, yet he'd dated several women in the four years Zane had known him. No reason to doubt his defenses, strange as they sounded. Zane understood as well as anyone the ebb and flow of human sexuality.

Their workouts together dwindled to nonexistent in the days following their last impromptu sexual encounter, which involved the light kissing. Zane had no issue with Langston. He had a good time with him at work, at the gym, and the "three times he'd scratched Langston's itch," he often mused about their trysts.

"Crazy," Josh said, blue eyes twinkling. "Now what about me? Are you ever going to scratch my itch?"

The recollections of his stint with Langston poking his mind, added to his own bubbling yearnings for Joshua, Zane let himself go. Worry that Dana and Langston might hear a mere twenty yards from their tent failed to hold him back. He unzipped his sleeping bag, climbed inside with Joshua.

Coated in DEET, their oily bodies slid against each other. Zane did not care if he ingested some of the insect repellant smeared over Joshua's taut body. He savored the taste mixed with sweat, like bitter apples. He wanted to devour Joshua, reconcile the lost moments. He stopped, gazed down at him.

"I didn't bring any protection," he said.

Joshua reached for his hiking pants and dug through the pockets. Brandishing a package of condoms, he grinned. "Good Boy Scouts come prepared."

Chuckling, Zane slipped on the condom and took Joshua into his arms, rubbed his lips and tongue over his bitter-tasting body. He allowed his mind to tunnel in on one reality—Joshua's firm muscles beneath him and the rugged Alaskan wilderness pressing down on them. An ecological three-way. Sex with Josh certainly made his tryst with Langston seem nothing more than hanging out with a beer-drinking buddy.

Amid a distant burst of thunder over the mountain range, Zane flooded the condom.

"I have it," he said, sitting upright minutes after his softness had slipped out of Josh. "It's the letter B."

"What're you talking about?"

"The answer to your riddle. It starts off big, can be sharp, and is never first. The letter B."

Joshua laughed. "That's right. You finally got it."

"Yeah," Zane said, rolling back on top of Joshua and nibbling his lips. "I finally got it."

CHAPTER 15

"WHAT is it, Greg?" Zane said the following Monday morning into his cell phone.

"I'd rather speak in person. Can you meet me in my office at noon?"

"Sure, I'll be there."

"Come alone, Zane."

Zane clicked off his phone. What secretive news did Greg need to share in private? Had he uncovered a pathogen in the bears? Infection, meningitis, a spreading virus that might cause violent behavior? Spurring the bears to consume their victims, like the two that had killed Uncle Ted, Harold Bloomington, and Vishva Rakesh? But why had Greg sounded so mysterious?

The unspoiled Chugach Range, highlighted by the late Monday morning sun, failed to capture Zane's imagination the way it normally would on his drive along Muldoon Road to the University of Anchorage. He wrapped his concerns around the throbbing lobes of his brain and the troubled tone of Greg Gomez's voice.

"I didn't want to make a big issue out of this," Greg said when Zane stepped inside his small office twenty minutes later. He glanced into the hallway and shut the door. "But let's keep this between those who need to know until we understand the situation more fully."

"What's going on, Greg?"

"I ran more assays on the blood from the bears that killed Dr. Krum and the two most recent victims. Similar anomalies showed up in both tests. Take a look." Greg gestured toward his computer.

Zane placed his palms on Greg's cluttered desk and leaned into the brightly lit monitor, overheated and humming from excess use. A spreadsheet of some kind filled the screen. "What's this? Some sort of data?"

"It's serum testosterone from the grizzly that killed Dr. Krum. Same results in the black bear responsible for the deaths of Drs. Bloomington and Rakesh. I ran another test on both samples using the HPLC-MS, a rather expensive instrument which provides the most concrete data. The HPLC-MS allows a narrow window for false positives, unlike the blood assay. The most artifact-free we have. The HPLC-MS confirmed the initial findings. Extraordinarily high concentrations of testosterone."

Greg scrolled down, revealing peaks and valleys from a line chart. "This right here shows the levels of testosterone." He maximized another datasheet. "Now check that out. It's the test results from the black. Same indications. See?"

"Is it that alarming to find high levels of testosterone in bears?"

"This time of year, a grizzly's grams per deciliter concentration is usually about sixty. In late summer and autumn during the mating season and prior to hibernation, a grizzly's grams per deciliter concentration will increase by up to ten times, more than six thousand g/dl. The grizzly that killed Ted Krum displays upward of one hundred thirty thousand g/dl, and those are findings for a sow. What you're looking at, for the black, is about one hundred thousand g/dl."

Dr. Gomez's numbers registered in Zane's mind, like scree sliding from the side of a rocky slope. He could hardly fathom such massive increases. "That's about twenty times higher than the normal spike in late summer and autumn."

Greg nodded. "Initially, I considered hyperaggression as an explanation, especially considering the magnitude of the destruction. Stress does increase testosterone production."

"But not likely?"

Greg shook his head. "Not at the levels we're observing. I double checked Eugene's findings in both necropsies. We found no tumors that might have increased the production of testosterone."

"That's far out," Zane said, gulping a mouthful of air. "What do we do now?"

Greg nudged Zane with his shoulder and maximized a second page. Another datasheet filled the screen, covered with decimal numbers and stubby equations. "It's the other results which startle me more, quite frankly."

Zane straightened. "What is it?"

"Toxicology tests reveal an odd chemical in the blood of both samples, enough to give me pause. You can see the analysis here. I conducted the tests twice to be certain."

Zane gazed at the spreadsheet, unsure what he observed.

"That's benzoylmethylecgonine," Greg said. "In layman's terms, cocaine."

Zane peered at Greg over his shoulder. "Cocaine?"

"Pure, unadulterated cocaine, Zane."

He shook his head, trying to organize his muddled thoughts. "How on earth did cocaine get into the bears' blood?"

"There's more still," Greg said. "Both bears show a trace amount of another alkaloid." He maximized and minimized pages. A line chart appeared on the screen. Inhaling, he straightened and allowed Zane to take in the charts. "It's an ingredient common in over-the-counter nasal decongestants. Levomethamphetamine."

"People use that to make crystal methamphetamine," Zane said.

"Yes, I know."

"Can the body produce cocaine and methamphetamine naturally?"

"There's a peptide which produces cocaine-like neurotransmitters in the brain," Greg said. "But not quite in the same compound as I found, and not in bears. To be honest, there's little research."

Zane stood straight, questioned Greg with wide eyes. "We've got a drug problem in the local bear population, is that what you're telling me? Bear junkies?"

"Maybe." Greg snorted a chuckle. "You think someone might be deliberately poisoning the bears in the area. Like Dr. Krum, maybe?"

"No." Zane thrust his shoulders forward. "I'm sure he wouldn't have done that. Not after how Josh raves about him. Not based on what I've read in his journals. And we didn't find a trace of any drugs at his cabin. The medical examiner didn't find any drugs in him either. Besides, what would explain the black bear's blood test? That attack occurred thirty miles northeast of Krum's cabin."

A shadow of apprehension eclipsed Greg's brown eyes. "I have tremendous respect for Dr. Krum's research too, Zane. That's why I telephoned you. These findings are extremely odd."

They studied each other's sharp expressions under the buzzing fluorescent lights. Zane trusted Greg's expertise, perhaps more than anyone else in the field, except for Dr. Sands's. Little reason to doubt his judgment.

"Might the bears have gotten into the drugs from somewhere else while foraging for food?" Zane said. "They do sometimes have a huge appetite for the unusual. Maybe they got into it by accident."

Bears often travelled long distances to feed off the protein-rich garbage in the Anchorage area, wandering across the Knik Arm, following the wooded valleys along the Glenn Highway. Anchorage still had a long way to becoming "bear proof" like the island of Kodiak, where bears, common as human residents, held title as the largest land-dwelling omnivores on the planet. Residents had fortified everything on the island with the mind to keep the giants out. Anchorage lagged behind adapting to local wildlife. And like any American city, Anchorage had more than its share of drug pushers.

"Any drug activity going on lately?" Greg asked. "More than usual?"

"I'm unaware of any new flood of illicit drugs into the area," Zane said. "I'll have to check with the Bureau of Investigations and some of the other agencies. Dr. Orowitz didn't find anything unusual in the digestive tracts, did he, other than human remains? Hypodermic needles, latex gloves, anything commonly found in drug dens?"

Greg shook his head. "Only clothing, oatmeal, grasses, berries, other high-sugar-content foods. Bears digest food awfully fast, Zane. What I found in the scat appeared no different than what Eugene found. Foodstuff from area trash, perhaps, but no drug paraphernalia."

"Geez, Greg, this could be major, far more than I imagined. Bears eating drugs? Nothing like this has ever happened before. Have you shared this information with anyone else?"

"Most in the department are aware of the findings. Eugene, Sylvia…. But they don't have any explanations or care to provide one. Everyone agrees we should refrain from going public until you guys decide what to do."

"What connection does all this have with the testosterone levels?" Zane asked. "You think wherever they're getting the cocaine and methamphetamine they're also getting steroids? Or can the cocaine and meth spur some kind of overproduction of testosterone?"

"If anything, it should do the opposite."

Zane pondered what Greg had told him. "The bear assaults occurred around Birchwood and Twin Peaks," he said, thinking aloud. "Something might be going on in those areas. I would guess they're involved in the illegal steroid trade too."

"That's my guess, Zane."

"Thanks for the information, Greg. I'll certainly look into this. If what you say is true, then we might have more bears—and more people— at risk. In the meantime, back to business and keep our fingers crossed, I guess."

Greg chuckled. "I grew so excited about the results I've missed my morning run."

"I suppose we all could use some stress relief after this."

Was it possible? Local bears snatching drugs from local meth labs?

Too strange, Zane thought as he headed back to headquarters.

LATER that afternoon, Zane hit the gym hard. He lifted heavier than he had since high school. Extra energy demanded release. Whenever he worked out, he'd imagine himself engaging in manual labor required for a subsistent lifestyle. Weighted walking lunges—hoisting heavy logs or carrying water from a distant stream. Cable rows—sculling a canoe on a bucolic river in search of fish. Dumbbell curls—dragging a caribou carcass along a hillside.

Sweat dribbled down the sides of his face, coated his forehead and chest and back. He did the smith machine until his glutes felt loaded with cement. Pressed the leg slide, shaking with dizziness after each set. Completed six sets of calf raises, using six forty-five-pound weights, that made him leap to his feet after each set and walk off the lactic burn.

Earlier in the day, he'd shared Greg's findings with a few of his fellow troopers, many of whom were at the gym with him. Langston had scoffed. "Ridiculous," he'd said. "Greg is always trying to agitate things around the university." The two troopers with the Bureau of Investigations had stared at him the same way they might a man sprouting wings. What could they say? Dana had shrugged. "Sounds weird."

The theory did sound ludicrous. But who could explain Greg's findings? The data hadn't lied. Testosterone, cocaine, and nasal decongestant in the bears' systems. What were the odds both showed the same results?

He hadn't expressed his concerns to Col. Lund. Dozens of other issues, new and ancient, already occupied his commander. He was still miffed at Zane for the failed Baxter brother stakeout. Since the AST evaded official investigations into bear attacks regardless, Lund would've reacted with resentment. "I got no time to deal with rogue bears," he'd say. "Let DNR or Fish and Game worry over it."

Zane had put in a request for reports of recent drug raids and any active meth labs in the area. None of his colleagues from the Bureau of Investigations had recalled any offhand. The narcotics sweeps from last summer had, at least temporarily, slowed down the proliferation of new meth labs and street cocaine.

But again, perhaps their effectiveness forced the pushers to hide farther out, into the bush, closer to bear habitats, away from the state's ever watchful eyes. Maybe that's where the bears were getting into the drugs?

Dealers might've established labs nestled in the Chugach Range close to Anchorage and the Mat-Su Valley, near the site of the attacks. Or maybe locals living in isolated cabins who cooked meth in their kitchens, too strung out to have realized they'd discarded valuable ingredients in their composts, had inadvertently allowed bears to rummage their waste.

He worried about Josh. Was he safe out in the bush, in the heart of what might be a nascent drug haven? Safe from the unwary drug-crazed bears and meth runners living in ramshackle cabins? Had the Alaskan bush evolved into a swath of drug dens?

He'd promised Greg to keep awareness of the bears' blood test within a tight circle. Joshua was already in too deep. He certainly did not wish to insinuate that Uncle Ted had abused or peddled narcotics.

Musings of Josh had filled Zane's head since their backpacking trip to Magpie Peak during the weekend. That night in the tent by the lake with Josh, cocooned in Josh's sleeping bag, rolling around like wolves, had been spectacular. Did it matter what Dana and Langston might hear? Perhaps they had been too busy making their own noise to notice.

Zane had spotted Dana crawling out of Langston's tent the follow morning before the mist had a chance to lift off the lake. So they had some fun that night too. Zane never considered the two might hook up the same way he had with Dana—and Langston. Jealousy had nibbled inside Zane's stomach. But for whom? And why?

Everyone had their private lives, he'd judged. How much of their secrets had entwined in each other's worlds more than anyone would admit? He and Joshua had made love perhaps the same time Langston and Dana had. The idea made him snicker. He dropped the barbell on the rack after fifteen reps of triceps presses and shook his head.

Peering across the gym floor, he spied Langston doing dumbbell curls with what appeared a hefty ninety pounds in each hand. Must still be on the juice, Zane speculated. He wondered who Zane had used to inject him with steroids since he and Zane had stopped working out together. Unless he'd overcome his fear of needles, Langston needed someone to shoot him up. Perhaps another trooper. Zane had seen him working out with Allan Colton a few times, another investigator with the AWT, a buff man in his late forties, married, with four daughters.

Did Allan ever scratch Langston's steroid-induced itch?

Best to shake off the strange sensation, pump more iron, forget about the drama that swirled around workplaces. He laid his head back on the bench, inhaled, blew out a heavy breath into his next lift. Ten repetitions later, he rested, breathing heavily.

Should he visit Joshua at the cabin after his workout? If only Joshua had cell reception. Nothing to worry about. Surely the whole idea of meth labs and drug-crazed bears derived from mere fancy.

He grunted, pushed into the barbell, imagined lifting a hefty spruce log outside his rustic cabin in the bush.

CHAPTER 16

HE STOMPED down the trail. No matter how hard he shook his head, trying to make it leave, the fury intensified. Steam from his breath covered his body like a smoldering forest fire. He chomped at the grasses growing alongside the foothill, ripped them from their roots. Scrub and alders pinched at his nose and one good eye like fanged mosquitoes. He hunkered behind the scrub, inhaling oxygen for all its worth. But his throbbing legs permitted him to stand still for only a short time. He must keep moving. Every muscle burned and cried out for release.

His one good eye took in every rustle of the alders, every flutter of a bird. He swept his head from side to side, missing not a stir, relying on his acute sense of smell. Animals in those colorful, sleek skins he'd become accustomed to seeing—and smelling—ambled nearby. A few. But enough to bother him. Did they detect him? Most likely not. He always marveled how close they allowed him to approach without them ever noticing his presence.

Guttural growls emerged from deep inside his belly. Keep quiet, keep quiet, his instincts warned him. He crouched lower, ensuring his shoulder blades remained below the grasses. The creatures would assume the movement as wind sweeping the brush.

His entire life they'd snarled at him, brandishing their bright teeth behind shiny colored armor that clinked and wrinkled with movement. A long time ago, one had caused him great pain. Yet he found little reason to fear them. He sensed their helplessness against him. But this time, hatred for them clawed inside his body, reaching toward his brain and grabbing hold like an eagle with its prey. Especially for the one whose scent had been seared into his brain.

He wanted the man he followed to stop stomping on the path. Every move enraged him. The ground swayed and swiveled, a sensation similar to falling from a tree. He remembered that happening to him once during his sixth summer. He'd climbed a tree for a bird's nest and had slipped from a branch, months before the hunter had taken out his eye. He'd heard bones shatter near his shoulder area. He'd lain there for days, waiting to die. But he'd survived. All on his own. His young adult bones had healed. Until he'd run into that dastardly bow hunter.

Piercing hot blades of grass singed his skin. His teeth ached like muscles exploding with a driving force. Hatred for that cruel world, mined with deathtraps, pushed him into a lower crouch. His ears filled with white hot blood, enough to crest a small creek. He kept his head in a sweeping motion, his one eye focused on the feet of the two-legged animal pounding the earth in front of him. The one with the familiar stink.

He opened his mouth and flexed his snout. A distraction. More human creatures. They grunted and squealed from the distance, away from the foothills. Only a few lingered closer to him. One of their species lurked even nearer. The man creature again. Running along the path, stomping on the hard ground like a herd of caribou. An ear-splitting, gut-wrenching pounding.

With his head low to the ground, he followed the man, using wide steps. He loped to the side and leaped into the high brush when the man glanced behind him. Had he heard, smelled him coming?

The runner's body language indicated he'd only momentarily startled him. The man faced ahead, his breathing heavy with each swing of his two legs and two arms. He was trying to get away, yet retained a steady rhythm. Would others view him? Did it matter?

He shot out of the bush like an arrow.

Grunting and heaving, he grabbed the runner by his calf, flung him to the ground. Instantly the head cracked open. Blood pooled on the ground. The man bellowed, screamed out. The smell of fear and confusion scratched at his brain as his teeth sunk into flesh.

Let him squirm. The more fight he gave, the more he wanted to rip him into shards to blend with the twigs and duff. He flipped the runner facing the sky. Snapped his neck. Instant death. No doubt. Instinct instructed him how to kill with precision. He'd needed no lifetime of experience to aid him.

He tore into him, shook him like a ground squirrel. Limbs swatted his sides, enraging him even more. Two of his teeth had broken when he'd bit into bone. Several more cracked. But he harnessed enough bite to tear and rip whatever he set his mind to.

He flung the corpse onto the ground, stepped on it. Blood coated his teeth, dribbled down his snout, burned his one eye. He dragged the corpse into the brush. Part of his victim's foot remained by the trail.

He paused, glanced around. More of the species squealing. They were stomping his way. They'd noticed the man's pleading. But too late. He bit into his scalp, tore flesh from bone. Fangs dug into eye sockets, locked onto nostrils. He yanked his head upward, pulled with all his massive strength, a power even he'd failed to realize he possessed until that moment.

"Someone was screaming for help over there!"

People rushed toward him. He smelled them coming with jolting fear. Spread wide, he protected his kill. A scream. A bone-chattering shriek. They wanted to snatch his cache.

"There! Lying in the brush. Someone help him!"

"O Gott, O Gott! Entsetzlich zu miterleben!"

Raising his head, he realized there were too many of them to face off. They came fast. Like a crazed herd of caribous rushing across the tundra from a swarm of black flies. With one last bite into the man's upper back, he bolted for the safety of the trees.

SUNDAY evening, hundreds of concerned citizens packed the University of Anchorage's Taggart Hall, and many more pushed against the entrance outside. Inside, cameras and lights were aimed at the podium, where five men and two women of grave appearance sat on metal chairs behind one of those long folding tables typically used for receptions.

Zane watched from the back in plainclothes, arms locked across his chest. He too took an interest in the affairs, like any concerned citizen. His mind still whirled from the news of the latest bear mauling. As vicious as the first two. Only this time, the crazed bear had attacked someone he knew. A good friend and collaborator.

Zane's heart had stopped when Dana's quivering voice on the other end of his cell phone pierced his ear early Wednesday morning. He sat firm against his headboard, trying to understand her blubbering. "What's wrong, Dana?" he said, almost afraid of her response.

"Bono…. Bono…."

"Dana, take a deep breath and tell me."

"There's… there's been another… another fatal bear attack. A black bear… in Bicentennial Park."

Zane's mouth dropped open. The phone trembled in his hand.

Dana began wailing without restraint. Zane had never heard her in such hysterics, not even when he'd comforted her the day after her father's unexpected fatal heart attack.

"Bono, this time… this time it's Greg. Greg Gomez, Bono," she said. "A bear mauled Greg Gomez. Like the others. Greg Gomez is dead."

Her crying escalated and Zane went mute. Hot thrumming deadened his hearing. He held the phone, an object reeking with disgust, away from his face. None of it was real. How could a man he'd spoken with face to face a mere two days ago be dead? He inhaled, concentrating on his professional deportment. Slowly, he brought the phone to his mouth.

"Does Col. Lund know?"

"He's with Karen here at headquarters. Poor Greg. Oh, Bono. All hell will break loose once the media finds out there's been another fatal attack."

"Anyone at the scene?"

"Langston and some others are there now."

He reassured her again, using his softest voice, and clicked off the phone. He stared into a vacuum of nothingness. It couldn't be happening. It couldn't. Not again. Not Greg Gomez this time.

But it was happening. The nightmarish past five days had confirmed the brutal reality.

Dana's prediction about a media frenzy had proved true. A hound after a fox exerted less energy. He refused to read the *Daily News*, which contained headlines and sidebars about the bear attacks each edition since Greg's mauling death. After fifteen-hour days, Zane crashed in bed with the memory of phones buzzing in his ears. He dreamed of voices screaming of retaliatory bear kills and brash reporters fishing for scoops.

The media withheld details of the victims' partially eaten corpses at the state's request. How long would the media hold out? Enough eyewitnesses had seen the brutalized body of Greg Gomez. Gossip spread. Like with the attacks of Drs. Bloomington and Rakesh, disparate views had erupted. Half those on the scene had said without doubt the untagged bear protected its kill after eating part of it. The others had stated it had run off into the forest immediately after the attack without consuming the victim. Six witnesses, two differing viewpoints.

What else was new?

"He was jogging, Bono," Langston had said when Zane arrived on the scene after Dana's call. "Even bumpkins understand jogging can spur a chase response."

"Good God, Banks. Did you see him or not? The bear tore his face off. His pancreas, liver, all gone."

Langston turned away, cringed. The medical examiner, standing next to them, shuffled toward his sedan, head heavy, after he'd ordered the body packed in the polyethylene bag.

People nearby frightened the bear off before the bear could ravish the rest of the body. Officials found running shorts and a T-shirt worn by Greg, torn to ribbons and lying in the brush. Only Greg's one sock remained on his severed foot.

When officials arrived on the scene, the bear, still hovering near its kill on the higher elevations of a nearby foothill, was grunting and chomping its teeth. Municipal police flushed it from the woods and used lethal removal. Taking it down required six slugs to the chest cavity and head.

The German taxi driver, resting in his cab in the nearby parking lot at the time of the attack and one of the first on the scene, told Zane the bear had acted "verruck"—insane. Once Zane learned the details, conversing with the cabby in broken German, he sent him home with one of his business cards.

Another witness, a bird-watcher with the local Audubon society, fainted after she retold Zane and Langston how she'd found the condition of Greg's body. The ambulance that had responded to the 911 dispatch raced her to the hospital. Greg, beyond medical help, was left for the medical examiner.

Dr. Sylvia Linden had tested the third bear's blood. Cocaine, methamphetamine, and testosterone were present. Identical results as the first two bears. Something seriously wrong pumped through the bloodstreams of those bears. State law enforcement and the researchers agreed to remain tight-lipped about the discovery. Officials wanted to flush out the offending drug dealers from the bush without the media disclosing police strategy.

Thursday and Friday, a massive aerial patrol searched for drug hideaways. Two Robinson choppers—one from Anchorage, the other from Palmer—crisscrossed the entire Mat-Su Valley and Anchorage regions, an area the size of Massachusetts, only to return to their home bases with no news. Backcountry rangers in Chugach State Park and the National Forest reported zilch also. Cabins near Eagle River and Birchwood, already loaded with daring summer tourists, appeared tame.

The bear had terrorized Greg while jogging in Bicentennial Park, a popular four-season, four-thousand acre municipal playground (five times larger than New York City's Central Park), treasured by Anchorage residents. Now that a death had occurred closer to home, ten miles from downtown, the citizens lost patience. Not the first time a bear had assailed anyone in Bicentennial Park, but the first fatal mauling. Like during the summer of 2008, Anchorage area residents demanded action. And they wanted it fast.

Zane gazed around the packed hall. Reporters around him jabbered in a slew of languages: Japanese, Chinese, German, Russian. The entire world's eyes focused on south central Alaska. Were crazy bears dismembering hikers and joggers out of spite?

The two bear experts from Colorado and British Columbia, Drs. Birkeland and Cummings, flown in to investigate and offer their theories, insisted the bears had acted without malice. Zane had spoken to each briefly at headquarters Friday morning. He did not care for either man. They displayed a pompous air, sneering with every sentence uttered, contemptuous of the uproar. Silly humans getting upset over nothing, both had said.

Marauding bears hadn't ripped to shreds their good friend or family member.

Greg's father and eldest sister had flown in from Texas to mourn their loss and return his body to San Antonio. Zane empathized—how horrible for his family to identify his remains, which included not even a face to gaze down upon. Greg, too dedicated to his work, had never married. Good thing no wife would suffer through the anguish.

Neither Greg's sister nor father attended the meeting at Taggart Hall. A tight-knit family, they only wanted to take what remained of Greg and return to Texas. They'd departed on the midnight flight to San Antonio last night. Zane had spoken briefly with Greg's father, a short-statured, proud-looking man with grief oozing from his black eyes like oil, before they'd left for the airport. Zane had told him over and over how dependable and talented Greg was. Mr. Gomez had merely nodded, his dark eyes moist.

Zane clung to his belief the bears had attacked randomly—as farfetched as the idea seemed—but even he demanded answers. The public's worries rose beyond his own grief for Greg. Out of habit he kept glancing around for him as part of the symposium. He would not participate this time, nor would he ever again.

Karen Flecks, ready to represent the AST's position, sat squeezed between Dr. Sands and a representative from the Department of Natural Resources, Rylan Zelenje. Officially, the AST backed off investigating bear attacks. Not after this third time. The public and the state had given them little choice. The gravity of the situation had escalated beyond the university's research team or the two biologists with Fish and Game. Juneau insisted law enforcement do something. Four state representatives flew in for the meeting, planted in the front row of the lecture seats in dark suits. The fatal attacks, coming at the start of the tourist season, had become political.

Joshua also attended. He sat in the fourth to the last row, had smiled with tight lips at Zane when he'd spied him squeeze inside the hall. Zane had promised Joshua much less than he had Mr. Gomez.

Dr. Sylvia Linden tapped the closest of the three microphones on the table and cleared her throat. The buzzing crowd quieted, a ripple of murmurs absorbed by the beige slab walls. Cameras snapping and shutters grinding eased into background noise. Zane shielded his eyes from the blinding flash of bulbs and tried to concentrate on the doctor's comments.

"We're going to try to provide you with answers and elucidate our findings in a moment," Dr. Linden began, leaning into the microphone. "After that, we'll have open mic. I know everyone is anxious, so let's please do this orderly. We'll have time to address everyone's concerns once the panel speaks."

People stirred, huffed. Muffled chatter rose to the tiled ceiling. Dr. Linden gestured for Karen Flecks. She leaned into a microphone with her stunning beauty and asserted how the Alaska State Troopers, "in coordination with research efforts," sought to understand and safeguard both the public and the bear population, "using every available resource."

One man sitting in the center of the hall shouted, "You care more for the bears than us," but the crowd hushed him. Zane's blood chilled, the hairs on his nape stood erect. He sensed a raucous crowd. The speakers would have to choose their words with care.

Dr. Orowitz spoke next. He took a deep breath and began by explaining the nature of the bears' overall health. No worries for disease. He highlighted the nature of the bears' physical conditions in relation to behavior patterns, indicating that the bears had acted alone, unrelated to each other. The Department of Natural Resources' Rylan Zelenje provided his worth. He delineated why bears attack, how few bear attacks have actually occurred, and how to bear proof garbage.

The two bear experts from Colorado and British Columbia, Drs. Birkeland and Cummings, took turns mirroring each other's viewpoints, affirming their opinions, and attributing a "seemingly bizarre situation" to chance. Their expertise, haughtiness, and command of the crowd intrigued Zane. Each had spent half his lifetime speaking before such concerned citizens about his beloved bears. Their steadfast manners proved effective in quelling dissent. They would make excellent expert witnesses for a defense, Zane thought.

Dr. Sands turned his head toward a microphone, cleared his throat to gain attention. He corroborated the two biologists' theories, and insisted the physiology and evolution of bears made it impossible for them to attack without provocation.

"Dr. Krum might have been feeding or intimidating the bears," he said. "He lived alone in a cabin submerged in their natural habitat, on the watershed, their prime foraging and feeding grounds. Harold Bloomington and Vee Rakesh trekked in generational bear grazing territory holding a basket full of wild berries when the black bear encountered them. Dr. Gomez had been jogging in the park, close to the forested foothills, where bears often rest in seclusion. Running signals a bear to chase. How often have we witnessed such events in Alaska, right here in Anchorage, in Bicentennial Park?"

Some people in the crowd moaned, yet a sizeable number nodded in agreement. The worst reaction came from Joshua. When Dr. Sands had indicated Uncle Ted might have harassed the bears into an attack, Joshua had noticeably cringed, sat stiff, almost raised a hand to speak out. Zane noted the red blotches that had emerged over his nape. Dr. Sands's words had struck him like a baseball bat.

"Bears do not seek to destroy for sport," Dr. Sands continued. "They cannot behave like serial killers. Never could. Only man is capable of such behavior. The occurrences of the past few weeks can be deduced as bad luck, a result of people taking calculated risks, as they do each day in the wilds of Alaska."

"The wilds?" a middle-aged woman exclaimed, jumping to her feet. "But they're happening in our own backyard, right in Bicentennial Park, across the street from here."

"Let the man speak," a woman shouted.

"Stop interrupting," another exploded.

Dr. Linden begged the crowd for patience and order.

Dr. Sands dismissed the woman's outburst with a grin and shake of his head. Once the crowd settled, he said, "Anchorage lies in the heart of some of the wildest land on the planet. Even a municipal park like Far North Bicentennial, if it lay in the Lower Forty-eight, would boast national park status. You cannot live in a place like Alaska—whether in urban centers or the bush—and not expect to run into bears, especially when taking such risky behavior as jogging, berry picking, and feeding and baiting wildlife."

The crowd's murmurings escalated. Dr. Linden consulted with her podium mates. She announced people could approach the stage for open mic. A rush of individuals filed in line. Zane counted at least sixty. Dr. Linden insisted each person pose one brief question.

"What's the best way to educate the public about bear awareness?" a red-haired college-aged woman asked.

"Symposiums such as these," Dr. Cummings said. "Public service announcements on television or radio. In British Columbia, we post prominent signs and billboards throughout areas with high concentrations of bears to keep people aware of the dangers when entering into the bears' home."

"No one has addressed the nature of the attacks," an elderly man next asked. "Why such brutality?"

The speakers exchanged gapes, assessing who should answer. Their eyes fell on Dr. Sands.

"As I stated previously," he said with a tight grin, "a bear responds in proportion to how he perceives a threat. Proximity can trigger how aggressive, or if he bothers to respond at all. In most cases, a bear will turn and leave before you will even detect his presence. Perhaps the best safety tip I could give, on the rare chance you will find yourself face to face with a bear, is to keep as far a distance between you and him as possible."

"Is it true the bears have eaten their victims?" the man asked.

His question angered the crowd. "One question only," several waiting in line behind him shouted.

Dr. Linden hushed the crowd, and the next person approached the microphone while Dr. Sands answered the man's question.

"Bears, especially black bears, do not look to humans as dinner. Their diet consists overwhelmingly of vegetable sources. Black bears in particular consume ninety-five percent of their calories through roots, nuts, and grasses." He chuckled. "Their major meat source derives from insects."

"Can you guarantee our children are safe playing in our backyards?" the next questioner said, wringing her hands. "Do we have to watch them like hawks to make sure no bear will kill them?"

Dr. Birkeland from Colorado responded in his heavy Norwegian accent. "No bear wishes to harm your children. Bears do not seek the company of humans. Bears fear people more than you fear them. You have succeeded in killing each of the offending bears. You should be happy, ya? Humans will always come out the victor, as it goes."

Another woman stepped forward. "Why did the bear break into the trapper's cabin?"

"She was seeking the food source," Dr. Sands said. "A bear's intelligence supersedes most other mammals. The bear you refer to acted on a conditioned response. She had learned where the trapper stored his food."

The man following took his turn at the mic. "Some of the newspaper accounts say the bears were defending their turf. Where exactly is their turf?"

Dr. Sands made a sweeping gesture with his right hand. "This is their turf. All this lies in bear territory. This university sits in the heart of bear territory. Downtown Anchorage is in the middle of bear territory. Sometimes we pay the price for intruding into their world with our lives."

Karen Flecks, harboring a profound understanding for damage control, quickly leaned toward the microphone closest to her. "One of our own has been killed," she said. "A renowned researcher the AST has worked with for many years, Dr. Greg Gomez. He worked for this very university. We all mourn his loss, and the loss of the other victims. But you must be aware that a rational understanding of bear behavior, explained by our expert panel, and common sense are the best solutions. The AST, along with other agencies and the university, will continue to examine the situation surrounding the attacks, and use what we learn to educate the public to prevent future fatal encounters with bears. Understanding and education safeguards your children and yourselves."

"Hundreds of people jog in Bicentennial Park each day. Are you telling us we have to lock ourselves in our homes the entire summer?" the next questioner said.

"That's not what I was implying," Karen stated.

Another woman nudged the questioner aside, grimaced at the podium. "What is the state and city doing to investigate the shootings of the bears? I see no reason why the bears should have been shot just for being bears. Especially since we're on their turf."

Many shouted their agreement. Others hissed and booed. Cameras clicked and snapped. Standing this time, Dr. Linden lifted the microphone.

"Please, please," she said. "Order. Let's have some order. Many more people wish to ask questions."

"We will take strong actions against anyone retaliating against the bears," Rylan Zelenje said in response to the woman's query once the crowd eased. "The state of Alaska has laws protecting wildlife, and we will uphold those laws to the fullest. We at the Department of Natural Resources and the other state agencies have the situation under control, and there is no need for citizens to raise arms against the bears. In regards to the killings of the three bears, we have concluded those involved acted in appropriate self-defense within their rights."

"The bears have rights too," someone shouted.

"Animals can't have rights," another retorted.

"Let's keep order," Dr. Linden pleaded. "Or we'll end the symposium."

Dozens more people posed questions, many repeating what others had already asked. An hour after the first person had posed her question, Joshua reached the microphone. Zane, beginning to tire in the back, stood firm and clenched his fists by his sides, eager to hear what he had to say.

"Dr. Sands, you mentioned the reason for the grizzly attack on Dr. Krum was to get food inside his cabin, yet the bear hadn't eaten any of the food. Can you explain that?"

Straight for the jugular. Zane swallowed a chuckle. He hardly blamed Josh for his forthright approach. Of course only a few others knew about the food being left untouched by the grizzly. Joshua had stewed for more than three weeks over his uncle's death, and all the experts had told him—from the AST to the present panel—was Dr. Krum had the gruesome death coming.

A hush covered the crowd like a heavy woolen blanket. Wide eyes peered at the sturdy man standing by the microphone. They sensed someone of high intelligence and rationality before them, representing the finer qualities of their community status. A citizen emissary. Several coughs masked a heightened, perhaps uncomfortable, consciousness.

Zane, unsure if Dr. Sands recognized Joshua from the two times he and Zane had visited his bear sanctuary, observed the doctor shifting his eyes about the expansive hall. His grizzled hair seemed to brighten, as if blood had rushed to the tips.

"No evidence suggests bears can act indiscriminately vicious," he said with a wobbly voice. "You must understand, bears respond to humans only to the same degree that humans provoke them. By virtue of stepping into their territory, we can instigate an aggressive response. Should we fault bears for behaving like bears?"

"You once told me that fatal bear attacks, the likes of what we've seen recently, occur one in a million," Joshua continued without protest from the silent crowd, "yet it's happened four times in two weeks."

Dr. Sands's eyebrows fused. His lips puckered. Even from the back, Zane detected his discomfort—and anger.

"The nature of coincidence dictates that an event can happen at any time," Dr. Sands finally said. "There's no gauging random actions. That's why we call them random. Ad infinitum. Anything might happen repeatedly at some point, but natural law does not order when those events must fall within the continuum."

Zanc watched Josh walk back to his seat, his chin raised high. Dr. Sands had not defeated him. Thus far, he'd posed the sole question coming close to stumping the panel. Yet Zane failed to figure out the riddle himself.

Cumbersome worries exploded around his head along with the flash of cameras. The similarities of the attacks. Mere coincidences? The necropsy had revealed the black bear that had killed Greg was in near perfect condition, despite its advanced age at twenty-two or twenty-three. Other than broken teeth from the mauling, nothing plagued the bear. Ancient scar tissue indicated the eye injury had occurred years before. No other details that would make a bear stand out, would make it attack and kill.

Except maybe if it were under the influence of illicit drugs?

Zane agreed that bears were incapable of revenge. He understood much of what the experts on the podium had said. Still, the nature of the attacks jabbed him like a hunter gutting a kill. Were more bears roaming the wilderness around Anchorage, consuming cocaine or other drugs from garbage bins, primed to attack someone new?

CHAPTER 17

WORRIES swirled inside his mind like the wind off the Chugach Range. Tidbits of understanding, swept away by a gale of fear. A bore tide, rushing up Turnagain Arm, filling canyons twenty feet deep in mere minutes. Soon enough, leaving the same flat, empty bed for miles. Greedy, ruthless quicksand wider than three football fields. Life ebbed and flowed the same.

Where would his muddy musings carry him this time? He must follow his thoughts carefully, tread gingerly. A consideration, like a drop of water into a pond, leaving ripples of nothingness. Expansive, like the white stucco ceiling of his mobile home.

He lay in bed, fingers woven atop his naked belly, eyes fixed on the ceiling. Bright sunlight streamed through the tears in the tinfoil covering the windows. He glanced at his alarm clock—9:33 at night. Outside, the wind howled like a bassoon in the black spruce that surrounded the mobile home park. His mind's wanderings always terminated the same.

He closed his eyes, pictured himself lying in his former cabin north of Denali, relaxing after a long day's toil. Life in the bush had eluded him. He'd failed to harness his dream. Aborted his efforts less than a year after moving from Rhode Island. What other avenue had he? Julie had needed to reach Anchorage. The aftermath of her accident had left scant doubt. Julie could not return to the bush. Their marriage had tapped out by then, anyway. Zane and the bush proved less a match than he and Julie.

Wouldn't he rather lie exhausted after chopping wood or fishing than from handling frustrated mobs and lawless rednecks?

He'd always salved his ego by recalling what his father had once told him. "At least you followed your dream," he'd hear him say in his broken English, like a ghost whispering in his ear. "At least you gave a try."

Is that the only ingredient that comprised a man? Tenacity? Hadn't Greg Gomez embodied the same spirit when he'd journeyed from Texas to Alaska to study bears at a world-renowned research institution? His life had ended clenched in the jaws of one of his subjects. What had either Greg or Uncle Ted or Zane to show for their efforts but grief?

The horror of the past few weeks enervated him. He tried to focus on the investigative aspects to strengthen his spirits. How much, if anything, did the illicit drugs in the bears' systems have to do with the attacks? Had someone intentionally poisoned them? A sociopath out for kicks?

"You know why I moved out here?" the hermit Grason Boyd had said to Zane just before stepping into the helicopter, after Zane and Jasper had spotted the naked woman running for her life the day they'd trailed the Baxter brothers. "I was wee close to becoming a killer."

Had his hands been free of the cuffs, he'd probably have made a pinch gesture with his thumb and index finger. A symbol for a life reduced to pure survival. Panicky lambs running from the fangs of wolves. Who could tell one from the other?

Samples of the bears' blood had already been sent to two labs for second opinions. One to Boston, the other to Seattle. Zane had insisted in the face of the university's objections. They waited for either confirmation or denial of the university's initial findings. Dr. Linden and the other researchers had already scoffed at Greg's results—and their own. Natural neurotransmitters often masquerade as cocaine-like substances, they'd said. And the high testosterone levels? False-positives. But Greg had used the HPLC-MS, a state-of-the-art foolproof apparatus permitting near zero false-positives. No one had budged from his or her position. Wait for the findings from Massachusetts and Washington.

Good enough, Zane affirmed. At least their stanch theories might postpone public hysteria.

But again, Greg had expressed alarm at the blood tests. He'd spoken in secret. Zane hadn't taken Greg for one with a taste for hyperbole.

Drug-crazed bears?

No new drug raids. No abnormally high proliferation of meth labs. Even the impoverished native villages tinkered in their typical way, quiet and uneventful. Alcohol, the preferred means for escaping a dissatisfied life.

Perhaps the attacks were merely nasty coincidences and the tests nothing alarming, like the bear panel had insisted. Perhaps his mind churned for no reason.

A hand reached out to him. Soft, yet firm and strong, resting upon his chest. He turned his head and smiled at Joshua, who'd climbed into bed next to him. Zane had been waiting for him to step out of the bathroom. He gazed at him, mesmerized for a moment by his sparkling blue eyes and firm jaw line. His time with Joshua, more than a means to pass a dull evening, grew precious to him.

"Feels good to get a hot shower," Joshua said, his freshly shaved face beaming with warmth.

"Hard to live without modern comforts."

Josh eyed Zane. "You okay?"

"I'm good." He reciprocated Josh's touch. The back of his hand rubbed against the smoothness of his cheek. "You confuse me, though."

"How so?"

"With you I don't know who I am."

"You're a man. One of the last of a dying breed."

"I'm unsure about that." Zane sighed. "If I was any kind of a man, I'd still be living out in the bush, with a wife and children."

"You reflect about life in the bush a lot, don't you?"

Too often, Zane realized as wind rattled the windowpane. He inhaled. "It's no big deal. Stuff happens, that's all."

But Joshua read the truth behind Zane's cryptic words. "What happened out there, Zanebono?" he said. "Tell me. What haunts you about your time in the bush?"

Zane turned from Josh, rolled to his side. "I'd rather not talk about it."

"Did something horrible happen? Like with the bear attacks? Why won't you tell me?"

"Maybe some other time," Zane said toward the opposite wall. "It's a long story. I'm beat. Some meeting tonight, huh?" He wanted to shift the subject. "You sure did wallop Dr. Sands."

"I needed some reasonable answers."

"I was surprised how many in attendance defended the bears."

Joshua hunkered down closer to Zane. "Wildlife junkies talk about how humans encroach on animal territory, but they never question their own encroachment. Back home when I was a kid, I'd go on overnight hiking trips with church groups, and we'd run across hunters and Boy Scouts, like us. Now when I hike the trails, besides other hikers, all I see are state-funded wildlife conservationists with their dart guns and clipboards. The arrogance staggers me. Same kind of thing Uncle Teddy despised. He used to criticize the selfish hypocrisy relentlessly. That's part of what got him kicked out of the university. They refused him tenure because of his stance."

Zane flushed. In a way, Josh had described him. Zane's government job stipulated he safeguard wildlife, including bears. And he held no conflict with his duties. Yet he understood Joshua's complaints. Arrogance reared itself more often than not in Zane's circles. Protecting wildlife for some had metamorphosed into a form of ministering.

Zoolatry, he sometimes referred to it, always making sure to refrain from uttering the term aloud whenever around colleagues. Except sometimes Dana.

"I remember what you said when we went camping at Crystal Lake," he said. "About people worshiping animals the way we used to thousands of years ago."

"That's the kind of thing my uncle fought against," Joshua said. "He used to say it flew in the face of science. In the end, his struggles were shot down. One man against a torrent."

Zane pulled Joshua closer, held him firm to his bare chest. Good to feel body heat emanating from someone he admired and had become drawn to. Did he love him?

What constituted love, anyway? He'd met Joshua a little over two weeks ago, and in that short elapse of time, he'd come to recognize that Josh demanded something from him. But what? Was it what he'd asked from Julie and Dana?

The only essentiality for the moment—Joshua's clinging to him.

"I'm glad I came to Alaska," he said into Zanebono's chest. His breath tickled the dark coarse hairs. "I only wish it had been under different circumstances."

"Weird how fate works," Zane whispered.

"Do you believe in fate?"

"I believe in going wherever life takes you without resisting. To follow the open path."

"Do you like where you're going?"

Zane stroked Joshua's wavy hair. "Do I have a choice?"

They remained silent, Zane caressing Josh's hair, Josh twirling Zane's chest hairs around his index finger.

Joshua, his voice sober, said, "Before the town meeting today I went to see Dr. Bloomington's and Dr. Rakesh's relatives."

Zane pressed his chin to his sternum and grimaced at the top of Joshua's head. "You're full of bombshells, aren't you?"

"Sounds crazy. But I had to talk to them. One loved one to another. They talked about them like they were the staples of their lives. Dr. Bloomington grew up in Wasilla. Knew bears like the periodic table, his brother told me. They reminisced how Dr. Bloomington and his wife, Vee, would pick berries in the summer each Sunday evening and watch the sun set over the mountains at midnight. They said they never once had any trouble with wildlife. They actually had more trouble with humans. About a month ago someone had broken into their car while parked at the Twin Peaks trailhead, stole some jackets and an old duffel bag. Probably one of those itinerants who wander the backwoods. Dr. Rakesh would use the berries to make chutney pies. They'd usually get home late, they said, past midnight. Only this time, they never made it back."

"Did you rile them with ideas?"

"Don't worry. I didn't tell them about the bears eating the victims. Dr. Bloomington's brother identified the bodies, but he never mentioned anything grotesque. Maybe he wanted to spare the rest of his family the details. They were in academia, wildlife biologists, like Uncle Ted." Josh lifted his eyes to Zane, eyebrows arched high over his forehead. "And like Dr. Gomez."

Zane gaped at Josh.

Joshua rested his head back over Zane's unsteady heartbeat. "The people mauled by the bears were in the exact same field," Joshua continued. "All three bear experts, all retired, except for Greg. What're the odds, huh?"

Not until that moment had he realized Greg, too, fit the exact profile of the other three victims. A lot of coincidences, that's for sure. Too many. Zane wanted to mention the information Greg had discovered about the odd chemicals found in the bears' bloodstreams. Zane saw now that he must keep his mouth shut. Joshua might let slip what he'd learned. And since he was taking it upon himself to meet with the families of the victims, best Zane told him as little as possible. Plus, he did not want Josh to fear his uncle might've been involved in illicit drugs.

"I'm sure it's no big deal," Zane said, his voice low.

"It's probably nothing," Josh agreed. "Not like bears would seek revenge against bear biologists, would they?"

"Of course they wouldn't," Zane said. "Not for any reason. Bears are smart, but not that smart." Did his voice sound as uncertain to Joshua's ears as his own?

Joshua inched his fingers down Zane's abdomen and grabbed onto him. A symbol of his manhood, in the clutches of another man, in many ways stronger and more potent than Zane. His masculinity portended the allure. Joshua had willingly submitted to him, more than once. The ultimate surrender. The preeminent seizing of power. The wolf devouring the burly lamb.

Zane rolled on top of him, let his weight fully engulf his body. Their lips sealed onto each other's. Joshua resisted enough to entice Zane further. He clutched his hands, squeezed them against the headboard, stopped momentarily to gaze into Josh's eyes.

Why did Zane feel they were soldiers on their last day of leave before returning to battle?

CHAPTER 18

DANGER!

1 jogger fatally mauled by black bear Wed. 6:00 a.m., 6/8/11. Bear euthanized. High concentration of bear activity may exist near foothills.

PROCEED AT OWN RISK!

AK Dept. Fish & Game

BEAR activity. So that's how Fish and Game had described it, Zane brooded, gazing at the handwritten sign posted along the trail where a black bear had mauled Greg to death almost a week prior. Zane recognized Jasper Bohler's choppy script. Like he hadn't wanted to write it. The same warning Fish and Game had tacked to the kiosk display at the Twin Peaks trailhead after the deaths of Drs. Bloomington and Rakesh. Someone had placed a bouquet of flowers by the sign. But for whom? Greg or the bear?

He glanced around, kicked at the damp duff, shuffled along the muddy trail about one hundred yards. No joggers or hikers. No bears. Quiet and stillness masked the horror that had unfolded a handful of days before.

Little remained of the ambush, except the brush still lay flat where the three-hundred-seventy-five pounder had pinned Greg's body. Rain from the past two days had washed the blood away, seeped into the earth. Scavenging rodents absconded with whatever tiny particles of Greg investigators had left behind.

Gone faster than the wind. Like Uncle Ted's ashes. Nothing but an illusion.

Cheery chirping from the white-crowned sparrows and tree swallows lightened his heart. But only for a moment. High atop their perches in the birch trees, they'd been the only true witnesses to the horror that had befallen Greg Gomez. Could birds shriek in terror like humans? Or had they gazed over the landscape with indifference, as they appeared to now?

A porcupine waddled ahead of him, oblivious to Zane, the way they were apt to behave in front of larger mammals. They had little to fear. Coated in thousands of spiny quills, porcupines scoffed at potential predators.

What did man have for self-defense? A massive brain, corroding from the daily barrage of a modern world Zane understood less and less each day.

Even Greg, one of the most intelligent men Zane had encountered, possessed scarce defenses against a raging black bear hell-bent on destruction.

It had taken municipal police six rounds to bring down the offending black.

Zane pondered the life of a bear. Their mothers gave birth to them inside a warm and cozy den, protected from winter's deadly hold. For all practical purposes, they lived happy-go-lucky lives. Until a boar would snap one in its jaws. Or a fall from a tree or cliff resulted in a slow, agonizing death.

Or a moose would stomp one to a pulp.

Fifty percent of bear cubs failed to reach their third summer. Hunters, Zane knew from enforcing state laws, accounted for a mere fraction of bear deaths in Alaska. Strict hunting guidelines put into effect years ago helped reduce unnecessary kills.

Other bears caused the overwhelming remainder of cub deaths.

Contemporary society censured Zane and others for uttering the fact aloud. Not even back at headquarters did Zane toss around notions of infanticide. One of those truths the AWT accepted as truth, yet no one dared to mention. He chuckled. Didn't people used to handle the subject of sex the same way decades ago?

How odd that existing scientific facts should now be considered taboo.

Dr. Sands had insisted only humans kill for no reason. Zane had learned firsthand that other animals took down prey without need. During his tenure working with the AWT, he'd come across dozens of animal carcasses in the backcountry killed by wolves and left to rot. Why had they killed them if they had no intention of eating them? For sport? To harness their predatory skills? He recalled the stunned silence at Taggart Hall when Joshua had mentioned that the grizzly responsible for breaking into his uncle's cabin hadn't eaten any of his food.

People clung to one uptight notion after another. Surpass one phobia, conjure more.

Self-imposed blind sacrifices to a greater power in one form or another.

He glanced toward the foothills through a clearing in the birch grove. Fireweed grew from the south-facing slopes. Brilliant bursts of blood-red blooms, brushing the ashen sky. He waved mosquitoes from his face and peered closer. What other predatory bears might lurk there?

"Come get me," he murmured, hand hovering instinctively near his Glock. "Let's have it out, snout to snout."

The call of ravens rebuffed his challenge.

Back at headquarters, Zane sat at his desk, unable to shake the most recent attack from his head. More pressing concerns demanded his attention. The gallbladder harvesting failed to pull him back to the paperwork under his nose.

Coincidences. A lot of them. Joshua had uncovered a fairly obvious commonality. All four victims had studied bears.

Even the media had failed to detect that little tidbit and the media lived for such worthless information to spread before the public, like manure.

Or was it worthless?

He retrieved a notepad from his drawer, gripped a pencil, and drew three columns. He labeled each column after the four victims: Krum, Bloomington and Rakesh, Gomez. Next he compiled a list of facts about the attacks in the subsequent rows and made a check mark under each column if the fact related to the victims.

1. Grizzly bear—he checked Dr. Krum's column. 2. Black bear—checked the other two columns. 3. Fatal—checked all. 4. Partially eaten—all. 5. Early morning attack—Krum, Gomez. 6. Late night attack—Bloomington and Rakesh. 7. Biologists….

Zane paused. The most imposing common imprint. Alaska had its share of scientists, but enough that the odds favored four biologists encountering the same atypical, unrelated deaths? Sighing, Zane checked under each of the columns and crossed off the rows with fewer than three check marks. He gazed at his work. The visible rows revealed what he'd already known. The tangible table helped organize the jumble in his head. Each of the victims had died, each had been partially consumed, and each had at one time practiced in the same field of study. How would a bear, although pushing toward the top of the list of intelligent mammals, plot a premeditated hit on a select group of humans based on their careers?

Tearing off the sheet, he attacked a fresh page and made a table similar to the first. This time he labeled each column Bear 1, Bear 2, and Bear 3. He listed the bears' overall health, strengths, sizes, weights. No starvation. No brain disease. Healthier than a bear in a zoo. No tags or collars. Unfamiliar to the AWT, DNR, and Fish and Game. Blood work the same. Until the list ran off the page.

Frustrated, he balled the latest list and tossed it into the trashcan, shaking his head. Why did he even care? For Josh's sake? Col. Lund had swiped the issue from his hands. The AWT didn't conduct investigations into bear attacks, even with the state on their backs. Who did those over-paid bureaucrats in Juneau think they were, anyway? Let Karen or Fish and Game handle publicity.

"Looks like you could use some lunch, Bono."

He lifted his head from his hands, grinned at Dana at her desk, signature Bad Ass coffee at her lips. "Yep," he said. "I guess I could." He stood with a determined screech of his chair. "Let's blow."

THEIR favorite luncheonette bustled with workers on their lunch breaks. After they waited in line five minutes, the host seated them at a booth, quickly wiped and cleaned by Henrietta, the smiling twentysomething waitress who usually served them. She, like many others, had moved to Alaska for the outdoor adventures, but needed to make a living between mountaineering excursions.

"Same old?" she asked, tanned hands on athletic hips.

"Same old," Dana said.

"Back in a scramble."

Zane avoided eye contact with Dana, understanding her well enough after working with her three years. She wanted to pry open his brain like a walnut. Still suffering from the shock of Greg's death, she labored to grasp what might have happened. He had little to share with her. He comprehended the bear attacks as much as she did.

But the question she flung at him from across the Formica table sideswiped him like a wayward football.

"What's the deal with you and Gaffner?" she asked.

Zane gulped his water, wiped his mouth. "Wouldn't you rather talk about the bear attacks?" he said.

"You're not turning gay on me, are you?"

Although they'd already ordered, Zane concealed his flush by reading the menu. He envied the pictures of hamburgers and fries. An inanimate still life, more at peace with themselves than he felt in his own world, he brooded, sliding down the slick, fabric seat. With his restless leg convulsing, he said, "What on earth do you mean?"

"You two have been spending a lot of time together since he arrived."

"I'm helping him with his uncle's death, that's all."

"You've never put that much effort into helping anyone who lost a loved one from an animal attack."

"They never asked for help like him." Bravery replaced the burning in his cheeks. With a cool resolve, he raised his chin. "He needs me," he said. "In some way, he needs me, and isn't afraid to say it."

"Is that what you want in a relationship? Someone helpless?"

"He's hardly helpless. And no, that's not what I want." Not completely, he mused.

The greasy air absorbed the chatter around them into one humming murmur. Grateful their voices scarcely carried beyond their booth, he gazed outside at the gray clouds shuffling eastward over the Chugach Range. Traffic on nearby Glenn Highway raced past, adding to the blurry babble inside the diner. Commercial trucks, cars, and RVs packed the parking lot. Was there a way to avoid Dana's meddling?

"I know about what happened between you and Banks," she said out of the blue, forcing Zane to snap his attention back her way.

He held the menu under his chin, his face burning white hot.

"Don't be embarrassed," she said, eyes penetrating him. "Banks let it slip when we heard you and Joshua fooling around in your tent at Crystal Lake."

Zane figured they might've heard, recalling the moment Dana had crawled out of Langston's tent that chilly morning. Shivers had nibbled on his neck when he'd spotted her. Jealousy? But why? He supposed no one liked rejection for another. "You mean while you guys were playing musical tents?"

"This isn't about me and Langston, it's about *you* and Langston."

"What did he tell you?"

"How you guys used to do steroids and how it makes you horny, or something like that."

"He actually told you that?"

"I forced him to fess up. But I'd already figured something had happened between you two anyway. Don't get all red in the face. I doubt it's uncommon around here. In Alaska there're ten guys for every woman. Someone's going to either go without or make do with what they got. Alaska might have the highest rape rate in the country, but ninety-percent of men never resort to that."

He tried to conceal his burning face by scratching his forehead. "Sometimes the way you talk, Dana. I like it best when you mind your own business."

Dana giggled. "I can read you easier than you realize, Bono. I don't always need you to speak to figure out what's on your mind."

He wanted to change the subject. "So are you and Langston dating?"

"It was one of those things. Like with you and me. Hey, don't give me one of those reproachful looks, Bono. I haven't slept with that many men. I've probably been with the same amount of guys as you."

"Dana…."

"I'm merely trying to make a point."

"If there're so many men to choose from, why haven't you settled down? How old are you? Twenty-six, twenty-seven?"

"Twenty-six. And I didn't say they were all marriageable men. This is Alaska. Between the antisocial types and the itinerants, what's left?"

"Me?"

She fiddled with her placemat with a cartoon rendition of a map of the state of Alaska and inane trivial facts for tourists. "You're too old-fashioned." She snickered. "You even take your hat off whenever you eat at restaurants."

Zane glanced at his trooper cap lying on the seat beside him. "Used to be a time when women liked chivalrous men."

"Back in the Victorian period. I love working with you, Bono, but if we ever lived together we'd drive each other nuts. Put you in a time machine and you'll be fine. In a way, your foray with Joshua Gaffner and Banks…. Well, that's old-fashioned too, odd as it sounds. Appearances can deceive, like the backcountry. You're an anachronism, living at a time when the man was the man."

"I'm probably more likely to experience that with another man, these days," Zane said, stunned by his own forthrightness.

"Exactly." Dana nodded. "Now you get my point."

"You sound like my ex. I'll never figure out you women."

"Maybe you're better off with Joshua. A lot of guys are. Better off with each other, I mean. If you can swing that way, why not?"

"Can we eat in peace, please?" he said, noticing Beatrice balancing a tray toward them. "Can we eat?"

"Zane, don't get uptight. I still consider you the biggest stud on the ranch, way bigger than Langston. You're the ideal alpha male. Understand why I'm not interested in dating you? I want the top dog position too."

"Now, that makes a whole lot of sense," Zane said, rolling his eyes while Beatrice dealt their lunches on the table.

CHAPTER 19

"HI, ZANE. How have you been?"

"I'm… I'm doing good. And you?"

"I'm fine. Good to see you."

"You too." He peered over her head from the threshold to his doublewide. "How did you get here?"

"Paratransit." She giggled with a shrug and downturn of her mouth. "I ride free. Remember?"

"Come on in." Zane stepped aside and helped her wheelchair over the small hump. Builders had not equipped the mobile home for special needs. Zane should have realized that before closing. Maybe she would've visited more often. This was only her third visit in five years. He wanted to ask her what had made her come, but he feared sounding standoffish.

"You're probably surprised I'm here," Julie said, "especially since it's only been about a month since the last time we saw each other."

"Either way I'm glad you came. But you should've phoned me to pick you up. I know how unreliable municipal transit can be."

"Especially on Sundays." Julie straightened her wheelchair over the shag carpet in Zane's living room. She hated using the motor while indoors. Although she had partial function of her arms, she demonstrated smoother finesse when pulling on the wheels. She blew a puff of wind under her bleached bangs. "Took two hours for them to show after I called."

"That's horrible."

"I didn't mind. I spent the time needlepointing. I've made you something." She lifted a small, square canvas from the pouch on the side of the chair. "You like?"

"I love it." Zane grinned at the cross-stitched scene.

"It's the Chugach Range," Julie said. "Not bad for one of my first creations, huh?"

"I'll have to have it framed." He laid it on the nearby dining table and stepped back into the living room. "You're lucky you caught me," he said. "I only got home about a half hour ago."

"Good thing the bus was late then," she said. "I took a chance you were home. I tried to call you a few times over the weekend, but your cell went straight to voice mail. Were you working?"

What could he tell her? That he'd spent another weekend with Joshua Gaffner, a man, the third in a row? That they'd stayed at his cabin near Birchwood, like he and Julie had in the bush before her accident? A stress free weekend, exactly what Zane had craved, with his state-issued satellite phone hooked to his battery pack to prevent him from slacking on his duties? During their dinner at the posh downtown restaurant, Julie had confessed she knew about his bisexuality. Still, he resisted mentioning Josh.

"I was taking care of some things," he said. "My cell wasn't working so great, sorry."

"I started to feel bad for you, Zane." She flashed him her sage eyes. "I've been imagining those people killed in the bear attacks. Hard to believe what happened to Greg Gomez. I remembered you mentioning him. The AWT must be stressed to the limit."

He scratched at his greasy two-day old beard, worried a moment he looked a mess. "If it wasn't for pressure from Juneau and the media circus and the crazy nuts out to seek revenge against every hairy creature that walks on all fours, we wouldn't have to worry much about it." He sat in an easy chair across from her. "The media's in more of a feeding frenzy than the bears. It's starting to subside somewhat." His attempt at laughter came out as a snort. "I'm rude. Would you like something to drink? Food?"

"Water would be nice."

Zane scurried to the kitchen, filled a glass with ice water from the refrigerator door, headed for the living room. With a snap of his fingers, he turned back for the kitchen. Luckily, he had a drawer full of straws from past fast food delivery orders. He never used them, but saved them. For what reason? The Italian in him, he supposed. Or perhaps the Alaskan?

"Here you go." He made sure she had a good grasp before letting go. "It's nice and cold."

"Thanks." She sipped from the straw, rested the glass in her lap.

Zane followed her gaze at his laptop set on the coffee table next to a notepad and ballpoint pen. "Started to ready some work," he said. "Figure I'd do research on bears while watching the Mariners with the sound down."

"Sorry."

"No problem. You know me, always finding something to tinker with. In fact, I was considering calling you."

"About what?"

He let his shoulders fall. "I'm unsure."

"It's that time, Zane." Julie shook her head. "Happens every year. You still kick yourself for what happened."

He dropped into the easy chair and sighed. "I don't think about it much." A bold-faced lie.

Memories of his past life in the bush with Julie stomped through his mind more often than the wind blowing off the Chugach Range. But each winter breakup, the reflections tumbled faster, more harshly, until they collapsed on top of him in an avalanche of despair. June twentieth. The day Julie had suffered her accident. Seven years tomorrow.

Hollow emptiness gnawed into his gut. He imagined Julie sitting alone, in her one-bedroom government-subsidized apartment with nothing to do but watch cable television and needlepoint. Not long ago, life had poured from her once sturdy limbs. At least she still possessed an independent streak. She'd traveled to his mobile home park on her own without needing him. Isn't that partly why they'd divorced?

"Sure you don't want anything to eat?" he said, swallowing the painful recollections. "I've got some leftover lasagna in the fridge."

She giggled. "You always have leftover lasagna in the fridge. You're worse than our dads."

He shrugged. "I can't make anything else. Maybe it's genetic. I miss your cooking." Should he have said that? He didn't want to lead her on. Did he?

She maneuvered a few inches closer. "I was considering asking Mom to send Mikey up for his ninth birthday. It's on a Saturday this year, and I'm sure he'd love to celebrate along with the Fourth here in Alaska. It's short notice, but Mom and Dad can swing the cost. Dad's pension kicked in last month."

Zane forced himself from jumping to his feet. In his mind a small boy rushed to him, arms open, toothy grin. And today was Father's Day. "I'd love to see him again. He comes to my mind often. But I'd like to pay for his ticket."

"I'll ask. Might be easier from their end." She glanced around the living room, her eyelashes fluttering. "I can't guarantee anything."

Julie had far more sway with her parents than Zane ever had. His former in-laws rarely budged whenever Zane requested Michael come for a visit. The past few years he'd quit nagging.

"I'm already making Mikey an embroidered pillow with a picture of a clown." Julie laid a shaky hand on Zane's thigh. "I hope I can give it to him in person."

Zane struggled to smile, wanted to appear cool. Was she coming onto him? She rarely touched him. How long had she gone without companionship? One of the many topics they avoided. She'd mentioned dating in the past, but refrained from expounding about any of the men.

Was she desperate now? Is that why she'd traveled to see him using undependable paratransit?

He should probably explain to her about Joshua. Their relationship had cemented the past few weeks, like the mudflats in low tide grabbing onto wayward skiffs. And with their budding romance, their lovemaking during the weekend had taken on an amplified fervor. The woods brought out the animal in Zane. Julie might remember that.

At the cabin, Zane had heard strange sounds emerging from his mouth while chopping wood for the stove, repairing the leaky roof, hauling water from the creek. Sounds he made only when good emotions grabbed hold. Did they have anything to do with Josh? How long since he'd hummed his favorite tunes? Not since living in the bush with Julie and Mikey, along with the music made from his saw or ax.

He and Joshua had tacitly made a commitment to each other. Josh had said he'd ended his relationship with his last boyfriend because of his "two-timing." Zane resisted destroying the novel trust they'd built together by fooling around with Julie.

He squirmed, cleared his throat. "You want to sit outside? Nice and warm tonight."

"Zane, you're blushing."

"I'm not."

"You always turn red when embarrassed."

Why couldn't he blurt out: "Julie, I'm dating someone. A man from Oregon named Joshua Gaffner. We've been seeing each other close to one month, and we've become rather serious." But he couldn't. He wasn't ready. Not yet.

"I have high blood pressure, that's all," he said.

An awkward silence cast a long shadow over them.

She sighed, released her hand from his thigh, let it drop like a draft snake in her lap. "There's actually a reason why I wanted to come in person." She reached into the same pouch in which she had stored her needlework and took out some papers.

"What's that?"

"Forms. I'm afraid I need a cosigner for a loan."

"A loan? For what?"

"I'm going to start taking online courses." She smiled, widened her eyes. "I'm hoping to get an associate's degree in Holistic Health. Maybe get a part-time job with the Access Alaska Center. They do fine work with the disabled."

"Great, Julie. But why don't you let me pay? Why do you put yourself through this red tape when I should be paying you alimony anyway?"

"I refuse to take any alimony from you, Zane. We've been over that. It's hard enough for me to ask you to cosign. I'm certainly not going to ask you for a loan."

"I didn't say a loan."

"Zane...."

He took the papers from her hand, skimmed over the cobweb of fine black print. Cold blood ran along his arms.

"You don't need to worry," she said. "I don't plan on going back on the payments. I received an increase for my SSI and disability coming this fall."

Zane shivered. "I'm not concerned about that," he said, his lips tight. "But can I ask why you came to me when your father would happily sign? You could fax him the forms."

"Take your pick, Zane. Either Dad signs or Mikey visits. You won't have both. You know I can't ask my parents for more than one thing at a time. They get pretty picky and exasperated. The smallest request overwhelms them. And I need to get this form out by Wednesday."

Sighing, Zane grabbed the pen from the coffee table and signed, initialed, and dated on the appropriate lines. "I could've come to your place to do this." He handed her the forms, wrinkled from his strong grip. "You didn't have to fuss with coming out here. I work only ten miles from your complex."

"I thought it would be more respectable to see you. After all, I'm the one asking for a favor."

But gratefulness and satisfaction avoided him. Instead, he felt only wasted and spent. He was good enough for a signature, but nothing more. She'd rather take the public's money than his.

Julie's accident crippled him perhaps more than her, and the image of her present life, of how their world had unraveled in the bush in a mere wisp of the arctic wind, made him sick to his stomach. And tomorrow marked the seventh anniversary of the tragedy.

He squeezed the pen with his fist. "At least let me give you a lift home."

"That I'll accept."

An hour and a half later when he returned home from dropping Julie at her government subsidized apartment complex on Fifth Avenue, Zane rushed to the bathroom and vomited into the commode.

He wiped his forehead with the back of his hand and vomited again.

CHAPTER 20

THE heavy glass doors slid open. Langston, mouth and eyes puckered, pushed the handcuffed man through the vestibule and forced him into a chair by his desk. Zane stared from a pile of paperwork.

An hour before, the Anchorage Police had called the AWT to the house of a man who'd allegedly shot and killed two bears foraging in his backyard. The third "retaliation" shooting since Greg's fatal mauling two weeks ago. Most of south central Alaska sat on pinecones waiting for the next attack. Despite no other bear attacks since, fear gripped the public. Zane assumed the man at Langston's desk the latest culprit.

"What's the story, Banks?" Zane said.

"Two dead blacks, sow and male subadult."

The man, squirming like a roped chicken, shouted he'd shot the bears in self-defense.

Sneering from his swivel chair, Langston said, "I still don't believe you're telling the truth. I think you shot them because you thought you could get away with it."

"You can't hold me for defending myself."

"I'm holding you for hunting outside bear season. We'll find out whether you shot them in self-defense soon enough. From what I uncovered, there's no indication either of those dead bears charged you."

"You mean I have to wait for one to come at me before I can shoot?"

"That's the law."

"You brown shirts are nuts."

"Are you fessing up you failed to wait for a charge?"

The man grimaced, sealed his lips tight, and glanced around the office while wriggling in his chair. Only nine o'clock in the morning and the desks sat half-empty. Dana had taken a personal day off.

"I thought they were coming at me," the man grunted again. "They glared at me with those sinister black eyes of theirs. The big one stood on its hind legs."

"That's not a sign of aggression," Langston said. "That's a sign she was minding her own business."

"It's my backyard."

"You live in Anchorage, Alaska. You're in *their* backyard."

"That's crap. I'm not waiting around for some bear to eat me or one of my kids for breakfast."

Langston leaped for the man, got into his face. Spittle formed at the corners of his mouth. "The law's the law, and you're not above it, understood?"

Zane jumped from his desk and pushed Langston back into his seat. "Calm down, Banks. Just relax, will you? Now, both of you keep your heads." He'd observed Langston unravel a handful of times, but nothing close to violence. What had set him off? The bear shootings? Lots of people shot bears senselessly. He demonstrated commitment to his job— never at such a zealous level. Perhaps everyone was on edge from the attacks and the pressure that rested on their shoulders to ensure Greg's death was the last.

Amanda, seated at her desk with the phone receiver buried in the crook of her neck, gave Zane one of her "I don't understand what the heck is going on" looks.

"Langston, go get some coffee, I'll take care of this guy."

Langston shrugged off Zane's hands and strutted for the kitchenette. Zane shook his head, reached into his pants pocket for a set of keys. He unlocked the man's handcuffs and sat at Langston's desk. "Sit back and relax and give me your statement, sir. Straight out with minimal personal commentary."

"What's going to happen to me?" The man shook his hands and rubbed his wrists.

"You're not under arrest."

"Do I have to pay a fine? How much?"

"If we conclude you shot without provocation, you could face a fine of fifty thousand dollars. Depends on the age and gender of the bears."

"Fifty thousand dollars? I can't afford that. A bear can attack a man without provocation, but a man can't fend off a bear? Is that how it goes?"

"You'll have a right to a hearing. Let's get your statement, please."

"This state's becoming worse than anything in the Lower Forty-eight. Why did I ever bother to move from California? It's spreading like cancer."

"Alaska's got laws like any other state."

"Stupid laws, if you ask me."

"We protect the wildlife for the public's sake as well as theirs. Why did you move here if you don't like bears wandering around?"

"A man has a right to live without worrying about a bear killing him or his family, don't he? What are you guys doing about those poor people who got eaten to death, huh? The public knows all about it, and you don't care. All you care about is your far-reaching authority."

"Sir, give me your statement about the shooting, please. You're only succeeding in detaining yourself longer than either of us want."

The man leaned back in the chair. Beginning with a guttural moan, he recounted his tale how he'd come to shoot the two blacks trespassing in his backyard. Zane, dazed and tired, inputted the information into the computer. A straightforward investigation would most likely find the man culpable for killing the cub, but not the sow. The AWT would waive the fine and sentence him to a weekend of educational courses on gun safety and bear behavior. Zane thanked the man for his cooperation and allowed him to use the phone to call his girlfriend to pick him up.

The remainder of Summer Solstice passed in the same pestering manner. Irritating, disruptive. The entire office, the entire city, pulsed with jittery unease with a stubborn sun that wouldn't disappear until past midnight—and then only for four hours. One colossal PMS, Amanda had described it. To make matters worse, Julie called Zane after lunch to inform him she'd been unsuccessful persuading her parents to let Michael travel to Alaska for his birthday, shattering his hopes. She was optimistic they might allow him to visit during Christmas. After hanging up, Zane began to mimic Langston's surly attitude.

When the German cabby called Zane on his cell phone right before seven o'clock, Zane worried he'd never step foot inside his comfy doublewide again.

The cabby had been thinking hard about something he'd noticed the morning of Greg's mauling. Switching back and forth between German and English, he told Zane he'd been dozing, like he often did whenever he worked the night shift, shortly before the attack, around five in the morning, when a loud banging awoke him. A trailer—white or gray, he thought—was backed close to the trailhead. A man walked around the back, inspecting it. Eskimo looking, the cabby said, or possibly a light-skinned African American. He shrugged it off, dozed again, only to awaken to the sound of the trailer driving away. He glimpsed two men in the cab of the SUV, both the same ethnicity. He didn't think anything of it until later. For some reason, he couldn't shake it. The cabby was unable to memorize the license plate number, but remembered the SUV's color. Green or gray or possibly blue, coated with dirt. Five minutes after the SUV drove off, Greg's screams jolted him from his taxi.

What connection the cabby's recollections had with the black bear that assaulted Greg Gomez, Zane had no idea. Perhaps the truck drivers had witnessed the attack and took off in shock. Or maybe they were shady criminals dealing in stolen goods from the back of their trailer and had escaped the scene before the law caught them. Maybe Zane should locate them for interviews.

Zane jotted notes, thanked the cabby in German, and leaned back in his seat, sighing loud enough to force Col. Lund to shut his office door with a groan.

Work the next morning began even worse than the previous day. Lying on his desk, leering at him, was the headline story in the *Anchorage Daily News*: BEAR VICTIMS' FAMILIES SPEAK OUT. The media refused to let the story go. Joshua Gaffner, the bereaved nephew of the first victim, Dr. Theodore Krum, was one of the primary interviewees.

Standing by his desk, Zane skimmed through the article. Two minutes later, he sat and reread it a second time, making sure to devour each word. Joshua hadn't revealed anything too top secret. No mention of the bears eating their victims (although people were already talking). But he did state the similarities between the victims' professional backgrounds. The *Daily News* reporter, Liz Scribner, spent four subsequent paragraphs highlighting each victim's academic careers.

Dr. Theodore Krum had worked as a bear expert at Ochoco State University in Oregon. He'd written several papers on bear ecology. He was considered a prodigy by his late teens, even before receiving his doctorate in ecology from the University of Oregon. During his high school years, he worked his summer vacations for the National Park Service, researching bear behavior in Yosemite.

Drs. Bloomington and Rakesh, husband and wife researchers, had spent seven years studying bears and cougars at Thurston College in Tacoma, Washington, before retiring to Alaska. They'd written two books on animal behavior, *Beasts Stalk the Cities*, about cougars in urban environments, and *Habituated North American Black Bears of Olympic National Park*.

And the most recent victim, Dr. Gregory Gomez, a local scholar from the University of Anchorage. He'd received his doctorate in animal science at Texas A&M and had written several "controversial" papers on bears. Scribner had interviewed Greg's father via telephone in San Antonio. He said, "We prized Greg for his intelligence, dedication, and understanding." Seemed only yesterday Zane and Greg had spoken in his dingy office about the odd findings in the bears' blood tests.

Dana must have read his mind. "Your blood tests from Washington and Massachusetts came in," she said. "The university faxed them earlier this morning. I put them on your desk."

"About time," he grunted.

Zane pushed the newspaper aside and snatched up the report. He compared the results with a copy Greg had printed of his own tests. If Zane interpreted the numbers correctly, the testosterone and methamphetamine content in bear three appeared more elevated than the other two. No doubting the University of Anchorage's findings now. Four different experts had uncovered the same results. The question remained: How did the drugs get into the bears' systems?

He presented the findings to Col. Lund, who grumbled about the investigation being a wasted effort. "Bears who consume drugs die from poisoning," he grunted. "They don't go on murderous rampages."

Aggravated, he decided to kick the report at the Bureau of Investigations's feet.

"And unless you're a senator in Juneau, I don't want to hear any more about it," he said before ushering Zane out of his office.

Zane agreed with his superior. Drug-crazed bears killing people who'd studied them, as the *Daily News* reporter had alluded, held no logic.

But did anything related to the attacks make sense?

"Where's Banks?" he asked Dana, once back at his desk, hoping to suppress his irksome worries.

"He took a personal day."

Good, Zane contemplated. He needed one. After the other day, Zane imagined Langston might explode from the mere clank of a paperclip. Testier than a wolverine. "I guess I'm next in line for time off," he said. "I could sure use some."

"Langston's been in a mood lately," Dana said.

"You noticed, huh?"

"I think he's miffed about you know what."

"What?"

She glanced around the office, lowered her voice. "Telling me about you guys."

Heat pinched under Zane's collar. "Let's drop the whole subject," he whispered through clenched teeth. "Don't ever mention it again, please. Especially here in the office."

"I don't have a problem with it—"

"Dana...."

Dana shrugged and turned back to her paperwork.

Shaking off Dana's prying, Zane surfed the Internet for facts on bear behavior for the remainder of the morning. Despite his commander's initiative and his own weariness over the entire ordeal, the issue lodged in his mind like a splinter in the foot.

He yearned to help Joshua. Somehow. Nothing pained him more than telling Josh time and time again he held no answer to why his uncle had to die so horribly.

He discovered a study revealing that when massive doses of testosterone were injected into mice, they reacted violently and had resorted to cannibalism, even autocannibalism. Another mice study showed methamphetamine and cocaine caused similar behavior. Could the results of the mice translate into the same indications for large bears?

With the bear research out of the way, he googled the four victims' names. He discovered dozens of papers written by each. Several articles he read in entirety beyond the abstracts. Interesting the scholars had the same take on bear behavior. Contrary to many of their contemporaries' beliefs, their overall conclusions: bears behaved as unpredictably as humans. But enough that they might act like murderers, even while drugged out of their minds?

Zane discovered another interesting morsel. Dr. Barry Sands had worked at Thurston College during the same period as Drs. Bloomington and Rakesh. The three had worked in the Department of Physiology and Biology. Zane wondered. Might the bears target Dr. Sands next?

Surely bears don't intentionally kill people who study them. Too outlandish. Too incomprehensible. If bears held a grudge, why not go after those responsible for the gallbladder poaching, a recent crime the AWT had yet to solve?

He chuckled. Regardless of the peculiar prototypes of the attacks, he could hardly fathom the notion. He clicked out of the web pages. Col. Lund was right. A wasted effort.

CHAPTER 21

STEAM curled from a pot of what smelled like vegetable soup simmering on the stove. Zane had driven straight to the cabin after work without planning. Returning there was like coming home. Josh wiped his hands on a towel and peered at the copy of the *Anchorage Daily News* Zane had planted on the table.

"Are you angry with me?"

"Liz grasped for straws when she tried to connect the attacks with some kind of strange revenge plot by the bears," Zane said, taking off his trooper's cap and tossing it onto the table next to the newspaper. "But I'm not mad at you for talking. At least you got your chance to speak on your uncle's behalf, clear his name like you wanted. Now everyone realizes he never fed or baited the bears and he was an honest scholar."

"Not an honored one," Josh said, turning back to the stove. "He deserved more respect."

Zane draped his jacket on the back of a ladder-back chair and embraced Joshua from behind. His taut muscles twitched from Zane's touch. Another long day. Zane looked forward to an evening of warmth and lovemaking. Josh rotated to face him, and they kissed long and needful.

"Hungry?" Joshua asked, breaking their lip-lock and smiling into his eyes.

"Absolutely."

"Should be ready in about ten minutes. Let me make sure the soup doesn't burn. I'm still getting used to cooking over wood heat. I have to constantly move the pots and pans on and off the burners. Not that I was ever a great cook to begin with."

Zane sat at the table and kicked back while Josh put his nose to the pot. Like with Julie in their old rustic cabin.

"I kinda hoped you'd show tonight," Josh said.

"Why's that?"

"Just did. I was going to ride out where I could get cell reception and call you to come out before the weekend if you could." Josh nodded toward an untidy stack of Uncle Ted's journals that sat on the table beside Zane. "Have you read all of what was legible in them?"

"Not all. Why?"

"I read through the last one today," Joshua said, releasing the stirring spoon with a dull clank and sitting opposite Zane. "The more I read, the more I realize the bears never posed a problem for Uncle Teddy, not in the ten years he lived here. When I stayed here with him a few summers ago, I never saw a single grizzly. We spotted a few black bears, but usually only their rumps getting smaller and smaller as they scurried into the scrub."

"Your uncle believed bears are unpredictable. They proved him right when three killed him and the others for no apparent reason."

"And like with the Bloomingtons," Joshua went on, darting around Zane's comment, "the only concerns he had, even living way out here, were with other people. Crooks had broken into his cabin three times. One time someone stole two rifles."

"He should've reported that."

"He did. The next day he wrote he hiked into Birchwood and called the state troopers. Happened only this past spring, a few months ago."

"Report probably landed on the Bureau of Investigations' lap. I'll look into it."

"Funny thing, they stole a pile of his dirty clothes at the same time."

Zane scrunched his forehead. "I would guess a desperate and hungry sourdough. Out here they'll scavenge far more than bears."

"Listen to this entry dated March 15, 2011." Joshua opened a dog-eared section of the journal lying on top of the stack. He scanned the page with his blue eyes and stopped halfway down. "'No human being has crossed my path since the sun began rising at seven in the morning. Yet the strangest things have occurred that defy explanation. Today while fetching water by the creek, someone broke into my cabin for the third time in as many weeks. I had been gone a mere half hour. It's as if the burglar (or burglars) had been lying in wait, watching me.'" Josh glanced up from the journal. "Creepy, isn't it? Wait, there's more. 'I had fewer issues with property theft when I lived in Oregon. I believe I am being targeted, but whoever it is lives outside the area, I'm certain. My neighbors, who I have always regarded as law abiding and sensible, have told me they've witnessed no unusual activity, and they have witnessed no strangers lurking around. And doubly odd, none have had the same issue with thefts as I. I consider myself a good judge of character. My neighbors appear above suspicion, as far as I'm concerned. After the theft, like the other two times, I hiked to the road and checked for human prints and tire tracks. I found a single set of unfamiliar boot prints that led to tire markings crisscrossing in the mud and snow piles about half a mile away, but I could not judge how old they were. The three thefts baffle me.'"

Joshua closed the journal with a slap. "He goes on to say he plans on filing a report in the morning. That was the last entry about it. I guess the lengthening daylight hours shut down any more problems with snoopers."

"Strange," Zane said, massaging his chin.

Josh gazed out the window, remained silent a moment. "Lots of crazies out there."

"No worse than anywhere else, I guess."

"What's really weird, I started to feel someone watching me lately, even before reading that entry, like the trees have eyes."

"Living out here alone can make a man hear and see things. I get the same way even in Girdwood." Zane dropped his head in his hands and rubbed his temples.

"What's wrong, Zanebono," Joshua said. "Bad day at work?"

"Bad month."

"All this bear stuff?"

"That's part of it." Zane revealed his face, exhaled. "My son, Michael, has been on my mind a lot lately. He's turning nine next week.

Julie got my hopes up he might come to Alaska for his birthday, but she told me he won't be coming."

"How long since you last saw him?"

"Couple of Christmases ago."

"Maybe you can fly down for a visit."

"Yeah, maybe. Before the summer's over, I guess. I've got some vacation time coming."

Josh reached across the rough-hewn table and touched Zane's arm. "I guess you're still not ready to tell me why you or your ex doesn't have custody of him."

"Nothing personal. It's difficult." The wood burning stove had sapped most of the moisture from the small cabin, and Zane could feel the dryness on his chapped lips. For a moment, he wished he hadn't come to see Joshua. He wished he'd gone home to Girdwood, where he kept a refrigerator full of cold beer and could stew in his thoughts.

"You don't like to talk about them much," Joshua said.

His blue eyes, dark like sapphires, seized Zane's attention. He wanted Josh to understand. "With Mikey," he began, his words falling off his dry lips like a plea for forgiveness, "it was easier to let him return to Rhode Island and live with his grandparents. He'd have more stability. Julie had her disability, and I could hardly raise him alone. I didn't even have a job at the time, and being with Julie at the hospital day and night, I had no time for him. My fault everything happened. Julie's parents cursed me for taking Julie and Mikey to Alaska. Told me I was an arrogant fool. I suppose they were right."

"Don't let people browbeat you, Zanebono. You followed your dream, nothing wrong with that."

Zane chuckled. Almost the same words his father had once used to console him for the same reason.

"It's not your fault, whatever happened," Josh went on, his voice deep and solemn. "The same way it wasn't Uncle Ted's fault a grizzly attacked him, or Dr. Gomez's fault, or the fault of the Bloomingtons, despite what the University of Anchorage or the others say."

Joshua's words soothed Zane's melancholy. He stood, stretched, and walked to Josh, held Josh's head against his abdomen, his Glock rubbing

Josh's shoulder. He wanted to nudge the issue behind them. The smell of vegetable soup thickened the air. His stomach rumbled. Joshua must've heard. He smiled up at Zane.

"I'll get dinner ready," he said. "You relax a bit, okay?"

They ate piping hot vegetable soup and grilled cheese sandwiches, after which Zane helped Joshua wash the dishes in a tub of murky water. Silence dominated the evening. The clank of dishes, the splash of sudsy water, the skid of a chair were the only noises. By nightfall, with the sun still hovering high above the canopy of the spruce, aspens, and pines, they fell onto the twin mattress Joshua had bought before moving in to replace the one torn to bits by the grizzly, and made an unhurried, drowsy kind of love.

The sensation they were weary soldiers on leave bridled Zane's mind again. Soon, they'd be marching off to a hidden war, thousands of miles away. Yet merely by stepping outside, Zane entered a battleground. One filled with chilling reminders of desperation and cruelty. Trooper Zanebono Fusca, esteemed soldier of the Alaska State Troopers, wildlife division.

Little to show for his efforts. His two most pressing concerns had failed to summit a conclusion. Bears attacking people, people attacking bears. An endless cycle of blood splatter.

"Joshua, my job is to ensure people adhere to regulations protecting wildlife," Zane had told him during their last weekend together, when Joshua had pressured him for more answers. "We're doing the best we can, trying to figure out why the bears attacked. But things like that sometimes happen." He'd turned his face away, ashamed of the burning on his cheeks. Same response he'd given him weeks ago when they'd stood in the parking lot of headquarters the first day they'd met.

"I don't believe Uncle Ted died for no good reason," Josh had said. "I want to ensure his death wasn't in vain."

"Things out here never happen for a good reason," Zane had snapped, recalling his own failed attempt at life in the bush. "It's the raw wilderness. People in Alaska die from stepping outside in winter. You come from your urban world and expect everything to have a reason. You want explanations, nice and packaged. Well, the real world doesn't provide snap answers. Especially not up here."

It had been at that moment, after their boisterous exchange, when Zanebono had told Josh he loved him and would do anything for him within his power. The words had slipped out, like steam from cold breath. Joshua had not reciprocated vocally, but his actions revealed enough. He'd fallen into Zane's arms, held onto him with a rugged strength Zane had never experienced from a partner. Failure had disappeared, flew up the stovepipe in a hunt for some other subservient fool. Desire had eclipsed Zane's heart.

After that, Joshua skipped across Zane's mind like a stone flicked over the surface of a pond. And now that Joshua—his boyfriend, in the true sense of the word—had made the non-existent investigation tangible, even if they did disagree on certain issues, the drive to help him spurred for a resolution against his commander's advice. To protect Joshua from whatever evil, real or imaginary, lurked in the forest surrounding his uncle's tiny shack.

"Zanebono," Joshua whispered after their sleepy lovemaking, his face turned toward the log wall, the smell of vegetable soup still heavy. "I miss the night. I mean, I miss the darkness."

Zane sat against his pillow and snickered. "Wait until December. You'll have almost twenty-four hours of it."

"I'm not going to wait."

Zane peered at the back of Josh's head. "What do you mean?"

Silence. "I'm returning to Portland."

Zane's lack of words pushed him to say more. "You were right, Zanebono. I did everything I could. You've done everything you could. Everything within your power, like you told me. There's no point. All I have are memories of Uncle Teddy now. An empty urn. Too painful." He paused, perhaps waiting for Zane's reply. When he still refrained from speaking, Joshua said, "Zanebono, I've sold the cabin."

Zane snapped his head. "You what?"

"I ran into a man in Birchwood. He knew my uncle. Said he would be interested in buying it for his hunting guide business. He wants to use it for a warming hut when he and his clients hunt fox and lynx in the winter. He's serious about buying, and I told him okay. We're going to meet in Eagle River tomorrow afternoon."

Suddenly, Zane felt like a moose caught in a tree. He remained silent, entangled in the spindly branches of shock and dismay. The earth opened, swallowed him whole.

"It's tough living out here without plumbing or electricity," Joshua mumbled. "I'm tired of traipsing to town to take a shower or do laundry. Things were different when I visited my uncle, or when you're around. Your job requires you stay closer to town, near roads. When you lived in the bush, you had a fulltime wife. Besides, my dad needs me back home to help with the business."

Rejected by Joshua too. No different than a woman. Than society in general. Joshua didn't need him to guard him from woodland beasts. No one did. He'd used Zane for a mere reprieve while trudging through the trauma of losing his uncle, much like how Dana had used him after her father's death. And the others who'd used him.

"I won't leave for a few weeks," Joshua said. "I have to stick around and take care of selling the cabin." Josh rolled over and faced Zane. "I was hoping you might help me sell my truck."

"Sure," Zane said in a low voice, after a moment's deadened consideration. "Sure, I'll help you sell your truck."

"What would life be like for us, Zanebono? You're not even gay, not completely." Joshua sighed. "I don't even know what you are."

"A dying breed, you once told me," Zane said toward his toes, his mind full of jagged introspection.

"Zanebono, if one good thing's come out of this, it was meeting you. But I have to go home. I can't stay here."

Zane nodded. "I understand. I think I always knew that." He forced a shaky smile, gazed at Joshua, a blurry streak of flesh. "It's been fun, knowing you. Being at your cabin."

"After reading Uncle Ted's journals, I realized I have to go through with selling the cabin. Nothing's here for me anymore. I can still see the blood stains on the walls and floor. The worst part is wondering which stain belongs to my uncle or the grizzly."

"Then come live with me," Zane let slip. Why had he uttered those words? He hadn't noticed them coming. They spouted from his mouth like gravel kicked up from a truck's tires. Spat out in a desperate attempt to cling to Joshua. Or to force Joshua to cling to him.

"I can't, not right now," Joshua said, almost as rashly. "Please understand. We don't have to say good-bye. You can come down and visit me in Portland. Or I can come up here. It's only a four hour flight. I want to stay in touch."

The same way I stay in touch with my son, Mikey, Zane wanted to say. Or Julie, who lived ten miles from AST headquarters, but whom he only visited once or twice a year.

Were each of his relationships destined to remain long distance, far from his grasp?

Zane tossed the covers back and leaped to his feet. "Well," he said, mustering an upbeat tone. "I guess I better head to Girdwood. Gotta get up early tomorrow for work."

"Zane, wait. Don't go."

"I have to, really I do." He pulled on his underwear and his socks, followed by his navy blue trooper pants and brown shirt. Inhaling a gulp of false nonchalance, he squatted by Josh and kissed him on his forehead. "We're both pretty busy these days. Can't put off the real world much longer."

"But, Zane. You and I are the real world. We can fit into it. Only not here. Not in Alaska. Not me."

Zane gazed at Joshua, slurped in his baby blues, perhaps for the last time. Wanting to hold them long enough to remember. Why had he imagined a man like Joshua might need or even want him?

Zane had streaked past Joshua's sky like a meteor. Quick fun to kill a dull afternoon. Nothing more.

"I'll keep you posted if anything new comes up about the bear investigation," he said, jumping to his feet. "Oh, and if anyone's interested in buying a second-hand truck, I'll let you know about that too." *The old Ford Ranger and I have a lot in common*, Zane snickered to himself.

Squaring his shoulders, he slipped on his Danners, grabbed for his holster from the kitchen table, and marched out the door.

CHAPTER 22

EVER-present ravens yapped overhead in the trees, mocking Zane as he walked past the two trucks and white trailer in the parking lot of Dr. Sands's bear sanctuary and onto the footpath behind the cottage. Dana kept tight to his side. She'd never visited the sanctuary before.

"Amazing," she said, gazing around wide-eyed. "I've heard about this place, but never imagined. How many bears does he have?"

"About eleven right now," Zane said, his mouth taut. "A few died during the winter."

Zane had business. Acting like a tourist dragged far from his intentions. He'd brought Dana along to show her the source of much of the AWT's knowledge. They'd come wanting Dr. Sands's advice. Advice how to quell the hysteria surrounding the recent bear attacks. Zane and Dana's goal was to thwart any more retaliatory killings against bears.

Several bears roamed inside the habitats, pawed at the pesky flies and mosquitoes buzzing around their snouts. A few more lounged on the grass and gazed at the blue sky, while one adult black ran about, huffing and snapping at an invisible adversary.

"Is that him?"

Zane, following Dana's gaping brown eyes, slipped on his sunglasses to block the unusually bright sun. His view through the polarized lenses revealed a crystal clear image of Dr. Sands standing inside the farthest bear habitat from the cottage. His assistant, Leslie, watched from outside Pingaq's mesh enclosure, arms stiff by her sides, while Dr. Sands waved a shirt at the brown bear's snout. Next he threw the shirt, and when Pingaq returned with it, Dr. Sands reached into a pouch attached to his belt and tossed the bear a treat.

"Like he's playing fetch with a dog," Dana said.

"He's a bit eccentric," Zane whispered as they approached closer to Pingaq's cage, "but smarter than a whip. Understands more about bears than anyone I've encountered."

"What's that on the bear's nose?"

"A scar," Zane said. "Got it trying to fend for itself after its mother died, before Fish and Game rescued it."

"Dr. Sands," Leslie hollered. "ASTs are here."

Taking his watchful eyes off the bear for the first time, Dr. Sands glanced at Zane and Dana. In a frantic heartbeat, Pingaq swiped at its master with its serving-platter-sized paw. Dr. Sands dodged the speedy assault, stumbled backward, leaped to his feet. He shouted a string of odd-sounding guttural commands at Pingaq. Foreign words which Zane failed to recognize. Sounded Italian. The bear, reluctantly, retreated inside its den.

"Don't ever force me to take my concentration away from the bears," he shouted at Leslie, already on the verge of tears. "Especially in front of Pingaq. I don't care who's here."

"I'm sorry, Dr. Sands," she blubbered. "I forgot. Please, I'm sorry."

Dr. Sands exited the cage, stared down Leslie before barking a command at her in the same strange tongue he'd used with Pingaq. She scurried past the two troopers toward the cottage, her face in her hands. Brushing off his pants, he smiled at Zane and Dana.

"I'm sorry," he said. "These things happen. We must tread carefully. Their playful antics can sometimes mean life or death to mere humans like us."

Exhaling, Zane removed his hand from his Glock. He'd reached for it when Pingaq had lunged for Dr. Sands, an instinct honed during his six years on the job, particularly since the recent fatal bear attacks. Dana too had clamped onto her sidearm, ready to fire if needed.

"Be careful," Zane said, shaking off the tension with a chuckle. "Your little girl there has outgrown you quite a bit."

Dr. Sands waved away their hypervigilance. "Pingaq didn't mean any harm," he said. "She hardly knows her own strength. Bears in captivity rarely do. They don't often have a chance to use the power Mother Nature has bestowed on them. Who have you brought along with you this time, Trooper Fusca?"

"This is Trooper Dana Chernikoff."

Dana and Dr. Sands greeted one another.

"Your Kodiak is a remarkable bear," Dana said. "How old is she?"

"She's going on eight. Has many years ahead of her, I hope."

"Did you lose another bear?" Zane asked, scanning the other habitats. "You're down another one from my last count, unless it's hiding in its den."

"No, another died last week. A black bear. Major, we called him. Twenty-two."

"Ripe old age for a bear," Dana said. "What do you do with their carcasses once they die?"

Dr. Sands soured his bronzed face, stroked his goatee, and narrowed his eyes at the bright yellow sun. "The SPCA buries them for us at their cemetery north of Wasilla. We'd do it here, but I hate the idea of the sanctuary sitting atop a mass grave."

They gazed around the sanctuary, observing the bears' antics. Seasoned pine scent swept in from the evergreens abutting the Eagle River, masking the intermittent whiff of bear scat. A northern harrier flew against the powder blue sky, a luckless lemming clutched in its talons.

"What do you feed your bears?" Dana asked.

"A variety of foods. Grains, pinecones, grasses, berries, beetles. Whatever they would find in their natural environment. We supplement their diets with vitamin injections, of course. Primarily B-12 shots. A luxury of the domesticated bear."

"They must live a lot longer in the sanctuary than in the wild," Dana said.

"Major was my oldest until his death, the first I ever brought to the sanctuary after he survived a near poaching by a bow hunter. My oldest living, Denali, is seventeen."

"They're beautiful animals," Dana said.

"Thank you. Now what can I do you for?"

"People are on edge, wondering when the next bear attack will come," Zane said. "Every bear spotted has become a suspect killer, I'm afraid."

"Is the attitude anything new?" Dr. Sands said. "Man has regarded bears as intruders since the Middle Ages."

"We're worried about retaliatory shootings," Zane said. "You might've heard we've had a few already. Four bears shot dead. Three of them cubs."

Dr. Sands grimaced. "Yes, I have. It's a war out there. But then again, what's different from the way things existed before the attacks? Man has always sought to exterminate bears."

"You wouldn't happen to have any idea how we can guarantee the public there's no chance of it happening again," Dana said. "I mean, seriously, what are the odds?"

"There's no guarantee." Dr. Sands studied the two officers and stared off at Pingaq poking its snout out of its den. "Might be one next year, next week, maybe even tomorrow. Your guess is as good as mine. The fundamental issue, we must remind the public they live in bear country. This domain belongs to them. We are visitors in their kingdom."

"Have any of your bears ever escaped?" Dana asked.

Zane gaped at her. He considered the question odd, but was glad, nonetheless, that she'd asked.

"Never." Dr. Sands continued to gaze toward Pingaq, unfazed by Dana's abrupt question. "Not in sixteen years since we opened has one escaped, even for a minute. We have a state-of-the-art facility. Sturdy mesh purchased from a reputable company in Texas. Foolproof." He snickered with his eyes turned back toward Zane and Dana. "Even humans couldn't tinker with these cages."

Roughhousing from the bears challenged the chirping birds and bustling breeze. A subadult grizzly rattled its cage, bit at the air, rushed inside its den, frightened. Dana and Zane exchanged curious glimpses.

"I suppose you're right," Zane said. "We need to keep educating the public about bear safety and understanding that bears are, like you once titled one of your books, monarchs of the forest."

"You might like to learn that I'll be doing a radio program on the bear attacks next Tuesday," Dr. Sands said. "KAKM invited me for an interview."

"Wonderful," Zane said. "Perfect opportunity to calm people's nerves."

"I doubt that's possible," Dr. Sands said, pondering the ground. "Like I've mentioned, we humans, we're prone to whims created by hysteria. We haven't changed since the days of primordial man. We live in a perpetual tribal-like mindset of hatred and revenge."

In coming to the bear sanctuary, Zane wanted also to give Joshua one last offering before he returned to Oregon. A going away gift, perhaps. He sought Dr. Sands's assurance that Dr. Krum had done nothing to incite the grizzly that had attacked and partially eaten him. Even if he must force the doctor to belie his convictions. Coaxing a salmon from a grizzly might prove easier.

The more Zane considered what Joshua had told him Wednesday at the cabin, the more he agreed. Best Joshua left Alaska. Joshua had far less experience living in the bush than Uncle Ted, who'd spent a good deal of his adolescence working alone in the Yosemite's backcountry. Yes, he'd convinced himself over and over with burning eyes, good he'd decided to leave.

"Any experiences you've encountered, Dr. Sands, when a bear has attacked a person without any explicable reason?" he asked, choosing his words with care. "Let's say, Dr. Theodore Krum. An educated scholar, much like you, who understood more than anyone the dangers bears pose."

"Dr. Krum's view of bears was quite different from mine," Dr. Sands said. "If you're asking if I agree bears can behave the way I have described man, the way Dr. Krum and a few of his peers believed, I must say no, I do not."

"There's no case of someone taking every conceivable precaution against a bear attack and still failing?"

"Perhaps," Dr. Sands said, averting his eyes from the glare of the sun and Zane's steady gaze. "But none ever recorded. Trooper Fusca, I've analyzed every single bear attack in North America since people began recording them in the late nineteenth century. *Ursus arctos*, *Ursus americanus*, *Ursus maritimus*, fatal and nonfatal. Of the mere one hundred encounters, I believe in each case the attacks could have been averted."

"By staying home?" Dana interjected.

Dr. Sands chuckled. "What was it the venerable journalist Horace Greeley once said? 'Abstinence is favorable to the head as well as to the pocket.'"

Zane nodded and sighed. His last attempt to appease Joshua crushed into dust. "Dr. Sands, why don't you show Dana your grounds," he said, wanting to break away. "I'd like to make a few phone calls, if you don't mind."

"Of course," Dr. Sands said, his character showmanship bubbling forth. "I'd love to. Come along, Trooper Chernikoff. We have nearly five acres to explore. Do you know that some brown bears have been clocked at speeds faster than greyhounds and that…."

Zane actually had no calls to make. He wanted to escape from Dr. Sands and Dana, to ponder. He walked the footpath to the cottage, his mind weighty, yet blank, like water vapor.

Inside, Zane propped his sunglasses atop his cap and glanced around the cluttered space. More boxes from benefactors around the world stacked the floor and shelves. Tissues. Petri dishes. Bleach. Phosphorus. Iodine. Dehydrated fruits. He wandered into the small front office. More clutter. Must be a method to his madness, Zane pondered, eyeing the mess.

"He's a man of imminent importance to bear ecology."

Zane looked up. Leslie, Dr. Sands's assistant, examined him from the threshold to the office, her eyes red and glassy.

"Without men like Dr. Sands, bears wouldn't stand a chance in today's world," she said. "Not with man's nature. Always trying to kill and take what doesn't belong to him."

Zane, suppressing the burn blossoming on his cheeks, forced a grin. "Perhaps you're right. Dr. Sands has been invaluable to the AWT's efforts in safeguarding bears."

Leslie stared at him, her eyes far away. Dr. Sands had brought her onboard two years ago, straight out of college from what Zane had gathered, but he'd never shared more than a few words with her. The past two years he'd wondered if she and Dr. Sands had become lovers. He never learned how many bedrooms were on the second floor of the cottage where they slept. Leslie exuded aloofness, someone maybe with Asperger's syndrome. Perfect fit for Alaska.

"Do you believe the bears who killed those people are bad, Trooper Fusca?"

Zane scratched under his cap. "I wouldn't call them bad. Overly territorial, maybe. Perhaps even suffering from some kind of unidentified illness."

"Do you believe bears can take revenge against humans for all the trouble we've caused them? Dr. Sands says bears are incapable of vengeance."

"You differ?"

Leslie shook her head. "I agree with him. Only humans kill for revenge."

"I suppose." Zane, grinning with discomfort, shifted his eyes around the muddled office. A handwritten sticky note dangled from an antiquated computer monitor. At first glance, he assumed Dr. Sands had jotted down some kind of recipe for a compound, for the words were foreign. "Planto magis $C10H15N$, dico frater adepto magis $C17H21NO$, attero nepos." Then he recognized the Latin. He could make out a quarter of the note, since he'd studied Latin-based languages. He understood "tell," "brothers," "get," and "more" but nothing else. Attero nepos? An eccentric, erudite researcher, Zane guessed.

"He's a great man." Leslie stood motionless, like a statue. Or a deer caught in headlights. Unsure how to describe Leslie, Zane continued to grin at her.

"I agree," he said, his tone soft, calming. "A fine man."

"Any man who would sacrifice his life for another living creature must be great. Don't you think?"

"Yes, I do."

"You know what I call him? I call him the Mother Teresa of bears."
Leslie giggled. "He doesn't like it, but that's how I see him."

Zane nodded, lips firm. "A fitting description."

"Ready to go, Bono?"

Zane peered over Leslie's shoulder at Dana, who stood by the exit.
He moved his eyes back to Leslie, but she'd already darted off. A few
seconds later, he watched her through the office window grab a hose
outside and drag it toward a bear cage.

"Sure," Zane said, relieved. "Let's get out of here."

CHAPTER 23

FIREWORKS rocketed from the grounds of Mulcahy Stadium, and burst against the backdrop of the Chugach Range. He'd hoped to have brought his son to watch Anchorage's favorite baseball team, the Bucs, take on crosstown rivals, the Glacier Pilots, before enjoying the Fourth of July spectacle. With that dream squashed, he'd volunteered his services to help patrol the event, along with dozens of other state and municipal law officers. His feet ached inside his Danners after standing ten hours. Half past midnight, and the big climax had only started.

The stirring pyrotechnics contradicted the reality of Zane's life, which cycled forever on dull. No Michael. No Joshua. No answers to any of life's puzzling mysteries. The bear attacks, the illegal gallbladder harvesting, the hollowness of his one-sided relationships. He faced his duties, the only tangible feature of his life, like he might an avalanche.

Joshua and he hadn't spoken to each other since Zane had walked out of the cabin more than a week ago. Once during last weekend, Joshua had phoned him without leaving a message. Zane hadn't returned his call. Why bother? Joshua wanted neither love nor security from Zane.

Most likely he'd called only to check if Zane had found any parties interested in buying his rundown pickup truck.

Yi shi zu cheng qian gu hen. The Chinese proverb flashed across Zane's mind along with the latest multicolored fiery burst against the cobalt sky. "One error is the sorrow of an entire life."

He'd ventured to Alaska for an opportunity to live off the land. He'd succeeded in destroying his ex-wife's life and hampered his relationship with his young son. One choice, one final decision to leave Rhode Island, and he'd forever pay for the mistake.

In some respects, meeting Joshua Gaffner had only rubbed the scabs raw.

The night wore on. One by one, the festive partiers departed the grounds along with smoke from the last smoldering firework display. Zane returned to his doublewide, too exhausted to even strip off his clothes. He awoke in his wrinkled uniform, unshaven and disoriented. He ate cold cereal and orange juice, showered, and was at his desk, dressed in a crisp uniform, by eight.

The threat of a major rainstorm scented the mild July air. Normally, he enjoyed a good summer downpour. Reminded him of July in Rhode Island. Zane continued to rack his brain for answers to all that plagued him. Pieces rattled inside his head. But what and where did they fit?

Should he care? Joshua had ended their relationship. Soon he'd be returning to Oregon, back home where he belonged, helping in his family's small kitchen remodeling business. Still, Zane could not purge the drive for resolution, if there was any, to the bear attacks. For Joshua's sake and his own.

Last week he'd listened to Dr. Sands's interview on public radio station KAKM. The bear expert had provided little new information. He'd come across the radio with the charm and eccentricity listeners had perhaps tuned in for. Dr. Sands remained unwavering in his defense of bears. Most of the callers had mirrored his position.

"Why can't we learn to leave the bears alone?" one female caller had said.

"They were here first," a man had agreed, reiterating the previous caller's sentiments.

A crackly-voiced woman had called from a Wasilla retirement home. "The state should ban hunting altogether," she'd said. "I used to hunt bear and Dall sheep with my father in Kenai as a girl, and I'm ashamed to admit it today."

But what about the tranquilizer guns, injections, and traps that wildlife biologists used with impunity at taxpayer's expense? No one had mentioned that, Zane had noted.

He took out his list of victims. Anything to add? More similarities?

Thieves had stolen items from Dr. Krum, and Joshua had mentioned someone had stolen items from Drs. Bloomington and Rakesh's vehicle a few weeks before their deaths. What might those crimes have to do with the bear attacks?

On a whim, Zane called the University of Anchorage Police and Campus Security. His fellow lawman and sometimes beer buddy Rob Tupelo answered. He didn't sound too surprised when Zane asked whether Dr. Greg Gomez had ever reported anything stolen from his office. People called all the time, he said, reporting strange things.

After digging through past records, Rob found that Greg had, indeed, filed a theft report one month prior to his death. Someone had stolen his gym bag, filled with soiled running clothes, from his office. Rob recalled one of his coworkers mentioning the theft and judging it strange. Why would anyone want to steal someone's smelly running clothes? They never found the stolen items and considered the offense too minor to pursue. Rob guessed Greg might have misplaced the bag.

Zane thanked his friend and replaced the receiver. More stolen clothes? A freakish amount of curious similarities. But nothing made sense. Where did everything lead?

Zane googled "fatal bear attacks Alaska." Two hits for the past five years, not including the most recent ones, which showed enough articles Zane had to filter out any attacks for the year 2011. Nothing stood out about the other two. In 2006, a black sow killed a female field worker mapping a quadrant for the Alaska Geological Survey one hundred miles west of Fairbanks. Alone in the bush, the worker had no means for help. The three-hundred-pound bear crushed the woman's thoracic cavity seconds after she radioed an SOS. The medical examiner declared the cause of death asphyxiation. Dr. Sylvia Linden from the University of Anchorage suggested the woman had angered the sow when she'd stepped too close to her three cubs hiding in the scrub. The offending bear and cubs evaded capture.

The following summer, a husband and wife on a ten-day rafting excursion in the Brooks Range were attacked by a grizzly while they slept inside their tent, fifty yards from the Alatna River. The boar killed the wife, but the husband, an Anchorage car dealer, managed to escape downriver and seek help at a nearby native village. Zane recalled with a chill a similar experience, when he'd fled to Kalida after Julie's accident. Official statement after Fish and Game captured and euthanized the boar: "Grizzlies in Alaska's interior require wider territory for survival, and the bear viewed the campers as threats to fragile fish supply in nearby Alatna River."

He broadened his search to the entire North American continent. Dozens of attacks the past twenty years alone, eleven fatal. One grabbed his attention. In 1994, a rare grizzly in northeastern Washington State had mauled a man to death. Curious, he read the seventeen-year-old article from the archives of a Coeur d'Alene newspaper. He hardly believed his eyes. The man, Dr. Jacek Zawadzki, was an ecologist at Thurston College in Tacoma, Washington, along with Harold Bloomington and Vishva Rakesh—and Dr. Barry Sands.

Dr. Zawadzki had been on an expedition, searching for evidence of grizzlies in Washington State, when, ironically, a grizzly had killed him. He hadn't gone on the expedition alone. Dr. Sands, associate professor at the time, had accompanied him. Zane shook his head, widened his eyes, wondered if he'd misread.

Dr. Sands, the lone survivor, had provided the reporter his account of the attack. They'd been staying at a small National Forest cabin during the night after spending their days searching for signs of grizzlies. They'd made the mistake of cooking indoors, capturing the odors in a tiny space. Late at night they began to hear sounds outside their cabin. Bears approaching. Eventually the bears began making appearances during the daytime. All blacks. But in the distance, they noticed a curious blond-coated bear. Larger and more rippled than the others.

They'd found what they'd come for. The elusive grizzly of the Kaniksu National Forest.

Soon the grizzly began advancing, maintaining a safe distance from the humans. Yet whenever the men returned from their scouting trips during the day, clearly a bear had tampered with the door. Deep, wide claw marks striated the wood. No doubt they belonged to their blond beauty, which Dr. Sands had dubbed "Aurum." Latin for "gold."

Against their acumen, the two scholars decided to bait Aurum. Within two days, Aurum rummaged near the door to the small shack while the men huddled inside, shaking with fright and excitement. Each night, Aurum left before causing any destruction.

One day while the researchers were scouting a mile from the cabin, they turned a corner in dense brush and came face to face with Aurum.

She'd been following them. Dr. Zawadzki, leading their hike, took the full brunt of the assault. Although officials on the scene wondered why Sands hadn't tried to shoot the bear—for both men carried rifles—they'd accepted his explanation that he'd frozen in terror.

The reporter quoted Dr. Sands as saying, "Dr. Zawadzki pulled his rifle on the bear, and that's when the bear attacked. I don't believe he would have attacked Jacek if he hadn't felt threatened. The rifle flew out of his hands. But I couldn't move to grab it or even raise my own. I was petrified. Frozen in awe. You can imagine how stunned I was when Aurum left me untouched."

Zane googled Dr. Jacek Zawadski's name. Why hadn't it surprised him to find several articles, written with the same philosophy as Greg's, Uncle Ted's, and the Bloomington's? Bears, capable of the same meaningless violence as humans. A view eschewed by the majority of their contemporaries.

Zane's law enforcement training prevented him from denying too many coincidences existed. But what did any of it mean? He felt like a blind man feeling his way down a wide trail, tripping and stumbling over stones and roots.

By noon, the rainstorm predicted by the National Weather Service pummeled the Anchorage bowl. Ropes of rain fell from the dark sky. Sinister black clouds obscured the peaks of the Chugach Range. Only a partial glimpse of the streaking snow off the crags materialized when the rain eased for a moment, like claw marks raked down the side of the mountains.

Zane stayed in for lunch, like his partners, and ate microwavable lasagna from the vending machine in the kitchenette. Hardly appeased, he sat back at his desk, his mind still inching its way over every detail of what he'd read that morning.

What about that sticky note he'd come across in Dr. Sands's office? Since reading it, he couldn't shake the obscure meaning. Like a stubborn leaf refusing to let go of the windshield of his truck after a rainstorm. Something about telling brothers to get more…. Get more what? What brothers? Attero nepos. Zane googled the term.

He was about to check the numerous hits, when the sliding glass doors to the vestibule slid open and two rain-soaked men hurried inside.

"We need help," the larger of the two said. They were native Alaskans. Athabascan. Perhaps Tanaina.

Suddenly, Zane recognized them. Standing at the entrance to the AST headquarters in a growing puddle of rainwater, were the Baxter brothers, the AWT's most sought after suspects in the gallbladder harvesting case.

Zane sat frozen at his desk. Col. Lund shuffled outside his office and stared at the two men. Dana, Langston, Amanda, and the others also gaped, unable to speak.

Breathing heavily, the older brother came closer. "We went to our mom's church, St. Fyodor's, before coming here. The head priest told us to turn ourselves in, to ask for help."

"All right," Zane said, his voice even. "That's what we're here for."

Karl Baxter, who Zane knew was the older of the two, dropped into a chair. He took a moment to steady his breathing.

"He's trying to kill my brother and me," he blurted. "He's crazy. Craziest Cheechacko I ever eyed. Totally nuts."

"Wait, wait," Col. Lund said. "Let's settle down. Who is doing what now?"

"First, we want guaranty you'll give us immunity."

"Immunity from what?" Col. Lund demanded.

Karl swallowed. "We got information about the gallbladder harvesting and the bears that killed all those people."

CHAPTER 24

FAST moving wiper blades pushed the pouring rain off the Escalade's windshield like a fan of mindless water. Zane and Dana, racing along the Glenn Highway, held their breaths. The siren screamed in their ears. Emergency lights flashed blurry in the downpour, bouncing off the wet blacktop of the highway. Cars, obscured by the swift sweep of water, pulled off to the sides to let them pass.

The story the Baxter brothers had recounted in the interview room at headquarters still resonated surreal in Zane's ears. Yet everything they'd said made sense. Suspicions Zane had carried for weeks suddenly had fallen into place.

The Russians train bears to ride bicycles for the circus, for goodness sakes. Dr. Sands's voice, hollow and stern, had echoed inside his head while listening to Karl narrate the horror that ensnared them.

Like he's playing fetch with a dog, Dana had said during her first experience at the bear sanctuary last week while they'd watched Dr. Sands toss a balled-up shirt for Pingaq.

Throughout their story, the Baxter brothers had insisted on immunity, refusing to go forward unless Zane promised. Despite having a difficult time digesting everything the brothers had been telling them, Zane had promised to speak with the District Attorney and ask for a reasonable deal in exchange for their help in the investigation and to testify in court, should it come to that.

"The man's crazy," Karl had uttered for the twentieth time. "Crazier than those aphrodisiac salesmen from Shanghai. Once he found out we were the ones behind the gallbladder harvesting, that's when he freaked."

"You told us everything?" Zane had demanded.

"Everything we figured out. He kept us in the dark with the details, but we knew bad things were going on. Real bad things."

Zane had jumped to his feet, knocking over his chair, after they'd ended the interview. Outside in the main room, the others had been watching on closed-circuit television. The same disbelieving expressions had marked their faces. Col. Lund, already on the phone in his office, had barked information to the Bureau of Investigations. Dana had followed Zane for the Escalade.

"Careful, Bono," Dana said, bracing her hand against the dashboard. "The rain's making everything slick. We'll get there quicker if you slow down."

Took forever to travel the thirty miles to Eagle River. RVs and trucks on the Glenn Highway posed as obstacles in a virtual game—a deadly game with unknown rules or consequences to losing.

"What's the chemical formula for crystal methamphetamine?" Zane said toward the rain-smeared windshield.

"What?"

"Do you know it?"

"CH or C something. I can't remember. Why?"

Stacked on shelves and the floor in Dr. Sands's cottage, boxes of phosphorus, iodine. Those were some of the ingredients used to make crystal methamphetamine. Could it be possible? Is that where the bears had gotten into the drug stash? The same drugs Greg had found in their systems? Had the brothers been speaking the clear-headed truth back at headquarters?

"Call the SPCA and ask them if anyone has requested any bears be buried in their cemetery in the past two months."

Dana fumbled with the satellite phone, requested the SPCA's phone number from the operator, and dialed. A minute later, she clicked off.

"They said no, no record in the past two years. You think those bears that attacked Greg and the others were—?"

"I'm unsure," Zane said, his mind whirling like the rain around the truck. "I really don't know."

The raging Eagle River gurgled with white froth to their left as Zane sped along the frost-heaved-covered road leading to the sanctuary. Minutes ticked by. They bounced along the curvy blacktop for what seemed hours. Zane switched off the emergency lights and siren. He did not want to give anyone forewarning of their arrival.

When he pulled into the parking lot, the first thing Zane noted was the missing white trailer and one of the trucks. Ducking from the rain and small hail smacking against their faces, they scurried for the cottage.

Inside, Zane checked the small office for the sticky note. Gone. He rummaged through the desk, drawers, file cabinets. Nothing added up.

"Check the habitats," he told Dana. "I'll look upstairs."

The two bedrooms lay empty, like cavernous chasms. Clearly the doctor and his assistant had been bedding together in the main bedroom. Remnants of their life together—shards of dirty laundry, toiletries, paperwork, books—scattered the floor and tabletops.

A minute later, "Bono, hurry!"

Reaching for his Glock, Zane dashed downstairs and out the door to find Dana crouching on the footpath by the closest bear habitat. Leslie's head was cradled in her arm, blood gurgling in the downpour and streaming into a drain. Deep lacerations streaked her face and arms.

"Did one of the bears escape?" Dana shouted at her above the downpour.

Unable to speak, Leslie gestured with her bloodied fingers toward a habitat. It was empty, the gate wide open.

"Darted for us like a Doberman pincher," Karl had said in the interview room back at headquarters. "Never in our lives, even when we were boys in Port Raven, have we come that close to a bear."

Karl had said Dr. Sands had stood by the gate to one of the black bear cages, had opened it like he'd wanted to step inside. He'd shouted in some strange language, and the next thing the brothers had realized, they were running from a two-hundred-pound black bear.

"The damn bear was jumping on the truck," Karl had said. "I swear. You can see the indents and claw marks for yourself. Dr. Sands ordered the bruin to come straight for us. The bear wouldn't give up until it tore us with its fangs." Luckily, the tires finally grabbed hold of the slick gravel,

Karl had said, and they took off down the road in their truck. A beige Toyota with the license plate number: XRL 547. The one he and Jasper had chased west of Knik Arm. Leslie had most likely been the driver.

Zane squatted next to Leslie's bloodied head. "Where's Dr. Sands, Leslie? Can you hear me?"

Her white and glassy eyes stared through him. "Brilliant," she muttered. "Brilliant. I told you, didn't I? Mother Teresa…."

"How many bears were in the habitat, Leslie?" Zane said. "Can you tell me? How many bears escaped?"

Zane stood with his Glock ready, realizing Leslie was minimal use to them in her condition. Dana hustled inside the cottage to call for an ambulance. Seconds later, she hurried back to Leslie's side with an armful of medical supplies she'd grabbed from inside.

"This is no good," she cried. "We have to get her into the cottage."

Zane stopped eyeballing the grounds long enough to help Dana and Leslie reach the cottage. "Take care of her best you can until the paramedics arrive. I'm going to check the back."

Eyes wide, concentration heightened, Zane ignored the sheets of cool rain when he stepped back outside. He peered from side to side, nostrils flaring. He treaded down the footpath, careful to keep his Glock poised when turning blind corners around the bear habitats. But what good would his sidearm or bulletproof vest do to ward off an attack by escaped drug-crazed bears? Or worse, Dr. Sands, certainly almost as volatile as any deranged bear, might kill him in a rage.

Could it be true?

No noise other than rain and wind and pelting hail. He neared the river, rising fast and jumping with foamy swells. No bears. No Dr. Sands. Rain washed away any signs of bear tracks or human footprints.

He came around the backside of the sanctuary toward the far habitat. Pingaq's enclosure. He peered in. No sign of the nine-hundred-pound Kodiak. It must be hiding inside its den, waiting out the storm. A prima donna, for sure. He called for it above the downpour. No response.

He cornered the front of the habitat, shrinking from the BB-sized hail that stung his cheeks, and noticed deep tire grooves in the muddy earth and leading to Pingaq's cage. The tracks gurgled with water like a roaring stream. What he observed next shook his spongy socks inside his Danners.

Pingaq's gate, like the one near Leslie, stood gaping open.

Attero nepos. He'd forgotten to follow through with his Internet search back at headquarters. Now, the Latin words flashed in his mind like bolts of lightning. Attero nepos. Even as he inched closer to Pingaq's gate, the phrase refused to leave his head. The words washed over him like the rain gushing down his face, inside his collar, along his nape and back, sending chills through his bones.

Attero nepos.

Attack? Nepos. Nephew? Attack nephew?

He froze. Latin for "attack nephew."

"Joshua?"

He closed his gaping mouth only after rainwater lodging in his throat choked him.

Coughing, he sprinted down the footpath to Dana, who was venturing outside the cottage. He nearly slipped into her.

"What's going on?" she demanded.

"Get back inside and wait for backup. I've got to get to Joshua."

"Bono, what?"

"Bolt the doors," he said. "Keep an eye out for the other bears. I have a feeling I know where I can find Pingaq and Dr. Sands."

"Pingaq? What do you mean?

"Cage door's wide open. It's missing."

"Where are you going? Zane...."

"Keep your Glock ready."

Zane rushed through the cottage and jumped inside the Escalade. Like the Baxter brothers, he had a tough go getting the tires to take hold of the wet gravel. He turned the steering wheel, pumped the gas pedal. Finding traction, he took off down the winding road and headed back for the Glenn Highway.

CHAPTER 25

DEMAND for a helicopter to land at Joshua's cabin, site of the first vicious bear mauling, was denied.

"Sorry, Bono," Jasper Bohler's voice cracked over the two-way radio. "Storm's got choppers grounded from Anchorage to Palmer."

"There may not be any other way back in there," Zane cried. "This rain's turning the highway into a torrent. The side roads have to be worse. I'll need backup."

"Sorry, nothing I can do. We'll remain on standby and continue to keep a lookout for Dr. Sands's trailer and vehicle. Ground support is on way to assist Dana at the Eagle River Sanctuary."

Zane clicked off, anger fixing on his cheeks like hot wax.

He still could not wrap his mind around the horror that flooded his head. Dr. Barry Sands, celebrated bear expert, author of several books on bear ecology, a man the AWT had sought for guidance—an egomaniacal sociopath who might be on his way to harm Joshua Gaffner.

And his prized bears, he'd manipulated into drug-enraged henchmen.

But why go after Joshua?

Might he have misconstrued that odd note written in Latin?

No, his gut told him. He had not jumped to conclusions. Dr. Sands, missing for God knew how long, orchestrated something sinister for the "nepos." The nephew. Dr. Theodore Krum's nephew. The man who'd humiliated Dr. Sands in front of hundreds of attendees at the town meeting at the University of Anchorage's Taggart Hall.

He tried to call Joshua's cell phone for the umpteenth time. Still no reception.

A minute later, he took the exit at milepost eighteen and hastened across the Alaska Railroad tracks for the turnoff to the cabin. Mud on the primitive road grabbed at the thick tires of the Escalade. Exactly as he'd feared. Almost worse than mudflats. Zane shifted gears, zigzagged to maintain control over the sturdy vehicle. He skidded, became stuck. Cursing, he slapped the steering wheel, begged for help from whatever sources availed themselves. God? Karma?

"I failed in the bush with Julie," he muttered toward the rain-streaked windshield, "don't let me fail again. Not with Joshua."

He held in a breath and tried once more. Tapping the gas pedal, he shifted to low gear, turned the wheel completely to the right, next to the left. The truck jerked, spun out. His head jerked back against the headrest. He was free.

Riding the berms to avoid the river raging down the middle of the narrowing trail, he drove steady and resolute. Sopping spruce and alder branches scratched and banged the truck and flicked the antenna. Twigs snapped in half from the sturdy truck rambling past. He peered through the rain-smacked windows for Dr. Sands and his white trailer. The same the German cabby had seen parked at the Bicentennial Park trailhead prior to Greg's death. The same trailer in which Dr. Sands had instructed the Baxter brothers to haul the bears around to different locations for him to lodge his twisted attacks against arch-nemeses in his field, the brothers had said.

Joshua. He must reach him.

ZANE parked the truck as close as possible, before the road turned into a narrow hiking trail, about one-hundred yards away from the cabin. By the time he exited the truck, the downpour had changed to a drizzle. Joshua's missing truck surprised him. Was he out running errands in such horrible weather on a road even the Escalade had nearly failed to navigate? Had he sold his truck? Had he already returned to Oregon? They hadn't spoken in nearly a week. Maybe when Joshua had last telephoned him, he'd wanted to say good-bye.

Or perhaps Dr. Sands had beaten him to the cabin and done something awful to him, and confiscated his truck to conceal his crime.

Gooey mud clutched onto his boots along the hike to the cabin, his Glock leading the way. Low level clouds churning in the gray sky made it difficult to distinguish smoke rising from the chimney, but he detected the aroma of wood burning fireplaces. Might be from any of the cabins strewn across the area. A scant light emanated from the single smeary window. Joshua had to be home. He had to be.

A blast of dry heat smacked Zane in the face and sapped the sopping wetness off his clothes when he stepped inside the cabin. Another surge of warmth welled inside him. Joshua sat at the table, chopping potatoes, carrots, and onions.

His blue eyes, shiny like shards of frosted glass, grew wide above his busy hands. "Zanebono, what on earth are you doing here?"

Zane stared, smiled. "I drove out to check on you," he said flatly, suppressing an urge to laugh out loud.

"In this storm? Check on me for what?"

"You're okay? Nothing wrong?"

"I'm fine. What's going on, Zanebono?"

Zane replaced his gun, took off his cap and Turtle Tracks, and shook off the rain. "Long story," he said. "I better have a cup of that coffee I can smell brewing on the stove first."

Seated at the table, taking intermittent sips of his steaming mug of black coffee, Zane repeated the story the Baxter brothers had told them at headquarters, including the blood results that Greg had found, along with Zane's own suspicions. All the while, Joshua listened, hands busy chopping potatoes, carrots, and onions. Not until Zane finished did Joshua show emotion.

He shook his head. "Hard to swallow everything."

"What's to understand?" Zane sipped his coffee, relishing the warmth and Joshua's wellbeing. "I'm glad you're okay. My head was spinning with worry driving over here."

"Why did you think he'd come after me, of all people?"

"I don't know. That strange note written in Latin. The connection with your uncle. Plus, you're alone out here, an easy target. By the way, where's your truck?"

"It's in Birchwood. I was in town a few days ago doing some grocery shopping and the starter conked out. I left it at the mechanic's. I figure I should have it fixed if I'm to sell it. I hiked back here along the roads carrying what perishables I could. The rest I left in the truck."

Zanebono settled a prolonged squirm after Joshua had mentioned he still intended to sell his truck. That meant he hadn't changed his plans to return to Oregon. "You missing any clothes?" he asked through tight lips.

"Like what Uncle Teddy wrote about in his journals? Hold on, let me check." He returned a minute later, standing before Zane wide-eyed. "Some of my hiking clothes are gone. You think someone broke in while I was in Birchwood? You think it was Dr. Sands or those Baxter brothers?"

"Maybe," Zane said. "I'm still piecing everything together. I'm unsure, but it appears Dr. Sands trained the bears to follow scent, like bloodhounds."

"Can bears do that?"

"They can smell a drop of blood a mile away. I'm sure they can be trained to do the job of a bloodhound."

"Remarkable," Joshua muttered.

"At least everything's calm here, nothing to worry about. I'm sure Dr. Sands decided to lay low rather than waste effort coming here with half the law enforcement agencies in Alaska hunting for him."

"Still hard to digest."

"I'll have to hang out here a while," Zane said. "The road's nearly washed out."

"Sure, that's fine."

While Joshua made dinner, Zane trekked to the outhouse. He kept his hand poised by his Glock, in case. Ground squirrels rustling in the wet duff startled him. Two or three came out from their underground hideaways to drink from the puddles left by the storm. He wanted to peck off the rodents with his semi-auto for the way they'd somersaulted his heart. Squawking above jerked his head skyward. Two golden eagles flew over the crowns of the spruce and pines toward the creek and the rainbow trout that had surely washed onto the banks from the storm.

After using the outhouse, he plodded through the mud to the Escalade, coated in sludge and ensnarled with leafy twigs. He tugged at a few twigs wedged between the wiper blades and the windshield and hopped inside the cab.

"Hello, Clarice," he said into the radio. "This is Trooper Fusca. What's going on with the Sands case?"

"Troopers have his place swarmed," the dispatcher responded. "No sign of him. There was one sighting of him in Eagle River, buying supplies at a local supermarket. Witnesses observed him get into a green or blue Suburban hauling a white trailer. No one's got a clue which direction he took off in. We've got check points on the junction of Glenn and Parks Highways, and one on the Seward Highway before the Whittier Glacier."

"They find the bears?"

"They found and euthanized one black lingering by the river they're pretty sure belonged to Dr. Sands. Based on recent records, all the other bears have been accounted for, except the Kodiak."

"Dr. Sands probably absconded with that one. Any narcotics?"

"They've confiscated some undetermined chemicals."

"Baxter brothers?"

"In jail."

"Dana and the other girl okay?"

"Dana's A-OK, still at the sanctuary. Ambulance rushed Leslie Kultas to Providence Hospital. No word on condition."

"I'm staying out here at the Krum cabin near Birchwood. Road's too impassible right now. I requested helicopter support earlier, but you can put that on hold. I'll bring the Escalade in tomorrow. Keep me posted. I'll have the Stratos with me."

"Okay, Zane."

"Over and out, Clarice."

He grabbed the battery pack for the Stratos phone from the strongbox between the front seats. No telling how many hours he might be trapped at the cabin with Joshua. Overhead, a short break of the clouds allowed a glimpse of the Chugach Range to the east. Snowfall had left the mountains white capped. Zane noted more ominous sky edging closer from the west.

He walked through the tall marsh grass and saxifrage searching for any clues a bear might have wandered by. No tracks. No scat. Everything appeared undisturbed. Hard to imagine such beauty had borne witness to the bloodshed dealt to Dr. Krum, allegedly at the hands of Dr. Sands. He noticed the darkening clouds edging closer and headed inside.

"Another storm's on the way," he said to Joshua, leaving his muddy boots by the door. "Thirty minutes, from the looks of it. We better hunker down for the night."

"We're trapped here?" Joshua said from the stove, frying hamburgers.

"We'll head out in the morning." Zane set the Stratos on the table and plugged it into the battery pack. "Got word everything's quiet thus far. No one can find Dr. Sands. Like I figured, the venerable Dr. Sands decided to high tail it out of the area instead."

"Where can someone run in Alaska? There's no state line to cross, and only one road leads into Canada."

"We've got more than a half million square miles to get lost in." Zane noted the worry lines break across Joshua's forehead. "If we don't find him trying to escape on one of the highways, we'll find his abandoned truck and trailer somewhere, and they'll lead the way to him."

"I won't be surprised if everything the Baxter brothers said about Dr. Sands winds up true," Joshua said. "I told you from the start my uncle hadn't elicited a bear attack. What happened here was no bear wandering through the forest searching for human food."

"Looks like you were right all along," Zane said. "We'll learn more once we get back into town and pump the brothers for further information. Leslie, if she pulls through, will certainly aid us. One thing confuses me, though. How did Sands know your uncle lived out here?"

Joshua turned down his mouth and gazed toward the plank floor, his hand gripped over the spatula. "Maybe they ran into each other once or twice. In Eagle River while shopping for supplies. Dr. Sands did mention he was familiar with Uncle Ted's work. He probably would've recognized him. They probably chatted, and Uncle Ted mentioned where he lived. Those academics run in tight circles."

"I found that out earlier today. Did you know Sands worked with the Bloomingtons at Thurston College in Tacoma?"

"He seems to have an association with all of the victims."

Zane shrugged. "Like I said, we'll learn more once we nab him."

"I hope they get him. I want him punished for each and every offense he's committed." Joshua knitted his brows. "Whatever they are."

"He'll get what he deserves. For now, I've worked up an appetite. Dinner about ready?"

Zane helped Joshua set the table and prep the remainder of dinner. Felt good to work side by side again. Domestic partners. Deep in the woods in their cabin. Surrounded by thousands of acres of woods. The nearest neighbor nearly a half mile. Yet the reality of their lives had scarcely altered since learning of Dr. Sands's closeted criminal lifestyle. From what Zane had gathered, Joshua still aimed to sell the cabin and truck and return to Oregon.

Zane refrained from mentioning Joshua's plans during dinner. They ate hamburger patties without buns and fried potatoes, carrots, and onions mostly in silence. Now and then, Joshua wondered aloud about the intricacies of Dr. Sands's scheme. Zane merely shrugged and speculated himself.

"At least it's over," Zane said, finishing the last bite on his plate. "By the time we get back into Anchorage tomorrow, Dr. Sands will already be behind bars, like his precious bears."

Patter on the roof indicated the next line of rainstorms had poised overhead. Joshua glanced toward the ceiling. "I'd better get some more wood and give it a chance to dry before the rain picks up. I doubt the shed will keep out the water for too much longer."

"Need some help?"

Joshua pulled on his gaiters and boots by the door. "That's okay. I've got it—"

A massive smash against the door jarred Joshua to his feet. Zane dropped a dish into the tub, splashing soapy water on his already damp clothes. He rushed to Joshua's side. Instinctively, he grabbed his arm and yanked him away from the door. Another sharp rap, this time rattling the entire cabin.

The hairs on Zane's arms and nape stood stiff. "Keep back," he shouted. "Stay clear from the door and window."

"What's going on?" Joshua cried, bracing onto Zane's bicep and cringing against another strident bash against the door.

"Keep back!"

Zane nudged Joshua backward. Joshua stumbled on his snaking bootlaces and clutched for a chair. Raising a hand for quiet, Zane peeked out the rain-streaked slider window. A head taller than the cabin itself, a Kodiak brown bear stood on its hind legs, exposing its rock-pick-sized fangs. Zane recognized the two-inch tan scar running across its snout. It was Pingaq, Dr. Sands's nine-hundred-pound princess. And it was fighting to get inside.

CHAPTER 26

ANOTHER resounding crash against the door.

"Quick, help me with the table!"

Zane and Joshua upturned the dining table, unconcerned with spilling the plates, drinking cups, or anything else on top, and slammed it flush against the door.

"Grab a hammer and nails while I hold it in place. Hurry."

Joshua scuttled through the small cabin, opening drawers and cabinets and tossing the contents to the floor until he found what Zane had requested. Zane grabbed the hammer and nails from him, held several nails in his mouth, and began hammering one, sometimes two nails at a time into the table to reinforce the door.

"Will this stop it from getting in?" Joshua asked.

"Put some of the chairs against the table," Zane murmured through stiff lips. "Add anything heavy to help strengthen the resistance."

Joshua piled chairs, small tables, boxes filled with heavy books, sixteen- and thirty-two-ounce cans of creamed corn, baked beans, stewed tomatoes, and whatever else he could pile against the door while Zane hammered. The bear pounded in retaliation. Hammered nails began to pry loose from the wall, dislodging millimeter by millimeter. Zane hammered and rehammered, his hand cramping.

"Here." Joshua handed Zane another handful of nails. "I found these in a box under the basin table."

Zane glanced at the galvanized, six-inch nails. "Thanks, these should take better hold." But for how long, Zane fretted.

Pingaq's pounding ceased right when Zane hammered the last nail. He sensed the bear had moved off to size up the cabin for another means inside.

"Help me with the mattress. Put it against the window. Quick!"

Pingaq's jug-sized muzzle rubbed against the pane as Joshua and Zane slammed the mattress against the window. Sudden darkness engulfed the cabin. For a moment, peace stole into Zane's edgy insides. But only for a millisecond. Pingaq's huffing outside intensified. Scratching came from the left side of the cabin, next from the windowless back.

While his eyes adjusted to the dimness, Zane fumbled through the cabin searching for boards, shelves, anything to fortify the barriers to the door and window. Joshua followed behind him, sensing the urgency.

Fierce growling outside the cabin set thousands of rolling pinecones down Zane's spine. If Uncle Ted hadn't been able to keep out a three-hundred-pound grizzly, how would Zane and Joshua prevent a nearly half-ton Kodiak from breaking in?

Zane grabbed for his gun belt from the floor, where it lay after they'd upset the dining table. Strapped around his waist, he pressed his hand against the Glock for security. Without any windows, he had no way of gauging the bear's whereabouts or gaining view of a target to shoot.

"I'll have to move the mattress aside a little," he told Joshua. "I need to look out. Stand back and keep quiet."

With care, Zane slid the mattress until a thin, dull strip of daylight cut across the cabin's floor. The sow backed off, roared on its hind legs, dropped to all fours and shook until its dark brown fur stood out like the quills of an angry porcupine. Water splatter struck the window in a grenade-like explosion. Unprepared, Zane fell to his haunches. He straightened himself and peeped out the window from his knees. Pingaq loped sideways, forward, lowered its snout to the ground.

Zane shouted to Joshua, "Get into the far corner. She's going to charge." He wrenched the mattress to cover the window, pressed against it with all his weight. Joshua, disregarding his command, joined him. Together they strained. Zane's stocking feet slid on the wood floor. *Remember to put boots on*, Zane made a mental note as he struggled to force his weight into the mattress.

He waited for the inevitable shatter of glass, the ensuing resistance of the mattress against their bodies. The ripping and shredding of the stuffing out of the mattress—and Zane and Joshua. Nothing came. Silence.

Zane whispered, "Step back a bit. Let me check what's going on."

They gradually released pressure against the mattress. Zane nudged the mattress inchmeal. Joshua stood back, hands clenched by his sides.

Holding his breath, Zane edged around the mattress and peered through the narrow slit. On the other side of the windowpane, Pingaq's black, glassy eye met Zane's.

Roaring vibrated the glass and the entire cabin. The bear's gaping mouth covered nearly the entire window. Zane was certain the snot- and blood-smeared glass would explode from the sow's penetrating growling. Fangs larger than Zane's fingers dripped with saliva. Its scar like a worm crawling across its snout.

Pingaq huffed, bit at the air, but slipped on the mud when it lunged for the window. Disoriented, it lumbered in a circle. To Zane's relief, Pingaq turned and bolted for the forest, disappearing under the canopy of the thick grove of pine and spruce.

"It's backed off," Zane said, permitting himself to exhale.

"For good?"

"I doubt it. Most likely it's taking shelter from the rain. Even wild animals hate a downpour."

"Should we make a run for it? Can we reach your truck?"

"And then what? If we get stuck in this rain, we'll be sitting targets. The Escalade is covered with windows. The drug dealer who used to own it had the windows bulletproofed, but I doubt he had it bear proofed."

"We're trapped in here like rats, is that what you're saying?"

"More like mice."

Zane scoured the cabin. Locating the satellite phone in the corner where it crashed from their turning over the table, he dashed to retrieve it. He waited for the usual humming. He shook it, held it to his ear. Dead.

"Dammit," he grunted. "Must've busted when it fell to the floor." They shouldn't have upended the table before clearing it, he reproached himself.

Joshua peered over his shoulder. "Let me have a look."

"Are you any good with electronics?"

Joshua took the phone from Zane's hands. "I'm not too mechanical. I'm better with carpentry. But maybe I have some kind of magical touch."

Zane wanted to say, "You sure do," recalling their times making love, but now was not the time. Would another opportunity come?

"See what you can do," Zane said. "I'm going to keep an eye on that beast. I'll crack the window. Maybe I'll get a shot at it."

"You're going to kill it?"

"What would you rather I do, dance with it? The number one issue is to get out of here alive, wouldn't you say?"

Joshua turned back to fiddle with the satellite phone, his downcast eyes full of despair.

From the narrow opening in the window, Zane scanned the outside, the patter of heavy rain filling his ears. The rain-streaked window revealed a sopping wet boreal forest. In the small meadow, the downpour flattened the saxifrage and grass. Nothing four-legged appeared to move over the spongy turf.

Reassuring himself that his sidearm was still holstered against his hip, he wedged his body a few inches between the mattress and window. He stretched his arm along the windowpane, the coolness of the glass penetrating his brown shirt. He walked his fingers to the fastener until he could get a decent hold. Undeterred, he unsnapped the latch. Careful to avoid making too much noise, he slid the window open piecemeal until a rush of coolness and a strong stench of urine mixed with rain-soaked boreal forest battered his face. He squinted, shielded his eyes from the stinging rain.

He wanted to call for the bear, to entice it out of its hiding. He glanced down at his Glock, barely able to make out its shape in the murky shadow of the mattress. Even if he could get a good shot, how might mere bullets stave off an attack by a massive brownie?

The bullets might spur it to more aggression, like he'd witnessed dozens of times in the past.

He eased the window shut, slid out from behind the mattress, and pressed it more firmly against the window. Shaking the water droplets from his hand, he eyed Joshua, still tinkering with the radio. "Do you have any lanterns?"

Joshua kept his eyes focused on his task. "A few, but they're empty."

"You don't have any extra fuel?"

"I didn't buy any because it's always light outside. I didn't want to bother with the expense."

"I'll build up the fire in the stove," Zane said. "I'll keep the firebox open. Might give us some more light in here."

Several minutes later, Zane had stoked the fire to a full blaze, filling the cabin with a comforting, oscillating glow. Proud of his small accomplishment, Zane stared at the firebox burning bright orange. Thermal waves distorted the wall behind the stove.

The tiny cabin heated in no time. Zane stripped off his brown shirt, leaving on his white T-shirt. Joshua watched him, frowned.

"Sounds like the rain's letting up," he said. "Maybe we can drive out of here."

"Maybe not so good," Zane said. "The bear's been avoiding the rain. It might venture back out from hiding once the rain stops. Rain's probably what's kept it from tearing this place apart already. Remember, bears can reach speeds of about forty miles per hour. Even if we could guarantee the truck will make it out of here, we might not make it to the truck before the bear makes it to us."

"Do you think this is the same horrible situation Uncle Ted found himself in?"

Zane suppressed a cringe, recollecting the details of the attack scene after he, Dana, Greg, and Jasper had descended in the helicopter. How long had the grizzly stalked and terrorized Uncle Ted before it ripped Uncle Ted and the cabin to shreds? Zane needed to calm Joshua. "From what I'd pieced together from the scene," he said, "I'd say he didn't have any idea what hit him." Lying, in this case, seemed the better choice.

Joshua rested his hands atop the satellite phone and sighed. "I can't fix this stupid thing. Something's wrong with the components. It won't matter much anyway. It's a satellite phone, and stuck inside with this storm we probably won't get any—"

A massive slam against the door shook the cabin, followed by fierce growling and huffing. Joshua, jumping to his feet, dropped the Stratos to the floor, spilling out more of its innards. The cabin shook and screeched, like a scream from arthritic pain.

"Not again," Joshua bellowed.

More chewing, biting, clawing. The table buttress quivered and rattled. Top nails loosened. Zane sprinted for the door. He grabbed for the hammer and began pounding in the loosened nails. The smashing stopped. Zane persevered with his hammering until a sudden, heavy stomping from above froze his hand in midmotion.

"It's on the roof," Joshua shouted. "It's on the roof!"

The old cabin creaked and shimmied under the weight of the nearly one-thousand-pound Kodiak. Sounded like two large men in army boots jumping up and down. A pounding that made the earlier downpour nothing more than a brushing of tree limbs on the roof.

The chimney pipe began to shake. Zane hurried for the stove, hammer gripped in hand, and peered along the aluminum pipe to the ceiling. A slight gap between the pipe and roof revealed the dark behemoth roving back and forth. The pipe rattled, gyrated, and screeched.

"I must've agitated the bear when I was fussing with the stove," Zane said. "If that bear's under the influence, any noise might set it off. I should've realized."

"Not your fault," Joshua hollered above the roaring. "Watch it! He's trying to pull out the pipe."

Zane dropped the hammer and grabbed hold of the searing hot stovepipe. His flesh sounded like frying bacon. He screamed in pain, but held tight.

Wood shavings from the ceiling fell like rain onto Zane's face. Joshua hurried over to help. Zane raised his leg to keep him back. He did not want Joshua to burn himself on the hot pipe.

"Grab me some rags, my shirt, anything, and dip them in the tub of dishwater."

Joshua scooped up Zane's shirt and what other fabric he could find scattered about the cabin and soaked them in the water before helping

Zane wrap his hands with them. With the added shield, Zane grasped the blistering hot pipe more firmly.

Pingaq yanked hard from the roof. Shredded insulation floated down like snow. Smoke billowed in from the fist-sized gash in the pipe.

"Douse the fire," Zane hollered. "We'll asphyxiate."

Coughing, Joshua tossed what water was left in the tub into the stove's firebox. Wood hissed like a thousand snakes. Steam and smoke choked the cabin.

Sudden silence. Only the drumming beat of a driving rain on the roof.

Zane released the stovepipe and scrambled between the mattress and the window. Pingaq loped back for the safety of the trees. Zane shook the damp garments from his hands and wrenched open the slider. His right palm, rigid like melted plastic coated the skin, stung against the receiver to his Glock. Stiff fingered, he fired ten rounds, until the magazine emptied. He was certain at least three had hit the bear, one possibly in its neck. It had shaken off the bullets like falling pine needles.

"It's retreated back into the woods," he said, stepping out from behind the mattress and breathing heavily. "I hit it, but it didn't do any good. Let's get this place aired out while we got a chance."

Zane holstered his Glock, and he and Joshua pulled aside the mattress. Zane slid the window fully open, stopping a moment only when a strident screech surpassed the pulsating rain, and continued until enough smoke, accentuated by the flood of daylight, escaped outside. Once the cabin aired sufficiently, Zane inched the window shut and slid the mattress back into place. He leaned against the mattress, dropped to his haunches, dangled his pulsating hands between his legs.

Joshua balanced in a squat in front of him. "You're injured. Your hands."

Zane examined his palms for the first time. Red inflammations had already broken out. Sticky yellow pus gelled over the blisters. With the adrenaline rush subsiding, the biting sting began to creep into his consciousness.

"It's not too bad," he lied. "Maybe second-degree burns."

Kneeling before him, Joshua held his hands, inspected them. His solicitous touch sent a warm shiver along Zane's spine. He wanted to hold him, stroke his stubble-coated cheek. If only the pain in his hands had been swept out the window along with most of the smoke.

"It's far worse than a second-degree burn," Joshua said. "They might get infected. You need help."

He rushed to the back of the cabin and returned with a first aid kit. Zane relished the sudden cool relief of the ointment Joshua applied over his palms. But the reprieve was short lived. Within minutes, the burning broke through again, traveling along his palms and into his fingertips and halfway up his arms.

"We've got to get out of here," Joshua murmured, wrapping gauze around each of Zane's hands.

Zane locked onto his blue eyes. "We'll be okay," he said. "That bear can't last like this forever. Eventually, it's going to either die or pass out. And then we can radio for help from the truck."

"How long will that take?" Joshua said. "If what you and the Baxter brothers say is true, and Dr. Sands injected his bears with all those drugs, it might last through the night. I've seen what those kinds of drugs can do to people back in Portland. They party all night, into the morning, and can't sleep for days. I broke up with my boyfriend because of such antics."

Zane winced from Joshua's bandaging. "Give me enough room to move my fingers, will you?" He flexed his hands, sucked in another wince. He must be strong for Joshua, for both of them. He needed to convey resolute strength.

Joshua pivoted against the mattress beside him. "Maybe we should burn down the cabin and escape when the bear gets distracted by the flames. I haven't officially sold it yet. Uncle Ted wasn't insured, but it won't matter."

"A bit extreme."

"Any other solutions?"

No, Zane realized. He harbored no other way out.

Resting his head against the mattress, Zane gazed heavenward. Remnants of foul smoke rubbed against the ceiling. Surreal swirling movement of empty space.

Spazio vuoto, he recalled the term in Italian.

Zane had made a situation worse once before when he'd tried to rescue Julie seven years ago. Failure had reared itself like a crevice in the earth, pulling Zane and his entire world down with him.

Gazing at his bandaged hands, he feared he might fall short again.

CHAPTER 27

SILENCE cut into the cabin like vaporous claws, save for the rain and the constant drip of water in the pot they'd placed under the gash in the roof. Every nook and crevice held in an anxious breath. Suffocating quiet left the hairs on Zane's arms erect. Most of the smoke had settled, leaving only the pungent smell of damp, smoldering firewood. Difficult to judge the passing of time from the murkiness inside the cabin. Zane's wristwatch showed quarter past five in the afternoon. The bear had held them captive for three hours.

He glanced outside the small gap between the mattress and windowpane, the twentieth time in the past half hour. Gray, swirling clouds concealed the sun. Rain fell heavily now. All afternoon it had come and gone, heavy at times, light at others. Intermittent hail had broken the monotony of relentless drumming with high-pitched pattering. The grassy meadow, matted and motionless, concealed no crouching bear. The forest revealed no secrets.

Zane's last glimpse of it was about forty-five minutes ago. Pingaq had lumbered out of the forest, stood in the meadow like a statue for a good five minutes, eyeing the cabin. Then a sudden hail storm had pummeled from the sky. Pingaq had bit at the frozen raindrops like a madwoman, roared, and bolted for the protection of the forest.

The Escalade's pull grew almost painful. What if they failed to make it to the truck? And even if they did make it, what if the muddy river masquerading as a road hindered any escape? Then what? The sow would have them trapped inside a prison smaller and more perilous than the one they were already in. They'd be sitting ducks. The bear's next meal. Steak tartare.

Each time Zane had reached behind the upturned mattress for the window latch, unable to hold back, visions of the sow's fangs and claws had stood in his way. Any movement might release the bear's drug-crazed fury. The slightest vibration and it might come barreling out of the forest, roaring and charging. Best they lay low, wait and see.

Zane gazed at the dripping landscape. Exhausted from the marathon of worries racing through his mind, he leaned against the side of the mattress. Something should make a sound. A foraging rodent, a creaking tree, the howl of the wind. Other than the patter of rain, the boreal forest remained encased in painful stillness. As if woodland creatures cowered from the marauding bear.

Coarse brushing distracted him. He turned. Joshua was sweeping the floor again. He'd already straightened most of the cabin, stacked what items he could in front of the door or window for reinforcement. His slow movements and drooping face had revealed how futile the effort was. He'd right-sided boxes and useless lanterns, mopped black water from around the stove, striving to do something normal, any household chore on a typical summer afternoon.

Zane studied him, troubled by his waning spirits. They hadn't spoken to one another in more than an hour, other than, "Do you want more pretzels?" Fretful lines pulled down the sides of Joshua's normally firm, strong mouth. Luster in his eyes had diminished to a dull matted hollowness. His bangs, streaked with dust and soot, clustered over his brooding forehead like tangled cobwebs.

The sweeping sound stopped. Joshua clutched the broom, leaned against it. Across the room, Zane continued to stare at him, speechless.

"Do you want something more to eat?" Joshua asked without meeting his eyes.

Zane waited to answer. Had Joshua expected a response? Did he speak merely to fill the agonizing void, like the other times in the past few hours?

"No," Zane said finally, facing back out the window. "I'm good."

Scratching again. Through the small partition of windowpane, Zane watched Joshua glide the broom over the wood floor. He hovered near the stove, the broom reaching far under the black iron, over the same areas, again and again. Turning, Zane went to him. He grasped the broom, held it stationary. Joshua still refrained from meeting his eyes. Did he blame Zane for all the troubles that had befallen them?

"Why don't you rest a while," Zane whispered, wanting to reassure Joshua in some way. "You're more fidgety than a rat."

Joshua lifted his blue eyes, peered unmoved at Zane. "You mean a mouse."

He released his grip on the broom and returned to his former position, seated on the floor against the wall, his face buried in the crook of his arm. Zane leaned the broom in a corner and placed his hand on Joshua's shoulder.

"I'm sorry for everything."

"Not your fault," Joshua said into his arm, his voice faraway and murky, like salvation. "I'm tired of waiting." He revealed his red eyes. "Isn't there something we can do?"

"I keep wanting to race to the truck," Zane muttered, "but I fear I might make things worse, whether I leave you here stuck in the cabin or if you come with me." Indecision burrowed into his skin like maggots.

Joshua flashed Zane hopeful eyes. "Maybe the bear's dead. Maybe when you shot it, you fatally wounded it, and it's lying dead among the trees, and we're worrying for nothing?"

Zane shook his head. He wanted to buoy Joshua's hopes, but reality obscured shallow deception. A few shots from his semi-automatic had not brought down the nine-hundred-pound brown bear. Zane had witnessed bears—even blacks—survive five, sometimes ten, bullets. Slugs as old as Zane's son, Mikey, had been pulled from bear carcasses during necropsies. Some had lived years with bullets lodged in the thickness of their skulls. He recalled stumbling upon Uncle Ted's bloodied cabin. The grizzly that had killed him survived for hours after Uncle Ted had blown off half its muzzle.

"I didn't get a good enough shot," he said, dejected. "If anything, it's more agitated. Besides, if it's going to drop dead, it would have soon after I hit it." He swallowed, and said with reservation, "I saw it roaming around about an hour ago."

He glanced into a corner, where he'd placed Uncle Ted's Remington rifle, the one that had survived the grizzly attack a month earlier, loaded with the three bullets he'd found. Even those would do little to harm the sow, he speculated.

They had enough provisions to last a week. If Zane failed to show for work, someone would come looking for them. He'd briefed Clarice on his whereabouts. But for how long would Pingaq remain quiet?

"Best thing to do is to stay calm, sit and wait, as quiet as possible," he uttered. "We'll figure a way out of this."

"Let's try our cell phones again," Joshua said. "Last time I got one bar for a split second. Maybe I can hold it longer and reach 911." He turned on his cell, waved it around from his seated position on the floor, trying to gain a signal. His face falling, he clicked off the phone and shoved it back inside his jeans pocket. "Nothing," he groaned.

"I'll tinker with the Stratos." Zane moved to a chair by the door where he'd set the satellite phone the last time he'd tried to fix it. Off and on the past three hours, he and Joshua had taken turns fiddling with the phone, to no avail. But even if they got it working, they still had to find open sky to transmit.

His bandaged hands made tinkering with the phone difficult. The raw pain had ebbed to a dull ache, like a bad sunburn. If he stretched his palms, the pain lessened. Of course, that made doing almost anything impossible.

He peeled back the gauze and cringed from the sight. The red blisters had transformed into purple sores encircled by black crusts. He did not show Joshua. The man had enough to worry over.

Again the Escalade summoned him. Inside the cab, a two-way radio waited, untouched.

"I'm getting cold," Joshua said, hugging himself. "How about you?"

"We can't make a fire because of the stovepipe," Zane said. "We'll asphyxiate. It would be nice to have some more light, though."

The darkness Joshua had craved, Zane mused. But not quite under such circumstances.

"Wait." Joshua jumped to his feet. "I remember Uncle Teddy storing candles in one of these boxes."

"Okay, but be quiet," Zane warned. "Try not to attract the bear's attention."

Joshua rummaged through several boxes, using whispery movements. "A lot was destroyed in the attack," he said. Then with a triumphant smile, he brandished two small votive candles. He placed them on the stove and lit them. The small flames flickered, grew in strength. Two small rounded swaths of light oscillating against the dank walls. Joshua carried one to his spot on the floor and set it by his feet.

For a short time, the diminutive candles provided the only means of comfort. Zane glared at the pieces of the phone. Another puzzle to figure. At least the gallbladder harvesting mystery had ended, Zane considered while toying with the Stratos. The Baxter brothers had admitted to the killing, on condition of immunity. Most likely they'd receive a sentence similar to those who killed bears outside of hunting season. A weekend in a motel listening to lectures and watching films on how to respect bears. A small price to pay for the needless killing of bears for their organs. Considering the Baxter brothers' usefulness in ending Dr. Sands's rampage, a worthy price.

After a while, Zane ditched the satellite phone and slid alongside Joshua and the candle. Zane studied his Danners, the mud crusted and flaking, much like his soul.

"Why would he do it?" Joshua said, pressing his head against the wall. "What would make a man do such a thing?"

Sighing, Zane cupped his bandaged hands across his bent knees. He remembered what his good friend and colleague Greg Gomez had once said. "Beliefs shouldn't be idolized." Those words pierced him now.

"Religion," he spat.

Joshua gaped at him. "Religion?"

"Dr. Sands's obsession with bears transformed into a religion—a cult," Zane said, stating aloud for the first time what he'd theorized for quite some time. "He worships bears like gods. He's become a zealous nut, a crazed follower of his own philosophy. Remember what you said about how man started off worshiping animals, and here we are, thousands of years later, doing the same thing?"

"But why would a man who loves bears risk their lives?"

Zane gazed at the wood floor. Hard to imagine harboring enough passion about something that a person might choose murder. "I guess once a person's ideology and identity merges," he said, "that's when he turns into a radical. The slightest criticism of his beliefs, and in his twisted mind, he believes you're challenging his existence. Self-preservation is never debatable."

"I never imagined an educated, accomplished man like Dr. Sands resorting to such madness," Joshua said. "I took him for a stodgy eccentric, but to go to such extremes?"

"I think Dr. Sands first got the idea for his plan when he'd gone searching for grizzlies in Washington State with his old colleague Dr. Zawadzki," Zane said. "He'd witnessed firsthand how quickly bears learn, and how vicious they could be, making the smartest and deadliest hound no more intelligent or intimidating than a scarecrow."

"Why inject the bears with cocaine, meth, and steroids?"

"Who knows? To make them murderous like him. So that they'd do his dirty work for him."

"Such a wasted life," Joshua muttered, shaking his head.

"Dr. Sands has helped our department with many cases," Zane conceded. "At some point, somewhere in his mind, his research became about more than preservation of bears—Sands was saving himself."

"You sound like you've experienced this kind of behavior before."

Zane straightened his legs to release more blood flow. "Not near as fanatical as Dr. Sands, but many share his sentiments. I see it even within the AWT."

"Dr. Sands murdered Uncle Ted"—Joshua lowered his eyes—"and the others, merely because they'd disagreed on a few issues, despite their shared love for bears. Makes me sick to my stomach."

They remained in silent rumination, the full weight of Dr. Sands's deeds hitting Zane—and certainly Joshua—for the first time. Dr. Sands's bear assassins, Zane mulled. And one stalked them from the woods, hankering to get at him and Joshua.

"Where do you suppose Dr. Sands is right now?"

"Maybe authorities have already caught him and we'll be rescued soon."

Joshua's somber expression proved he did not fall for Zane's desperate stab at hope. "I almost feel sorry for the bears," Joshua said under his breath. "It's not their fault. Even the one that killed Uncle Teddy."

"No, I suppose not."

Joshua laid his hand on Zane's thigh. "You're willing to forgive the bears. Why not yourself?"

"What do you mean?"

"Tell me about your ex-wife," Joshua said. "What have you been beating yourself up over for all these years?"

Zane pressed his chin against his chest. "You have to ask me that now?"

"You blame yourself for Julie's accident. Why, Zanebono? What happened when you lived out in the bush?"

Like a river overflowing with muddy water, the recollection of his stint in the bush overcame Zane. He grasped firmly onto his legs, despite the ache underneath his bandages. Did he truly wish to travel back to that time? Where mounds of accumulated misery lurked?

He'd navigate clear of those sour memories at least a dozen times a week. They'd taunt him until he'd either dismiss them with police work or face them head on and allow the shards to grind into his brain. Almost seven years ago to the day. The catastrophe that had shattered his and Julie's hopes and dreams.

Joshua remained still. He'd brought his hand back into his lap. Waiting. Perhaps Zane should tell him everything that had transpired in the bush. Maybe then Joshua would return to Portland, realizing he'd left behind a man with little to offer him but misfortune and uncertainty, and he'd escape the residual guilt for his sudden exit.

He eyed the votive candle on the floor between them, mesmerized by the flame's simplistic stoicism. A mere flame, one miniscule, vertical, raindrop-sized conflagration. Yet he could start a forest fire with it, if he chose to, on a less rainy day.

Mustering strength from that one aspiring flame, Zane settled against the wall, journeyed back to June 20, 2004, ten months after he, Julie, and baby Michael had landed in the bush, north of Denali National Park.

He recalled the brilliant sunshine beating down on the cabin. They were enjoying the endless hours of daylight, trapped on the other side of the Alaska Range throughout winter, like a beach ball caught in a gutter. Even two-year-old Mikey had awakened to the unabashed sunshine. His first unaided footsteps had taken place across their dusty cabin floor the day the sun lifted fully above the mountains, drenching the snow-dappled valley in a blaze of lavender and orange.

Julie had been particularly headstrong. She wanted to fish at the nearby pond they'd dubbed "Fusca's Pond," now that she had warm sunshine to sit under. "I'm sick of eating moose and caribou," she complained.

Zane stayed behind, wanting instead to fix the cabin's roof from a pesky leak and to ensure their cache hadn't weakened from a freak early summer snowstorm. A foot had fallen in central Alaska four days prior. He encouraged her to stay closer to the pond's shoreline. "There's still some ice on the pond," he warned. "Keep clear of any flowing water."

"I know, I know," Julie grunted.

Snowshoes fastened to her mukluks, she traipsed down to Fusca's Pond, fishing pole, bucket of bait, and auger in hand. High atop the cache, Zane watched her stomp through the remaining snowfields, alight with late morning sun. They'd already worn a path between the cabin and the pond from chopping ice and drilling for water throughout winter and spring. Zane began to drool for the succulent grayling he imagined she'd catch.

He lost sight of her once she descended the small hill covered with dwarf spruce. An hour later, Zane, cold and shivering, climbed down the cache ladder. He realized he'd better check on Mikey, asleep inside the cabin. The toddler had collapsed, exhausted after a morning of copious frolicking. Zane hadn't recalled laughing so much with his young son that his ribs hurt.

He was gazing down on the sleeping Mikey, in the midst of pulling the woolen blanket closer to his soft chin, when a horrendous shriek stopped his heart. Another cry, an ear-splitting guttural bellow. He ran from the cabin.

More strident crying out. He raced over the hill toward the pond, slipping on the sun-smoothed snowfields. A dwarf spruce stopped his slide. He shook himself, leaped to his feet, scanned for the source of the horrific screaming.

Julie's fishing gear lay toppled about ten yards from the pond's shore, near the termination of the surface ice. He tried in vain to locate the source of the shrieking. Not until he cleared the spruce trees did the surreal sight along the shore meet his gaping and burning eyes.

Julie was kicking and squirming beneath an adult Alces alces. The moose was stomping her to death. Julie's stinging cries stirred Zane. He reached the attack scene right when the moose head butted Julie with its full weight. She somersaulted at least six feet into the air and landed on her back. Her slick parka slid her on the icy area of the pond near to the center. She lay motionless. A bone-chilling splintering sound echoed through Zane's head.

"Julie!"

Zane chased the moose off, but it remained near the pond, grunting and squealing. It was then Zane noticed a calf shaking by an alder bush, calling for its mother. The cow must've perceived Julie as a threat to its suckling and had attacked in a protective rage. Scorning the moose, Zane hurried to reach Julie before the frail ice broke and released her into the life-sucking, frigid water.

Laying spread eagle on his belly to distribute his weight, he pulled himself across the surface. "I'm coming, Julie," he reassured her in a whisper, terrified the slightest noise might break the thinning ice. "I'm coming."

But she lay frozen. Not even her chest appeared to rise with breath. The ice creaked. He felt a rip race under him. Closer to Julie, water gurgled under the thin ice.

He inched closer, holding in his breath until his sides ached. Two feet away, he reached for her. With his hand on an exposed section of her neck, he checked for a pulse. Relief raised his spirits. A gentle thump drummed against his fingertips. He had no choice but to pull her away, even if he worsened what injuries the moose cow might have inflicted on her.

Slowly he pulled her back, inch by inch, holding his breath. Her bloodied head left a red streak over the ice where he'd dragged her to the shore. Right when he gathered her in his arms, the fragile ice collapsed, and muddy pond water gurgled over the thin sheets. Unable to fret over doing her more harm, he raced for the cabin, slipping and sliding. Mikey was crying when he stormed inside. He scurried to undress Julie, checked for injuries, stopped the bleeding as best he could. Their remedial first aid kit, even with its suturing gear, would not save her. She needed help.

He secured Mikey in swaddling and fabricated a makeshift crib on the floor to prevent his wandering off. "Our lives are over," he muttered, tears searing his face, while he upturned the dining table and tied blankets between the legs and nudged Mikey's spill-proof drink cup into the crook of his arm. "I've ruined everything. Our lives are over."

With tears chilling his cheeks, he raced toward the western horizon, toward Kalida, the closest village with a year-round population. When he arrived four hours later, panting and heaving, the villagers surrounded the man wearing a blood-drenched down jacket in bewilderment. Struggling for breath, he begged for help and collapsed.

He awoke to the sound of a helicopter landing in the village center. Alaska Search and Rescue had arrived to take Zane back to the cabin. When they reached the cabin, Zane and the two officers found Mikey asleep next to Julie. Somehow, he'd wiggled out of the tight swaddling, climbed out of the makeshift crib, and scaled the bed to snuggle beside his mother. Julie was still unconscious. Rescuers, surprised she'd survived, rushed to save her.

During the helicopter ride to the hospital in Fairbanks, an SAR medic expressed shock Zane hadn't even an HF radio at his cabin. Red-faced, Zane realized how naïve they'd been, venturing into Alaska's rugged wilderness. Mere children playing a deadly game in the woods. Their surviving winter had been a fluke.

"I would've done the same thing," Julie murmured two days later from the hospital in Anchorage, where another helicopter had transported her from Fairbanks for what would be a total of eighteen hours of surgeries. "If a moose had gotten between me and Mikey, I'd have kicked and stomped too." She tried to flutter a laugh, but she barely summoned enough strength to speak.

Zane anguished by her side for days while doctors and nurses at Holy Cross safeguarded her condition. He squeezed every ounce of hope inside himself that she'd regain use of her legs and arms. Neurologists were less optimistic. "Her cervical spine fractured in two places, Mr. Fusca," they told him. "People with broken necks don't walk."

"Is it possible I might have made her condition worse when I carried her back to the cabin?" Zane later asked one of the doctors outside Julie's hospital room, his voice low and shaky.

"Of course, Mr. Fusca," the doctor said, matter-of-factly. "Anything might have caused the final snap. We'll never know."

The worst part was facing Julie's parents. His in-laws had traveled from Rhode Island to assist their daughter and grandson before the helicopter from Fairbanks had even landed at Holy Cross, but not without interspersing their tender loving care for Julie and Mikey with harsh words for Zane.

"You idiot," Mr. and Mrs. Gagliardi shouted at him time and again whenever alone with him. "You headstrong, idealistic idiot. Look what you've done. Look… what… you've… done!"

"You actually saved my life, Zane. I could've died from hypothermia," Julie said while he watched her during one of her physical therapy sessions. He was grateful she had regained partial use of her arms and upper body a mere month after the accident. "Look on the bright side. Thank God I didn't have Mikey strapped to my back," she said, huffing while cranking the arm ergometer. "That moose would've killed him instantly."

Zane cringed, recalling the same horrible scenario many times. How close had she come to taking baby Michael fishing with her, as she was apt to do? She and Mikey had become fastened at the hip out in the bush.

"That's why you joined the troopers, Zane," Julie said about a year later in her new subsidized apartment on Fifth Avenue, two months after their divorce finalized. "You couldn't control what happened to me out in the wilderness. You want to save everyone and everything else. It's your way of sacrificing yourself."

That word again. Sacrifice. Dana had once referred to him as a "sacrificial lamb." Is that how Zane viewed himself? Is that what defined a man, how much he sacrificed his life for others?

"It's somehow your strange way of seeking absolution for what happened," Julie said three years ago while they dined together for the first time in more than a year, eager to show off her new electric wheelchair. "But you were never to blame to begin with. Things happen, completely out of our control to change the course. That's how life is."

Zane held back from chronicling for Joshua what took place at the hospital and afterward. Too much emotion to put into words. Too embarrassing to reveal. He guarded those nasty feelings for himself. Somehow, Joshua had added two and two.

"The SAR medic was wrong, Zanebono. Nothing we do in life guarantees us security or safety. Or even love. You did what you wanted. You moved into the bush. For almost a year. You couldn't control what some crazy moose did. You can't even control what some crazy bear does." His voice fell hollow and empty. "There's no comparing you to a man like Dr. Sands, Zanebono. Dr. Sands wanted to control everything, manipulate the entire world for his own ego, all while condemning mankind for the same things he was doing. You're not like that."

Zane exhaled, releasing seven years of anguish. "But the worst part is living with guilt for not being around to help Julie. Even though it was her idea for a divorce, I still feel responsible for her care."

"Because that's the kind of man you are," Joshua said. "You've done nothing dishonorable."

"I haven't?"

"Your strength, your masculinity, your nurturing nature. That's what attracted me to you."

Zane dropped his head to his knees. "I can't even get us out of this cabin."

"If you hadn't raced here to be by my side, I'd be alone right now, scared out of my mind," Joshua said. "You saw those other bodies, the ones attacked by Dr. Sands's bears. You saw how that grizzly had torn through the door. You're the one who rebuilt it. It's ten times sturdier because of you. I'd probably be dead now if not for you."

Zanebono allowed the tingly warmth of Joshua's words to flow through him. He gazed into his baby blues, allowed a tight smile to grace his lips. But shouldn't Zane be reassuring him? Without holding back this time, he swept the mussed bangs from Joshua's forehead, unconcerned about the throbbing in his hand.

"I've missed you a lot," he said.

Joshua inched his hand toward Zane. "I've missed you too."

Zane let his hand fall between his bent legs. "Does missing each other mean anything?" he said, scrutinizing the light three-day-old beard around Joshua's jaw line. "Do… do you still plan on leaving for Portland?"

Joshua stood and wandered to the defunct stove, where the second votive candle struggled in the draft coming out of the hole in the roof. Nearby, on the one small stool they hadn't used as a barricade, he touched with his fingertips Uncle Ted's journals he'd organized earlier in a neat stack, as if wanting solace from them. Facing Zanebono, he said, "I should go back. I left things up in the air. My family often treats me the same way they did Uncle Ted, but… I have responsibilities."

"I understand," Zane said. "Sometimes we have to return home, for whatever reasons." Like spawning salmon, he almost said aloud.

"Have you ever considered moving back to Rhode Island," Joshua said. "To be nearer your son?"

"I'd make things worse. What would I do there? Hard to imagine leaving Alaska behind. Sad as it sounds, I barely know Mikey."

Zane stood and peered out the small opening of the window. The sky was clearing to the west. The rain would ease in about fifteen minutes. If he was going to make a move, he'd have to soon. No more dillydallying. How much longer could either of them stay penned inside the cabin without water or heat?

In the far end of the visible woods, Pingaq skirted the marsh, headed out of sight behind the cabin. Zane suppressed a shudder. The first sign of the sow in an hour. Zane realized Joshua hadn't seen it. He withheld mentioning anything. He'd only panic, make too much noise. Cause the restless bear to charge. He blocked the window opening with his body.

"We better stay still and keep away from the window," he said. "We don't want to draw the bear's attention. Let's go sit down."

"How are your hands?" Joshua asked once they settled back in their spots on the floor.

Zane relished the soothing touch when Joshua gently lifted his hands and examined them. "They're doing okay," he whispered.

Flushing, Joshua sighed and shrugged. "I wish we could build the fire. I sure could use some coffee."

"I'll buy you a steaming sixteen-ounce mug from Bad Ass once we're out of here."

"You think we'll make it?"

Zane chuckled. "You say that like we're standing at death's doorstep."

"Feels like we are."

No sooner had Zane mentioned death's doorstep, when a sharp ruckus jolted them. Alert, Zane jumped to his feet and peered around, gauging the direction of the clamor.

"Sounds like Pingaq's tearing down the outhouse," Zane said, cocking his head toward the back wall of the cabin, where the outhouse stood, fifty yards away in a small dell. "Maybe it'll unleash all that drug-induced rage."

Joshua vaulted off the floor and clutched onto Zane's arm. "Let's leave now. Let's go."

"I'm not letting you risk going out there." Zane softened his voice. "You're still safer inside here. You stay behind and I'll go."

"It's me it wants. It's zeroing in on my scent, not yours."

"At this point, that bear won't care which one of us it gets a hold of. I need to reach the radio. Enough time to place a distress call. Then I'll be back."

Smashing and splintering wood continued to reverberate outside while Zane rushed to get into his boots, shirt, and vest. Too many items were stacked against the door. He judged the window a simpler way out.

"I have to get going now if I'm to do this," he said. "Make sure you shut the window quietly after I leave, and push the mattress back into place. Remember, stay clear of the door and window while I'm gone. Hold onto Uncle Ted's Remington and use it if you have to. It's loaded with three bullets. Cock, aim, and pull the trigger. That simple."

"How do I let you back in?"

"Keep the mattress ajar and watch out for the bear. If it comes before I reach the house, do what your gut tells you. Don't let me in if it means compromising your own safety. If the cabin goes, run a straight line for the sturdiest and tallest tree and scale it like you've never done before. Pingaq is too heavy to climb a tree. Now I have to go."

Zane held Joshua firm by the shoulders, making sure to keep them both from shaking. Together, they tightened their arms around each other. Zane kissed Joshua, full on the mouth, warm and comforting like the heat from a wood burning stove. A prolonged, penetrating kiss.

The kind of kiss a soldier gives to his beloved before heading off to war.

Without another word, Zane slid the window open enough for his body to slide through. Before bringing his left leg completely outside, he smiled at Joshua, gave him a wobbly thumbs up, and crept toward the truck parked one hundred yards away.

CHAPTER 28

MUD sucked at his boots. Each slurping sound hit Zane's ears like the roaring of a jet engine. He could still hear Pingaq mangling the outhouse. How much longer did it need? The outhouse was only so big. Keep steady. Focus ahead. Eyes wide. Inhale. The truck beckoned. Ninety yards, eighty-five yards, eighty yards….

Drizzle tickled his nose. He suppressed the urge to scratch. Steady. Keep walking. Hand poised by sidearm. Ignore the itching. Ignore the slurping. He hesitated a second to check the wind. He sensed it came from his back. Good. The outhouse was on the other side of the cabin, downwind from the bear's supersensitive sense of smell.

Splintering wood reverberated throughout the forest. Breathe. Quick and easy. Sixty yards, fifty-five….

Zane's mind balanced between failure and an incessant drive to persevere. He refused to allow any harm come to Joshua the way he had with Julie. His future with Joshua also weighed in the balance. But even if today might be their last together, he must save him. For both their sakes.

Forty-five yards, forty yards….

He caught the first glimpse of the Escalade parked at the trailhead. Broken twigs and leaves from the relentless rain showers blemished the truck. About thirty more steps and he'd be inside. Safe and dry, calling for help on the radio.

Pingaq roared, chomped into what sounded like wooden planks. Maybe it would fall into the pit and drown, Zane hoped. About twenty-five steps more. Twenty. Fifteen. Or maybe it would collapse and die from exhaustion. Ten steps. Five.

Relief coursed through Zane's limbs when he reached the driver's door. Holding his breath, he grabbed the door handle, the wet bandages rubbing his blisters raw. Then, the forest went dead.

Stone cold deathlike calm.

Zane's hand froze.

He jerked his head. Pingaq's rampaging of the outhouse had ended. Hurry. Get inside the truck without attracting that beast.

Zane clutched at the door handle, grateful for the bandages for the first time, since they muffled his movements. *Click.* He stopped. Did the bear hear? Another squeeze, slow, purposeful.

The door creaked ajar.

Zane glanced around the sodden forest. Nothing moved, save for the rain cascading through the boughs of the spruce and pine trees. Fortified with determination, he opened the door in one sweeping motion, disregarding the abrupt screech of the door. He slinked inside, inhaled, and shut the door as tightly as possible without slamming it.

Releasing a breath, he concentrated his strength to focus on priorities. He peered down the trail through the leaf-speckled windshield. The thick trees concealed the cabin. Joshua would be fine, he assured himself. Next, his Glock. He needed to load his 9mm with fresh bullets. Moving his arm like a cautious snake, he reached inside his holster pouch for the keys to the strongbox between the front seats. The slightest noise and he'd stop, glance outside, and, more confident, continue.

With the clip loaded, Zane, forgetting stealth in place of urgency, grabbed for the radio. "Hello. This is Trooper Fusca," he whispered into the mouthpiece. "I need support at the Theodore Krum cabin near Birchwood. SOS…. Hello?"

He grimaced at the mouthpiece, shook it, spoke again. "Trooper Fusca here. Clarice? Hello?" He shook it again. Fumbled with some buttons. "Trooper Fusca, requesting backup support. SOS. Hello?"

"Zane?"

"Clarice, you there?"

"Yes, Zane. Sorry, we've had some trouble with the storm. You okay?"

"I need helicopter support at the Krum cabin. I've got a thousand-pound bear trying to—"

Smash!

The massive thump knocked the mouthpiece from Zane's battered hand. He fumbled it off the seat, gazed behind him. Pingaq slammed headfirst into the back of the truck. Zane jerked forward, clutched onto the dash to absorb the shock.

"Zane? Zane? What's going on? Zane?" Clarice's voice faded in and out, between gnarly static and dead silence.

Pingaq rammed again. The truck crashed against a birch tree, denting the hood. Loosened leaves tumbled down and coated the truck. Zane braced himself for another impact. *Boom.*

"Get me help," he hollered into the radio. "ASAP."

"Zane, you there? I can barely hear you."

Zane dropped the mouthpiece, pulled out his Glock. He aimed, tried to zero in on the crazed sow's head through the window. He pulled the trigger. Bullets thudded like baseballs against the glass and exploded into twisted metal. He'd forgotten. The Escalade had bulletproof windows.

Pingaq reared up, slammed shoulder-first into the Escalade again, a truck five times the bear's weight. Yet Pingaq had no trouble nudging it two, three feet at a time. Raw power, the kind Dr. Sands had boasted about.

The bulletproofed rear window shattered from the bear's tenth impact. Perfect. Zane shot five rounds. Did he hit it? Difficult to judge from the thick fur. Pingaq backed off, huffing and chopping. It circled the truck, trapping Zane like a ground squirrel in its den. His worst nightmare. Pingaq rose to its full ten-foot height, striking the birch tree branch with its massive head. Roaring, Pingaq rocked the Escalade from side to side like a toy truck.

Grasping onto the leather seats to steady himself, Zane lowered the driver's window and pointed his Glock again, this time emptying the magazine into Pingaq's stomach, wider than an oak dining table and probably as thick. Crouching, the bear roared louder than a bore tide barreling up Turnagain Arm, and head butted the side of the truck. Zane crashed against the passenger door, grunting in pain. He lost the bandage on his right hand fighting to close the window to keep out Pingaq's overpowering paws. Blisters on his palms oozed what felt like burning acid.

Pingaq jumped onto the truck's hood, the steel pulsing and flexing under the sow's half-ton mass. Pan-sized dents were left where it trod. The sow bit at the windshield. Snot and blood glazed the glass. Its two-inch scar twisted and stretched with each roar. With his Glock spent, he grabbed for the bear spray stowed in the glove compartment and lowered the passenger window. He leaned out the window and waited for a change in the wind before dousing the bear with the potent pepper oil. Pingaq reeked of raw sewage from the outhouse. Unable to get a useful shot, he tossed the container to the floor with a sneer.

Pingaq growled. Drooling fangs gnashed into the windshield. Zane jumped back, awaiting the worst. It slapped the windshield with its massive paws. The radio antenna poked its snout. Infuriated, the bear pivoted, bit at the fluttering appendage, and with one sweep of its paw, tore it from the hood, wires and all.

The sky unleashed a pounding downpour. Pingaq slid off the hood, roared at the truck, slapped it two, three times, and scurried back into the forest. Zane caught his breath. He tried the radio again. Nothing but static. Without the antenna, the two-way was useless.

He shouted into the mouthpiece nonetheless. "Can anyone hear me? Clarice? Get backup! Get backup! Clarice! Can you hear me?"

Frustrated, Zane tossed the mouthpiece. It bounced off the floor and struck him in the knee. He kicked at it, released a tidal wave of expletives.

Six, eight slugs in Pingaq, and still it refused to go down.

Zane didn't worry how long his reprieve might last. He had to reach Joshua before the bear, now infuriated with burning slugs in its gut, went for the scent it had been trained to hone in on—Joshua Gaffner's.

He pictured helping Joshua clean Uncle Ted's blood from the cabin. He refused to have more blood and flesh to scrub. Not if Zane had any power over it.

The heavy rain subsided. Light sprinkles rustled the landscape. Beyond the drizzle tapping the steel frame of the truck, the forest fell silent. Loud and echoing in his ears, filling an empty void the size of the entire state.

Zane was about to step outside the truck, creep to the cabin, when something shattered the lull. A sharp growl. Pingaq, roused and enraged. Again.

Whacking against wood. Reverberating and relentless. This time, Pingaq was attacking the cabin—with Joshua alone inside.

His heart racing, Zane honked the horn, screaming for the bear out the window.

"Hey, bear. Come get me! Come get me!"

He honked and honked even after his injured palm bled and oozed fresh pus. Stinging pain shot up his right arm, but Zane persevered.

"Hey, Pingaq! Come get me!"

Barreling down the trail, Pingaq charged. A plume of muddy duff swept ten feet into the air. Like a runaway Mack truck, it pressed hard, snout low, lips peeled back. Relieved for Joshua's safety, Zane braced himself for the inevitable and violent impact.

When it hit, Zane landed in the back seat, dazed and shaken. He peered above the front seats. The front end was smashed in, almost to the windshield.

Pingaq ground its head into the grill, pushing until the truck stopped against a spruce tree. Growling and spitting blood, the bear rolled the truck. Zane grabbed onto whatever his hands reached for, disregarding the throbbing pain. The turnover bounced him into the hatch. He struck his head on the larger strongbox carrying winter gear, flares, the tranquilizer gun.

The tranquilizer gun!

His keys. He fumbled for them, dug deep into his pockets. Searing pain ripped and tore at the tender, bleeding blisters on his palms. Pingaq rotated the upended truck, like a top. Metal screeched against gravel and mud. Realizing the keys were still in the strongbox up front, he scurried along the ceiling, snatched the keys, and hurried to unlock the box. He unhitched the lock, shielding his face from whatever unsecured contents spilled out. Pingaq came around the back, discovered the smashed rear window and reached its mammoth paw inside. Zane squirmed and twisted from its persistent grasping. He leaped back to the front before Pingaq squeezed its way inside.

Zane searched for the bear spray. Where had it rolled? Desperate, he dug through the glove compartment and brandished his last ditch weapon. He grasped onto it for his life and edged closer to the back, flinching from Pingaq's biting the leather sides and chomping its way farther inside. He aimed the green bottle within feet of its snout and squeezed.

The Polo unleashed a flume of hot scent that sent Pingaq reeling backward, growling and huffing mad. It stretched to its full height, swatted at its nose and eyes, and began circling the truck, head low, ears pulled back. Nice improvement, Zane scoffed.

Wasting little time, Zane unsnapped the tranquilizer gun and the syringes of Immobilon from the strongbox. Three darts should take down a bear the size of Pingaq. Then he remembered Dr. Sands had pumped it full of extra testosterone and cocaine and he loaded two more darts for assurance. He cocked the rifle and held it steady in front of him.

Like an infantryman, he crawled on his stomach across the ceiling until he reached the shattered back window. He peered outside. In the near distance, Pingaq was fighting with an alder bush that had snagged its paws. It uprooted the bush in a matter of seconds. Zane needed to act fast.

He leaped from the truck, stood, aimed, waited for the perfect moment.

"Pingaq! Desini! Exori!"

Zane peered over his shoulder. Dr. Sands stood along the narrow road, dripping wet and muddied, calling for Pingaq in Latin.

Pingaq stopped attacking the bush and sniffed the air.

"Veni, Pingaq."

Grunting, the bear stood on its hind legs, tasting the new scent. Recognizing its master, it trotted closer to Dr. Sands.

"Sede, Pingaq. Sile." Pingaq seemed unsure. Dr. Sands repeated the commands. Hesitantly, the Kodiak moved closer and sat beside Dr. Sands, like a trained hound.

Mesmerized, Zane lowered the rifle.

"Trooper Fusca, it's good to see you again," Dr. Sands called to him above the patter of drizzle.

Zane remained motionless, unsure what move to make next. Had Dr. Sands come to call off the attack? To spare Joshua and him?

"I'm doing it for the bears, you know," Dr. Sands said after an uneasy moment of silence arched between them. "It's not their fault that Mother Nature strings them along, forcing them to act solely out of instinct, without the capacity to murder, like man. They have a right to revenge, don't you think? You must witness firsthand the vicious things we humans do to them, Trooper Fusca. Killing bears for their gallbladders, like those deceitful Baxter boys, who, I'm sure, have provided you with all the grisly details of my scheme. I learned my victims' daily routines, then orchestrated their traps. They asked for it, of course. Imagine, carrying around beliefs like theirs. They cared nothing for wildlife. I'm only helping the bears along, pushing them to do what they would if they possessed the evilness of humans."

Zane swallowed. "Why Joshua Gaffner?"

"That's for me," Dr. Sands said with a wry grin. "I didn't exactly appreciate his questioning me during the little Q&A at Taggart Hall. I admit. I have a bit of an ego. All of academia does. Besides, he was getting in too thick."

"There must be at least four state law enforcement agencies searching for you, Sands," Zane said, trying to moderate his voice. "Maybe even the NFS. You have no way out."

Dr. Sands shook his head, his long, grizzled hair and goatee speckled with debris and dribbling with rainwater. "I'm not seeking a way out, Trooper Fusca. This is my final sacrifice to my beloved bears. My magnum opus, if you will, dedicated to them. Pingaq, she'll do my last bidding. Then it will be over. For all of us. You, me, Pingaq, and your boyfriend inside the cabin."

Zane recoiled from Dr. Sands's last comment. No matter. He had to protect Josh. Somehow. He would shout to the world the love that he harbored for Joshua if it meant saving him from Dr. Sands's and Pingaq's clutches.

"Your tranquilizer gun is no match against Pingaq," Dr. Sands went on. "I only have to give her one word, and she'll be on top of you, tearing you to shreds in a matter of seconds, much how she destroyed that bush over there."

The drizzle ceased completely at that point. The forest fell in a death knell of silence. Nothing stirred. Only the drip of residual drops off the trees. Not even a ground squirrel or the ever-present ravens uttered a squeal. Waiting, watching from their hideaways the two humans' standoff. Zane's index finger flexed over the rifle's trigger, the pain in his hands having submitted to numbness. The muscles in his shoulder contracted, preparing for action. He composed his breathing, sucked in more oxygen. Eyes penetrating.

"Serge, Pingaq. Perdi. Perdi. Interfice eum! Interfice!"

Pingaq leaped into a charge as if fired from a cannon. Zane raised the rifle, aimed for the bear's head. Pingaq stormed closer. Massive muscles flexing. Zane squinted, lined up the scope, and squeezed the trigger.

CHAPTER 29

THE two-legged creature—the pest she'd been fighting with for what seemed the entire day—fell backward when she'd tumbled on the wet gravel and grazed his side. The man's rifle blasted before his head struck the ground. She skidded to a stop and peered behind her. Her master, the man named Dr. Sands, who'd fed her, sheltered her since she was a cub— and, lately, hurt her in ways that confused her—grasped onto his shoulder. Something stuck out of it. The same sharp instrument Dr. Sands and his assistant, Leslie, had poked her with many times the past several weeks. Dr. Sands plucked it from his shoulder, eyed it, and fell forward.

Instinct told her to rush to his side. But what for? He might use what he'd pulled out of his shoulder and jab her with it. She was sick and tired of being stuck with sharp needles and made to feel funny. The other man wasn't moving either. She was confused. Were they both sleeping? Should she sleep too? She was tiring with another blistering headache but didn't wish for a nap.

She was glad the rain had ended. The downpour had felt like pesky mosquitoes gnawing into her flesh. They would be out in full force once the sun reemerged. Always did after rain showers. The wet ground soothed her injured forepaws from the dastardly stovepipe, the one that had made such a racket she'd wanted to tie it into knots.

Sweet stench of death blew under her snout. She followed it to her master, Dr. Sands. She poked her muzzle into his side, rolled him face up. Was he dead? She was unsure. What should she do now? Follow through with her training, with what her master had drummed into her head for the past week?

"Interfice eum, quaere vestigial," she heard her master's voice inside her head.

The scent again. Came from the cabin. Not death, but something alive. The scent Dr. Sands had instructed her to track. An odor mixed with fear.

She remembered that smell coming from her own mother when she'd fallen off the cliff where she'd once called home. The same odor had risen from inside her, watching her disappear over the edge. Horrible, stinking stench. The smell of hopelessness.

She remembered staring down the steep cliff into the white flumes of water bashing against the rugged rocks. Her mother struggled, tried to clutch onto the rocks to pull herself up, calling in distress. But the waves proved too powerful. With a brutal roar, the water pulled her under. Helpless, she could merely watch. She never laid eyes on her mother again.

She lay by the cliff for days, crying out for her. No response ever came, other than the growling of puffins and the scratchy chatter of bank swallows. And the crashing of those vicious waves. The need for food eventually lured her back into the brush to rummage for berries or rodents. Alone and confused, she no longer looked to her Kodiak home as a place of verdant discovery. It became a dark, ominous trap.

Jumping and cringing from every scent and sound, she foraged for berries and trapped small rodents. Her mother had taught her well. She learned quickly whose territory to avoid. The boars, standing three times as tall as she, bellowed and roared like thunder blasts whenever she wandered into their paths. Enough lush vegetation covered the island she had little worry finding another patch of earth to feed from.

Salmon fishing was the difficult part. She'd always had a tough go at catching them. They'd squirm and even bite. Her paws, although already the size of those funny things the humans wore on their heads, failed to hold the succulent salmon long enough to bring them into her watering mouth. She struggled and struggled, until people snapping photographs uttered heart-wrenching calls. She couldn't understand them, but she sensed their sadness. Did they mourn for the loss of her mother too?

A few days later, men and women with guns and tents showed up at the bay where she'd been struggling with the salmon. She smelled no fear or malice from them, yet their poised guns confused her. She'd experienced few hunters in her short two years, but understood the power they wielded. Her mother had always whisked her away whenever she'd catch wind of them.

Two of the humans chased off a large boar that had been harassing her for days. She remembered her mother behaving in the same way. She'd match them pound for pound if any tried to harm her cub.

Then one of the humans shot her.

Next, she realized she was awakening in a cage far from home, high above the mountains where she and her mother had roamed since the day she'd first emerged from their den. The roaring of whatever they carried her in was louder than all the cantankerous boars on the island combined, she was certain. Clouds whizzing past the window caused her to cower. The stench of fear again, this time coming solely from her.

She settled once she accepted they weren't going to fly into one of the mountains. When they touched ground hours later, new anxieties wrenched into her throat. They loaded her on another vehicle. This one carried her along more familiar turf. She could see the trees flying by out the small holes in the back.

At any moment, she expected any one of her human captors to kill her. Why did they prolong her misery? Did they not realize she was still alive? The cache they'd buried her in—the strange cage made from materials she'd never touched before—rattled with her clawing, yet they treated her like the invisible wind. All but one. The female human riding in the back put her face near the cage and showed her teeth. Why would the female snarl at her if she meant no ill will?

The big surprise came when they unloaded her cage from the van and placed her into a much larger cage—and opened the door to her plastic crate for her to escape. What did they plan for her next? She waited before venturing outside. She distrusted the humans.

Soon, she could no longer ignore the new smells that enticed her. She lumbered from the plastic crate and sniffed every corner, every crevice of her new, larger cage. The humans stood on the other side of the cage and snarled at her with tiny white teeth. A new man, who she suspected lorded over the territory of the larger cage, kept uttering a strange sound, "Pingaq," whenever he looked her way. After a while, she learned to snap to attention whenever she heard it.

Despite the erratic fears, she grew accustomed to life in her new surroundings. The nearby smaller bears, also in large enclosures, left her alone. And the man who called her Pingaq and his helpers gave her plenty to eat. She liked that she didn't have to hunt or forage for her own food. No more struggling with snapping salmon. The tender fish they tossed her were already dead. After a while, she settled into her new, luxurious life with little need for complaint.

But recently, her caretakers began to do strange things to her, things she didn't like. The man she'd come to recognize as Dr. Sands and his most recent assistant, Leslie, repeatedly poked her with sharp needles. Afterward, she'd grow angry, tired, excited, at the same time. The grating sensation in her mind lasted for days. Her heart would race like the water cascading down Eagle River in spring, and she'd fear her ever-growing chest might explode.

Enraged for mysterious reasons, she'd roar loud enough to wake her mother from her watery grave. She roared now. Roared for the entire forest to hear and tremble from her might. Roared from the scent that wafted from the cabin she'd been stalking for hours that housed the terrified man.

Interfice eum, quaere vestigial.

Recalling her stringent training to track and kill, she rushed the scent. Bashed through the forest, stomped the alder bushes and saplings. She heard the man patter inside the cabin. Smelled his rancid fear. He was deliberating, figuring out what to do next. He knew he was trapped and alone.

Perfect.

With surging anger, she raced for the cabin and smashed into the glass. The window shattered. Shards flailed off the strange contraption blocking the way inside and bounced off her thick coat. She smelled more mounting fear. The man with the scent was scrambling about and bracing for a fight.

Headlong, she rammed into the contraption blocking the window. Her head struck something sharp buried deep inside. She roared in pain.

The man swept the obstacle aside, with a strength uncanny for a human creature. He pointed a hunting rifle at her.

She flinched, growled, and charged again. He fired.

The bullet whizzed past her ear. She escaped around back and jumped onto the back of the cabin. Her claws peeled the wooden planks into toothpicks. Something hot blasted through the wood, grazed her throat. The man inside was firing at her again. More blasts. Smoke rose from the two holes left in the wood. She darted again for the front window.

Must be a way inside. She pushed hard into the barricade that the man had replaced. A crashing sound echoed inside her head. She growled, chomped manically at anything in her way. Fluffy white debris—not unlike snow, but not cold—swirled around her. No escape now. She had the man cornered. She'd be inside in a matter of seconds.

"Veni! Veni, Pingaq, veni!"

Familiar sounds, yet from an unrecognizable voice. She stopped, sniffed the outside air. The white stuff continued to fall. She turned. That man she'd been battling inside the large truck. He'd awakened and stood at the end of the trail, holding the same gun he'd used to kill her master.

"Pingaq, veni. Veni."

He was telling her to come. Her master was the only human who had the power to command her. Yet the words, so familiar.

"Pingaq! Veni! Veni, Pingaq! Veni!"

Why did he call for her? To get a good shot at her, like he had her master? He stood no chance against her bulk. In seconds, she'd barrel him in half.

A shrill grating sound came from the sky, where the sun had fully emerged from behind parting clouds. She jerked upward and braced herself against the brash wind and flying duff striking her face.

The rush of wind increased. Pellets of rock and soil stung her eyes.

Three, four piercing blows burned into her side. She peered at the man standing along the trail. She realized he'd shot her while the roaring from above had distracted her. He'd fooled her.

Drunk with confusion and fear, she stumbled toward the saxifrage, glistening under the sun. Wind from above continued to pummel her, but her mind and resolve grew weak. She lay down, let the sleepiness take hold. She gave one last wrench upward and watched the gargantuan machine (she recognized it as one of those birds that had taken her from her home on Kodiak Island) land nearby, helpless to battle it. Behind the flying contraption, a strange colorful arc streaked across the sky. So many colors, she could hardly make them out before she laid her head back down among the wildflowers and closed her eyes.

CHAPTER 30

HE WAITED on the South Terminal, Upper Level, at Ted Stevens Anchorage International Airport, pacing the long, brightly lit corridor outside the secured area. How long since he'd last seen him? Seemed ages. Like he was meeting him for the first time. He gazed out the window at the Chugach Range. Fresh August snowfall capped the higher elevations. Jets taxied on the tarmac closer to his view. Nearly two hours he'd been waiting. Anxious for his return, he'd left for the airport four hours before the flight was due.

He checked the monitor for the umpteenth time. Still read "On Time." Another forty-five minutes and he'd embrace him once again. Swing him toward the tiled ceiling. His hands began to sweat from clutching onto the gift he'd purchased for him. He hoped he liked it. His palms were still stiff from the burns he'd received grabbing onto the stovepipe. A few weeks of treatments had healed most of the blisters and minor infection. Otherwise, he had full use of his hands. Compared to Julie's accident, his had amounted to a mere stubbed toe.

Would they get along after so long apart? What would they say to each other? What time was it? He rechecked his wristwatch. Only five minutes had passed since the last time he'd looked. Why did time slow to a trickle at airports? He recalled the days, in his late teens, when a person could meet a party at the gate. That romantic era had withered like day-old roses.

Along with about a dozen other souls, he paced, rechecked the monitor, peered mindless out the picture window. Waiting. Hoping. Fearing. He sat on a hard chair, the tenth time in the past fifteen minutes, and studied the worn carpet. Only when he grew conscious of his restless leg bouncing, did he jump up, annoyed with his own nervousness. He inhaled, opened his eyes. Like when on a stakeout. But this was nothing like those times. This was a happy moment.

How would he react? What should he say to him when they met? Would they even recognize each other? Time hadn't elapsed that much since they'd last seen each other. But people change. Sometimes beyond anything recognizable. Zane had let his facial hair grow a bit. Did he look different? He checked his watch. The pilot should be about ready to make the descent, banking west from the Wrangell Mountains, two hundred miles southeast of Anchorage.

A flock of passengers exited the secured area, towing carry-on luggage and children. He studied their faces. Some acted excited, perhaps on their first trip to Alaska. Others dragged their feet, relieved to have made it home. He turned his back on the new rush of humanity and stared out the window. Hazy sun highlighted the metal on the taxiing jets. Korean Air. Delta. Pen Air. United. JAL. A British Petroleum 747. And of course, dozens of Alaska Airlines 737s. He inhaled. When would Alaska Flight 93 arrive?

He wandered to a kiosk and bought another bottled water, mostly for the napkins. He needed to wipe sweat from his forehead. He gulped the water empty, cold and revitalizing. *Calm down. Relax. Be strong. Nothing to worry about. It's not like you're strangers.*

On the way back to his seat, he checked the monitor. Still read "On Time." What do airports know? They never inform the public if the plane is delayed until fifteen minutes past due. Four fifteen. Twenty-five more minutes before the scheduled arrival. He returned to his seat, set the gift beside him, gripped the empty bottle. He flexed the plastic, irritating the middle-aged woman seated next to him. She sneered and walked to the near-empty security line, her screechy carry-on in tow.

The grinding of a jet's engines grabbed his attention. He glanced over his shoulder. An arriving flight taxied to a jet bridge. He squinted into the overcast sky. Sun would set a tad after ten that time of year. He hoped they'd have enough daylight to explore a few sites before heading home. Would he even want to explore? What if his plane arrived late and they'd only a few hours of daylight remaining? But they had two weeks together. No pressure.

Four thirty. His heart raced. Moisture evaporated from his mouth. Maybe the plane might arrive early. Airlines always scheduled arrival times later than the duration of flight to cover their butts in case of a late takeoff. He tossed his plastic bottle into the recyclable canister and rechecked the monitor. Breathless, he licked his lips. Alaska Airlines Flight 93—"Landed."

He was here, in Anchorage. Right at that exact moment. Perhaps grabbing his luggage from the overhead bin, waiting to deplane along with one hundred fifty other passengers. He breathed, focusing and calming himself. His cell phone clicked. "I'm here," his text message said. "Waiting for you," Zane wrote back.

Soon after, a new herd of passengers exited the secured area. He checked faces, surveyed for familiar struts. He spotted him. Dragging a navy blue carry-on. They approached each other.

"How you doing, sport?" Zane said.

"Good to see you, Pop."

It wasn't the rushing into his arms and swinging him around the way Zane had envisioned, but good enough. They hugged lightly, provided each other warm smiles. Everyone else in the airport vanished into wallpaper. All that existed for the moment was Zane and his nine-year-old son, Michael. Realizing the flight attendant who'd escorted Mikey from the airplane still stood waiting for his confirmation, he apologized and shook her hand to thank her.

"How was your trip, sport?" Zane said, grabbing his carry-on and leading him to baggage claim.

"Awesome," Mikey said. "Me, Grandpa, and Grandma got to spend the night in Boston so I could catch the flight this morning. Way better than last time. I flew all the way to Seattle in a big jet, nonstop, not one of those small ones out of Providence to New York or Philadelphia, all by myself."

"Sounds awesome." Zane grinned until it hurt. Now that the waiting was over, he realized he'd fretted for nothing. "I got you something," he said, handing Mikey his gift.

Mikey turned the baseball glove over in his hands. "Cool, Pop. Thanks."

Zane hoped they might take in a baseball game at Mulcahy Stadium one day during his two-week visit and watch the Bucs beat one of their crosstown rivals. Mikey might even catch a home run with his new baseball glove. Zane had Mikey call his grandparents in Rhode Island to let them know he'd arrived in one piece while they waited for his bag. Twenty minutes later, Zane, with his son seated beside him, pulled the Sierra from the airport's short-term parking lot, paid the attendant eleven dollars, and exited onto Minnesota Road.

Mikey, dazed-looking after his two flights totaling eight hours, but full of energy, peered out the window. "Check out those mountains," he said, unable to peel his eyes from the scenery. "Wow!"

"Last time you were here it was the dead of winter," Zane said. "Things look different in the daylight, huh?"

"I'll say."

"I was hoping to show you a few sites before heading home," Zane said. "Up for it?"

"Sure, okay."

When Zane pulled past the sign that read "The Alaska Zoo" fifteen minutes later, Mikey said, "The zoo? Why the zoo, Pop?"

"Thought you might get a kick out of it."

Zane paid for their tickets, and they wandered the grounds, casually glimpsing into the exhibits of seals, musk oxen, yaks, and coyotes. Zane had a particular exhibit in mind. Mikey's wrinkled forehead under his mop of wavy brown hair affirmed he knew his pop was up to something.

When they arrived at the brown bear exhibits, Mikey's eyes grew wider than chocolate-covered cherries.

"Wow!" he said. "Check out the size of that one. Must be a thousand pounds."

"Come take a closer look."

Zane guided Mikey down the handrail to a sign that provided information on the enclosed Kodiak brown bear. Mikey's eyes grew larger and larger the farther he read. Zane followed along, although he'd read the sign himself dozens of times. He'd helped create it. The zoo had requested his input.

The sign began with a clip from the *Anchorage Daily News*, dated July 10, 2011.

Terror in the woods

How Two Men Survived the Rampages of a Drug-crazed Bear

BY LIZ SCRIBNER

DR. BARRY SANDS, 61, trained his beloved bears to kill. His world-renowned bear sanctuary in Eagle River stood as the staging ground for his master plan: to rid the world of those with whom he disagreed. The terror that had begun a week before Memorial Day climaxed six weeks later at the site where it had all begun—the remote Birchwood cabin of Dr. Sands's first victim, Dr. Theodore Krum, 46. Wildlife trooper Sgt. Zanebono Fusca, 31, and Krum's nephew, Joshua Gaffner, 25, battled for their lives for four hours while Dr. Sands's beloved half-ton Kodiak brown bear, Pingaq, tried to tear down the cabin and do what she'd been trained for, to kill and devour the men trapped inside.

Trooper Fusca and Gaffner, next on Sands' hit list of victims—which included Krum, Dr. Harold Bloomington, 52, Dr. Vishva Rakesh, 39, and Dr. Gregory Gomez, 34—boarded up the door with tables, chairs, anything with weight, and blocked the mattress against the lone window. Pingaq, pumped up with more than 30 grams of crystal methamphetamine and 100,000 g/dl of testosterone, raged on a warpath. Nothing would bring the ferocious beast down, until an act of heroism by Trooper Fusca finally brought an end to Dr. Sands's sinister scheme....

Midway into the article, Zane stopped reading. He already knew the outcome. He'd lived through it. One of many stories the media had written about Dr. Sands's horrific scheme. The irony of Dr. Sands's plot, he'd turned the bears into creatures like himself. Aggressive, hostile, and keen to kill. In his mind, Dr. Sands had always wished bears would retaliate against man. Thus, he'd even the score for them.

Murder by proxy, Zane had told one reporter. "Dr. Sands himself had stated Mother Nature hadn't designed bears to seek revenge," he said. "That's when Dr. Sands stepped in to fix Mother Nature's shortcomings, from his perspective."

Zane had saved the day by using the command he'd heard Dr. Sands use to call Pingaq to his side. But it was Jasper, Dana, and Langston in the A-star which had startled Pingaq and allowed him to get in the shots needed to bring Pingaq down.

Pingaq, spared by authorities, had gone through a kind of bear rehab. Authorities had closed the Eagle River Sanctuary until further notice. The other bears had been shipped to zoos across the globe. Five to the Lower Forty-eight, two to Canada, one each to Thailand and Japan.

Despite being left for dead, Leslie, recovering from fifty separate injuries (including losing her right thumb), remained steadfast in defending Dr. Sands. She never cleared herself from culpability or asked for immunity. Once well enough to leave the hospital, authorities reprimanded her to the Sixth Avenue jail, where she still awaited trial.

She told authorities everything, validating and adding to what the Baxter brothers had contributed—how Dr. Sands had used the brothers to purchase cocaine and other narcotics, how he and the brothers had hauled the bears to where the doctor had learned the victims would be at certain hours, how he'd trained the bears to obey his orders and track specific scents with the clothes Dr. Sands had ordered the brothers to steal from the victims. She'd even confessed to occasionally hiding the brothers and driving them to make drug runs in their pickup truck in out of the way locations to throw off authorities. She'd apologized for none of it. Her confession had come with an air of pride and defiance. Prison would accentuate her tenure with Dr. Sands with a final flourish.

Officials had reduced the Baxter brothers' charges from aiding and abetting and distribution of narcotics to criminally negligent homicide, a class B felony that would most likely net each brother three years behind bars, (including a lengthy weekend at a motel seminar to learn respect for bears upon their release) for their help in nabbing Dr. Sands.

The media frenzy following the ordeal had turned Zane into a short-term celebrity. Yet Pingaq still grabbed most of the public's notice. Sands's bears were victims, much like Zane and the others. Some didn't see it that way. They considered Dr. Sands's antics a mark of heroism. They agreed with his views. Dr. Barry Sands in his death had become a cult hero to them. One who'd stepped over the line of sanity on behalf of bear conservation. His books on Amazon had spiked in sales, including *For the Love of Bears*, which had rocketed to number one on the "Nature and Ecology" list. A documentary was already in the making of the man and his life. Zane imagined the tone. Mawkish, much like Dr. Sands's view of his beloved bears.

Pingaq, famed bear, survivor of Dr. Sands's twisted plot to eradicate anyone who disagreed with him, loped in its enclosure, queen of a new land. How passive Pingaq appeared now, Zane mused, gazing at the sow inside its lush home. It licked its paws, swatted at invisible flies. He wondered if it recognized him. Bears were one of the most intelligent land mammals on earth. Of course it remembered. But then again, it *had been* drugged out of its mind.

"You're a hero, Pop," Mikey said after reading the article. "A real authentic hero. Grandma and Grandpa told me something way cool happened to you, but—wow!" He gazed at Zane as if he were a superman of sorts. Zane hated the notoriety but cherished his son's doting. His grin reached to his earlobes.

Even Julie had been impressed. She'd telephoned a few days after the incident hit the media to express her admiration. She'd blushed when they'd met for dinner a few weeks later to discuss Mikey's coming to Alaska. She'd been even further delighted when Zane had recounted to her how he'd put his foot down with his former in-laws.

"Mr. Gagliardi? This is Zanebono."

Zane had stepped outside onto his porch for all of the mobile home court—all Alaska—to hear his private phone call. With his hands still bandaged, he conjured courage from the towering and powerful Chugach Range. He inhaled the entire state, its rugged power, vitality, brutality.

He stood, more immovable than the aspens and mountains.

What was the time in Rhode Island? Ten at night? Zanebono didn't care. Mr. Gagliardi told him he'd heard about the bear attacks, and

Zanebono's role in stopping them. His voice, unusually shaky, had overflowed with esteem.

"I want Mikey to come up before school starts," Zane said flat out, without pause. "It's in the best interest of the kid and me."

Mr. Gagliardi hushed his wife in the background. "Certainly, Zane," he said. "You have every right. The boy should spend more time with his pop. I agree."

"I want him up here for at least two weeks. I figure the first two weeks of August is a good timeframe. He'll be home in time to start school. I'll e-mail you the ticket in a few days."

"Certainly, Zane. Certainly."

He hadn't allowed a half-ton bear to push him around; he wasn't going to let two former in-laws complicate his life. The chirping swallows and ravens seemed pleased with his newfound boldness, as well.

"Ready to go, sport?"

"Okay, Pop. Whenever you are."

Hand in hand, they walked through the remainder of the zoo, toward the Sierra. Before heading home, they stopped by Julie's apartment complex. Mikey, untarnished by years of compiling adult-riddled fears, leaped into her lap undaunted by the wheelchair. Julie laughed and rubbed his floppy hair. No one had given Mikey the full account of his mother's tragic accident as far as Zane knew. He understood she'd had a run-in with a moose, but he appeared to hold little grudge against the ungulates (he'd merrily spotted five since leaving the airport). Mikey had stated in the past he harbored few memories of his short life in the bush, traipsing in the snow with his pop or strapped to his mother's side while she toiled in the root garden.

Julie gave him a belated birthday gift—the pillow she'd embroidered with a picture of a clown. Mikey seemed to understand the effort needed for her to make it, and he hugged her with gratitude. They spent the remainder of the afternoon with her. They dined at a roadhouse-style diner and explored the Anchorage Museum—the one place Mikey had remembered from his last visit during Christmas. Mikey had talked endlessly about the earthquake machine reenacting the 9.2 Good Friday earthquake of 1964. He couldn't wait to give it a go again. Julie waited in the lobby for them and greeted them with a smile when they exited.

They hugged good-bye around eight o'clock outside the sliding glass doors to Julie's apartment complex which reflected the Anchorage skyline, and they said they couldn't wait to spend more time with each other during the next few weeks. Zane promised to take them hiking on a wilderness trail in Eagle River. "Wheelchair accessible," he emphasized. Mikey insisted that Zane promise to show him the infamous site of Dr. Sands's Bear Sanctuary too.

On the Glenn Highway, they passed AST headquarters. Zane didn't bother to inform his son. Zane watched the stately, three-story building surrounded by evergreens and a spotless blacktop parking lot shrink in his rearview mirror. He recalled back to two weeks ago, when he'd stepped into his commander's office after returning from his leave of absence to allow time for his hands to heal. Dana, already aware why he'd scheduled private time with Col. Lund, had scurried for the women's restroom, hands to her face.

Langston had gone about his business at his desk, like any other day. Amanda had hugged him the moment he'd stepped from the vestibule, until he feared he might suffocate. She'd said something about his Ivy League hair and "pecan-brown" eyes.

"I can't believe you're thinking about going through with it," Dana had said to him at her Campbell Park duplex a week before.

"Please understand," Zane had said, sitting on the same sofa where they'd made love two years before, after her father's death. "It has nothing to do with you, anyone else, or the department."

"No one cares if you're gay," she'd said, brown eyes wide, almost pleading. "Karen Flecks is a lesbian. The AST is okay with it."

Zane had flushed. "I'm not gay, Dana. But that's not the point. That's not what this is about. It's about why I had left Rhode Island for Alaska in the first place."

Her downturned, taut lips had implied a desire to comprehend, yet she'd labored. And with her rushing to hide in the bathroom, Zane figured she still had a tough time understanding.

Inside Col. Lund's office, he and his commander had locked eyes. By the expression on Col. Lund's face, he'd gotten wind of why Zane had asked to speak with him. They'd expressed few words. Zane had emphasized the certainty of his decision. Dressed in plainclothes, he'd laid his badge on Col. Lund's desk, along with his holster and gun.

The notion to leave the AST had first struck Zane as selfish—was he enjoying his time off too much? But the idea lingered, like the scent of pine after a rainstorm, and he realized the decision he must make.

He intended to stay in touch with his colleagues, especially Dana. She'd always remain a part of his life, if she wanted him. Zane couldn't imagine "scratching Langston's itch" again, but he hoped they might continue their annual weekend camping trips in the mountains and share a beer now and then.

Headquarters vanished with a bend in the highway. At milepost eighteen, Zane exited for the Birchwood Loop Road. Mikey gaped at the impinging woods. His seatbelt barely contained him. He watched with fascination while they waited for the Alaska Railroad loaded with tourists to pass northbound. He grew bored with the long train and, furrowing his eyebrows, looked to his father.

"What happened to the trailer you used to live in? Didn't you used to live in a trailer park?"

"I put it on the market," Zane said. "We can still stay there a few nights if you like, but I hope to have it sold by next summer. I'm probably going to rent it this winter for skiers at Alyeska. In the meantime, I've got something better you might like."

"Cool." Mikey said, and he went back to ogling everything outside the window once the train passed and Zane headed forward.

Zane went down the checklist of wildlife precautions. "Animals are unpredictable," he said, for the tenth time since leaving Julie at her apartment. "You have to respect them. They aren't pets or something you watch only on the Discovery Channel. They're wild creatures that live by instinct, not emotion. Remember."

"I know, I know," Mikey grumbled.

Just like his mother, Zane conceded with a snicker and shake of his head. Stubborn.

The primitive road narrowed. Zane parked the Sierra next to the old pickup where the road became impassible. Excited, Mikey jumped from the truck, spread his arms wide.

"It's like the real Alaskan woods."

"It is the real Alaskan woods," Zane said with a hearty laugh.

With Mikey's luggage and pillow from Julie in hand, they hiked the trail to the cabin. Smoke curled from the newly installed stovepipe. The patched roof held it steady. A warm glow in the recently fitted window pulled them closer.

"Hey, I was wondering what happened to you guys." Joshua stepped outside the cabin right when they reached the door. Grinning from ear to ear, he patted Zane's shoulder and eagerly shook Mikey's hand after Zane introduced them.

Joshua seemed to sense Mikey's amazement with his surroundings and suggested they put his things away so he could explore before dark. Inside the cabin, Mikey glanced around. The cabin still smelled of fresh white wall paint. He mentioned the cabin's small size, but cared less where he slept. Joshua and Zane had already set a cot near the new cast iron stove.

Mikey set down his luggage and tossed his pillow and ball glove on his cot. He ogled the brand new mattress in the corner, halfway concealed by a privacy divider. "Do you guys live like husband and wife?"

Zane scratched his head. Joshua snickered.

"Well… umm," Zane said. "Yeah, we do, I guess." No point fudging the issue. Uncanny how well kids gathered things.

Mikey eyed the mattress and shrugged. "Cool," he said and turned his attention to more pressing issues, like insisting he wanted to venture outside and explore.

Zane and Josh followed Mikey outside, chuckling over the boy's enthusiasm. Surrounded by the golden saxifrage, Mikey shouted he wanted to live in the woods forever. It was "way cooler than Cranston." And perhaps he might move in with them, Zane considered, watching his son turn over stones, peer into the forest, study a pinecone. If he chose to force the issue with his former in-laws, now more compliant. Mikey showed as much enthusiasm about the Alaska vastness as Zane had when he stood his height and had first noticed Alaska on the United States wall map in grade school. The yearning for immense, unexplored places might lodge deep within their genes, like with his own pop, who'd immigrated from Italy to a country he'd never stepped foot in before.

Zane wondered if any of Mikey's early experiences in the bush had somehow imbedded into his subconscious and helped shape him into the happy, venturous boy who frolicked before him. Would he have grown into a troublesome child if he'd never dragged him and Julie into the bush north of Denali, regardless of his grandparents' strong values and discipline?

Mikey wandered behind the cabin to inspect the outhouse. Zane and Josh had completed the construction last week. Nice to have more privacy than a moldy tarp when taking care of Nature's Business. The wood still exhaled a fresh scent of pine. Joshua himself had carved the crescent moon in the door—with a smiley profile.

Two days after the Pingaq incident, Joshua had returned to Portland to tie up loose ends. Ten days later, Zane picked him up from Ted Stevens, ready to embark on their new adventure together. Like Zane, Joshua officially resigned from his family's kitchen remodeling business. With Joshua's former world stored away, Zane looked forward to a future with him.

They'd concluded too much had happened between them to leave things dangling. Josh said he'd connected with Zanebono in a way he'd never experienced. Zane too relished a special symbiosis with Josh. Living at Uncle Ted's cabin would make a grand start to their adventure together. Neither man cared for the silly trappings of the loud, modern world.

Julie knew about their relationship. Her grin had twitched into something conniving when he'd told her the night they had dinner that he was in love with a man and they'd planned to move together into a small cabin in the woods.

She sat quiet, studying him across the Formica table. Her grin, the same grin she carried with her the way a woman carries a purse or other accessories, curled higher. First the right side of her mouth, next the left, until her gray-green eyes vanished in folds of flesh. "That's so cute."

"Cute?"

"It's adorable."

"I'm moving in with a man, not a puppy."

Zane had once lamented that Joshua's presence had aggravated his horrible memories of the bush. After the ordeal with Pingaq and Dr. Sands, Zane realized Josh had forced Zane to surpass them. Josh's strength and determination, but also his vulnerability, infused Zane with a sense of self and understanding.

Tenacity might define a man in part—finding one's own path in the face of contempt. But the remainder? Josh had underscored the true meaning for him. Josh looked to Zane for a source of fortitude and resilience.

Zanebono would have thrown himself under Pingaq's monstrous claws if it had meant saving Josh from the sow's ferocious grasp, for one reason: Because Joshua had expected him to. Josh hadn't voiced the expectation while Pingaq had trapped them inside the cabin like mice for four hours. Zane sensed Josh yearned for his strength to pull them out alive.

Together, they'd share a sourdough's life, far from the madding crowd. Not quite the remote cabin like the one he and Julie had lived in north of Denali, but rustic enough for Zane. An acceptable compromise.

Perhaps it was Zane who needed to feed off Josh's vulnerability more than Joshua required Zane's strength.

"Can we go fishing?" Mikey asked, rushing back to the front and brushing his hands over the tall grass in the meadow, the same meadow in which Pingaq had lain down to sleep after Zane had shot it with three darts. "Last time it was too cold and dark to fish. I want to go fishing. Can we?"

Zane draped his arm around Josh. "Sure," he said. "Sure we can go fishing. Tomorrow we'll all go fishing."

Mikey wandered to the edge of the meadow and peered into the dense forest. Zane, with one eye on his twirling and giggling son, kissed Josh on the lips. Pure and unadulterated. Potent like the Alaskan wilderness. As real as the love that surged inside him.

SHELTER SOMERSET enjoys writing about the lives of people who live off the land, whether they be the Amish, nineteenth-century pioneers, or modern-day idealists seeking to live apart from the crowd. Shelter's fascination with the rustic, aesthetic lifestyle began as a child with family camping trips into the Blue Ridge Mountains. When not back home in Illinois writing, Shelter continues to explore America's expansive backcountry and rural communities. Shelter's philosophy is best summed up by the actor John Wayne: "Courage is being scared to death but saddling up anyway."

Romance from SHELTER SOMERSET

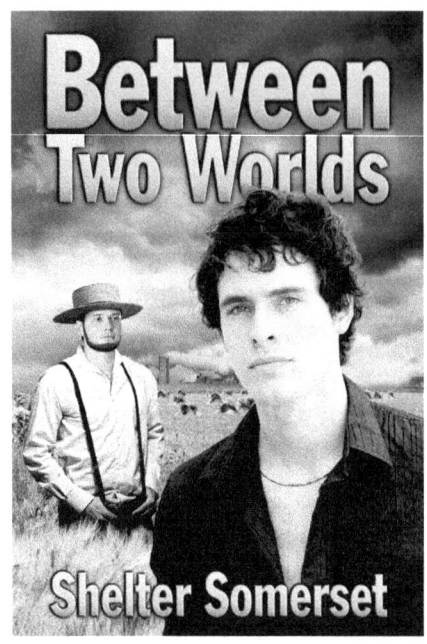

http://www.dreamspinnerpress.com

Also from SHELTER SOMERSET

SHELTER SOMERSET

ON THE TRAIL TO
MOONLIGHT GULCH

http://www.dreamspinnerpress.com

www.ingramcontent.com/pod-product-compliance
Lightning Source LLC
Chambersburg PA
CBHW051542260626
47170CB00003B/1067